BETTY NEELS

Because Of You

MILLS & BOON

BECAUSE OF YOU © 2023 by Harlequin Books S.A.

THE SECRET POOL
© 1986 by Betty Neels
Australian Copyright 1986
New Zealand Copyright 1986

First Published 1986
First Australian Paperback Edition 2023
ISBN 978 1 867 28741 4

HEAVEN IS GENTLE
© 1974 by Betty Neels
Australian Copyright 1974
New Zealand Copyright 1974

First Published 1974
First Australian Paperback Edition 2023
ISBN 978 1 867 28741 4

RING IN A TEA CUP
© 1978 by Betty Neels
Australian Copyright 1978
New Zealand Copyright 1978

First Published 1978
First Australian Paperback Edition 2023
ISBN 978 1 867 28741 4

Except for use in any review, the reproduction or utilisation of this work in whole or in part in any form by any electronic, mechanical or other means, now known or hereafter invented, including xerography, photocopying and recording, or in any information storage or retrieval system, is forbidden without the permission of the publisher.

This book is sold subject to the condition that it shall not, by way of trade or otherwise, be lent, resold, hired out or otherwise circulated without the prior consent of the publisher in any form of binding or cover other than that in which it is published and without a similar condition including this condition being imposed on the subsequent purchaser.

All rights reserved including the right of reproduction in whole or in part in any form. This edition is published in arrangement with Harlequin Books S.A. Cover art used by arrangement with Harlequin Books S.A. All rights reserved.

This is a work of fiction. Names, characters, places, and incidents are either the product of the author's imagination or are used fictitiously, and any resemblance to actual persons, living or dead, business establishments, events, or locales is entirely coincidental.

Published by
Mills & Boon
An imprint of Harlequin Enterprises (Australia) Pty Limited (ABN 47 001 180 918), a subsidiary of HarperCollins Publishers Australia Pty Limited (ABN 36 009 913 517)
Level 19, 201 Elizabeth Street
SYDNEY NSW 2000
AUSTRALIA

® and ™ (apart from those relating to FSC®) are trademarks of Harlequin Enterprises (Australia) Pty Limited or its corporate affiliates. Trademarks indicated with ® are registered in Australia, New Zealand and in other countries.
Contact admin_legal@Harlequin.ca for details.

Printed and bound in Australia by McPherson's Printing Group

CONTENTS

THE SECRET POOL 5

HEAVEN IS GENTLE 167

RING IN A TEACUP 321

Romance readers around the world were sad to note the passing of **Betty Neels** in June 2001. Her career spanned thirty years, and she continued to write into her ninetieth year. To her millions of fans, Betty epitomized the romance writer, and yet she began writing almost by accident. She had retired from nursing, but her inquiring mind still sought stimulation. Her new career was born when she heard a lady in her local library bemoaning the lack of good romance novels. Betty's first book, *Sister Peters in Amsterdam,* was published in 1969, and she eventually completed 134 books. Her novels offer a reassuring warmth that was very much a part of her own personality, and her spirit and genuine talent will live on in all her stories.

CHAPTER ONE

THE EARLY MORNING sun of a midsummer's day morning shone with warm cheerfulness on to the quiet countryside, the market town tucked neatly into the Cotswold hills and its numerous windows. These included those of the Cottage Hospital, a symbol of former days, fought for and triumphantly reprieved from the remorseless hand of authority, and proving its worth tenfold by never having an empty bed.

Inside the grey stone walls of this Victorian edifice, the day's work was already well advanced. Its thirty beds were divided between surgical and medical patients, with two beds for maternity cases who couldn't make it in time to Bristol or Bath, and one private ward used for any child too ill to move or anyone too ill to nurse in the wards. There was a small outpatients' department, too, and a casualty room where the local GPs could be called to attend any accident. Small it might be, but it did yeoman service, easing the burden of patients on the big Bristol hospitals.

It was staffed by the local doctors, ably supported by Miss Hawkins, who still insisted on being called Matron, two ward sisters and their staff nurses, and four pupil nurses, sent from

Bristol and Bath to gain experience. There was a night sister, too, and a handful of nursing aides, local ladies, whose kindness of heart and willingness to work hard when everyone else was fast asleep more than made up for their lack of nursing skills. Miss Hawkins was nearing retirement age, an old-fashioned martinet who had no intention of changing her ways. Until six months ago she had had the willing co-operation of Sister Coffin on the medical ward but that lady had retired and her place had been taken by a young staff nurse from the Bristol Royal Infirmary, who had accepted the post of sister in preference to a more prestigious one at her own hospital. It was agreed by everyone, even the grudging Miss Hawkins, that she had proved her ability and was worth her weight in gold. She had a happy knack of getting her patients better, coping with emergencies without fuss, carrying out the various doctors' orders faithfully, and lending a sympathetic ear to the young nurses' requests for a particular day off duty.

She sat at the desk in her office now, the sun gilding the mousy hair pinned neatly under her frilled cap, warming her ordinary face, escaping plainness only by virtue of a pair of fine hazel eyes, thickly lashed, and a gentle mouth. The desk was more or less covered by charts and a variety of forms and she had a pen in her hand, although just for the moment she was doing no work at all, her thoughts far away, if rather vague. She was normally a sensible girl, prepared to accept what life had to offer her and not expecting anything very exciting to happen. Indeed, the three elderly aunts with whom she lived had imbued her with this idea from an early age. They prided themselves on their honesty and plain spokenness and had pointed out on a number of occasions her lack of good looks and amusing conversation. They had done their best to dissuade her from training as a nurse, too, but she had been surprisingly stubborn; despite their certainty that she was too quiet, too shy with strangers, and lacking in self-assurance, she had gone to Bristol, done her training, and emerged at the end of it with flying colours:

Gold Medallist of her year, the prospect of a ward sister's post in the not too distant future, and a circle of firm friends. The girls liked her because she listened to the details of their complicated love lives with sympathy. The young housemen liked her because she listened to them, too, about their fleeting love affairs and their dreams of being brilliant consultants. She sympathised with them when they failed their exams and rejoiced with them when they passed and, when on night duty, she was always a willing maker of hot cocoa when one or other of them had been hauled out of bed in the small hours.

But she had declined the ward offered her and had instead applied for and been appointed to the medical ward of the Cottage Hospital in her home town. All because her youngest aunt, Janet, had had a slight—very slight—heart attack and it had been impressed upon her by Aunt Kate and Aunt Polly that it was her duty to return home.

So she had come back to the small town and lived out, going to and fro from her aunts' rambling old house not ten minutes' walk from the hospital. And because she was a good nurse and loved her work, she had taken pride in changing the medical ward, with patience and a good deal of tact, into the more modern methods Sister Coffin had ignored. It had been uphill work but she had managed it so well that Matron considered that she had been the instigator of change in the first place. If she regretted leaving her training school and the splendid opportunities it had offered her, she had never said so, but just now and again she wondered if life would have been different if she had taken the post at Bristol. She would have kept her friends for a start and used her nursing talents to their utmost; and who knew, perhaps one day she might have met someone who would want to marry her.

She stifled a sigh and looked up with a smile as her staff nurse came in. Jenny Topps was a big girl, always cheerful and amiable and with no wish to be anything but a staff nurse. She was getting married in a year's time to a rather silent and adoring young farmer and her ambitions lay in being a good wife. She said now,

'We're ready, Sister. There's time for a quick cup of tea before Dr Beecham gets here. I've sent the little nurses to coffee; Mrs Wills—the nursing auxilary—is in the ward.'

'Good. Yes, let's have tea, then I'll go over to the Women's Medical. It's quiet there and Staff can cope, but I'll just take another look at Miss Prosser. Mr Owen's not responding to his antibiotic, is he? I'll see if Dr Beecham will change it. He might be better off at the Infirmary.' She took the mug of tea Jenny had fetched from the ward kitchen and sipped it.

'You must miss the Infirmary,' observed Jenny. 'It's pretty quiet here—bad chests and diabetics and the odd heart case...'

She studied Sister Manning's quiet face on the other side of the desk; she liked her and admired her and although she wasn't pretty she had a pretty name—Francesca.

'Well, yes, I do, but I do need to be nearby my aunts...' She finished her tea, got to her feet and said, 'I'll be back in five minutes. Get the nurses to start making up that empty bed, will you? There is a diabetic coming in at two o'clock.'

The ward was quiet, the men waiting for the bi-weekly round from the consultant. Most of them were on the mend. Mr Owen worried her a little, and the new patient who had come in during the night, a suspected coronary, might spring something on them. She went slowly down the old-fashioned but cheerful ward, stopping for a word here and there and casting an eye on these two, and then went through the door into the women's side.

Here she was met by her second staff nurse, a small dark girl who like herself lived out.

'All ready for Dr Beecham?' asked Francesca. 'How's Miss Prosser? She was a bit cyanosed when I did the round this morning.'

'Still a bit blue. She's had some oxygen and she's quite bright and cheerful.'

They stood together and looked along the facing row of beds.

It was a small ward with pretty curtains at the windows and round each bed, and plenty of flowers. Half the patients were up, sitting by their beds, knitting or reading or gossiping. Francesca walked slowly to Miss Prosser's bed and made small talk while she studied that lady. They had had her in before and she was by no means an easy patient; she would have to talk to Dr Beecham about her. She smiled and nodded at the other patients and went back to her office, tidied the top of her desk, and with a glance at the clock went back to the men's ward. Dr Beecham would be there at any moment now.

He came through the door within moments, a short stout man with a fringe of hair on a bald head and twinkling blue eyes. She had known him ever since she had begun her training; he had been one of the first lecturers she had had and as she became more senior he had occasionally explained some unusual case to her. She liked him and the smile which lighted up her face made it almost pretty.

He had someone with him. Not just Dr Stokes, who was the RMO; a tall man with massive shoulders, fair hair with a heavy sprinkling of grey and the good looks to turn any woman's head. Francesca sighed at the sight of him. She knew him, too: Dr van Rijgen, a specialist in tropical diseases who had come to the Infirmary at regular intervals to lecture the students. He lived in Holland and worked there as far as she knew, although he seemed equally at home in England. Years ago when she had begun her training she had had the misfortune to drop off during one of his lectures; even after all these years, she remembered his cold voice, laced with sarcasm, very quietly reducing her to a state bordering on hysteria. They had encountered each other since then, of course, and she had taken care never to allow her feelings to show, and he for his part had never betrayed any recollection of that first unfortunate meeting. He eyed her now with a kind of thoughtful amusement which made her fume inwardly. But she replied suitably to Dr Stokes and Dr Beecham and then bade him a frosty good morning.

He had a deep slow voice. 'Good morning, Sister Manning. I see that I must congratulate you since we last met at the Infirmary.' He glanced round the ward, half the size of those in a Bristol hospital. 'Hiding your light under a bushel?'

She said in a voice which made his fine mouth twitch, 'If I remember aright, sir, my light was a very small one—a mere glimmer.'

He gave a crack of laughter. 'Oh, dear, you have a long memory, Sister.'

'A useful thing in a nurse,' interpolated Dr Beecham cheerfully. 'What have you got for us today, Fran?'

Dr Beecham prided himself on the good terms he enjoyed with the ward sisters and none of them minded that he addressed them by their Christian names when they were away from the patients.

'Nothing much, sir. There's Miss Prosser...' She didn't need to say more, they both knew that lady well enough. 'And Mr Owen who isn't so well. All the rest are making good progress.'

'Right, shall we see the ladies first? I want Dr van Rijgen to look at Mr Owen.'

The round wound its usual way, first through the women's ward and then the men's, to spend some time with Mr Owen; this time Dr van Rijgen did the examining. At length he straightened up. 'I agree with you, John,' he told Dr Beecham, 'he should be transferred to the Infirmary as soon as possible.'

He sat down on the side of the bed and addressed himself to Mr Owen. He explained very nicely, even Fran had to admit that, with a mixture of frankness and confidence which cheered the patient. 'And if Sister can arrange it, perhaps your wife would like to travel with you in the ambulance?'

He glanced at Dr Beecham who nodded and then turned his cold blue eyes upon Fran. 'Sister?'

'Mrs Owen lives close by, I am sure something can be arranged.'

They had coffee next, squashed in her office, discussing the round, pausing from time to time to alter drugs and give her instructions.

They had finished their coffee when Dr Beecham reached for the phone. 'I'll warn the medical side, Litrik. What about his wife?'

Dr van Rijgen turned to Fran and found her eyes fixed on his face.

'Mrs Owen? Can you get her here so that we can have a word with her, Sister?'

He frowned impatiently when she didn't answer at once. She had never thought of him as having any name other than van Rijgen; the strange name Dr Beecham had said made him seem different, although she didn't know why. A strange name indeed, but quite nice sounding. She realised that he had spoken to her and flushed a little and the flush deepened when he repeated his question with impatience.

'Certainly, sir. I can telephone her, she lives less than five minutes' walk away.' She spoke crisply and thought how ill-tempered he was.

Dr Beecham had finished with the phone, and as she dialled a number he said, 'Right, Fran. We'll go along to X-Ray and look at those films. Litrik, will you talk to Mrs Owen?'

He patted her on the shoulder, said, 'See you later, Litrik,' and went away, taking Dr Stokes with him.

Mrs Owen was a sensible woman; she asked no unnecessary questions but said that she would be at the hospital in ten minutes. 'I'll not ask you any questions, Sister,' she finished, 'for I'm sure the Doctor will tell me all I want to know.'

Fran put down the receiver and glanced at Dr van Rijgen, sitting on the window ledge, contemplating the view. She had no intention of staying there under his unfriendly eye; she picked up the charts on the desk and got up.

'Don't go,' said Dr van Rijgen without turning round. 'However sensible Mrs Owen may be, she'll probably need a shoulder to cry on.'

He spoke coldly and she, normally a mild-tempered girl, allowed her tongue to voice her thoughts. She snapped, 'Yes, and that's something you wouldn't be prepared to offer.'

The look he gave her was like cold steel; she added, 'sir' and waited for his cold calm voice to utter something biting.

'It is a good thing that my self-esteem does not depend upon your good opinion of me,' said Dr van Rijgen softly. 'Would it be a good idea if we were to have a tray of tea? I have found that tea, to the English, soothes even the most unhappy breast. Come to that, the most savage one, too.'

Fran didn't look at him but went in a dignified way to the kitchen and asked Eddie, the ward maid, to lay up a tea tray.

''As 'is nibs taken a liking for it?' asked that elderly lady. 'Not like 'im, with 'is foreign ways.'

Fran explained, knowing that if she didn't Eddie was quite capable of finding out for herself.

'Give me 'arf a mo', Sister, and I'll bring in the tray. Three cups?'

'Well, yes, I suppose so. Mrs Owen won't want to sit and drink it by herself.'

She would rather not have gone back to the office but there was no reason why she shouldn't. Dr van Rijgen was still admiring the view and he didn't look at her when she sat down at her desk. Indeed, he didn't move until one of the nurses tapped on the door, put her head round it in response to Fran's voice and said that Mrs Owen was there.

Fran sat her down: a small plump woman, her round face so anxious. 'It's Jack, isn't it, Sister? He's not so well. I'm that worried...'

Fran poured the tea and said in a quiet way, 'Mr Owen has been seen by Dr Beecham and Dr van Rijgen this morning, Mrs Owen.' She handed the doctor a cup. 'Dr van Rijgen will explain how things are...'

He had got to his feet when Mrs Owen had been ushered in; now he sat on the edge of the desk, half turned away from Fran.

He looked relaxed and unworried and Mrs Owen's troubled face cleared. His explanations were concise and offered with matter-of-fact sympathy; he neither pretended that there was much chance of Mr Owen recovering, nor did he paint too dark a picture of his future. 'We shall do what we can, Mrs Owen, that I can promise you,' he told her finally and Fran, listening, was aware that if she were in Mrs Owen's shoes she would believe him; what was more, she would trust him. Which, considering she didn't like the man, was something to be wondered at.

Dr van Rijgen went away presently, leaving Fran to give what comfort she could, and Mrs Owen, who had kept a stern hold on her feelings while he had been talking, broke down then and had a good cry, her grey head tucked comfortingly into Fran's shoulder. Presently she mopped her eyes and sat up. 'So sorry,' she said awkwardly, 'but it's a bit of a shock...'

Fran poured more tea and murmured in sympathy, and Mrs Owen went on, 'He's nice, isn't he? I'd trust him with my last breath. Funny, how you can feel he means what he says. Though I suppose he has to talk to lots of people like that.'

'Oh, yes, I'm sure he must. He's a very eminent doctor even though he's not English, but that doesn't mean that he doesn't understand your husband's case, Mrs Owen, and have every sympathy with you both.'

'And you, you're a kind girl too, Sister. My Jack thinks a lot of you.'

Fran made a comforting murmur and, since Mrs Owen was calm again, embarked on the business of ways and means. 'I still have to arrange things with the ambulance; it'll be some time tomorrow morning, quite early, if you could manage that? If you could come here? The ambulance will have to come back here, but I expect you'd like to stay for a bit and see Mr Owen settled in? Do you have friends in Bristol where you could stay?'

Mrs Owen shook her head.

'Then I'll phone the Infirmary and ask them to fix you up—they have a room where you can be comfortable and they'll see that you get a meal. There is a morning bus from Bristol, isn't there? And another one in the late afternoon. I should take an overnight bag.' She added in a gentle matter-of-fact voice, 'Are you all right for ready money, Mrs Owen?'

'Yes thank you, Sister. You don't know how long I might have to stay?'

'Well, no, but I'm sure the ward sister will tell you and you can ask to see Dr Beecham and Dr van Rijgen.'

Mrs Owen went away presently and Fran went into the ward to cast an eye on things and to reassure Mr Owen that his wife would be with him when he was transferred. Other than that there wasn't a great deal to do; she sent the nurses to their dinner and Jenny with them and, leaving the aides in the ward, filling water jugs, went back to her office, where she sat down at her desk and started on the laundry list. She felt restless; perhaps it was the sight of the quiet country she could see from her window, or perhaps it was the knowledge that, after her busy days at the Infirmary, she wasn't working here up to her full capacity. Anyway, she felt unsettled and a little impatient with her life. Was she to go on for ever, living and working in this little country town? Her aunts were dears but they still treated her as though she were a child and she would be twenty-six on her next birthday. Another five years and she would be thirty... She shook her head at her own gloom; nothing ever happened. She turned back to the laundry list and Willy, the porter, came in with the second post. A handful of letters for the patients and one for herself. She got up and went into the wards and handed them all out. Jenny had done the dinners while she had been busy with Mrs Owen and the patients were resting on their beds for an hour. She made her quiet way round the two wards, stopping here and there to have a whispered word, and then went back to the office.

The letter on her desk had a Dutch stamp. It would be from a cousin she hardly knew; the aunts had had a brother who had died and his daughter had married a Dutchman and lived in Holland. Fran remembered her vaguely as a child when her own mother had taken her to visit the family. She had gone to her wedding, too, but although they liked each other their paths didn't cross very frequently.

She opened it now—it would make a nice change from the laundry—and began to read. When she had finished it, she went back to the beginning and read it again. Here was the answer to her restlessness. And one the aunts could not but agree to. Clare wanted her to go and stay. 'You must have some holidays,' she had written, 'two weeks at least. I'm going to have a baby—I was beginning to think that I never would—and I'm so thrilled, I must have someone to talk to about it. I know the aunts make a fuss if you go off on your own, but they can't possibly mind if you stay with us. Do say you'll come—phone me and give me a date. Karel sends his love and says you must come.'

Fran put the letter down. She had two weeks leave due to her and the wards were slack enough to take them; moreover it was a good time of year to ask before autumn brought its quota of bronchitis and asthma and nasty chests. A holiday might also dispel this feeling of restlessness.

She went to the office after her dinner and asked for leave and Miss Hawkins, aware of Fran's worth, graciously allowed it: starting on the following Sunday, and Sister Manning might add her weekly days off to her fortnight.

All very easy. There were the aunts to deal with, though. Fran, off duty that evening, tackled that the moment she got home. The ladies were sitting, as they always did of an evening, in the old-fashioned drawing room, knitting or embroidering, waiting for Winnie, the housekeeper, to set supper on the table. Fran, poking her head round the door to wish them a good evening before going up to her room to tidy herself, wondered anew at the three of them. They were after all not very old—Aunt Kate was the eldest, sixty-seven, Aunt Polly next, a year or two younger, and Aunt Janet a mere fifty-eight. And yet they had no place in modern times; they lived now as they remembered how they had lived in their childhood years between the two wars. It was only Fran's mother, five years younger than Aunt Janet, who had broken away and married, and had died with Fran's father in a plane crash when Fran had been twelve. She had missed them sorely and her aunts had given her a home and loved her according to their lights, only their love was tempered with selfishness and a determination to keep her with them at all costs. She remembered the various occasions when she had expressed a wish to holiday abroad; they had never raised any objections but one or other of them had fallen ill with something they had referred to as nerves, and each time she had given up her travels and stayed at home to keep the invalid company, fetch and carry and generally pander to that lady's whims. She had been aware that she was being conned, but her kind heart and her sense of obligation wouldn't allow her to say so.

She greeted them now, and whisked herself away and presently went downstairs armed with Clare's letter. Her aunts read it in turn and agreed that, of course, she must go. Looking after a cousin wasn't the same as gallivanting around foreign parts and, as none of them had ever lost their old-fashioned ideas about childbirth—a conglomeration of baby clothes, feeling faint, putting one's feet up and not mentioning the subject because it wasn't quite nice, eating for two and needing the companionship of another woman—they saw that Fran's duty lay in joining her cousin at once. She was, after all, their dear brother's daughter and Fran, they felt sure, was aware where her duty lay.

Fran agreed, careful not to be too eager, and in answer to Aunt Janet's question said that she thought that Matron would allow her to have two weeks, starting on the following Sunday. 'I'd better phone Clare, hadn't I?' she suggested and went to do that, to come back presently to say that Karel would meet her on Sunday evening at Schiphol.

'Sunday?' asked Aunt Kate sharply.

'Well, dear, he's free then, otherwise I'd have to find my own way...'

The conversation at supper was wholly given up to her journey. She said very little, allowing the aunts to discuss and plan and tell her what clothes to take; she had no intention of taking any of their advice but to disagree would be of no use. She helped Winnie clear the supper things presently, laid her breakfast tray ready on the kitchen table, wished her aunts good night and went up to bed. It was too soon to pack, but she went through her wardrobe carefully, deciding what she would take with her. Clare was only a few years older than she was and, contrary to her aunts' supposition, the last person on earth to lie with her feet up; a few pretty dresses would be essential.

There was no time to think about her holiday the next day. Getting Mr Owen away to Bristol was a careful undertaking and necessitated sending Jenny with him. Mrs Owen had arrived, breathless with anxiety and haste, and had had to be given tea and a gentle talk, so that the morning's routine started a good hour late, and that without Jenny to share the chores. Then, of course, there was a new patient coming into Mr Owen's bed and Miss Prosser was making difficulties, something she always did when they were busier than usual. It wasn't until Fran got home at last that she allowed her thoughts to dwell on the delights ahead. She was listening to Aunt Janet's advice about her journey and thinking her own thoughts when the image of Dr van Rijgen popped into her head, and with it a vague but surprising thought that she might not see him again for a long time. Not that I want to, she admonished herself hastily, horrid man that he is, with his nasty sarcastic tongue, and then thought, I wonder where he lives?

Surprisingly he came again at the end of the week, on his way back to Holland, to examine with Dr Beecham one of her patients who, recently returned from the tropics, was showing the first likely symptoms of kala-azar, or so Dr Stokes thought. To be on the safe side, Fran had put her in the single ward and had nursed her in strict isolation, so that they were all gowned and masked before they went to see the patient. Dr van Rijgen, being tied into a gown a good deal too small for his vast person, stared at Fran over his mask. 'Let us hope your praiseworthy precautions will prove unnecessary, Sister,' he said. She caught the faint sneer in his voice and blushed behind her own mask. She had, after all, only done what Dr Stokes had ordered; he had spoken as though she had panicked into doing something unnecessary.

Which, after a lengthy examination, proved to be just that. Acute malarial infection, pronounced Dr van Rijgen. 'Which I think can be dealt with quite satisfactorily here. It is merely a question of taking a blood sample to discover which drug is the most suitable. I think we might safely give a dose of chloroquinine phosphate and sulphate...' He held out a hand for the chart Fran was holding and began to write, talking to Dr Stokes at the same time. 'You were right to take precautions, Peter, one can never be too careful.' A remark which Fran considered to be just the kind of thing he would delight in; buttering up Dr Stokes after sneering at her for doing exactly the same thing.

He had the effrontery to look at her and smile, too, as he said it. She gave him a stony stare and led the way to the office where she dispensed coffee to the three of them and ignored him. It was as they were about to leave that Dr van Rijgen asked, 'Who takes over from you when you go on holiday, Sister?'

'My staff nurse, Jenny Topps.'

'I believe you start your leave on Sunday?'

'Yes,' and, after a pause, 'sir'.

He looked at her from under his lids. 'A pleasant time to go on holiday. Somewhere nice I hope?'

'Yes.'

It was vexing when Dr Beecham chimed in with, 'Well, the girl can't say anything else, can she, seeing that she is going to your country, Litrik?'

'Indeed! Let us hope the weather remains fine for you, Sister. Good morning.'

When they had gone she sat and fumed at her desk for a few

minutes. He had been nastier than usual and she hoped that she would never see him again. She got up and when she'd done her desk went in search of Jenny; it was almost time for the patients' dinners and the two diabetic ladies would need their insulin. There were several patients whom Dr Beecham wanted put on four-hourly charts, too. She became absorbed in the ward's routine and, for the time at least, forgot Dr van Rijgen.

There was a day left before she was to go on holiday; it was fully taken up with handing over to Jenny and, when she went off duty that evening, packing.

Her head stuffed with sound advice from her aunts, just as though she were on her way to darkest Africa, she took the early morning bus to Bristol where she caught a train to London, got on the underground to Heathrow and presented herself at the weighing-in counter with half an hour to spare. There was time for a cup of coffee before her flight was called and she sat drinking it and looking around her. A small, neat girl, wearing a short-sleeved cotton dress, sparkling fresh, high-heeled sandals, and carrying a sensible shoulder bag. She attracted quite a few appreciative glances from passers-by, together with their opinion that she was the kind of traveller who arrived looking as band-box fresh as when she had set out.

They were right; she arrived at Schiphol without a hair out of place, to be met by Karel and driven to Bloemendaal, a charming suburb of Haarlem where he and Clare had a flat. It wasn't a lengthy trip but they had plenty to talk about: the baby, of course, his job—he was an accountant in one of the big bulb growers' offices—Clare's cleverness in learning Dutch, the pleasant life they led...

The flat was in a leafy road, quiet and pleasant, within walking distance of the dunes and woods. They lived on the third floor and Clare was waiting at their door as the lift stopped. She was a pretty girl, a little older than Fran, and she flung her arms round her now, delighted to see her. The pair of them led her into the flat, both talking at once, sitting her down between them in the comfortable living room, plying her with questions. After the aunts' staid and sober conversation, they were a delight to Fran.

Presently Clare bore her off to her room where she unpacked and tidied herself and then joined them for tea and a lively discussion as to how she might best enjoy herself.

'Swimming of course,' declared Clare, 'if the weather holds.' She poured more tea. 'I rest in the afternoons, so you can poke around Haarlem if you want to. There is heaps to see if you like churches and museums. Then there is Linnaeushof Gardens and the open air theatre here and the aviary... Two weeks won't be enough.'

'You are dears to have me,' said Fran. 'It's lovely to—to...'

'Escape?' suggested Clare.

Fran, feeling guilty, said yes.

It was a delightful change after life in the hospital; Karel went early to work and she and Clare breakfasted at their leisure, tidied the flat and then took a bus into Haarlem or did a little shopping at the local shops; and after lunch, Clare curled up with a book and Fran took herself off, walking in the dunes, going into Haarlem, exploring its streets, poking her nose into its many churches, visiting its museums, and window shopping.

It was on the fourth day of her visit when she went back to St Bavo's Cathedral. She had already paid it a brief visit with Clare on one of their morning outings but Clare hadn't much use for old churches. It was a brilliant afternoon so that the vast interior seemed bathed in twilight and she pottered happily, straining to see the model ships hanging from its lofty rafters, trying to understand the ornate memorial stones on its walls and finally standing before the organ, a vast affair with its three keyboards and its five thousand pipes. Her mind boggled at anyone attempting to play it and, as if in answer to that, music suddenly flooded from it so that she sat down to listen, enthralled. It was something grand and stirring and yet sad and solemn; she had heard it before but the composer eluded her.

She closed her eyes the better to hear and became aware that someone had come to sit beside her.

'Fauré,' said Dr van Rijgen. 'Magnificent, isn't it? He is practising for the International Organists' Contest.'

Fran's eyes had flown open. 'However did you get here?' And then, absurdly, 'Good afternoon, Dr van Rijgen. I was trying to remember the composer—the organist is playing like a man inspired.'

She studied his face for a moment; somehow he seemed quite friendly. 'Do you live here?'

'Utrecht.'

'But that's the other side of Amsterdam...'

'Thirty-eight miles from here. Less than that; I don't need to go to Amsterdam, there is a road south...'

She was aware that the music had become quiet and sad. 'You have patients here?'

'What a girl you are for asking questions. I came to see if you were enjoying your holiday.'

She goggled at him. 'Whatever for? And how did you know where I was staying, anyway?'

He smiled slowly. 'Oh, ways and means. Your cousin told me you would most probably be here. She most kindly invited me back for tea. I'll drive you, but there's time enough. Shall we wait till the end? The best part, I always think.'

Fran opened her mouth and then closed it again. What was there to say in the face of such arrogance, short of telling him to go away, not easily done in church, somehow? But why had he deliberately come looking for her? She sat and pondered the question while the organ thundered and swelled into a crescendo of sound and faded away to a kind of sad triumph.

Dr van Rijgen stirred. 'Magnificent. Do you like our *Grote Kirk?*'

'It's breathtaking; I didn't know it was so old...all those years building it. I must get a book about it.'

'I have several at home; you must borrow one.'

Fran stood up and he stood up with her, which put her at an instant disadvantage for she had to look up to his face. 'You want something, don't you?' she asked. 'I mean,' she hesitated and blushed. 'You don't—you aren't interested in me as—as a person, are you?'

'That, Francesca, is where you are mistaken. I should add that I have not fallen in love with you or any such foolishness, but as a person, yes, I am interested in you.'

'Why?'

She spoke softly because there were people milling all round them now.

'At the proper time I will tell you. Now, if you are ready, shall we go back to your cousin?'

She went ahead of him, down the length of the vast church, her mind in a fine muddle. But I don't even like him, she reminded herself, and then frowned quite fiercely. Once or twice during their strange talk, she had liked him very much.

CHAPTER TWO

SHE PAUSED OUTSIDE the great entrance to the church and he touched her arm. 'Over here, Francesca,' he said and led her to a silver grey Daimler parked at the side. On the short drive to Clare's flat he made casual conversation which gave Fran no chance to ask questions and once there she saw that she was going to have even less opportunity. Apparently whatever it was he wanted of her would be made clear in his own good time and not before. And since she had no intention of seeing him again while she was in Holland, he would presently get the surprise he deserved.

Her satisfaction was short-lived. She was astounded to hear him calmly telling Clare that he felt sure that she would like to see something of Holland while she was there, and would Clare mind if he came on the following day and took her guest for a run through the more rural parts of the country?

She was still struggling for words when she heard Clare's enthusiastic, 'What a marvellous idea! She'll love it, won't she, Karel?'

Just as though I'm not here, fumed Fran silently, and got as far as, 'But I don't...'

'Oh, don't mind leaving Clare for a day,' said Karel. 'I shall be taking her to the clinic tomorrow anyway—you go off and have fun.' He gave her a kindly smile and Fran almost choked on the idea of having fun with Dr van Rijgen. Whatever it was he wanted of her would have nothing to do with fun. She amended the thought; perhaps not fun, but interesting? All the same, such high-handed behaviour wouldn't do at all. She waited until there was a pause in the conversation. 'I had planned to visit one or two places,' she said clearly and was stopped by Dr van Rijgen.

'Perhaps another day for those?' he suggested pleasantly. 'It would give me great pleasure to show you some small part of my country, Francesca.'

There was nothing to say in the face of that bland politeness. She agreed to go, the good manners the aunts had instilled into her from an early age standing her in good stead.

He left shortly after with the suggestion that he might call for her soon after nine o'clock the next morning.

'Don't you like him?' asked Clare the moment the sound of his car had died away.

'Well,' observed Fran matter-of-factly, 'I don't really know him, do I? He gave us lectures when I was training and he's given me instructions about patients on the wards... He was absolutely beastly to me when I was a student and I dozed off during one of his lectures. I think he laughs at me.'

Clare shot her a quick look, exchanged a lightning glance with Karel and said comfortably, 'Oh, well, I should think he's forgotten about that by now—or perhaps he is making amends.'

A fair girl, Fran said, 'I shouldn't have fallen asleep, you know—I expect it injured his ego.'

Clare gave a little chortle of laughter. 'You know, love, once you've got to know each other, I think you and Dr van Rijgen might have quite a lot in common. He's very well known over here; did you know that?'

'No. He comes to Bristol to lecture on tropical diseases, that's all I know about him.'

'Well, he goes to London and Edinburgh and Birmingham and Vienna and Brussels—you name it and he has been there. A very clever laddie.'

Fran had turned her head to look out of the window; Fran was a dear and Clare studied her... She was a thought old-fashioned but that was the aunts' fault, and save for her lovely eyes she had no looks to speak of. But, her hair was fine and long, and her figure was good, if a trifle plump. Clare, with all the enthusiasm of the newly wed, scented romance.

There was no romance apparent the following morning. Dr van Rijgen arrived exactly when he said he would, spent five minutes or so charming Clare—there was no other word for it, thought Fran indignantly—and then led the way to his car.

'Where are we going?' asked Fran and, when he didn't answer at once, 'where are you taking me?'

He was driving south, through the country roads criss-crossing the *duinen* so that he might avoid Haarlem, and there was very little traffic about. He pulled in to the side of the road and turned to look at her. 'Shall we clear the air, Francesca? You sound like the heroine in a romantic thriller. I'm not taking you anywhere, not in the sense that you imply. We shall drive across country, avoiding the motorways so that you may be able to see some of the more rural parts of Holland, and then we shall go to my home because I should like you to meet someone there.'

'Your wife,' said Fran instantly.

'My wife is dead.' He started up the car once more. 'On our right you can just get a glimpse of Heemstede, a suburb of Haarlem and very pleasant. And down the road is Vogelenzang, a quite charming stretch of wooded dunes; we must go there one day to hear the birds...'

Fran turned her head away and pretended to take an interest in the scenery; she had been snubbed, there were no two ways about that. If these terms were to continue all day then she began to wish most heartily that she had never come; she hadn't wanted to in the first place. She voiced her thoughts out loud.

'No, that was only too obvious, but it was rather difficult for you to refuse, wasn't it?'

'I cannot think,' said Fran crossly, 'why you are bothering to waste your time with me.'

'I dare say not, but now is not the time to explain. And now, if you could forget your dislike of me for an hour or two, I will tell you where we are going. This road takes us the long way round to Aalsmeer. We shall go through Hillegom very shortly and take a secondary road to the shores of Aalsmeer which will take us to the town itself; there we shall drive down its other shore and take country roads, some of them narrow and brick, to Nieuwkoop. We have to drive right round the northern end of the lake and pick up the road which eventually brings us to the motorway into Utrecht. My home is on the far side of the city in the woods outside Zeist. We will stop for coffee at one of the cafés along the Aalsmeer.'

'It sounds a long way,' observed Fran.

'No distance as the crow flies, and not much further by car. We shall lunch at my home.'

She gave him a sideways glance. His profile looked stern; he couldn't possibly be enjoying himself so why had he asked her out? He turned his head before she could look away. His smile took years off his face. 'I haven't had a day out for a long time—shall we forget hospital wards and night duty and lectures by disagreeable doctors and enjoy ourselves?'

His smile was so warm and friendly that she smiled back. 'Oh, I'd like that—and it's such a lovely day.'

His hand came down briefly on hers clasped in her lap. 'It's a pact. Here we are at Aalsmeer. I'll explain about the flowers...'

They stopped for coffee presently, sitting down by the water's edge while he drew a map of the surrounding countryside on the tablecloth. 'There are motorways coming into Utrecht from each point of the compass. We shall join one to the south, going round the city, and then turn off towards Leusderheide—that's heathland...'

'You live there?'

'No, but very near. It's only a short run from here.'

They got back into the car and drove on through the quiet countryside with only the farms and small villages studded around the flat green fields. But not for long. They joined the motorway very soon and presently the outskirts of Utrecht loomed ahead and then to one side of them as they swept past the outskirts. Dr van Rijgen drove fast with an ease which was almost nonchalance, slipping past the traffic with nothing more than a gentle swish of sound, and once past Utrecht and with Zeist receding in the distance he left the motorway and slowed his speed. They were on a country road now, with Zeist still visible to one side, and on the other pleasantly wooded country, peaceful after the rush of the motorway.

'We could be miles from anywhere,' marvelled Fran.

'Yes, and I need only drive a couple of miles to join the road into Zeist and Utrecht.'

'And the other way?'

'Ede, Appeldoorn, the Veluwe; all beautiful.'

'You go there often, to the—the Veluwe?'

He didn't allow himself to smile at her pronunciation of the word.

'Most weekends when I am free.'

It was like wringing blood from a stone, she reflected, wringing bits and pieces of information from him, word by word. She gave a small soundless sigh and looked out of the window.

They were passing through a small scattered village: tiny cottages, a very large church and a number of charming villas.

'This looks nice,' she observed.

'I think so, too,' said Dr van Rijgen and swept the car with an unexpected rush through brick pillars and along a leafy drive. Fran, suddenly uneasy, sat up, the better to see around her, just in time to glimpse the house as they went round a curve.

It was flat-faced and solid with a gabled roof and large windows arranged in rows across its front; they got smaller and higher as they went up and they all had shutters. The front door was atop semi-circular steps, a solid wooden affair with ornate carving around its fanlight and a tremendous knocker.

Fran didn't look at the doctor. 'You live here?'

'Yes.' He leaned over her and undid her door and her safety belt and then got out himself and went round the bonnet so that he was standing waiting for her as she got out, too. She said quite sharply, 'I wish you would tell me why you've brought me here.'

'Why, to meet my small daughter. She's looking forward to seeing you.'

'Your daughter? I had no idea...'

He said coolly, 'Why should you have? Shall we go in?'

The door had been opened; a very thin, stooping, elderly man was standing by it. 'Tuggs,' said the doctor, 'this is Miss Manning, come to have lunch with us. Francesca, Tuggs has been with us for very many years; he runs the place with his wife, Nel. He is English, by the way.'

Fran paused at the top of the steps and offered a hand. 'How do you do, Tuggs,' and smiled her gentle smile before she was ushered indoors.

It was a square entrance hall with splendid pillars supporting a gallery above it and with a fine staircase at its end. Fran had the impression of marble underfoot, fine silky carpets, a great many portraits, and sunlight streaming through a circular window above the staircase, before she was urged to enter a room at the back of the hall. She paused in the doorway and looked up at her host. 'I'm a bit overwhelmed—it's so very grand.'

He considered this remark quite seriously. 'One's own home is never grand, and it is home. Don't be scared of it, Francesca.' He shut the door behind them. 'Nel will bring coffee in a few moments and you can go and tidy yourself—she'll show you where. But first come and see Lisa.'

They were in a quite small cosy room with chintz curtains at the windows and a wide view out to a garden filled with flowers.

The furniture was old, polished and comfortable, and sitting by the open window was a buxom young woman with a rosy face, reading to a little girl perched in a wheelchair.

The young woman, looking up, saw them, put down her book and said something to the child who turned her head and shrilled, 'Papa!' and then burst into a torrent of Dutch.

She was a beautiful child, with golden curls, enormous blue eyes and a glorious smile. Dr van Rijgen bent to kiss her and then lifted her carefully into his arms. He said something to the nurse and she smiled and went out of the room and he said,

'This is Lisa, six years old and as I frequently tell her the most beautiful girl in the world.'

Fran took a small thin hand in hers. 'Oh, she is, the darling.' She beamed at the little girl, careful not to look at the fragile little body in the doctor's arms. 'Hullo, Lisa.'

The child put up her face to be kissed and broke into a long excited speech until the doctor hushed her gently. 'Let's sit down for a moment,' he suggested and glanced up as a stout woman came in with a tray. 'Here's Nel with the coffee.' He said something to her and turned to Fran.

'This is my housekeeper; no English worth mentioning, I'm afraid, but a most sensible and kind woman; we'd be lost without her.' He spoke to her again—she was being introduced in her turn, Fran guessed—and then got up as he said, 'Nel will show you where you can tidy yourself.'

The cloakroom into which Fran was ushered, tucked away down a short passage leading from the hall, was so unlike the utilitarian cubbyhole in her aunts' house that she paused to take a good look. Powder blue tiles, silver grey carpet, an enormous mirror and a shelf containing just about everything a woman might need to repair the ravages upon her make-up. Fran sniffed appreciatively at the bottles of eau-de-toilette, washed her hands with pale blue soap and felt apologetic about using one of the stack of towels. She dabbed powder on her nose in a perfunctory manner, combed her hair and went back across the hall.

Father and daughter looked at her as she went in and she had the strong impression that they had been talking about her—naturally enough, she supposed; and when asked to pour out she did so in her usual unflurried manner.

Lisa had milk in her own special mug and sugar biscuits on a matching plate but they were largely ignored. She was a happy child, chuckling a great deal at her father's soft remarks, meticulously translated for Fran's benefit.

A very sick child, too, the charming little face far too pale, the small body thin above the sticks of useless legs. But there was no hint of despair or sadness; the doctor drew her into the talk, making a great thing of translating for her and urging her to try out a few Dutch words for herself, something which sent Lisa into paroxysms of mirth. Presently she demanded to sit on Fran's lap, where she sat, Fran's firm arm holding her gently, examining her face and hair, chattering non-stop.

They were giggling comfortably together when the young woman came back and Dr van Rijgen said, 'This is Nanny. She has been with us for almost six years and is quite irreplaceable. She speaks little English. Lisa goes for a short rest now before lunch.'

Fran said, 'How do you do, Nanny,' feeling doubtful that such an old and tried member of the family might look upon her with jealousy. It was a relief to see nothing but friendliness in the other girl's face and, what was more puzzling, a kind of excited expectancy.

Alone with her host, Fran sat back and asked composedly, 'Will you tell me about Lisa? It's not spina bifida—she's paralysed isn't she, the poor darling? Is it a meningocele?'

He sounded as though he was delivering a lecture on the ward. 'Worse than that—a myelomeningocele, paralysis, club feet and a slight hydrocephalus.' His voice was expressionless as he added, 'Everything that could be done, has been done; she has at the most six more months.'

The words sounded cold; she studied his face and saw what

an effort it was for him to speak calmly. She said quietly, 'She is such a happy child and you love her. She would be easy to love...'

'I would do anything in the world to keep her happy.' He got up and walked over to the French window at the end of the room and opened it and two dogs came in: a mastiff and a roly-poly of a dog, very low on the ground with a long curly coat and bushy eyebrows almost hiding liquid brown eyes.

'Meet Thor and Muff—Thor's very mild unless he's been put on guard, but Muff seems to think that he must protect everyone living here.'

He wasn't going to say any more about Lisa. Fran asked, 'Why Muff?'

'He looks like one, don't you think?' He bent to tweak the dog's ears. 'Would you like to see the gardens? Lisa spends a good deal of time out here when the weather's fine.'

There was a wide lawn beyond the house bordered by flower beds and trees. They wandered on for a few minutes in silence, with the doctor, the perfect host, pointing out this and that and the other thing which might interest her. But presently he began to ask her casual questions about her work, her home and her plans.

'I haven't any,' said Fran cheerfully. 'I would have liked to have stayed on at the Infirmary; at least I'd have had the chance to carve myself a career, but the aunts needed me at home.'

'They are invalids?'

'Heavens no, nothing like that. They—they just feel that— that...'

'You should be at their beck and call,' he finished for her smoothly.

'Oh, you mustn't say that. They gave me a home and I'm very grateful.'

'To the extent of turning your back on your own future? Have you no plans to marry?'

'None at all,' she told him steadily.

He didn't ask any more questions after that, but turned back towards the house, offering a glass of sherry while they waited for Lisa to join them for lunch.

She sat between them, eating with the appetite of a bird, talking non-stop, and Fran, because it amused the child, tried out a few Dutch words again. Presently they went into the garden once more, pushing the wheelchair, Fran naming everything in sight in English at Lisa's insistence.

They had tea under an old mulberry tree in the corner of the garden and when Nanny came to take her away, Lisa demanded with a charm not to be gainsaid, 'Fran is to come again, Papa—tomorrow?'

He was lying propped up against the tree, watching her. 'Are you doing anything tomorrow?' he asked. 'We might take Lisa to the sea—the sand's firm enough for the chair.'

'If she would like me to come, then I will—I'd like to very much.'

She was quite unprepared for the joy on the child's face as her father told her. Two thin arms were wrapped round her neck and she was kissed heartily. In between kisses she said something to her father and squealed with delight at his reply. Fran looked from one to the other of them, sensing a secret, probably about herself. She certainly wasn't going to ask, she told herself, and wished Nanny goodbye, encountering that same look of pleased anticipation. It was time she went home, she decided and was instantly and blandly talked out of it.

They dined in a leisurely fashion in a room furnished with an elegant Regency-style oval table and ribbon-backed chairs and a vast side table laden with heavy silver. Fran was surprised to find her companion easy to talk to and the conversation was light and touched only upon general topics. Lisa wasn't mentioned and although she longed to ask more about the child, she was given no opportunity to pose any questions.

She was driven back to Clare's flat, her companion maintaining a pleasant flow of small talk which gave away nothing of himself. And at the flat, although he accepted her invitation to go in with her, he stayed only a short time before bidding them all good night and reiterating that he would call for her at ten o'clock in the morning.

Clare pounced on her the moment he had gone. 'Fran—you dark horse—did you know he'd be here? Did he follow you over to Holland?'

Fran started to collect the coffee cups. 'Nothing like that, love, we don't even like each other. He has a small daughter who is very ill; I think he has decided that it might amuse her to have a visitor. We got on rather well together, so I suppose that's why he's asked me to go out with them tomorrow.'

'His wife?' breathed Clare, all agog.

'He is a widower.'

'And you don't like each other?'

'Not really. He's devoted to Lisa, though, and she liked me. I like her, too. You won't mind if I'm away tomorrow?'

Her cousin grinned. 'You have fun while you've got the chance.'

The weather was being kind; Fran awakened to a blue sky and warm sunshine. She was ready and waiting when Dr van Rijgen and Lisa arrived. She got in beside Lisa's specially padded seat in the back of the car and listened, only half understanding, to the child's happy chatter.

It was a successful day, she had to admit to herself as she got ready for bed that evening. They had gone to Noordwijk aan Zee, parked the car and carried Lisa and her folded chair down to the water's edge where the sand was smooth and firm. They had walked miles, with the shore stretching ahead of them for more miles, and then stopped off for crusty rolls and hard-boiled eggs. They had talked and laughed a lot and little Lisa had been happy, her pale face quite rosy; and as for the doctor, Fran found herself almost liking him. It was a pity, she reflected, jumping into bed, that he would be at the hospital at Utrecht for all of the following day; it was even more of a pity that he hadn't so much as hinted at seeing her again. 'Not that I care in the least,' she told herself. 'When Lisa isn't there he is a very unpleasant man.' Upon which somewhat arbitrary thought she went to sleep.

She spent the next morning quietly with Clare and Karel, and took herself for a walk in the afternoon. Another week, and her holiday would be over. She hadn't mentioned Dr van Rijgen in her letters to the aunts and upon reflection she decided not to say anything about him. She thought a great deal about little Lisa, too; a darling child and happy; she had quite believed the doctor when he had said that he would do anything to keep her so. She went back to the flat, volunteered to cook the supper while Clare worried away at some knitting and went to bed early, declaring that she was tired.

Karel had gone to work and she was giving Clare the treat of breakfast in bed when the doctor telephoned. He would be at the hospital all the morning, he informed her in a cool voice, but he hoped that she would be kind enough to spend the afternoon with Lisa. 'I'll call for you about half past one,' he told her and rang off before she could say a word.

'Such arrogance,' said Fran crossly. 'Anyone would think I was here just for his convenience.'

All the same, she was ready, composed and a little cool in her manner when he arrived. A waste of effort on her part for he didn't seem to notice her stand-offish manner. To her polite enquiries as to his morning, he had little to say, but launched into casual questions. When was she returning home? What did she think of Holland? Did she find the language difficult to understand? And then, harshly, did she feel at her ease with Lisa?

Fran turned to look at him in astonishment. 'At ease? Why ever shouldn't I? She's a darling child and the greatest fun to be with. I like children.' She sounded so indignant that he said instantly, 'I'm sorry, I put that badly.' He turned the car into the drive. 'A picnic tea, don't you think? It's such a lovely day.' And, as she got out of the car, 'It would be nice, if you are free tomorrow, if you will come with us to the Veluwe—it's charming, rather like your New Forest, and Lisa sees fairies behind every tree. We'll fetch you about half past ten?'

'I haven't said I'll come,' observed Fran frostily, half in and half out of the car.

'Lisa wants you.'

And that's the kind of left-handed compliment a girl likes having, thought Fran, marching ahead of him up the steps, her ordinary nose in the air.

But she forgot all that when Lisa joined them; in no time at all, she was laughing as happily as the little girl, struggling with the Dutch Lisa insisted upon her trying out. They had tea on the lawn again and when Nanny came to fetch Lisa to bed, Fran went, too, invited by both Nanny and the child.

Being got ready for bed was a protracted business dealt with by Nanny with enviable competence. But it was fun, too. Fran fetched and carried and had a satisfactory conversation with Nanny even though they both spoke their own language for the most part. They sat on each side of Lisa while she ate her supper and then at last was carried to her small bed in the charming nursery. Here Fran kissed her good night and went back to the day nursery, because it was Nanny's right to tuck her little charge up in bed and give her a final hug. She had just joined Fran when the doctor came in, said something to Nanny and went through to the night nursery where there was presently a good deal of giggling and murmuring before he came back.

He talked to Nanny briefly, wished her good night and swept Fran downstairs.

They had drinks by the open windows in the drawing room and presently dined. Fran, who was hungry, ate with a good appetite, thinking how splendid it must be to have a super cook to serve such food and someone like Tuggs to appear at your elbow whenever you wanted something. They didn't talk much, but their silences were restful; the doctor wasn't a man you needed to chat to, thank heaven.

They had their coffee outside in the still warm garden, with the sky darkening and the faint scent of the roses which crowded around the lawn mingling with the coffee. She sighed and the doctor asked, 'What are you thinking, Francesca?'

'That it's very romantic and what a pity it's quite wasted on us.'

She couldn't see his face, but his voice was casual. 'We are perhaps beyond the age of romance.'

She snapped back before she could stop herself, 'I'm twenty-five!'

'On October the third you will be twenty-six. I shall be thirty-seven in December.'

'However did you know?' began Fran.

'I made it my business to find out.' His voice was so mild that she choked back several tart remarks fighting for utterance.

'More coffee?' she asked finally.

Their day in the Veluwe was a success: the doctor might be a tiresome man but he was a splendid father and, when he chose to be, a good host. They drove through the narrow lanes criss-crossing the Veluwe and picnicked in a charming clearing with the sunshine filtering through the trees and numerous birds. The food was delicious: tiny sausage rolls, bite-size sandwiches, chicken vol-au-vents, hard-boiled eggs, crisp rolls and orange squash to wash them down. Fran, watching Lisa, saw that she ate very little and presently, tucked in her chair, she fell asleep.

When she woke up, they drove on, circling round to avoid the main roads and getting back in time for a rather late tea. This time the doctor was called away to the telephone and returned to say that he would have to go to Utrecht that evening. Fran said at once, 'Then if you'll give me a lift to the city I'll get a bus.'

'Certainly not.' He sat down beside Lisa and explained at some length and then said, 'Lisa quite understands—this often happens. We'll get Nanny and say good night and leave at once; there will be plenty of time to drive you to your cousin's flat.'

And nothing she could say would alter his plans.

It was two days before she saw him again. Pleasant enough, pottering around with Clare, going out for a quiet drive in the evenings when Karel got home, all the same she felt a tingle of pleasure when the doctor telephoned. She had only two days left and she was beginning to think that she wouldn't see him or Lisa again.

'A farewell tea party,' he explained. 'I'll pick you up on my way back from Zeist—about two o'clock.'

He hung up and her pleasure turned to peevishness. 'Arrogant man!'

All the same she greeted him pleasantly when he arrived, listened to his small talk as they drove towards his home and took care not to mention the fact that in two days' time she would be gone. He knew, anyway, she reminded herself; it was to be a farewell tea party.

Lisa was waiting for them, sitting in her chair under the mulberry tree. She wound her arms round Fran's neck, chattering away excitedly. 'Is it a birthday or something?' asked Fran. 'There's such an air of excitement.'

Father and daughter exchanged glances. 'You shall know in good time,' said the doctor blandly.

They took their time over tea, talking in a muddled but satisfactory way with Fran struggling with her handful of Dutch words and the doctor patiently translating for them both. But presently Nanny arrived and Lisa went with her without a word of protest.

'I'll see her to say goodbye?' she asked, turning to wave.

Dr van Rijgen didn't answer that. He said instead, in a perfectly ordinary voice, 'I should like you to marry me, Francesca.'

She sat up with a startled yelp and he said at once, 'No, be good enough to hear me out. May I say at once that it is not for the usual reasons that I wish to marry you; since Lisa was able to talk she has begged me for a mama of her own. Needless to say I began a search for such a person but none of my women friends were suitable. Oh, they were kind and pleasant to Lisa but they shrank from contact with her. Besides, she didn't like any of them. You see, she had formed her own ideas of an ideal mama—someone small and gentle and mouselike, who would laugh with her and never call her a poor little girl. When I saw you at the prize giving at the Infirmary I realised that you were exactly her ideal. I arranged these days together so that you might get to know her—needless to say, you are perfect in her eyes...'

'The nerve, the sheer nerve!' said Fran in a strong voice. 'How can you dare...?'

'I think I told you that I would do anything for Lisa to keep her happy until she dies. I meant it. She has six months at the outside and you have fifty—sixty years ahead of you. Do you grudge a few months of happiness to her? Of course, it will be a marriage in name only and when the time comes,' his voice was suddenly harsh, 'the marriage can be annulled without fuss and you will be free to resume your career. I shall see that it doesn't suffer on our account.'

Fran gazed at him, speechless. She was more than surprised; she was flabbergasted. Presently, since the silence had become lengthy, she said, 'It's ridiculous, and even if I were to consider it, I'd need time to decide.'

'There is nothing ridiculous about it if you ignore your own feelings on the matter, and there is no time. Lisa is waiting for us to go to the nursery.'

'And supposing I refuse?'

He didn't answer that. 'You intend to refuse?' There was no reproach in his calm voice, but she knew that, in six months' time, when Lisa's short life had ended, she would never cease to reproach herself.

'No strings?' she asked.

'None. I give you my word.'

'Very well,' said Fran, 'but I'm doing it for Lisa.'

'I hardly imagined that you would do it for me. Shall we go and tell her?'

Lisa was in her dressing-gown, ready for bed, eating something nourishing from a bowl. The face she turned towards them as they went over to her was so full of eager hope that Fran reflected that even if she had refused she would have changed her mind at the sight of it. She felt her hand taken in a firm, reassuring grasp. 'Well, *lieveling,* here is your mama.'

She was aware of Nanny's delighted face as Lisa flung her arms round her neck and hugged her, talking non-stop.

When she paused for breath the doctor said, 'Lisa wants to know when and where. I think the best thing is for me to drive you back and you can discuss it with your aunts. And for reasons which I have already mentioned the wedding will have to be here.' He smiled a little. 'And you must wear a bride's dress and a veil.'

Fran looked at him over Lisa's small head. 'Anything to make her happy.'

He said gravely, 'At least we can agree upon that.'

CHAPTER THREE

THEY STAYED WITH Lisa for some time; she was excited and happy, talking nineteen to the dozen, full of plans for a future which would never be hers, but presently she became drowsy and the doctor carried her to bed where she fell instantly asleep.

Downstairs in the drawing room, over drinks and with the dogs at their feet, Dr van Rijgen observed, 'Thank you, Francesca, you have made Lisa happy. Now as to plans for the future... For a start, you must call me Litrik and, with Lisa, we must present at the least a friendly front. I suggest that I drive you home and we can tell your aunts together. You realise why the wedding must be here, of course? Lisa expects a full-blown affair, I'm afraid, and you are free to invite anyone you wish to attend. Are your aunts likely to disapprove?'

'Disapprove. Well, I don't know. You see they have made up their minds that I shan't marry, but I think that if we just told them at once they wouldn't be able to do much about it. I don't want them to know the real reason...'

'God forbid. How soon can you be free to marry me? It will take about three weeks for the formalities here.'

'I can be ready by then. It might help if you wrote to Miss Hawkins...'

'I'll go and see her. Do you want Dr Beecham to give you away? The service isn't the same as your Church of England, but I dare say you'll feel better if it's on familiar lines.'

It was rather like discussing the future treatment for a patient and just as impersonal and efficient.

'That would be nice.' She swallowed the rest of her sherry and wished that it would warm her cold insides.

'I will arrange your return here and for any family or friends whom you would like at our wedding.' He got up and refilled her glass.

'I must reassure you that you will be free to return to England after Lisa's death.' His voice was bleak. 'The annulment may take a little time but it can be dealt with here; you will have no need to be bothered with it.'

Fran tossed off her sherry. 'You had it all worked out, didn't you? Were you so sure of me?'

He smiled faintly. 'Certainly not. But Lisa was.' He got up and took her glass as Tuggs came in to say that dinner was served. 'And may I, on behalf of Mrs Tuggs and myself, wish you both happiness, Miss Manning and you, sir.'

'Why thank you, Tuggs. I shall be driving Miss Manning back the day after tomorrow; when I return we must make all the necessary arrangements. We hope to marry within the month.'

Nothing more was said about the wedding over dinner and when Fran said that she would like to go back to Clare's, Litrik made no objection. It was a warm quiet night and they had little to say to each other. Only when he drew up before Clare's flat did Litrik say, 'I'll come in with you, if I may—it may be easier for you.'

Karel and Clare were delighted at the news. Beyond remarking that it must have been love at first sight, and the hope that they would wait until she had had the baby before they married, Clare showed little surprise. She plied them with coffee and then tactfully retired to her kitchen with Karel so that Fran could bid her new fiancé good night—something she did in her normal calm manner, thanking him for her pleasant afternoon and asking if he would be good enough to let her know when he wished her to be ready for the journey back to England.

'Well, I'll let you know tomorrow. You will have to come and say goodbye to Lisa. Can you manage the morning? I've patients to see after lunch.'

'Very well.' She hesitated. 'I think I must be mad,' she said suddenly.

'No—compassionate, kind of heart and trusting, but never mad.' He was at the door. 'Remember that Lisa loves you.' He said quietly and closed the door softly behind him before she could answer that.

There was no chance of going to bed; Clare and Karel came back and spent the next hour talking about the momentous news. 'It's fabulous!' declared Clare. 'Fran, he's rich, and I mean rich, and well known and you'll have just about everything you can possibly want. I'm so thrilled. Whatever will the aunts say?'

'I think they will be struck speechless. I imagine Litrik will convince them; that's why he is going back with me.' Anxious to keep the talk light she added, 'Of course, you'll both come to the wedding, won't you? It won't be more than a month, so you'll be able to come; the baby's not due for about five months, is it?'

'Can't you wait till after Christmas so that I can wear something smart?'

'You'll look smashing—wear layers of chiffon like the models in *Vogue*.' She escaped to her room at last but she was too tired to think clearly by then. She got into bed and went to sleep at once.

She was fetched in the morning by Litrik whose manner towards her couldn't be faulted. He was a naturally reserved man so no one would have expected him to display his feelings in public; nevertheless he managed to convey a loving regard for

Fran which more than satisfied Clare. Not that it satisfied Fran. In the car she said forthrightly, 'Are we going to—to pretend all the time? I don't think I'll be much good at it. Calling you dear, and so on.' She turned her head to look at his inscrutable profile. 'You actually sounded as though you are glad that we are going to be married...'

'But I am glad—for Lisa's sake. Is that not a sufficiently good reason? And I am sure that, if you put in some practice, you'll manage a certain warmth towards me. No need to while we are on our own, of course.'

'You are impossible!' declared Fran crossly.

They spent a happy morning nonetheless. Lisa was full of plans for the wedding: the kind of dress Fran was to wear, the food they would eat at the reception, the picnics they would enjoy for the rest of the summer. The doctor translated patiently and when they had at last said goodbye to the child and were driving back to Bloemendaal, Fran remarked, 'I shall have to learn Dutch... I can understand a word here and there but not enough.'

'I'll arrange lessons for you once the wedding is over. In the meantime I know of someone in Bristol who will start you off. Your aunts won't object to her coming each day while you are with them?'

'I don't suppose so. Do I see you again once you have left England?'

'Unlikely. I will keep you informed as to plans. You do realise that you will need to wear bride's clothes? Lisa expects that.'

'You mean a veil and bouquet and a white dress? Yes, I know.'

'Good. Have you sufficient money, Francesca?'

Even if she hadn't a penny, she wouldn't have admitted it. 'Yes, thank you. At what time do we go tomorrow?'

'I'll be at your cousin's flat about nine o'clock. We'll go over by hovercraft from Calais. We should be with your aunts by teatime or a little after.'

Clare and Karel saw them off in the morning, her cousin bubbling over with excitement. The two men shook hands like old friends and the doctor made no bones about kissing Clare. 'We shall see you both at the wedding,' were his parting words.

They appeared to be, reflected Fran wryly, the very epitome of blissful love. But once they were on their way, Litrik reverted to his usual slightly mocking calm. 'Lisa sent you a book,' he told her. 'It's in the pocket of your door. You are to look at it and wear a dress exactly like the one she has encircled with chalk.'

It was a picture book telling the story, in a series of most delightful drawings, of a family of mice. And there, on the first page, was Mrs Mouse, in a wide skirted satin dress and a veil crowned with a wreath of orange blossom, her gentle whiskered face peering out from beneath it, tiny paws clasping a Victorian bouquet.

'Oh,' said Fran, and felt a lump in her throat. 'Does she really think of me like that—a mouse...?'

'The highest honour she can bestow on you, Francesca. Please copy the dress as far as possible; I will see that the bouquet is a replica.'

Fran turned the pages; Mrs Mouse's life was busy and happy; there were mouse babies in abundance, suitably bonneted and gowned, and several pictures of the cosy cottage in which they all lived. She said rather gruffly, 'I'll do the best I can about the dress; anything to make her happy.'

His stern profile relaxed. 'Thank you, Francesca.'

It wasn't until they were on the last stage of their journey that they discussed future plans, or rather, the doctor disclosed his plans. She was to leave the hospital within the next few days, merely going there long enough to hand over to Jenny Topps until such time as a new ward sister could be appointed. This, he observed casually, he had already arranged with Miss Hawkins. He would arrange for her to return to Holland in just over three weeks' time, with her aunts or on her own. He had telephoned Dr Beecham who would be delighted to give her away.

'You will, of course, stay at my home until the wedding; your aunts, too, of course, and anyone else you may wish to invite.'

He slowed the car as they approached the town, only another five minutes' drive away. 'My own family will be there, of course.'

'Oh.' She was startled out of her usual calm. 'Have you a family?'

He smiled faintly. 'A mother and father, two sisters, nephews and nieces, aunts and uncles. Is that so strange?'

'Yes,' said Fran baldly, 'you don't strike me as being the kind of man to need a family.'

'We have a good deal to learn about each other, Francesca.'

He had stopped before her aunts' house. 'Well, yes, but it'll be a waste of time, won't it?' A sudden thought struck her. 'Do your family know—I mean why you're marrying me?'

He had got out of the car and had opened her door. 'No, Francesca, no one knows. It will be our secret.'

They walked up the garden path together and at the door he thumped the brass knocker. It was opened almost immediately by Winnie who, after a surprised squawk, cast her arms around Fran. 'Well, love, there's a surprise—tomorrow we thought...' She took a good look at Dr van Rijgen. 'And who's this?'

'Dr van Rijgen, Winnie.' Fran planted a kiss on the elderly cheek. 'We are going to be married, only hush until I've told the aunts.'

Winnie hushed, only pumped the doctor's arm with warmth. 'They are having their tea, like always, in the drawing room.'

Without thinking Fran caught the doctor's hand in hers and led him down the hall and opened the drawing-room door. Her aunts were sitting as they always sat, each in her own particular chair, with Aunt Kate behind the small tea table. She had the teapot in her hand as they went in and when she saw them lowered it carefully on to the tray.

'Francesca—home a day early? You will of course tell us your reason for that. We are pleased to see you home again, child. Polly, ring for more cups and saucers and fresh tea.' Her rather prominent blue eyes were fixed on the doctor, standing by Fran, her hand still on his.

'I don't think we have had the pleasure...' began Aunt Polly.

Fran felt him give her hand a reassuring squeeze. 'Hallo, Aunts,' she said. 'This is Dr van Rijgen—Litrik. We're going to be married and he has driven me back from Holland so that you might meet him.'

The aunts weren't ladies to show their feelings but just for a moment they were caught off balance.

'Married?' asked Aunt Kate, and, 'How romantic,' sighed Aunt Janet, but it was Aunt Polly who rose to the occasion. 'This is unexpected news, you must forgive us if we are surprised. We had no idea...' She left the suggestion of a question in the air, but, since Fran didn't answer it, went on, 'Welcome, Dr van Rijgen, we are delighted to meet you.' She got up and kissed Fran and shook his hand and Aunt Janet and Aunt Kate followed suit before Aunt Kate told them to sit down. 'You will be glad of a cup of tea, of course.' Her eyes had slid to Fran's ringless hand. 'This is very recent, of course. And when do you propose to marry? Next summer, perhaps?'

'In three weeks' time, Miss Askew. In Holland.' Litrik's pleasant voice gave no hint of doubts about that.

'Three weeks—in Holland—that's quite impossible! Francesca, you have your hospital work to consider, and of course, you must be married here.' Aunt Kate, who liked to arrange other people's lives for them, poured their tea with a careless hand, her lips drawn into a thin line.

'Francesca is leaving the hospital in two days' time,' explained Litrik with what Fran secretly decided was his best bedside manner. 'That gives her time to buy anything she wishes for the wedding and join me before the wedding. We both hope that you will all come as our guests and meet my family. And my small daughter. I am a widower.'

He sat back and drank his tea while the three ladies digested this.

'But Holland,' murmured Aunt Polly, making it sound like a remote jungle in some far-flung corner of the globe. 'The church service...'

'Very similar to your own, Miss Askew. I live just outside Utrecht and have a practice there. Francesca will have plenty of friends and her cousin is only a short drive away. And I am well able to support her in comfort.'

'Your daughter...' began Aunt Kate, fighting a losing battle.

'Lisa and Francesca took an instant liking for each other.' He turned to smile at Fran and just for a moment put a hand over hers.

'She's a darling,' said Fran. 'I'm very happy and I hope you will all be happy, too.'

It was Aunt Janet who spoke. 'Of course we are, my dear. We never expected you to marry. We hoped you would be with us always, but it's all very romantic and sudden...'

'Not sudden,' said the doctor surprisingly. 'Francesca and I first met when she was a student nurse at the Infirmary. I go there to give lectures.'

The aunts, who believed in long engagements and knowing each other for years before deciding to get married, looked at him with approval. Here was a man who had taken some years to make up his mind; no flighty youth sweeping their sensible niece off her feet. 'That is different,' pronounced Aunt Kate. 'We should, of course, have preferred to have the wedding here, but you are a man of good sense, I feel sure, and Francesca and we shall be guided by you. You will, of course, stay for the night?'

'Thank you, that is most kind.' He was at his most urbane. 'I should mention that I have to leave by eight o'clock tomorrow morning—I have an appointment for the early evening in Utrecht.'

'All that way,' uttered Aunt Jane. 'You must be tired.'

Fran, casting a quick sideways glance at him, reflected that he wasn't tired at all; that he was enjoying himself in a secret way. Probably he hadn't met anyone like the aunts before.

Winnie was summoned and told to take their guest to his room. 'The car will be quite safe if you drive on to the grass verge by the gate,' he was told. 'Fran, go with Dr van Rijgen and show him.'

It was a lovely evening and the roses smelled sweet. Fran took several happy sniffs and asked, 'Do you mind? Staying the night, I mean?'

'My dear Francesca, I am delighted to do so. When do you report for duty?'

'I wasn't expected until Monday, but I'd like to go in at eight o'clock tomorrow morning.'

He wheedled the car on to the grass verge, got out and locked the doors before he spoke. 'I'll drive you there and have a word with Miss Hawkins.'

'There is no need...'

'Just leave everything to me. I see no possibility of us talking this evening. Do you suppose you could get up earlier and do a little planning over breakfast? Seven o'clock say?'

'The aunts are not called until eight o'clock, but Winnie will be up. I can get our breakfast—we'll have it in the kitchen. It'll be toast and boiled eggs. Winnie does the dining room before she starts cooking.'

They started up the garden path. 'When I'm at home I call the aunts with tea and get my breakfast; that gives Winnie a bit more time...'

'And does no one ever get up and get your breakfast, Francesca?'

'Heavens no!'

They weren't alone again for the rest of the evening; Fran helped Winnie with the supper, unpacked and got her uniform ready for the morning. She also put water, a tin of biscuits and, after an examination of her bookshelf in her room, a copy of an anthology of English verse on his bedside table. The idea of staying up late to talk to Litrik never entered her head. At least, it entered it, but was discarded at once; with four elderly maiden ladies in the house, it would have thrown a spanner into their stern way of life and quite spoilt the sober picture Litrik had presented.

She was up at half past six the next morning, trotting round the kitchen, laying the table, making tea, cutting bread for toast, boiling eggs. By the time the doctor got down breakfast was ready and they sat down together to eat it, he presenting an impeccable appearance while Fran, mousy hair hanging in soft swathes around her shoulder, buttoned into a sensible dressing-gown Aunt Kate had given her for Christmas, sat unselfconsciously opposite him, gobbling her food as fast as she could. 'I'll not be long dressing,' she told him, 'but I thought I'd better get breakfast over first—I don't suppose you like being kept waiting.'

There was no knowing what he might have replied, for Winnie came in then. Her good morning was severe. 'Miss Fran, you've no business gallivanting around as you are. It's a good thing your aunts can't see you now, sitting there in a dressing-gown—such goings on...'

The doctor's firm mouth twitched although he said nothing. It was Fran who spoke. 'Well, Winnie dear, if you take a good look at the doctor you'll see that he is not the kind of man to tolerate goings on.'

She was biting into her toast as she spoke and didn't look up, which was a pity for the gleam of amusement in the doctor's eye was pronounced. 'Besides,' she added, 'there is nothing of me showing.'

'Miss Fran, I am surprised at you! What the doctor must think!'

He offered his cup for more tea. 'Well, Winnie, times change you know. Francesca and I are to be married very shortly and as she points out, there's nothing visible to upset my normal calm.'

He glanced at his watch. 'Can you be ready in twenty minutes, Francesca?'

Fran bolted the last morsel of toast. 'Yes. Did you say goodbye last night?'

'Yes. I'll be outside in the car.'

She was ready in fifteen minutes, very neat in her uniform, a clean frilled cap perched on to smooth mousy hair. She had been to say good morning to the aunts and goodbye all at the same time, assured them that their guest had slept well and eaten a good breakfast and now she flung an affectionate arm around Winnie's shoulders and nipped down the path to where the car was parked.

'Will it make you late, coming with me?' she asked Litrik.

'No, I have allowed time for that. You have no problems? I will telephone you as soon as I can arrange a date for the wedding—the sooner the better, so try and get your shopping done and the packing within the next ten days or so. Are your aunts likely to delay matters?'

Fran considered. 'Well, they like to do things at their own pace and arrange things to suit themselves...'

'Three of the most selfish ladies I have ever met,' declared the doctor blandly. 'If they aren't ready to travel to our wedding then I am afraid they will have to miss it.'

'Well!' observed Fran. 'Well, I never... You mean that.'

'I always mean what I say, Francesca.' He parked the car at the hospital and turned to look at her. 'If they are not ready and willing to travel with you to Holland then I shall expect you on your own.'

She thought of Lisa. 'I'll promise to do that.' She took the picture book for herself from the pocket in the door beside her. 'May I keep this? So that I can copy the dress as nearly as possible. Tell Lisa that, and give her my love.'

They spent fifteen minutes or so with Miss Hawkins and Fran watched the doctor calmly getting everything all his own way while the unsuspecting Miss Hawkins agreed with all he said. They bade her farewell presently and Fran went back to the car with him. 'Have a good journey,' she begged him and offered a hand.

He took it and held it fast. 'We shall need to put in some practice,' he observed and bent to kiss her.

She stood watching the car gather speed. She had enjoyed the kiss; perhaps he was beginning to like her and not just because she was marrying him to make Lisa happy. The thought warmed her insides, but only for a moment; when she turned round it was to see faces at most of the windows. He had been seen and had seen them, too, and had acted accordingly; it would have been odd if a newly engaged couple had parted with a handshake. The pleasant warmth gave way to rage so her cheeks were fiery with it. The heads at the windows nodded and nudged each other and there were vague remarks about blushing brides, before those of the nursing staff who could leave the wards for a minute or two surged around Fran to offer congratulations.

She received them in her usual calm manner, her cheeks still pink, her eyes sparkling, her thoughts anything but romantic, and presently, since the day's work had to be done, they dispersed to their various duties leaving her and Jenny to go along to her office and begin the job of handing over.

It wasn't just the patients, it was every single article on the wards themselves which had to be accounted for. After a round of the patients and a few instructions to the nurses, the pair of them shut themselves in with a tray of tea and got down to work. Jenny had agreed to take over, at least until the new sister could be appointed, which made things a little easier, for she knew the patients and their treatments and understood the ways of the visiting doctors. All the same, what with the various interruptions from Dr Stokes and the dietitian, the dispensary and the laundry, and, over and above these, the treatments needed by the patients, it was six o'clock before they had finished to their satisfaction. Of course, there was still the ward inventory, a formidable undertaking by Miss Hawkins herself. Fran let Jenny go off duty, made sure that the patients were nicely settled and went into the linen cupboard. She emerged to write the report for the night nurse, phone her aunts to say that she would be home late, and plunged back into the welter of sheets, pillow-cases and blankets. She was still hard at it when the night nurses arrived and it was ten o'clock before she had arranged everything in orderly rows to her satisfaction. In the morning, Jenny could take over the ward, and she would see to the rest. The kitchen wouldn't take long; there was plenty of room in which to lay out crockery and cutlery; the beds could have the bedclothes turned back to make the counting of them easy. The nurses could have time to assemble the contents of the sluice rooms and the bathrooms. Fran went home at last, ate a hasty supper and fell into bed. The aunts would have liked to have talked about the wedding, but there would be time enough for that once she had left the hospital.

The following day was slightly worse although it had its mitigating moments. Fran, gobbling a hasty sandwich after Miss Hawkins's eagle-eyed inspection of ward equipment, was surprised and delighted to find her office suddenly invaded by the other sisters in the hospital, bringing a bottle of sherry with them and a large cardboard box gaily wrapped. She had opened it to find table linen and a rather sentimental card wishing her and Litrik every happiness and she had almost cried at the sight of it. The givers imagined that she was in love and marrying for that reason and she felt sad and guilty all at the same time. And the other good moment of the day was when Dr Beecham came, ruthlessly disturbing Miss Hawkins's inventory, to tell her that he was delighted and more than pleased to be giving her away.

'And I must say you are a fine pair, keeping it dark until the last moment. The wife's coming, of course, and she has bought a new hat, too. Must keep our end up with Litrik's family swanning around. Your aunts going?'

She had told him yes, and he had grunted. 'Gave them a bit of a shock, I dare say.' He patted her kindly on the shoulder.

'Well, you deserve a bit of the good life, Fran; you'll make a fine wife. Litrik's a lucky man.'

Litrik telephoned the next day, pleasantly brisk and businesslike. The date of the wedding was fixed, not quite three weeks away, and he would drive over three days before that and fetch her. Her aunts, he observed, would be taken care of by Tuggs, who would fetch them the day previous to the wedding and drive them back home again on the day following that. 'A short stay, I'm afraid,' he told her with no trace of apology, 'but I have an important conference in Brussels and there will be no chance to entertain them.'

'Do I have to tell them?'

She heard his quick impatient breath. 'I'll write to them. You have left the hospital?'

'Yes. Litrik, we are being married in church, aren't we?'

'Certainly. There is a civil wedding first, of course. The *dominee* is a personal friend of mine and he understands the situation. We will go and see him together. Cold feet?'

'Certainly not. How is Lisa?'

'In seventh heaven, bless her.' His voice warmed. 'She is really happy.'

Which made the whole thing worthwhile, reflected Fran as she wished him a rather sober goodbye.

She was neither impetuous nor impulsive; she spent the first day or so making lists and then took herself off to Bath, where she bought ivory satin, white tulle and fine lace and bore them off to the little woman who had made clothes for half the town for most of her life. If she was surprised to find that Fran wanted her wedding dress to be an exact copy of the mouse in the picture book she forbore from comment, but cut and stitched and fitted until an exact replica lay spread out in her workroom. When Fran went for a final fitting she allowed herself the observation that she had never expected the dress to turn out quite so exquisite. 'You'll look a treat, Miss Fran,' she declared. 'Mind you let me have a photo.'

There were other clothes to buy, of course, but first she had to drive the aunts to Bath so that they might purchase suitable finery. They had taken the news that they were to be fetched by Tuggs without too much argument, possibly because of the letter the doctor had written to them. Aunt Kate had been tart about the shortness of their visit to Holland, but, as Fran had pointed out with her usual common sense, he was a busy man and a prominent one in his profession and his work was very important to him.

Aunt Kate had sniffed. 'I suppose that, now you are to be married, we can no longer expect any care and attention; we three old ladies will have to manage as best we can.'

Fran stilled a rebellious tongue and took a deep calming breath. 'You are none of you old—why Miss Hawkins at the hospital is only a couple of years younger than you, Aunt Polly, and she works full time and housekeeps for her brother as well. And you forget that you have Winnie.'

'And that's another thing,' moaned Aunt Kate. 'Litrik insists that she should come to the wedding with us. I cannot think why.'

'I've known Winnie for years, Aunt Kate, she is my friend and Litrik knows that.' She added, with a touch of asperity, 'I'm taking her into Bath tomorrow to buy herself a hat.'

'I do not know what has come over you, Francesca. We have all said that you are a changed young woman.'

'I expect it's because I'm going to be married. I thought you would be pleased about that, Aunt.'

Aunt Kate looked uncomfortable. 'Of course we are pleased, but we had rather expected that you would stay here and look after us.'

'Well now I'll have a husband and a little stepdaughter to look after instead,' observed Fran cheerfully. She dropped a kiss on her peevish aunt's cheek and went upstairs to try on three pairs of new shoes, a Jaeger suit, two crêpe de Chine dresses, a tweed skirt, a jersey dress with a wildly expensive belt and a handful of sweaters and blouses. She had spent a lot of money, but she had never felt the urge to buy many clothes before; there had been no reason to do so. She had always looked nice but unspectacular; now she had gathered together a wardrobe she hoped would be suitable for a doctor's wife. There was still money in the bank; right at the back of her mind was the dim thought that one day she might need it.

She wrote letters to Lisa, in English but interlarded with an occasional Dutch phrase. Litrik had been as good as his word. A rather formidable lady had telephoned to say that she had been requested to give Fran as many lessons in Dutch conversation as possible. She was a hard taskmaster, but, by the time Fran had packed her bags, said goodbye to her friends and organised her aunts' journey so that they would have no worries, she had learned a score of little sentences off by heart, and any number of everyday words. 'The grammar will have to be learned later,' her teacher had told her. 'At the moment you have none, but persevere with what you have learned and practise daily. Your accent is tolerable and you can make yourself understood basically. I trust that Dr van Rijgen will be satisfied.'

'Oh, I am sure that he will,' declared Fran warmly. 'I can't thank you enough—I mean, Dutch doesn't sound like nonsense any more, if you know what I mean.'

She beamed at the lady, who found herself smiling back, at the same time wondering what Litrik van Rijgen could possibly see in such an ordinary girl. Nice eyes, pretty figure, sweet smile and a charming voice, but hardly scintillating.

He arrived exactly when he had said he would and was received by the aunts, sitting as they always did in their chairs in the drawing room. Fran, trotting to and fro between the kitchen and the dining room, hadn't heard the car. She opened the drawing-room door and poked her head round it. 'Aunt Kate, Winnie wants some sherry for the soup...' She caught sight of the doctor, who had got to his feet at the sight of her, and went a little pink. 'Oh, you're here—hallo, Litrik.'

He crossed the room and put his hands on her shoulders and kissed her. 'I wondered where you were,' he remarked blandly. 'I supposed you to be in your room doing last minute things to your hair or something. Are you cooking the supper?'

The faint edge to his voice made the aunts wince. 'Winnie's doing that,' Aunt Polly hastened to say. 'Francesca always helps.'

He had kept an arm round her shoulders. 'Can Winnie spare you for ten minutes? I'm sure your aunts will forgive us if we have a short time together, perhaps in the garden? There are several small points to settle and we must leave early in the morning.'

He smiled gently. 'We might take the sherry with us and go through the kitchen...'

Fran took the bottle from the sideboard cupboard, reflecting that there was more to Litrik than she had thought; the aunts hadn't a chance. She gave him a shy smile, assured her aunts that they would be ten minutes, no more than that, and led the way out of the room. She was rather warm from the kitchen and her hair had escaped its neat bun; she didn't feel at her best, but on the other hand, Litrik had smiled at her like an old friend.

Winnie took the sherry, ushered them out through the kitchen door and told them severely that they'd better be back in ten minutes otherwise the chicken would be overdone.

In the soft evening light, Fran turned to look at him. 'Don't you like the aunts?' she asked.

'Charming ladies; also, as I have already said, selfish to their fingertips. Do you spend all your time in the kitchen?'

'No—oh no, but you see Winnie is not as young as she was and there are little jobs I can do to help.'

'And can your aunts not help occasionally?'

'They are not used to doing anything like that.'

He took her arm and strolled across the stretch of grass behind the house.

'No last minute misgivings?' he wanted to know.

'Only that I might not fit into your kind of life.'

He let that pass. 'You will find Lisa not quite as well as she was. I think that perhaps we were a little optimistic...'

She looked at him appalled. 'You mean, less than six months?'

'I'm afraid so.'

'I'm so sorry. I can't bear to think of it.'

'Then don't. Let us think instead of securing her a happy life while she is with us.'

'Oh, I promise that I will do that—anything...'

'She is in transports over her new dress—did you manage to get a dress resembling her story book mouse?'

She answered him seriously. 'Yes, down to the last button. No whiskers or tail of course!'

He smiled down at her and put a hand out to tuck away a strand of hair.

'But mousy hair in abundance. You'll be ready to leave by eight o'clock in the morning?'

'Yes. I have two cases and my wedding dress in a box. Will breakfast at just after seven suit you?'

'Very nicely. We say goodbye to the aunts this evening.'

'Well, yes; they don't like to be disturbed too early.'

'Then let us go and join them. Did I tell you that Dr and Mrs Beecham will be driving over the day before the wedding? They'll be staying with us.'

'And the aunts?'

'Of course. The house is large enough. Nel is over the moon opening up the entire place.'

At the kitchen door, Fran paused. 'It'll work, won't it?' she asked him.

His voice was reassuringly warm. 'Oh, yes, Francesca, it will work.'

CHAPTER FOUR

IT WAS ALREADY warm when they left in the morning with Winnie to wave them goodbye. The aunts had been ready to bid them goodbye on the previous evening, managing to convey that although they were happy for Fran's future happiness they were themselves about to enter a period of deprivation caused by her permanent absence. Fran, remembering that as they drove away, felt vaguely guilty. She sat silently, wondering how her aunts would manage until Litrik spoke. 'Stop worrying, Francesca.' His voice was briskly friendly. 'Your aunts will manage very well; they do not really need you—they enjoyed making use of you. I am convinced that within a month we shall hear that they have found a suitable companion to take your place.'

He gave her a quick sideways smile which somehow reassured her. 'Now let us go over our plans for the next few days...'

A quite lengthy business which kept them occupied until they stopped for coffee. The hovercraft was full, for it was the height of the holiday season. Fran drank the coffee and ate the sandwiches which were brought to her and then sat quietly, not bothering to think, while Litrik, his briefcase open on his knees, wrote busily. He must have a great deal to do, she thought idly, but didn't pursue the thought; each time she had seen him he had appeared calm and unworried. She closed her eyes and nodded off on that reassuring thought.

They didn't stop again once they were on dry land and they were at the house as the clock on the dashboard showed the hour of five.

Litrik got out and came round to open her door. 'I've an hour,' he told her. 'We'll have tea, shall we, and then I'll have to leave you until about eight o'clock.'

He didn't wait for her answer for Tuggs was already coming down the steps to greet them and fetch the luggage. And, 'Welcome, Miss Manning,' he said warmly. 'We're all that glad to see you, and there's Lisa in such a state of excitement.'

'In the drawing room?' asked Litrik, and took Fran's arm as they went indoors.

The drawing room looked as lovely as she had remembered it, with the late afternoon sun pouring in and the soft colours of the furnishings glowing against its walls. And Lisa in her wheelchair, with faithful Nanny close by, her small face alight with excitement. The moment they went in she burst into talk and the doctor strode across the room and picked her up carefully and carried her to where Fran had hesitated.

'Mama,' shrieked Lisa and leaned from her father's arms to hug her. She broke into a babble of Dutch then and, obedient to a look from Litrik, Fran sat down and he put Lisa on her lap.

The child was thinner and paler although there was nothing in her manner to show that she wasn't as well as she had been. Fran glanced at Litrik in low-voiced talk with Nanny; he looked completely at ease and Nanny was smiling—perhaps he had become over-anxious… Fran settled down to one of the conversations she and Lisa so enjoyed, both understanding about half of what the other was saying and making up for the rest by a lot of giggling.

But soon Nel brought in the tea, smiling and nodding at Fran and shaking hands and presently Litrik came back and took Lisa on to his knees while Fran poured out.

'Nanny has gone to have her own tea; she'll be back presently so that you can unpack and rest if you want to. Dinner will be later than usual and Lisa will go to bed at her normal time. Tomorrow my family will arrive but not until lunchtime. I'll be at the hospital till about noon. And in the evening you and I are going to see the *dominee*.'

She had expected a busy few days before the wedding although the idea of meeting his family rather daunted her. Supposing they disliked her? And what about her clothes? It was still full summer and she had brought some pretty dresses with her as well as her new outfits. Would it be long dresses in the evening? She sat there, tell-tale thoughts worrying their way across her face.

'One thing at a time, Francesca,' said Litrik gently. 'Pour the tea, will you? Lisa wants to watch you unpack. Would you mind?'

'Of course not; in fact I'd like that very much.' She busied herself with the silver pot and the delicate china and joined in the cheerful talk about the wedding.

Nanny came back presently and Litrik went away, promising to look in on his small daughter when he got back home. His, 'Nel and Tuggs will look after you, Francesca,' were kindly uttered and she found it amusing that halfway to the door he remembered to come back and kiss her cheek.

She had wondered how she would fill in the time before he came home again but she need not have worried. Nanny wheeled Lisa's chair into the lift behind the staircase and, at a smile and a nod from Fran, left her in the large room which was to be hers. It was in the front of the house with a wide balcony. There was a bathroom and dressing room leading from it and it was furnished with beautifully polished pieces in yew and applewood. The floor was thickly carpeted and the three French windows were draped in old rose brocade, matching the spread on the bed. The dogs had joined them, sitting quietly side by side, satisfied now that they had got over the excitement of their master being back home.

Her cases had been unlocked and opened, both of them on a long chest against one wall, but the box with her wedding gown was unopened on the *chaise-longue* at the foot of the bed. She opened that first because that was what Lisa wanted to see most. The little girl's gasps of delight as she spread the dress on the bed more than repaid her for the trouble she had taken over getting it just right. She wheeled the chair close to the bed so that Lisa might finger the material and examine every inch of it and then opened one of the cases and unwrapped the present she had brought. A mouse dressed in a miniature replica of her own wedding finery. It had been a fiddly business making the mouse and then dressing it, but, at the sight of Lisa's ecstatic face, she had no doubt that it had been worthwhile.

The unpacking was hilarious, for she had to describe each garment in English while Lisa strove to copy her and then insisted on teaching her the Dutch, and when Nanny came to fetch Lisa she was drawn into it, too. But presently Lisa was borne away for her supper and bed, which gave Fran the chance to have a leisurely bath and change into one of the thinner dresses, sitting to do her face with extra care and arrange her hair with her usual neatness. And by then it was time to go and say good night to Lisa, a protracted visit as it turned out for Lisa wished to be told a story.

'In English?' asked Fran, mentally surveying her small stock of Dutch phrases.

English it seemed would do very well; it had to be a long story, lasting for several nights and never mind if she couldn't understand any of it, and it had to concern one of Lisa's beloved mice.

Fran, who had a splendid imagination, began an involved tale, interlarded with the odd Dutch word and helped out by a wealth of hand waving and a variety of voices. She didn't hear or see Litrik come into the night nursery; she was sitting on the bed beside Lisa, quite carried away while Lisa sat enthralled. When he sat down on the bed beside her she came to a halt, feeling foolish, although Lisa broke at once into delighted chatter. He put an arm across Fran's back and took his daughter's hand in his and said something to quieten her, then, 'Do go on,' he begged, 'I always enjoyed a good fairy story.'

'Well, that's the end actually; it's in instalments you see.' She felt shy and a bit silly.

'Then I must be sure and hear the second part.' He said something to Lisa and made her laugh and Fran got up and bent to kiss the child good night. The doctor did the same and the child tugged at his arm.

'It seems you are to be kissed, too,' he murmured to Fran and brushed her cheek lightly.

Fran caught sight of the child's eager little face watching them: she leaned up and kissed him with considerable warmth and felt his quick surprised breath.

They ate dinner, a delicious meal, at an elegantly laid table, the doctor completely at ease and Fran, outwardly at least, her usual calm self. They talked of this and that, made no mention of the wedding and discussed the weather. No one, thought Fran, spooning the luscious sorbet Tuggs had put before her, would know, just seeing us here like this, that we are going to be married in three days' time. She glanced up and found his eyes upon her and blushed guiltily as though she had spoken her thoughts aloud.

Tuggs had gone to fetch the coffee and take it to the drawing room when Litrik said blandly, 'We'll have to do better than this, won't we? Do you suppose we might forget our true feelings towards each other and pretend that we at least like one another? It will get easier once we start. Supposing we go to the drawing room and discuss the wedding like two old friends? In fact, could we not regard the whole exercise as an undertaking agreed upon between two people with one object in mind, to keep Lisa happy?'

Fran poured the coffee and handed him his cup. She said slowly, 'I've been selfish, I'm sorry—let's start again.'

'That's generous of you, Francesca, for the blame is mine; I have rushed you along without giving you time to, er—get into the part.'

He smiled at her with a charm to put her instantly at ease.

'Your family?' she asked him. 'I'm scared of meeting them, you know. I mean, do they think that we're...well, that you wanted to marry me?'

'I have told them that I have found the girl I want as a wife. That's true enough, isn't it? I am not a man to show my feelings too often and they wouldn't expect it.'

'And me?' Fran ignored grammar in her anxiety to get the matter clear. 'And what about my feelings?'

'I am sure that you will act your part admirably, Francesca. Shall we consider ourselves partners? I give you my word that I will do all in my power to make life easy for you.'

'And your friends?'

'They will come to the reception after our wedding, possibly we shall be invited out to dinner or drinks from time to time, but that should present no difficulties for you. You realise that your days will be largely taken up with Lisa?' He added bleakly, 'I very much doubt if she will be with us for Christmas.'

Christmas, from the viewpoint of early August, seemed a long way off. All the same Fran gave a little shiver. 'There is always hope.'

He didn't answer that. 'I have arranged to see Ivo Meertens, the *dominee,* after tea tomorrow. He understands the situation perfectly; you can say anything you like to him, ask him any questions, voice any doubts. We will go to his house and you can be sure that anything you say to him will go no further.'

'He—he does approve of what we are doing?'

'Yes. You see, Francesca, we are not hurting anyone, neither of us is emotionally involved, neither of us is hurting the other. On the other hand, we are making Lisa's remaining months happy ones.'

'I accept that,' she told him seriously. 'I promise you I will do my best to make Lisa happy.' Suddenly it was all a bit too much. She mumbled, 'Do you mind if I say good night? I'm tired...'

He got to his feet at once. 'Of course, it's been a long day. I breakfast at eight o'clock if you like to join me, but if you would rather, your breakfast will be brought to you in bed.'

'In bed? I can't remember when I had breakfast in bed. I'd rather have it here with you, Litrik.'

'Splendid.' He walked with her to the door and opened it and as she went past him stopped her for a moment with a hand. 'Good night,' he said and kissed her gently.

She had meant to go over the day's happenings in the peace and quiet of her bed but she was asleep the moment her head touched the pillow. In the morning, sitting up in bed drinking the tea Nel had brought her, there seemed no reason to do so. Besides if she was to have breakfast with Litrik she would have to get up and dress.

The faint lingering doubt that his friendliness and warmth of manner of the previous evening might have reverted to his usual chilly politeness was dispelled when she got downstairs, and she gave a small relieved sigh as he got up from his place at the table, wished her good morning and begged her to help herself to whatever she wished.

Breakfast was in a small room behind the dining room, with a round table and pretty rosewood chairs, a sideboard upon which were several covered dishes, and a wide window overlooking the garden. The sun streamed in making everything warm and bright and normal. Fran settled down to a good breakfast, all her overnight fears banished.

'Lunch will be at one o'clock.' Litrik's voice broke into her thoughts. 'Mother and the family will arrive about half past twelve; I shall be home by then.' He got up ready to leave. 'Have a happy morning with Lisa.' And since Tuggs had come into the room he paused by her chair and kissed her.

The morning passed quickly, walking round the garden with Lisa and Nanny; there was no lack of conversation even if it was a bit muddled. With Lisa borne away for her rest Fran hurried to her room and took an anxious look at her person in the pier-glass. She had put on a cotton dress in leaf green with a wide white collar and soft leather belt round her slim waist. There was nothing more she could do about her face and hair, she decided. She went back downstairs and wandered into the drawing room and found Litrik there.

Her, 'Oh, good, you are back,' was uttered with a warmth quite unlike her usual calm voice and he said, 'Nervous? You don't need to be. Have you had a pleasant morning?'

He was so casual that she bit back all the things she wanted to say. 'Very nice, thank you,' she told him.

He crossed the room and stood in front of her, picked up her left hand and slid a ring on to her finger. 'My grandmother's—I'm glad to see that it fits.'

She looked at the sparkling diamond surrounded by sapphires in an old fashioned gold setting, and then at him, a question in her eyes.

'No—Lisa's mother had no interest in the family jewellery, but I fancy that perhaps you will like it?'

'Oh, I do, it's so beautiful. Thank you very much, Litrik.' Rather awkwardly she lifted her face to his and kissed his cheek. She had wondered once or twice about a ring but now she was taken by surprise. She was bewildered by the sudden urge to burst into tears for no reason at all. Well, there was a reason; he had given it to her with a casualness which made a mockery of the giving. But what else was there to expect? She said quietly, 'I shall take great care of it while I am wearing it.' For, of course, she would return it within a few months...

There was the sound of a car driving up to the door and he said, 'Shall we go and meet my mother and father?'

She had no need to be nervous; his father was an elderly edition of himself, white haired, self-assured and with a warmth in his manner which Litrik lacked, and his mother was splendidly tall, beautifully dressed, with a face which had no pretentions to good looks and the kindest of smiles.

They greeted her with a pleasure she hadn't expected and his mother said at once, 'We are so happy to have you in the family, my dear, and I speak for everyone. There are rather a lot of us but don't let us overwhelm you.' She twinkled nicely at Fran. 'When we have a few minutes to ourselves we will go somewhere quiet and have a good gossip.'

Her English was faultless. Fran smiled rather shyly, 'I shall like that,' and found that Litrik had taken her hand while they were talking.

'Lisa is over the moon,' he told his mother. 'The two of them had an instant rapport.' He broke off at the sound of voices in the hall. 'The family,' he observed and flung an arm round Fran's shoulders. She needed it; her knees were wobbling with fright.

To Fran, who had no family other than her three aunts and Clare, the steady stream of aunts, uncles, cousins, nephews and nieces was quite bewildering. Litrik, standing at her elbow, meticulously introduced her to each and every one of them and she smiled and shook hands and kissed cheeks and forgot their names immediately. One or two of them stood out from the rest: Great Uncle Timon, a giant of an old man with a splendid head of white hair and a fierce moustache and a command of English which left her blinking. And the two aunts from Friesland, Tante Olda and Tante Nynke, formidable in elegant black dresses, gold chains draping their splendid bosoms, leaning over her from their superior height and, surprisingly, positively motherly towards her. There were children, too, well behaved and polite and palpably relieved when they were sent into the garden to play, taking Nanny and Lisa with them. There were perhaps twenty-five people there although it seemed at least twice that number. It was a mercy that they all spoke English with an ease she envied; there had been no need for her to have worked so hard at her Dutch lessons before she had left home for there would be no chance to air what little knowledge she had. Anyway, she would be terrified to try it out on these self-assured relations, even though they were behaving so kindly towards her.

She gave a little shiver; she was a fraud and it was all wrong that everyone should be so bent on making her feel that she was one of the family.

Litrik, chatting to a thick-set middle-aged man whom she vaguely identified as Uncle Hilwert, felt the shiver and drew her a little closer. He said lightly, 'Uncle Hilwert is anxious that we should have a large family. He was the eldest of ten children and he has six sons and daughters, all married.' He glanced down at her, smiling easily. 'We must do our best, mustn't we, Francesca?'

She managed a smile, trying to imagine Litrik surrounded by half a dozen children. Of course, he was marvellous with Lisa but then she was just one child and a very sick one to boot. Six all bursting with childish health presented rather a different picture. She had gone a little pink and given Litrik a quick look and found him still smiling.

Uncle Hilwert was joined by Litrik's sisters, Jebbeke and Wilma, who wanted to talk about the wedding. Fran liked them; they were friendly, anxious to put her at her ease and, at the same time, didn't fire questions at her. They teased Litrik gently and then carried her off to join a group of younger cousins.

'You can have Fran back presently,' declared Wilma cheerfully. 'After all you'll have her for the rest of your life and that's years and years...'

He let her go at once with some laughing remark and she wondered if he felt as bad about it as she did. She must stop thinking like that, she reminded herself as she crossed the room with Wilma and Jebbeke. She had promised that she would fulfil her side of their bargain and that was all that mattered. The circle of cousins opened out to absorb her and it wasn't until they had had their drinks and Tuggs had announced lunch that Litrik came looking for her.

They sat side by side with Lisa squeezed in between them. The little girl didn't say much; she ate her lunch carefully and, as Fran saw with some disquiet, with no appetite, but every now and then a small hand crept into hers and gave it a squeeze. Lisa at least was happy.

There was a general move into the gardens after they had had coffee, the grown ups strolling around, going from group to group, the children milling around happily, taking it in turns to sit with Lisa.

'Happy, darling?' asked Fran, sitting down beside her on the grass near to her chair. Lisa beamed at her. 'Happy,' she echoed. She had the mouse bride clutched under one arm and she was a little flushed. Fran sat quietly, for the child was tired; she took a small hand in hers and said, 'Go to sleep, darling,' and Lisa, understanding her, closed her eyes. Nanny, ever watchful, nodded and smiled at Fran, and wheeled the chair carefully into the house.

Litrik slid down on to the grass beside her. For such a large man he was remarkably light on his feet. If she had expected him to have made some soothing or encouraging remark, she was mistaken. All he said was, 'This isn't too good for Lisa, but she had set her heart on it, and she is happy. Do you like my family?'

'Very much.' If he could talk in that rather offhand way, so could she. 'They've all been very kind...'

He turned two suddenly cold eyes upon her. 'Naturally. You are to be my wife and I am the head of the family.'

She said tartly, 'Oh, I had hoped that they liked me for myself, not because I was marrying you.'

He smiled; the slow mocking smile she remembered so well from his lectures when some unfortunate nurse had given him a silly answer to his question.

'Do not allow such nonsense to cloud your common sense,

Francesca, but, if it will allay your fears, I assure you that, to a man, the family have taken you to their hearts.'

'I am glad to hear it. They must have been surprised; I don't think I'm at all what they expected...'

'What should they have expected?' he asked idly.

'Well, someone tall and willowy and fair, beautifully dressed and used to living in large houses.'

He said abruptly, 'They are two a penny, Francesca; you are unique.'

She wanted to ask him what he meant by that but his mother and the two aunts from Friesland bore down upon them and he whisked her to her feet and gave her a little push. 'Mother's dying to see your dress; you'd better satisfy her curiosity, my dear.'

She took the three ladies into the house and up to her bedroom and displayed her wedding gown and felt pleased at their admiration. 'You will be a pretty bride, my dear,' declared Mevrouw van Rijgen. 'You are so small and slender. You will not mind living in Holland?'

'Of course, she won't,' observed Tante Olda in a shocked voice. 'She will be happy wherever Litrik is. This is his home and now it will be hers.'

Mevrouw van Rijgen eased her feet out of her elegant pumps. 'Nevertheless, life will be different, I'm sure. Litrik has a great many friends and there will be entertaining. You will, I am sure, Francesca, be a delightful hostess and a splendid wife to Litrik—not the easiest of men,' she added with a twinkle. 'What is he like as a doctor? I have often wondered but how could I ask him?'

'He is a splendid doctor; the patients like him; they trust him, too, and that means a lot...'

'And the nurses, do they like him, too?'

Fran smiled. 'Oh, yes, but only from a distance, if you see what I mean; he is—well, he is a bit intimidating without knowing it.'

'He doesn't intimidate you?' queried Tante Nynke.

Fran shook her head. 'No, not in the least.'

'You are a calm girl,' stated her future mother-in-law, 'and an ideal wife for Litrik.' She got up and made her stately way in her stockinged feet to where Fran was sitting on the dressing-table stool. 'I am so very happy to have you for my third daughter, my dear.'

She kissed Fran's cheek and, for the second time that day, Fran wanted to cry. Here was someone she could learn to love, an ideal mother-in-law, and within a few months she would never see her again. Her pact with Litrik which had seemed so straightforward was getting out of hand.

They had tea scattered round the drawing room, with Lisa sitting on her father's knee. Probably the happiest person in the room, reflected Fran, listening politely to Great Uncle Timon booming the van Rijgen family history into her ear. She was rescued by Litrik.

'Time we paid our visit to Dominee Meertens,' he observed and whisked her out the room with the remark that they would be back in good time for dinner. Fran went to drop a kiss on Lisa's small cheek as they departed. *'Tot ziens,'* she whispered and Lisa giggled and answered with the 'bye, bye' Fran had taught her.

There were two cars at the door, the Daimler with Thor and Muff sitting patiently inside it, and a dark blue Bristol with Tugg's head inside its bonnet.

'Tugg's leaving in a few minutes to collect your aunts,' observed Litrik. 'He'll leave the car at Schiphol and fly over—there will be a car waiting for him at Heathrow. He'll drive down, spend the night at an inn and fetch your aunts in the morning. They'll be here by tea time tomorrow.'

They walked over to the Bristol and Tuggs withdrew his head to say, 'Just off, sir. Nel's got everything in hand. I should be back with the ladies by four or five o'clock tomorrow.'

'Good. Get a decent night's sleep, Tuggs. Wim will be in to

clean the cars and do any odd chores so take a couple of hours off when you get back here. Nel's got enough help in the kitchen and house?'

'Ample, sir. Never had so many willing helpers—there's nothing like a wedding...'

He beamed at them both and Litrik opened the Daimler's doors, urged Fran into the front seat, whistled to the dogs in the back and drove to the village.

The *dominee*'s house was by the church, an austere red brick edifice with square windows, a neat front garden and a half-open door. The *dominee* appeared at the door as they got out and as they reached it they heard a subdued confusion of sounds; someone was doing five finger exercises on a piano, children's voices were raised in fierce argument, a dog was barking, and someone, somewhere, was singing with more noise than talent. The *dominee,* probably inured to such domestic sounds, took no notice of them but merely raised his voice a little.

'Come in, Litrik.' He shook hands and turned to Fran. 'And this is Francesca.' He wrung her hand. 'Just as you described, too. The study will be the best place for our talk. My wife will bring coffee and then we can talk.'

His English was fluent but heavily accented and he had a booming voice which Fran considered might be of great advantage in church.

His study was a dark room, full of books, a massive desk taking up one corner. He waved them to chairs and when his wife came in with the coffee tray introduced her to Fran. She was a tall young woman with ash blonde hair and blue eyes. She shook hands with Fran, kissed Litrik and said in awkward English, 'Later when the wedding is over, we must become friends.'

'I'd like that,' said Fran, taking an instant liking to her. She saw her go with regret; the *dominee* was a bit overpowering and Litrik... She wished she knew him better.

She poured the coffee when she was asked to and sat drinking it while the two men discussed some knotty problem concerning the village hall. But presently they put their cups down and the *dominee* leaned back in his chair and addressed her.

'Litrik has told you that I am aware of your reasons for marrying. We discussed it at some length when he first decided to ask you to be his wife. His reasons, unusual though they are, are sound and compassionate and I have no doubt that you agreed to marry him for those reasons. You must dispel any doubts you may have, Francesca; you are hurting no one; you are bringing a great deal of happiness to Lisa for the last few months of her life. The fact that there is no emotional tie between the two of you ensures its success. You are, as it were, working together as you would to cure a ward full of patients, only in this case it is a small child.'

He had got up as he had been speaking and was pacing up and down the room. Now he stopped in front of her, frowning fiercely. 'Have I made myself clear? Your marriage will be as sincere as any other which I have performed; that it is undertaken for the reasons of which I have spoken is a secret between the three of us.'

Fran felt a bit overpowered; this, she felt, was only half-strength; she wondered what one of his sermons would be like when he could employ the full thunder of his voice. Yet she liked him; he was sincere and, she felt sure, fearless, and there was no denying that he had dispelled any doubts that might have been lurking. She looked at Litrik and saw that he was watching her intently.

'I don't think that I had any doubts, but I've not really had the time to think about that. I'm grateful and relieved that you agree with what we are doing and that we'll have your support. There is just one thing...' She cast the doctor an apologetic look. 'When we—when we no longer need to be married, will it be possible to annul our marriage quickly and quietly? Litrik has already told me that it shouldn't be a problem but I was thinking about his family.' She turned her shoulder to Litrik so that she couldn't see his face. 'They have been more than kind to me and accepted me...' She added fiercely, 'I'm not being saintly or anything like that, but I don't want them hurt or Litrik's career ruined.'

Litrik was staring at the back of her head from under lowered lids. 'What about your own career?'

'You said you'd see that I got a job,' she mumbled over her shoulder.

'So I did. I know that Dominee Meertens will reassure you about the annulment, just as I can reassure you that my career won't suffer in the least and we shall do the best we can, the pair of us, not to upset the family.' His voice was suddenly harsh. 'Marriages go on the rocks, you know. What has happened once can easily happen for a second time. Only we shall I hope part without rancour.'

'Remember Lisa,' said the *dominee* suddenly. 'Nothing is quite as important as her happiness.'

'No—no, of course not.' Fran studied the *dominee*'s face; he was a fierce man but a very good one. She smiled at him. 'While we are here, could you tell me if the service is very different to ours; my cousin who is married to a Dutchman wrote and described it to me, but it was all a bit vague.'

He beamed back at her. 'Ah, of course. This calls for more coffee and Siska.' He opened the door and raised his voice above the various noises coming from round the house, and when his wife appeared gave her the coffee tray. She was back within minutes and sat down by Fran and poured out and presently she and the *dominee* described the service between them.

'You know about the civil ceremony first?' asked the *dominee*.

'Oh, yes. Litrik explained.'

'Good. So you see that the ceremony is simple and short. The difference is that he will come with you to the church. You have bridesmaids?'

'No—you see Lisa can't be one...'

He nodded. 'Of course. It will be a happy occasion for her and for all of us.'

She and Litrik got up to go presently. They had nothing to say until he stopped the car in front of his own door but then Fran, unable to contain herself any longer, asked, 'Why didn't you say something? Why did you just sit there? You let Dominee Meertens do all the talking...'

'My dear Francesca, I had already stated my case. What was needed was a third party to give an unbiased opinion.'

'And just supposing he had opposed the whole thing? He might have changed his mind...'

'Which answers your question.' He got out and opened her door and took her arm as they went up the steps. Just in case someone was watching from the house, Fran thought peevishly.

They went together to say good night to Lisa and as they went down the staircase Fran paused halfway. 'Will everyone be dressed up?' she wanted to know.

'I imagine so. Eve of the wedding isn't it, more or less? Tomorrow there will be another dinner party but this evening is rather special—your welcome into the family.' He added kindly, 'Worried about what you will wear?'

'Well yes. I've only some summer dresses with me and some things I bought for later on. There is a skirt and top though... I don't want to let you down.'

'You would never do that. Supposing I got Wilma or Jebbeke to come along to your room presently?'

'Oh, thanks—they could tell me if I had the right things.'

The top and skirt were pronounced just the thing and indeed, surveying her person in the long wall mirror, she had to admit that they did something for her. Litrik, coming across the room to meet her when she got downstairs, bent to kiss her cheek and murmured, 'Charming, my dear. Did you show yourself to Lisa?'

She nodded, smiling shyly, feeling relief.

The evening was a thumping success; dinner, elaborate and

beautifully served, took up the greater part of the evening and afterwards the younger members of the party rolled back the silken rugs in the drawing room and danced.

Fran, who loved dancing and did it well, took to the floor with Litrik and presently everyone was dancing.

Her sleepy head on the pillow, she reflected with surprise that she was happier than she had ever been in her life; she wasn't sure how that was possible when she remembered Lisa, excepting that the little girl was happy, too. She smiled at the memory of the child's excited little face and the small delicate hand tucked into hers. Fran closed her eyes, her last thought of Litrik's light kiss brushing her cheek as they had said good night. Most of the family had been there watching, which was why he had kissed her; all the same it had been nice.

The lovely weather held. Litrik was called away to an emergency at the hospital during the morning and Fran took Lisa for a walk in her chair while the older ladies went to supervise the flower arrangements in the church. Litrik was back for lunch and they all scattered into the grounds of the house afterwards to sit about and gossip. But as they left the table Litrik had taken her arm, saying, 'You haven't seen the house yet, have you? We'll go round now.'

It had taken most of the afternoon; the drawing room, the dining room, a dear little parlour at the back of the house, Litrik's study, a billiard room and several small rooms used for mending and sewing and doing the flowers. Upstairs there were seemingly endless bedrooms, all of them beautifully furnished with bathrooms cunningly fitted into corners and most of them with balconies. There was a floor above, too. 'The nurseries,' explained Litrik in a disinterested voice, 'and more guest rooms. There is another floor above this one. Tuggs and his wife live there, and the maids.'

Fran, following him obediently from room to room, could think of nothing to say.

The aunts arrived at tea time and she bore them away to their rooms to tidy themselves and listen to their account of the journey. A most rewarding experience, they told her, they had been taken the greatest care of by Tuggs. The car had been comfortable and, since no mishap had occurred during their flight to Schiphol, they were willing to concede that flying was a pleasant mode of travel.

She led them down to the drawing room for tea and was relieved when Litrik took charge, introducing them to each member of the family and settling them finally with the two aunts from Friesland and his mother.

Dinner that evening was as elaborate as on the previous evening but there was no dancing afterwards. The civil ceremony was at ten o'clock on the following morning and everyone would have to be up reasonably early.

The party broke up soon after eleven o'clock and Fran, having escorted her aunts to their rooms and wished them good night, went soft footed to take a last look at Lisa. The child was asleep and there was no denying the fact that her small face looked pinched and white. Fran went to her room, undressed and got into bed. At least, she reminded herself, Lisa was going to be happy for a few months.

She woke early in another glorious morning, too lovely to stay in bed. She nipped to the window and pulled back the curtains and opened the door on to the balcony. It was quiet except for the birds; she leaned her elbows on the railing and took stock of the garden below and then became aware that Litrik was standing under the copper beech beyond the lawn. He had the dogs with him and was wearing slacks and an open-necked shirt.

'Come on down,' he urged her. 'We can have a few minutes' peace and quiet before we're engulfed.'

Fran tossed her mane of mousy hair over her shoulders, suddenly aware of wearing nothing but her nightie. 'All right, I'll be five minutes.'

Slacks and a top would do; she thrust her feet into sandals, washed her face and tied back her hair and trod quietly through the sleeping house.

He was waiting by the open front door, the dogs pacing to and fro, anxious not to miss their walk.

Litrik said without preamble. 'This is your last chance, Francesca. You're still willing to go through with it?'

She fell into step beside him, the dogs bustling around the pair of them. She had never been so sure of anything in her whole life before, although she didn't quite know why.

'I'm quite sure,' she told him in a steady voice. 'I went to look at Lisa last night before I went to bed—she looked so pale and ill. I'll not let her look like that...'

He tucked her hand under his arm. 'I beg your pardon for asking you that, Francesca. You are not one to back out of a promise, are you? Between us both we'll keep her happy.'

They turned back towards the house and saw Tuggs coming towards them.

'There's your early morning tea,' he told them and then, accusingly, 'you didn't ought to be seeing each other before you are wed.' He sounded severe. 'Unlucky, some say.' He added hastily, 'Not that you'll be unlucky, sir and miss.'

Litrik laughed and clapped him on the shoulders. 'Indeed we won't, Tuggs. Let's have some of that tea, shall we? Is everything going well?'

'Bless you, yes, sir. Nel's got everyone organised.'

He left them to drink their tea then and presently Fran said in a matter-of-fact voice, 'Well, I'll see you later,' and sped away to take a bath and have a good breakfast in her room as time-honoured custom dictated.

CHAPTER FIVE

LISA CAME TO watch her dress and various cousins and aunts and Litrik's mother paid admiring visits. 'Delightful,' pronounced Mevrouw van Rijgen. 'That is the prettiest dress—how proud Litrik must be, my dear.'

Fran murmured a nothing; she thought it very unlikely that he was even interested enough to notice what she was wearing, although presently, when everyone had left for the *raadhuis* and she went downstairs to the hall where Litrik was waiting for her, she felt a thrill of pleasure at his look of surprised admiration. He handed her her bouquet and they went together to where the Daimler, its windows wreathed with flowers, stood waiting with Tuggs, spruce and sporting a buttonhole.

'Now there's a sight for sore eyes,' he told them happily. 'I never saw a handsomer pair.'

Fran smiled at him. No one could call her handsome, although Litrik in morning suit and top hat fitted that description. Indeed, he looked to be every girl's dream of a husband; it seemed most unfair that he was, so to speak, to be wasted on her. But only for a few months, she reminded herself soberly.

There was a small crowd outside the *raadhuis* and the wedding chamber inside was packed. She saw Lisa, right in front with Nanny, and Dr and Mrs Beecham and her aunts and Litrik's parents; the rest was a blur of faces. The ceremony was short and when the ring was put on her finger she didn't feel in the least married. She signed her name obediently, received her marriage book and left the *raadhuis* on Litrik's arm, to get back into the car and be driven the short distance to the church.

Dominee Meertens was waiting for them there and this time things made sense; now she felt well and truly married. She glanced up at Litrik's face as they turned to go down the aisle and found him smiling; he would be happy now, she thought, because Lisa would be happy, too. The smile was really for her but that was to be expected. She must remember what Dominee Meertens had said: they were working together for the child's happiness.

They went down the aisle followed by the family and a great many people she supposed were friends of Litrik's. Almost at the door she saw Clare and Karel smiling and waving and she smiled back; they would be at the reception presently and she would be able to talk to them, perhaps invite them over for a day... There were more people outside the church now, as well as photographers and guests showering them with confetti and rose petals. Fran smiled and smiled and got into the car at last with Litrik beside her, her bouquet clutched in one hand, the other, with the gold wedding ring, on her silken lap.

She sought in vain for something to say; what did newly wed people say to each other? Or perhaps they just held hands, too happy to speak... It was a relief when Litrik said lightly, 'Well you should feel well and truly married, my dear, twice over.'

'Yes, well actually, I didn't feel awfully married at the civil ceremony. But I liked the church service. How pretty Lisa looked in that pink dress.'

It was easier after that; they talked about the reception and the number of guests who would be coming and the unfortunate manner in which Great Uncle Timon had blown his nose so violently during the prayers. By the time they reached the house, Fran had recovered almost all of her normal calm and when the first of the family arrived, she was standing in the drawing room by the open doors leading to the gardens, with Litrik beside her, looking composed and almost pretty in her wedding finery.

For the next few hours she lived in a kind of mosaic of voices and laughter, eye-catching hats, champagne and a seemingly never ending stream of people offering congratulations. Clare, radiant in yards of flowered chiffon, kissed her warmly.

'Darling, you look lovely. What a day—gosh, you must be over the moon!' She glanced around her. 'This gorgeous house, and I've never seen so much heavenly food. Is he very rich?'

Fran glanced at Litrik's broad back turned a little away from them while he talked to Dr Beecham. 'I expect so.' A reply which puzzled her cousin.

The aunts, determinedly British amongst so many foreigners, nonetheless assured her that they were reassured by the undoubted respectability of Litrik's family and friends, and confessed that they were enjoying themselves. 'It is a pity that our stay is to be so short,' commented Aunt Kate, 'but we do realise that Litrik is a busy man. We hope that you will pay us a visit before very long.'

Aunt Janet sighed. 'It is a pity about the little girl. She has a splendid Nanny, I am told.'

'Yes everyone loves her and she is always happy...'

'She seems to like you,' Aunt Kate sounded doubtful.

'We are both fond of each other. She is my little daughter now...'

Litrik had turned back to her; she felt his hand tighten on her arm, and when she looked at him he was smiling. 'Our Lisa is very precious to us isn't she, my dear?'

Aunt Kate, who prided herself on plain speaking, observed sharply, 'Such a pity that she is an invalid. Will she get better?'

Fran didn't wait for Litrik; she said impulsively, 'Of course she will. She has the very best of treatment.'

'Naturally,' declared Aunt Kate drily, 'with an eminent physician for her father.'

Only Litrik's hand on her arm stopped Fran from speaking her mind at that. He said smoothly, 'I am sure you would like to see round the gardens.' He had caught the eye of a youngish cousin, who made his way towards them. 'Lucas, Francesca's aunts haven't seen the rose garden. Would you like to take them there?'

It was Aunt Polly, who hadn't spoken at all, who lingered behind for a moment to whisper, 'I'm sorry, my dears,' before hurrying away to catch up.

They were surrounded by guests at once. There was no chance to say anything and after that there were the toasts, and since Fran was English a wedding cake to cut, and then more guests.

But presently, after the tea and cakes brought round by the waiters, everyone but the family took their leave. Mevrouw van Rijgen took off her hat and her shoes and settled on one of the sofas, the older ladies sank thankfully into comfortable chairs, the men went off to the billiard room and the young ones went out into the garden. There was to be a family dinner party and directly after that everyone would leave. Fran found it strange but when she mentioned it to Litrik he said blandly, 'But my dear, of course we are to be left alone; your aunts are to stay with my mother and father, Tuggs will go over and drive them home tomorrow.'

He took her arm. 'Let's go for a stroll and take Lisa with us?'

'Like this?' she said, looking down at her satin-clad person.

'Why not? You have to wear your wedding gown until the last guest has gone.'

'Oh, do I? Then let's go into the gardens—Lisa is looking tired, bless her! perhaps we could sit somewhere quiet for a while and she might doze.'

They sat under the mulberry tree, the three of them, not talking, and no one bothered them until it was time for Lisa to go to bed. Fran wheeled her round while she said good night to everyone and then handed her over to Nanny and said, 'Yes, I will come and say good night,' to the girl, knowing that she understood that.

'Papa?' asked Lisa.

'And Papa.'

They went upstairs together presently, she and Litrik, and sat on the small bed talking quietly about the wedding until the child's eyes closed.

Outside in the corridor, Fran said, 'I'll go and tidy myself ready for dinner.'

He gave her a casual glance. 'You look all right,' he told her and her bosom swelled with indignation. Brides didn't look all right, they looked lovely or charming or even beautiful. She turned away to cross the gallery above the stairs but he stopped her. 'Just a minute. Lisa expects to have her morning tea with us—I'll tell Nel to see that it's taken to your room and—I'll join you there.' He grinned, looking years younger. 'If you remember in the picture book of hers, Mama and Papa Mouse take tea together with rows of small mice tucked in between them.'

She was still smarting from his casual acceptance of her appearance. She said haughtily, 'I have already told you that I will help you in any way to make Lisa happy.' She opened her door and whisked through it before she would let him see the tears in her eyes. The day had been a happy one until now, she had actually felt married to Litrik, sure that they would be able to live together as friends, even enjoy each other's company, but now she wasn't so sure. She was just a means to an end, to keep Lisa happy for a few months; he didn't think of her as a person at all; he was a cold-hearted, autocratic, hateful man, and he hadn't changed one iota from the sarcastic egotistical lecturer of her student days.

She did her face and rearranged her veil and then went on to the balcony. The August day was fading into a soft glow and the gardens were quiet now. She would have liked to have stayed there but they might think it strange if she didn't join them. She went down to the drawing room and Litrik crossed the room and took her hand. 'Here you are, my dear. A champagne cocktail before we go in to dinner?' And he stayed with her, going from group to group, suave and charming. He should have been an actor, reflected Fran, whose drink had gone straight to her head.

Dinner, served a little earlier than usual so that everyone could get home that night, was magnificent: oysters, smoked salmon, devilled crab or creamed kipper fillets, followed by fillets of sole bonne femme and then crown roast of lamb or wild duck with black cherry sauce and finally trifle and a pavlova cake with a pear and raspberry filling. Fran, who had eaten only a couple of the tempting morsels served at the reception, enjoyed every mouthful, the whole having been helped along nicely by the champagne. It was a merry meal with a great deal of talk and laughter, but at the end of it, when everyone had gone back to the drawing room for coffee, the goodbyes were begun. Litrik's parents were the first to leave, followed by the rest of the family. Some of them were driving back to Friesland and as the last of them disappeared down the drive Fran asked, 'Did they have to go? Surely they could have stayed the night and gone in the morning?'

Litrik had turned to her with the faintly mocking smile she disliked so much. 'My dear girl—on our wedding night? An unheard of thing!'

She had blushed and walked away from him, back into the drawing room, suddenly feeling lonely. Even the aunts would have been company but they had kissed her good night and wished her well with a faint air of self-pity; they would miss her, they said, and Litrik, overhearing Aunt Polly's comment that they would have to manage as best they could now, allowed himself a smile.

He had followed her into the drawing room. 'Breakfast at

the usual time?' he asked her. 'With Lisa, of course. I've a full day's work tomorrow but I should be home by tea time. I'm sure you and Lisa will find plenty to do.'

She turned to face him. 'Oh, yes, we've so many plans… It was a very nice day.' She paused, it seemed rather a lukewarm way of describing one's wedding day but he, at least, hadn't even called it that. She would have to go to bed content with the fact that she had looked all right.

She said abruptly. 'Good night, Litrik,' and turned and flew up the stairs and into her splendid bedroom, where she undressed very fast and then spent far too long in a hot bath, having a good cry. He could have said something nice even if it wasn't true. After all it had been her wedding day. His family and friends had been sweet and admired her dress and said how pretty she had looked. She hadn't quite believed them but it had been nice to hear, all the same. She got into bed at last with a headache from too much champagne and crying, and then got out again to creep along the corridor to take a look at Lisa. There was a night light by her bed and she looked small and frail by its dim light. Fran turned and went back to her room, pausing to look over the gallery to the hall below. The house was quiet, although there were lights below. As she stood there she saw the study door open and Litrik come out and close the door behind him. She bolted back into her own room then and leapt into bed and turned out the lamps, which when she thought about it was silly and quite unnecessary.

She slept, although she hadn't thought she would, to be wakened by Nel with her early morning tea and a minute later a tap on the door and Nanny carrying Lisa, pink cheeked and eyes sparkling.

Nanny, settling her carefully beside Fran, said softly, 'Good morning, Mevrouw. There is fever this morning, will you tell the doctor?'

Fran nodded, 'Yes, of course, Nanny. He'll want to see you?'

'I think yes, Mevrouw.' Nanny slipped away and Fran lent

an ear to Lisa's happy chatter, understanding most of it. When there was a knock on the door and Litrik came in in his dressing-gown she stared at him open-mouthed and then remembered that he was to have his tea each morning *en famille* because that was what Lisa expected. His good morning was cheerful and he bent to brush her cheek before sitting down on the bed beside his daughter, embarking on a long conversation with her while Fran poured the tea, but presently he asked in English, 'You slept well?'

'Yes, thank you.' She wondered why he looked at her so intently, unaware that her nose was pink as were her eyelids from crying. She handed him a biscuit and after a moment offered him more tea.

'I must say this is a pleasant way in which to begin the day. Very domestic.'

'Yes. Nanny wants to see you before you go.'

He nodded calmly. 'Yes, I can see why. A quiet day if you can manage it, Francesca. There are several pleasant walks round here if you feel like it. If you can manage the chair down to the lake you could sit there—she loves that and she may sleep.'

'I'll do that. It'll give Nanny some time to herself, too.'

He put down his cup, ruffled Lisa's hair and kissed her gently and got up. 'I'll leave you to dress, both of you, though you look very nice as you are.' He smiled slowly at her look. 'And I mustn't forget this, must I?' He bent and kissed her again, this time without haste, and Lisa laughed and clapped her hands and gabbled something to her father.

'We are agreed, Lisa and I,' he told Fran, 'that you are a perfect mama.'

'That is at least something,' said Fran tartly, and, at his sudden cold stare, instantly regretted the remark.

Despite her outward serenity, she had been nervous about her new life, but she need not have been. Nanny and Nel and Tuggs nudged her carefully through the day, always appearing just when she was in doubt about something, gently suggested coffee, a walk in the grounds with Lisa, lunch with the little girl and Nanny on the shady veranda at the back of the house, and perhaps a swim in the pool, tucked away in a corner of the gardens, while the little girl had her afternoon nap.

When Lisa awoke, she took the little girl down to the lake on the other side of the lane running past the house. By the time Litrik got home she was feeling her feet sufficiently to greet him in what she hoped was a properly wifely fashion under Lisa's sharp eyes. The three of them played cards until Lisa was borne off to bed and Litrik went to his study, saying that they would see each other at dinner. Which left Fran free to go to her room and put on one of her new dresses.

She was agreeably surprised how pleasant the evening was. True, as soon as dinner was over, Litrik excused himself once more, but they had talked easily enough over the meal and he had observed that they might expect a good many friends to call within the next few weeks and, as well as that, dinner invitations. 'And I shall be free on Saturday—we might take Lisa to the sea for the day; this weather can't last much longer and it may be our last chance.'

They had had their coffee at the table and presently Fran said, 'Well, don't let me keep you from your work,' and got to her feet, followed with unflattering briskness by Litrik. 'I'm quite tired,' she told him mendaciously, and, since Tuggs was in the room, 'don't be late, will you?'

'I'll be as quick as I can, darling.' Uttered in just the right kind of voice. She blushed and Tuggs looked sentimental.

It was too early to go to bed; she went through the hall and into the drawing room. There was a grand piano at one end with a wall sconce shining invitingly on to its keyboard. The room was only dimly lighted but there was a log fire burning in the great hearth. Fran closed the door after her, went to the piano and sat down before it. She was by no means a brilliant pianist but she had talent and feeling. Perhaps if she played for a little while she might be able to throw off the vague feeling of disquiet... Half an hour of Delius, Chopin, Debussy and as much as she could remember of the score of *Cats* soothed her, uplifting her spirits sufficiently for her to embark on *Me and My Girl* when something made her pause and look round. At the other end of the room, sitting in the great wing chair by the fire, was Litrik, stretched out comfortably in the fire's warmth.

'Don't stop,' he begged her, but she got up, closed the piano and stood very straight beside it. 'If I disturbed you, I'm sorry,' she began.

'Not in the least, you play delightfully. Did you know that Lisa loves music? You must play for her some time.'

He got up from his chair and walked towards her. 'You did not find the day too difficult?'

'No, everyone has been so kind, I—I felt quite at home.'

'Good. One day soon we must go to Utrecht and you can buy some clothes.'

'There's no need.' The idea of spending his money bothered her.

'You are mistaken. We shall be invited out; I have a number of friends who will ask us to dine and later we must give a dinner party ourselves. For these you must be suitably dressed. I am a wealthy man and well known.'

She thought of her carefully chosen wardrobe which had seemed so right when she had bought it. Evidently it hadn't been suitable at all; he might even be ashamed of her. She swallowed mounting rage.

She said in a high voice, 'Ah—fringe benefits, how delightful. May I spend as much as I like?'

'Within reason...'

'Well, since I have no idea of your income, nor do I wish to know, that's going to be difficult, isn't it?' Her eyes glittered with temper. 'But don't worry, I'll do you proud—I've always wanted to wear *haute couture*.'

She went past him towards the door. 'You can always mortgage the house,' she told him flippantly as she closed the door behind her.

She didn't hear his low laugh; she was shaking with rage as she went up to her bed. Presently, sitting up in bed, she made a list on the back of an envelope. It was a long list; every single garment she could think of was on it and even roughly priced. The total cost ran into four figures. She cast paper and pen from her and turned out the light. She had married him to make Lisa's short life happy and for no other reason. He had said nothing about dinner parties and social occasions; well, if he wanted a dressed-up puppet he should have one. Pure silk, she reflected sleepily, cashmere, Gucci shoes and handbags and wildly expensive leather belts, she would have them all.

He played his part very nicely in the morning, joking with Lisa while they had their tea and Fran, because she had a promise to keep, was everything that Lisa expected of her. They spent another leisurely day, culminating in Litrik's return, tea on the veranda and a boisterous game of Ludo. In the evening, as the two of them sat down to dinner, he had an urgent call to go to the hospital in Utrecht, so that Fran ate alone and, since he didn't return, went to bed.

The days were falling into a pattern. It seemed that, for the time being at least, no one expected her to take over the housekeeping, something she hadn't wanted to do anyway. She was kept busy enough with Lisa, arranging the flowers, talking with Litrik's family on the telephone and, when there was a spare half hour, inspecting the cupboards Nel opened for her to look through. But as Tuggs was careful to explain, Lisa came first, the running of the house could come later.

The fine weather held; with an excited little girl cocooned on the back seat, they set out for Noordwijk aan Zee with the dogs and a picnic hamper and somehow, once they were there, with Litrik pushing the chair along the water's edge and Fran strolling along picking up shells and seaweed for Lisa to see, she dropped her guard, laughing and talking with a surprisingly friendly Litrik, a happy state of affairs which lasted all day. It wasn't until Lisa was safely tucked up in bed and they were sitting over their drinks before dinner that Litrik leaned across and tossed a cheque book into her lap.

'Lisa is due for a check up next week—on Monday morning. I suggest that you come in with us and go shopping while she is at the hospital.'

She stared down at the cheque book. 'Perhaps Lisa would like to come with me...'

'Far too tiring. Buy all you want and bring it home to show her.'

'All I want? You mean that, Litrik?'

'Did I not say so? Indulge yourself, Francesca. Presumably you like clothes as much as any other woman?'

She thought of her carefully made out list. 'Indeed I do. It will probably need more than one morning to buy all the things that I should like.'

'You can drive. There is a Mini in the garage—you can leave Lisa with Nanny.'

She said serenely. 'Thank you, I'll do that. And may I take Lisa for short drives around the country?'

'Why not?' He sounded faintly bored. 'The roads are quiet and you say you can drive.'

Tuggs came to tell them that dinner was ready and Fran was careful to keep their talk on safe grounds. The pleasant *bonhomie* they had enjoyed on the beach had gone; she supposed that it was all part and parcel of keeping Lisa happy—when she wasn't with them there was no need to pretend. Litrik was a reserved man and Tuggs and Nel wouldn't expect him to be otherwise, even though he was so recently married. She agreed pleasantly with him about the pleasure of their day; agreed, too, that they should accept the several invitations which they had received to dine with his friends. She accompanied him to the drawing room and poured their coffee, smilingly agreed, for Tuggs's benefit, that it was a pity that he had a lecture to prepare for his next teaching round, and picked up the knitting she had so fortunately packed, a soothing occupation, sorely needed. Her serene exterior masked a smouldering rage; Litrik had tossed the cheque book at her with the casual air of a man throwing his dog a biscuit. It had taken all her self-control not to throw it back at him, and now she was glad that she hadn't. She would go shopping and she would make sure that he wouldn't forget it in a hurry. Fran, usually so mild-tempered and kind, seethed with temper.

The knitting wasn't helping much. She went to the piano and lifted the lid and then went back to the big double door and made sure that it was closed before settling down on the piano stool. Litrik's study was on the other side of the hall and the house was large; if she kept her foot on the soft pedal, he wouldn't hear a note. She played Mendelssohn, Debussy and Grieg and at length closed the piano. She was crossing the room to pick up her knitting when a faint sound made her turn her head. Litrik was sitting in one of the big winged chairs in the bay window.

'Delightful,' he observed, 'but why the soft pedal?'

'How did you get in here?'

'Er—there is a small door from the back of the hall. I didn't want to disturb you. Even with the soft pedal down, it was obvious to me that you were taking your feelings out on the piano.'

Words—whole sentences of a vitriolic nature—were on her tongue. She swallowed the lot, wished him an icy good night and went out of the room.

Since the next day was Sunday, they went to church, sitting in the family pew under the pulpit with Lisa in her chair between them. Fran, listening with half an ear to Dominee Meertens thundering what sounded like warnings of eternal damnation, allowed her thoughts to wander. Nothing could have been pleasanter than Litrik's manner that morning and she perforce, with Lisa's eyes upon them both, had to match his manner with her own. The strain of being a supposedly loving wife was beginning to tell on her. Being a mother to Lisa wasn't hard at all; the child responded to love like a flower to sunshine and Fran had not found it hard to love her. So unlike her father: no feelings at all, rude, arrogant and too much money for his own good. He needed taking down a peg; she would enjoy doing that. She frowned; she had entered into her pact with Litrik meaning to do all she could to help him make Lisa happy, but somehow it wasn't turning out like that at all. She was allowing her personal feelings to take over and it was Lisa who mattered. She glanced down at the little face beside hers and smiled and tucked a small hand in hers, promising herself silently that she would keep a guard on her tongue and try harder to like Litrik. She would, she reflected, like him very much if only he were different. She was prevented from pursuing this line of thought by Dominee Meerten's rolling periods coming to a stop and everyone getting to their feet for prayers.

Presently they made their way down the aisle to shake the *dominee*'s hand and then chat with acquaintances of Litrik. It was a splendid opportunity for Fran to air her sparse Dutch, which she did reluctantly but with an unconscious charm which earned her a good deal of praise, even if it was unmerited. What with that and her good resolutions during the sermon, the day proved to be pleasant enough. Litrik laid himself out to be an amusing companion and Lisa was at her happiest; it wasn't hard for Fran to play her part.

Indeed the day had gone so well that before she went to sleep she had almost decided to tear up her shopping list and make out another one of three or four basic outfits, reasonably priced. It was unfortunate that when she went down to breakfast, dressed for the day in one of the jersey outfits, Litrik should look up from his letters to remark, 'Ah, Mama Mouse, shortly to be turned into a swan, if I may mix my metaphors.' His cool gaze took in her unassuming appearance. 'And very much the mouse.'

Tuggs wasn't in the room and Lisa for some reason hadn't yet joined them. Fran sat down and poured herself some coffee with a hand which shook slightly and helped herself to a croissant.

'What—nothing to say?' His voice was silky; he was needling her.

She buttered her croissant and took some black cherry jam. She had no idea why he was being so nasty but she didn't intend to let him see how much it could upset her. Mentally she added a few items, unnecessary and expensive, to her shopping list. She had her rage nicely under control by now; she said serenely, 'I expect you've had a bad night, you'll feel better when you've had your breakfast. Sleeplessness always makes one scratchy...'

She gave him a clear look and a kindly smile as she spoke and was rewarded by his look of affront. And then disconcerted by his bellow of laughter. Nanny came in then with Lisa who wanted to know why he was laughing and he became gentle at once, giving her some joking explanation which made her laugh, too.

At the end of the meal Litrik said, 'You'll come to the hospital with us, Francesca; you can say goodbye to Lisa there—the shops are close by. The car will be in the hospital forecourt but if you want to leave parcels let the porter have them. We shan't be ready until noon at the earliest.'

She agreed calmly and with a smile, careful to preserve her image for Lisa's benefit, and the two of them went off to get ready for their trip to Utrecht, happily engrossed in the peculiar mixture of English and Dutch which they had made their own.

The hospital was vast and impressive; Fran would have liked to have seen more of it, but once they were inside Litrik had suggested, in the pleasant voice he used when Lisa was with them, that she should say goodbye for the present. So she said, *'Tot ziens,'* in a cheerful voice, hugged the little girl, smiled at Litrik and took herself off. It was barely nine o'clock. She had three hours and some of that time must be taken up with spying out the land. She nipped smartly into the centre of the city, only a few minutes' walk from the hospital, and did a rapid survey of the shops. There were plenty to choose from and at the end of half an hour she had earmarked the boutiques which had taken her fancy. By eleven o'clock she was able to heave a contented sigh and pause for coffee. Sitting at a pavement café outside a fashionable department store, she conned her list. She was, to date, the possessor of two of the new season's suits, one in a rich bronze tweed, the other in a soft blue wool, a beautifully cut and frightfully expensive winter coat, a couple of gaily patterned knitted outfits, a dark green suede skirt and waistcoat with silk—pure silk—blouses to wear with them, three after-six dresses in strikingly rich colours and several pairs of shoes, high-heeled and impractical; it seemed only sense to have bought a pair of soft leather boots as well. She found time to buy undies, too, and a quilted satin dressing-gown and matching slippers. It only remained to go then to the particular boutique she had earmarked and see if she could find suitable evening dresses. Never mind if she didn't have the chance to wear them; Litrik had told her to buy all she wanted: and she very much wanted the peach pink organza dress she had seen in the window.

She had less than an hour and she would have to collect several of the dress boxes she had arranged to pick up at the end of the morning. Much refreshed by the coffee she set off briskly.

The pink organza was even lovelier on than it was in the window. She hardly recognised herself when she tried it on for it fitted to perfection. Heaven send she would have an opportunity to wear it... The saleslady was middle-aged and clever and she spoke English.

'We have some charming dresses if Mevrouw would care to look at them?' She suggested, 'If Mevrouw leads a social life now is the time to choose a gown of the first fashion.'

'Something for dinner parties.' Fran already had her eye on a deep apricot crêpe dress with long sleeves and a pretty neckline. 'And I believe we have to go the *burgermeester*'s reception...'

'Mevrouw's husband is well known in Utrecht?'

'He is a doctor. Dr van Rijgen...'

The lady's eyes gleamed. 'Ah, yes, a distinguished man indeed. The wedding was reported in the paper recently. My felicitations, Mevrouw. And may I suggest the apricot crêpe and perhaps this Prussian blue silk with the pleated skirt—just the thing for a dinner party.'

Fran bought them all, paid their astronomical cost without batting an eyelid and, since she was assured that the dresses would be packed and sent immediately to the hospital, set off to collect the rest of her shopping.

She had to make two journeys and, slightly alarmed at the pile of dress boxes the porter obligingly stacked in his office, she waited. He had barely finished when she saw a nurse wheeling Lisa into the entrance hall and went to meet her.

Lisa hugged her as though she had been gone for days instead of hours, and Fran knelt down beside the chair and put her arms round the thin little body. 'You were a really good girl?' she asked, and repeated it in her fragmentary Dutch so that Lisa shrilled with giggles.

'You were missed,' said Litrik from behind her. 'Next time you must come, too.'

Fran got to her feet. 'I would have come this morning, but I wasn't asked.' She spoke lightly because probably the nurse could understand English and Lisa was watching them both.

'She's been a good girl she tells me.'

'Very good. We must think of a little treat for her. You have done your shopping?'

She looked so pleased with herself that he studied her face thoughtfully.

'Yes, thank you. My parcels are in the porter's lodge.'

The doctor watched everything being loaded into the car boot with an expressionless face. Fran, busy getting Lisa comfortable, glanced at him once and decided that he was furiously angry, but when he got into the car and turned to look at her she was surprised to see that he was smiling, his eyes gleaming with amusement.

'Paid in my own coin,' he murmured. 'For a mouse you pack a hefty punch, Francesca.'

And before she could reply he said something to Lisa which sent her off into peals of laughter. 'I can see that there will be no need to amuse Lisa for the rest of the day; she will want to see the lot and, from the look of things, that's going to take hours.'

Fran thought it prudent not to answer that but let Lisa chatter for the short drive back home. She had indeed paid him back in his own coin but strangely she didn't feel happy about it.

CHAPTER SIX

THEY HAD LUNCH as soon as they got in for Litrik had to go to his consulting rooms in the afternoon and then on to the hospital at Zeist.

The boxes and parcels had been borne upstairs and Fran, eyeing their number, went down to lunch feeling guilty. But Litrik made no mention of her morning, the talk was light-hearted while Fran coaxed the little girl, now very tired, to eat something, and presently when the meal was finished she said, 'I'll take her up to her bed—shall I keep her there for tea?'

'A very good idea. Why don't you take your shopping to the nursery when she wakes up and keep her amused while she rests? She can get up for her supper if she wants to; I'll leave that to you—I'll not be back until late this evening.'

Nanny was waiting; Fran told her what Litrik had advised and then went downstairs again. He was in the hall on the point of leaving.

'Before you go, how is she?'

He had his hand on the door and turned to look at her. 'Not good, I'm afraid.' His voice held no expression. 'We must make the best of September and October.'

'Litrik, I'm so very sorry.' Her heart was wrung with pity; without stopping to think she ran across the few yards between them and put her hand over his.

He didn't say anything but he looked down at her hand clasping his, his eyebrows lifted and she snatched away her hand as though his had been red hot. If he had slapped her face she couldn't have been more shocked.

He opened the door then and went out without a backward glance, leaving her standing there, near to tears. When the sound of the car had died away she went into the drawing room and out into the garden through the doors at its end. The weather was still delightful but now there was a hint of early autumn in the air but her shiver had nothing to do with the cool wind. He was a monster, she told herself, and knew that that wasn't true. A monster couldn't love a child as he loved Lisa; go to such lengths to keep her happy. She went and sat under the mulberry tree until Tuggs came to find her. 'Mevrouw van Rijgen wishes to speak to you on the telephone, Mevrouw, if you would take the call in the drawing room?'

A dinner party, suggested Litrik's mother, quite an informal one, if they could manage the following Saturday evening. 'Just a few friends,' said Mevrouw van Rijgen kindly. 'I want to show you off, my dear!'

'It sounds delightful, but I'll have to ask Litrik. May I phone you back in the morning? He is not at home at present and I don't expect him back until later this evening.'

'Of course, my dear. How is Lisa?' And, when Fran hesitated, 'Things aren't so good, are they? I won't bother you with questions now. Ring me tomorrow, Francesca.'

Tuggs had put tea in the small sitting room, fussing gently around her, saying as he left her, 'We're all that upset to hear that Lisa isn't so well, Mevrouw. The doctor'll be cut to the heart and you, too—she loves you like you were her real mother.'

'Oh, Tuggs, I do hope so, but I've known her such a short time. You must all feel very bad about it. I—feel an interloper...'

He was quite shocked. 'Indeed no, Mevrouw. We're thankful that the doctor found you in time.'

'Thank you, Tuggs.' She remembered something. 'The doctor says that I may drive the Mini in the garage. I thought I'd take Lisa out sometimes—not far, but the country is so pretty and perhaps we can stop for tea or just to admire the view.'

'She'll like that. I'll see that the Mini is ready for you whenever you want it, Mevrouw.'

She smiled at his kind face. 'Thank you, Tuggs. You—all of you—have been so good to me.'

'A pleasure, Mevrouw. Will you be going to sit with Lisa this evening?'

'Yes. When I've had tea I'll spend the evening with her. The doctor will be back late this evening—you know that already?'

When he had gone she drank her tea and ate one or two of the little biscuits Nel had made and then presently went up to the nursery. Lisa was still sleeping but as Fran went in soft-footed, nodding to Nanny, knitting at the table, the little girl awoke.

'Tea,' she demanded, and to Fran, 'Mama stay.'

'Nanny, could you ask Nel to let us have a tray of tea? I've just had mine but Lisa might eat something if we have it together.'

And as Nanny got to her feet. 'I'm going to show the things I bought today to Lisa so we'll be all right until it's her bed time. Should we get her up for an hour or two do you think?'

'In her dressing-gown perhaps, Mevrouw. You will be all right?'

Fran nodded. 'Oh yes, Nanny. You go and have your tea in peace.'

Tea came and they shared the small meal together, and then Fran went to her room and fetched the pile of dress boxes.

She dressed in one outfit after the other with Lisa sitting in her chair clapping her hands and laughing with delight. The evening dresses were left until the last and by that time it was Lisa's time for supper and bed. Nanny, coming back, stopped in the doorway to exclaim, 'Mevrouw, what a beautiful dress—you look so pretty!'

Her warm admiration made Fran glow with pleasure; the pink was indeed beautiful and even in her over-critical eyes she looked less mousy in it. She said almost shyly, 'There's the *burgermeester*'s reception in a few weeks, would it do for that?'

The three of them spent a happy half hour examining everything and then Fran got out of the pink dress and into her sober jersey and, while Nanny saw to Lisa, took everything back to her room and hung each garment lovingly in the clothes closet. Tomorrow she would wear one of the knitted outfits, the saffron coloured skirt and patterned jerkin and one of those silk blouses. She sat down for a moment and took out her list. She had noted the prices of everything on it, now she added them up. The total made her gasp; even if Litrik were very rich, he would surely have something to say about the astronomical amount she had written down.

They played their part in the morning, with Lisa tucked up in Fran's bed with an affable Litrik sitting at its foot, drinking his tea. Fran scanned his face and marvelled that he was the same man as the coldly angry one of yesterday evening. Probably, she thought wryly, he'll look like that again when he sees how much I've spent.

She made an excuse to go down to breakfast before Lisa was dressed and found Litrik already there. He got up when she went into the room and she admired—for the hundredth time—his easy good manners.

She went straight to him and laid her neat list beside his plate.

'That's what I spent yesterday.' Try as she might her voice shook a little.

He waited until she was sitting down, pouring coffee with an unsteady hand, before he picked it up and read it. If she had expected anger or surprise she was to be disappointed. His face remained blandly calm and he showed no surprise. She said uncertainly, 'It's rather a lot of money...'

'I believe that I told you to buy what you wanted,' he observed, his voice as bland as his face. Without a trace of sarcasm he went on, 'Perhaps you didn't have sufficient time yesterday; if you need another few hours in Utrecht you can come in with me after lunch—I shall be home by noon—I'll be at my consulting rooms until four o'clock.'

She studied his face; it showed nothing but a disinterested politeness.

'I shan't need any more clothes for months,' she told him and saw the look of disbelief on his face. 'Besides, I've promised Lisa that we'll go for a short drive this afternoon—I'll be very careful.'

'Of course! We dine at Uncle Hilwert's on Friday, do we not? Not too many of us, I believe, and it won't be black ties.' He picked up the first of his letters. 'You'll forgive me if I read my post? There's not much chance once Lisa is here.'

So she drank some coffee and ate some toast, small and mouselike and unassuming despite the saffron skirt and the gaily coloured jerkin. For all the doctor cared, she might have been wearing an old sack; he hadn't even noticed... But Lisa did; she was examined, exclaimed over and admired by the little girl while Litrik smiled at her chatter and said nothing. Presently he got up to go, kissed his small daughter, and then paused by Fran's chair to brush her cheek lightly. 'I like the outfit—a great improvement,' he murmured.

He came home for lunch as he had promised but he had no time to linger over the meal. Nanny whisked Lisa away for her rest and Fran went in search of Tuggs to get a road map from him. The Veluwe would be too far, she had decided, but there was a good sweep of pleasantly wooded country and heath all around them. She pored over the country roads within a radius of twenty miles or so and planned their trip, avoiding the towns, criss-crossing the woods; the roads would be narrow but she was a good driver and there wouldn't be much traffic.

Under Tuggs's fatherly eye they set off presently, going eastwards from Zeist, taking a country road which would take her eventually in the direction of Doorn. She didn't intend to enter the small town, but by-pass it and drive on towards Maarn, turning north, making a rough circle. They had passed Maarn, gone under the motorway and taken a road between thick woods when they reached a crossroad. Fran had planned to go straight ahead, but Lisa had other ideas. The road to the left was nothing more than a narrow brick lane, overhung with trees, the signpost offering no more than four kilometres to Emminheide; not even marked on the map, when Fran looked for it. But nothing she could say would persuade Lisa to change her mind. She wanted to go to Emminheide and Fran gave in.

The road, being brick and rural, was uneven and only wide enough for one car. She drove slowly, since the road, unlike most Dutch roads, wound itself round a multitude of corners and the trees on either side prevented her from seeing any distance ahead. The woods on either side became, if anything, even thicker and she felt decided relief when they passed a small cottage, set back from the road. And presently they reached Emminheide: a cluster of small houses, a very large church and that was all. Fran drove on, wondering where the road led, for it must end somewhere, and after another half mile or so they saw another cottage, standing by itself in a small clearing; trees all around it, a well-tended little garden between it and the lane. There was an old woman in the garden and when she saw them she stopped picking the plums from a tree by the cottage and came down to the gate. Fran stopped and called good day and the old woman answered cheerfully.

'Tea?' asked Lisa.

There was no harm in asking. Fran drove the car carefully up to the gate and began a careful request for a drink for Lisa. She added politely in her best Dutch, 'I will pay you, Mevrouw.'

The old woman came out of the gate and peered into the car,

and she and Lisa carried out a brief conversation, at the end of which she turned to Fran. She spoke slowly now—Lisa must have told her that Fran's Dutch was fragmentary. Of course they could have tea. If Mevrouw would like to carry the poor little girl into the cottage they might sit in comfort and when they were rested, before they returned, they might like to see the lake behind the cottage. So beautiful, added the old woman, and very few people know of it.

There was plenty of time; Fran carried Lisa into the cottage and sat her down in the tiny parlour, seldom used except for important occasions such as weddings or funerals or family visits. It was overfull of tables and chairs and the walls were hung with old-fashioned pictures and photos, but there were some pieces of beautiful old china and a little cabinet housed silver spoons and dishes. They sat at the round table in the centre of the room and drank their tea and ate wafer thin biscuits, and when they had finished, Fran paid their modest bill and asked if they might see the lake. 'If it's not too far—I have to carry the little girl.'

The old woman nodded and smiled and led the way to the side of the garden and pointed to a path through the trees. Fran couldn't understand what she was saying but Lisa did and the child nodded and said, 'Two minutes, Mama.'

'You are learning English far quicker than I am learning Dutch,' said Fran, and laughed and at the same time sighed inwardly for Lisa's light weight seemed even lighter each time she picked her up.

The path was easy and well defined, leading through closely planted trees with no hint of what was to come. It ended abruptly at the edge of a fairy-tale pond, not large, but ringed with trees, fringed with rushes and reeds, its water a clear green dappled by sunshine. There were water coots among the reeds and the plop of fish. There was a willow tree drooping into the water and in season, Fran guessed, there would be kingcups, flags and meadowsweet. From where she stood she could see a water vole motionless on the bank. She heard Lisa's happy sigh and the skinny arms tightened round her neck. 'Pretty,' said Lisa. 'Stay.'

'All right, darling, just for a few minutes.' Fran walked carefully round the pond until she came to a fallen tree stump and then she sat down. 'Story,' demanded Lisa and, after a moment's thought, 'fairies.'

So Fran started off on one of her rather vague fairy tales, made up as she went along, half Dutch and half English. But Lisa didn't seem to mind that, she listened avidly to every word, nodding her small head from time to time and, when Fran paused for breath, urging her on again.

'Look,' said Fran at last, 'I'll ask the old woman if we can come here some afternoons and have tea and sit here...'

She tried again in Dutch and Lisa understood. *'Geheim,'* she said, so seriously that Fran did her best to understand her, but in the end she said apologetically, 'Sorry, darling, I don't understand.'

Lisa pondered. *'Niemand,'* she ventured. Fran knew that. 'No one.'

'Weet,' said Lisa hopefully.

'Know?' cried Fran truly triumphantly. 'You clever girl! Secret, of course.'

They hugged each other for being so clever and then Fran carried her back down the path to the car and settled her in it before going to speak to the old woman who had come to the door to watch them. It took a little time to explain and in the end Lisa did it for her. The old woman nodded, pleased to have visitors and to earn a few *gulden* and after a deal of handshaking, Fran turned the car and drove back the way they had come. They had stayed longer than she had meant to and even if Litrik wasn't home, Nel and Tuggs would worry.

They had time to tidy themselves up before he arrived and when he asked if they had had a pleasant drive Lisa burst into speech. He listened patiently and then said to Fran, 'I gather you've had an exciting afternoon, all very secret?'

'We had a lovely time,' said Fran, 'and yes, it's secret but quite harmless. I promised I wouldn't tell...' She hesitated. 'You don't mind?'

'Mind, my dear girl? Lisa has never been so happy. Far from minding I am deeply in your debt.'

He went over to little Lisa, sitting happy in her chair. 'What is it to be this evening?' he asked Fran over his shoulder. 'Snakes and Ladders or Ludo?'

He picked up the child and went to sit down in the big chair by the table and repeated everything in Dutch. It was to be Snakes and Ladders; Fran got the board and the counters and presently the three of them were deep in the game, cheating from time to time so that Lisa should win.

As Friday drew near, Fran found that she was nervous. She liked Oom Hilwert though he was a bit outspoken, but supposing there were people there she didn't know? Who couldn't speak English? Litrik would be ashamed of her... Common sense came to her rescue; everyone knew that her Dutch was of the kindergarten variety. She would wear one of her lovely new dresses and do her hair in the French pleat she had been experimenting with for the last day or two in the privacy of her bedroom. And if he didn't like it he could lump it, she told herself vigorously.

She took Lisa to the secret pool on Friday and they sat in the afternoon sunshine while she continued her fairy tale, and then she carried Lisa to the cottage where the old woman gave them tea. And when they got home, since Litrik hadn't returned, Fran took the little girl up to her room and showed her the dress that she was going to wear that evening.

Litrik was late home; Lisa was already in bed by the time he got in and there was barely an hour before they had to leave for Oom Hilwert's house. They went together, as they always did, to say good night to her and after a whispered promise that she would come back, dressed for the evening, Fran left the two of them together.

The dress was beautiful. Fran, who had never had couture clothes and had always thought of them as being wildly expensive, suitable only for the models in *Vogue,* realised that she had been wrong. The dress transformed her; it clung where it should, fell free in graceful folds when she walked, and made her feel like royalty. She had managed the French pleat, too, and put on a pair of high-heeled satin slippers which added both to her height and her self-esteem. She picked up her little beaded bag, which she had been unable to resist, and the soft angora stole and went along to Lisa's nursery. The child was still awake and Fran sat down on the side of the bed and showed her the contents of her bag, allowed her to sniff the fine white hanky scented with *L'air du temps,* and then pirouetted slowly so that the full glories of the dress might be studied.

'Darling Mama,' said Lisa sleepily as Fran kissed her good night.

Downstairs Litrik was waiting, immaculate in a dark grey suit and a richly sober tie. She had expected, or at least hoped, that he would say something about her dress, even tell her that she looked nice, but although he studied her through half-closed lids for several seconds, all he said was, 'I should like you to wear these,' and handed her a long velvet box.

There was a double row of pearls inside with a diamond clasp. She took it out with delicate fingers and looked at him, and when he didn't speak said quietly, 'The family expect it, of course...'

He nodded. 'Yes, they've been in the family for a very long time—they're handed down.'

'Or lent,' said Fran matter-of-factly as she fastened the clasp and went to take a look in the great carved mirror over the fireplace. They were magnificent and she touched them lightly while a dim memory became sharp in her head. 'Pearls around the neck, stones upon the heart': a proverb dredged up from something she must have read a long time ago. And oh, so true. She turned away from the mirror. 'Must I wear them?'

'Of course.' He sounded a little impatient. 'You are my wife.'

She stood in front of him, her head a little on one side, looking at him. 'No, I'm not,' she corrected him. 'I'm Lisa's Mama. We mustn't let the whole thing get out of hand, must we?' There was faint rebuke in her quiet voice. She gave him a kindly smile. 'It's difficult, isn't it? It seemed simple enough. Besides, I hate deceiving people, don't you?'

He said very evenly, 'I believe I made it perfectly clear that I will do anything to make Lisa happy for the next few weeks—we can go into the rights and wrongs of the matter at the appropriate time.' He turned away. 'If you are ready, shall we go?'

They hardly spoke in the car and when they got to Oom Hilwert's house there was no need to for they were at once surrounded by the other guests. Fran had to admire Litrik's manner towards her, though: the considerate husband, steering her from one guest to the other, making sure that she had the drink she wanted, bringing her into the conversation, encouraging her to take part in it, so that before they went into dinner she was quite at her ease. She sat on Oom Hilwert's right, with a youngish man, a distant cousin of the family, on her other side, and between them they flattered her gently, admiring her dress, remarking on the pearls, and reiterating their pleasure in having her in the family. 'And I daresay Litrik's loaded you with jewellery,' observed Oom Hilwert, 'though you have the good sense not to wear anything but pearls with that dress.'

'Litrik wanted me to wear them,' said Fran serenely. It was a pity that he was sitting at the other end of the table and couldn't hear.

After dinner everyone gathered once more in the drawing room, a vast apartment heavily furnished and rather grand and gloomy. The talk was largely of the *burgermeester*'s reception on one evening the following week and led to the ladies gathering together to discuss what they intended wearing.

'And you, my dear?' enquired Litrik's mother. 'You have a pretty dress, no doubt. You look charming this evening.'

Fran thanked her nicely. 'Well I found a dress in Utrecht—it's pink...'

'Just the right colour for you, Francesca. You will be able to wear the earrings.'

Fran said warily, 'Oh, yes...' and was saved from saying more by Litrik strolling over to join them.

'Francesca, Oom Hilwert would like you to play for us.'

She smiled up at him while her eyes flashed indignant fire. There was no point in making a fuss and she wasn't going to give him the satisfaction of knowing that he had spoilt her evening. She crossed the room to the grand piano standing in one corner and sat herself down, outwardly composed.

'What would you like me to play?' she asked Oom Hilwert. 'I'm not used to playing in front of people and I'm only a tolerable player.'

The old gentleman beamed at her. 'Play what you wish, my dear, and we will enjoy it.'

She ran her capable little hands over the keys; it was a splendid instrument and she would try and do it justice. She began with Delius and then Schubert and wandered on through Frans Lehar and Strauss and Grieg and then back to Delius, stopping as quietly as she had begun, sitting with her hands in her lap.

They had sat quietly while she played, now they clapped and crowded round her, making much of her and someone said, 'Lucky Litrik, to come home to that in the evenings,' and everyone laughed and someone else said, 'I'll settle for Francesca, never mind the piano,' and they all laughed again. Fran laughed with them, taking care not to look at Litrik.

Driving home presently he said blandly, 'You were a great success, Francesca.' They were driving fast down the almost empty motorway. 'You didn't mind my making you play?'

She was astonished to discover that she wanted to cry. She said stonily. 'I minded very much, it was a rotten trick.' She added childishly, 'It would have served you right if I had sat down at the piano and played chopsticks.'

'Yes, it would, wouldn't it?' he agreed affably, 'only I knew that you wouldn't do that. Do you want me to apologise?' His voice was silky.

'Certainly not. It's of no consequence to me. After all you are behaving as I would expect you to behave.'

'Now why do you say that?' He sounded interested and amused, too.

'Anyone—any man who can reduce student nurses to a mass of shaking nerves before a lecture hall of people, is capable of any mean trick he chooses to think up.'

All he said was, 'For a mouse you have sharp teeth.'

She would have liked to have gone straight to her room when they got home but she stood in the hall, waiting for him while he took the car round to the garages at the side of the house. He looked at her and smiled as he came in and locked the door behind him. 'Friends again?' he wanted to know, and she heard the mocking note in his voice.

'No. Here are your pearls. Thank you for lending them to me.' She was of half a mind to tell him what his mother had said about the earrings. Let him find out for himself, she decided and uttered a rather gruff good night as she went up the staircase.

Litrik was free on the following day; they drove to the Veluwe and had a picnic under the trees, Lisa in a woolly jacket and Fran in the suede outfit, for there was a distinct nip in the air. Litrik was at his most urbane and Lisa was as merry as a cricket. Fran, watching her, couldn't believe that she was going to die. Watching Litrik, too, laughing and joking with her as though he hadn't a care in the world, she stifled a sudden deep sympathy for him. He had, after all, known of the situation for months and must have become reconciled to it. He looked up and caught her watching him and for a moment they stared at each other and then he turned away to tease Lisa gently and presently they were all engrossed in Lisa's favourite occupation—teaching Fran Dutch.

Almost a week went by, each day with its gentle routine and two more visits to the fairy pond where they sat, the two of them, while Fran laboriously wove her fairy tale, almost as absorbed in it as her small listener. The old woman seemed to enjoy them coming, too; their tea was laid out for them in her little parlour and she liked a chat before they went home, sometimes leaving it to the last minute so that they were barely indoors and sitting in the drawing room before Litrik came back. For that was part of the secret; when he enquired as to their afternoon, Lisa would say that they had had a nice drive in the car and exchange a smile with Fran. 'Nice, Mama?' she would ask and Fran would answer, *'Geweldig,'* just to let Litrik see that she was learning Dutch fast.

They didn't go to the pond on the afternoon of the *burgermeester*'s reception; getting dressed for it would take up most of the evening and Lisa was to have a ringside seat from Fran's bed. As it turned out Litrik phoned to say that he would be home later than usual and they weren't to wait for him to have tea, so that the two of them, with Nanny for company, went up to Fran's room where she laid out the pink dress and, leaving Lisa in Nanny's company, went to take a bath. She had washed her hair the evening before and it hung very clean and shining around her shoulders—they wasted a good deal of time arranging it in various styles before she sat down in front of her dressing-table and did her face, applying the expensive new make-up she had bought. It didn't seem to make much difference and she turned her attention to her hair, putting it up in its usual French pleat, wishing the while that it was a dramatic black or dazzling blonde. It was time to put on the dress and she stood before the pier-glass studying her image while Lisa and Nanny uttered little cries of admiration. Well, the face and the hair might not be anything to shout about, but the dress certainly was. She danced a few steps round the room for Lisa's pleasure and stopped when there was a knock at the door and Litrik came in, dressed save for his tailcoat.

He dropped a kiss on Fran's cheek, hugged Lisa and wished Nanny a good evening and then sat down on the bed, his arm round the little girl, and studied Fran. Lisa babbled excitedly and he said, 'Very nice, very nice indeed, Mama—Lisa thinks you look like a princess.' He got up and fished the pearls out of a trouser pocket and, because Lisa and Nanny were watching, fastened them round her throat. 'Oh, and these,' he told her.

Pearl and diamond earrings, glittering and gleaming under the bright lights of the bedroom. She took them silently and went to put them on before the mirror and then, mindful as she was of their audience, turned to smile at him and thank him in her serene way.

'They look well enough,' he told her and went away to shrug himself into his tails, while she picked up the wide swansdown stole the saleslady had assured her was just the thing to wear with the gown. Litrik came back presently to say good night to Lisa and then stood patiently while she hugged and kissed Fran who bade Nanny good night and then rustled out of the room. She was scared stiff of the evening ahead of her. To anyone else she would have voiced her fright, but not to Litrik; instead she made rather vague small talk as he drove her into Utrecht.

She need not have worried. The *burgermeester* was a genial old man with white whiskers and twinkling blue eyes and his wife, small and round and grey-haired, was just as nice. Fran, with Litrik at her elbow, was introduced, chatted to and handed on to more dignitaries, all of whom appeared to be on the best of terms with Litrik and only too willing to get on the same terms with her. Presently there was dancing and they circled the floor rather sedately before Litrik relinquished her to one of the *wethouders,* who wanted to know if an English mayor and alderman were the same as the Dutch.

'All except for the names I think,' said Fran. 'This is a very handsome ballroom.'

She couldn't have picked a more suitable subject; she was treated to a long history of the *gemeentehuis* which lasted through the dance and a couple of encores before she was whisked away by one of Litrik's cousins, a young man, not much older than herself. 'You look beautiful,' he told her gaily and she laughed. 'It's the earrings,' she explained. 'I'm terrified of losing one, though.'

She danced without pause until supper was announced and Litrik very properly came to claim her. She thought that he looked a little severe and wondered guiltily if she should have sat out some of the dances with various of the elderly ladies. 'Shouldn't I have danced so much?' she asked anxiously, 'I rather forgot who I was...'

'I am delighted to see that you are enjoying yourself, Francesca. Certainly you may dance as much as you wish. I expect you would like to sit at a table with some of your partners.' He raised a hand to a half-filled table at the other end of the room and took her arm. There were half a dozen young men and girls there and she sat down happily while Litrik went to fetch her some food. He came back with an assortment of chicken patties, vol-au-vents and tiny sandwiches and sat down beside her. He wasn't severe any more. He seemed to be on such excellent terms with everyone there; indeed, she was vexed to see that he was deliberately charming the three girls, something he had never attempted to do with her. Deep inside her she felt sad and bewildered by it. She shook the feeling off and applied herself to the talk around her, laughing rather more than she usually did.

They danced together again after supper and for the last dance. She couldn't but help notice the sentimental glances the older ladies were casting upon them. Litrik had noticed, too; he said gravely to the top of her head, 'You do realise that I am considered to be a very lucky man?'

It was on the tip of her tongue to ask him if he considered himself lucky, too, but she refrained. Instead she said worriedly, 'Really, it would have been better if I weren't to meet so many people. I could have had a cold or something—I mean, it would be easier for later on.'

He said very quietly, 'Shall we cross that bridge when we come to it, Francesca?'

It was late when they got back home and the house was quiet. 'There will be coffee in the kitchen if you want it,' Litrik told her, but she shook her head. 'I'll go to bed. I'll take a peep at Lisa first.' She paused at the bottom of the staircase and asked in a forlorn voice, 'Did I look nice?'

She thought he wasn't going to answer her. 'Very nice,' he said at length in a dry as dust voice. He wasn't even looking at her, but brushing something off his coat sleeve. He looked very handsome standing there and quite remote. She took off the pearls and unhooked the earrings and retraced her steps and handed them to him. Her good night was uttered in her usual quiet voice although she didn't look at him. She went up the stairs carefully because her eyes were full of tears and she couldn't see very clearly.

She undressed slowly, hung up the pink dress and got into a nightie and then crept along to the nursery; Lisa was asleep and so was Nanny in her room leading off it. The little girl's face looked pale and thin in the dim light of the bedside lamp and Fran felt anxiety grip her; the child looked dreadfully ill... She gave a gasp of pure fright as a hand came down on her shoulder.

'Don't worry,' said Litrik quietly into her ear, 'she is no worse. It's just that when she's sleeping it's more obvious how ill she is.' He gave her a friendly pat. 'Go to bed, Francesca.'

She turned away. 'Yes, of course.' She gave him a brief glance and he said softly, 'Why, you've been crying.'

He bent and kissed her on her gentle mouth, not the usual peck she was offered for appearances' sake, but hard and urgent. 'Go to bed,' he said, suddenly harsh, and she went without a word.

Before she slept she decided that he had been sorry for her

because she had been crying about Lisa. But she had been crying before then, although she wasn't at all sure why.

September slid slowly towards October, taking with it a round of dinner parties, family meetings and lunches, pleasant leisurely drives through the Veluwe, and the now regular afternoon visits to the fairy pool. But it was getting too chilly to stay long by the water now. Fran, with Lisa wrapped in a rug on her lap, would sit on their favourite tree stump and add another chapter to her interminable story and then hurry back to the cottage for tea and a biscuit. And the day came when she knew that Lisa wasn't well enough to go there any more; fortunately the weather changed and they were forced to stay indoors and she continued her tale telling sitting comfortably in a high-backed chair drawn up to the log fire in the great hearth, with Lisa cuddled on her lap. She didn't need the sight of Litrik's grave face to warn her that there wasn't much longer to go now, although when he was with Lisa he presented a carefree manner and laughed and joked with her as he had always done. He said nothing to Fran, for there was no need, but she and Nanny, when there was no one about, talked about it and wept a little, something Fran thought Litrik wouldn't tolerate.

And the day came when Lisa stayed in bed and from then on Fran and Nanny took it in turns to be with her, only leaving when Litrik came home, to sit by the bed and always talk cheerfully to Lisa about his day's work and his plans for Christmas; and Lisa, lying propped up against her pillows with her mouse bride beside her, listened happily.

It wasn't long before there came a day when Litrik, too, stayed at home, sitting by the child's bed, her hand in his, talking to her in a perfectly normal voice with Nanny sitting knitting at the table and Fran on the other side of the bed stitching dolls' clothes which would never be needed. Tuggs brought trays of coffee and sandwiches and during the afternoon Litrik told Fran and Nanny to go into the garden for half an hour, but nobody wanted meals and nobody made any attempt to undress that night. Lisa died, as they had prayed she would, in her sleep just as the sun was turning a chilly dawn into a bright morning.

CHAPTER SEVEN

THAT EVENING, sitting alone by the fire in the drawing room after sharing a dinner with Litrik which neither of them had eaten, Fran went back over the long sad day. She had seen very little of Litrik; he had gone to his study and telephoned the hospital and Professor van Tromp, who had been looking after Lisa, and then he had emerged to shower and shave and drink a cup of coffee before shutting himself up in his study again. His face had been a grey mask of tiredness and he had hardly spoken to her. Professor van Tromp had come shortly after breakfast and when he had left again, she had gone to the nursery to help Nanny, thankful that in that kindly young woman's company she could cry if she wanted to. Litrik hadn't come to lunch; Tuggs had taken a tray of coffee to the study and she had sat at the table, pushing the food round her plate. In the afternoon she had wandered round the garden, longing to help Litrik in some way, but when she had offered to do so that morning he had told her curtly that he would do everything necessary and would telephone the family.

Even a walk with the dogs had been denied her for in the early afternoon he had emerged, whistled to Muff and Thor and left the house with them. When he had returned she had offered tea and been curtly thanked and refused.

It would have been so much easier for them both if they could have talked about Lisa and comforted each other, but he didn't want her sympathy nor had he any to offer her. Dominee Meertens had come in the morning and spent a little time talking to her but she had been too unhappy to listen, although she had been grateful.

She looked up in surprise as the *stoelklok* chimed midnight and Tuggs came into the room. 'Shall I lock up, Mevrouw?' he wanted to know. 'The doctor is in his study and I don't like to disturb him. The dogs are with him or I'd have given them a run...'

'You lock up, Tuggs, and I'll go and see if the doctor will go to bed. He must be tired; there has been so much to do.' She smiled at him from a sad face and he smiled back.

'It's been a bad day for us all, Mevrouw. Shall Nel fetch you up a nice warm drink before you sleep?'

She shook her head. 'No, thank you, Tuggs; if Nel would leave the coffee on the hob I'll get the doctor a cup if he wants it. You and Nel go to bed. You had a wakeful night and a long day, too.'

The house was very quiet once he had made it secure for the night. Fran sat on by the dying fire, thinking about Lisa and the fun they had had together. At least the little girl had been happy and had loved her a little, just as she had loved Lisa. When next she looked at the clock it was almost an hour later and she got up and crossed the hall to the study and knocked on the door and, without waiting for an answer, went in.

Litrik was sitting at his desk sprawled in his chair, staring ahead of him, his face a calm mask. He glanced at her briefly. 'What do you want, Francesca?'

'Litrik, come to bed, it's gone one o'clock and you had no sleep last night.' And when he took no notice, she went up close to him and said gently, 'Lisa was so happy and content, can you not try and think of that? And she loved you and you loved her as you always will. I—I'm so sorry, Litrik...'

He said with a kind of cold politeness, 'What can you possibly know about it? You haven't had a child!'

She didn't answer that. 'Would you like some coffee? Nel left it ready.'

'No, thank you. Go away, Francesca. Just for a time you and I have nothing to say to each other.'

He was wrong, of course, but she saw that she wouldn't be able to make him see that. Feeling defeated, she left him there alone.

He was at the breakfast table in the morning and wished her good morning and expressed the hope that she had slept well. 'I shall be at home today,' he told her. 'Family and friends will be calling. I've arranged the funeral for Friday, here in the village. Just family will come back here for a little while. Perhaps you will discuss with Nel what arrangements are needed to be made. I thought that we might send Nanny on holiday for a few weeks...'

'You're not discharging her,' said Fran quickly. 'I'm so glad—she would break her heart.'

He said evenly, 'She's been with us since Lisa was a year old—she is part of the household.'

'And I'm not,' thought Fran miserably. As soon as he decently could he would arrange things so that she could go back to England.

She drank coffee and crumbled toast, mindful of his remark that they had nothing to say to each other.

Litrik's parents arrived during the morning, and then his sisters; they were warmly sympathetic and Mevrouw van Rijgen observed very positively that although Fran had been Lisa's stepmother for such a short time, she had brought the child a happiness she had hankered after. 'So you mustn't grieve too much, my dear,' she said kindly. 'It has been a sad blow to all of us, especially to Litrik, but happily you are here to comfort him.'

Fran was profoundly thankful that he wasn't there to hear his mother say that.

More people came, friends—old friends of Litrik's who, it seemed, had known him for years. Fran said all the right things, dispensed coffee and tea and longed for the day to be over. The visitors went at last and they dined together, carrying on a polite conversation, not a word of which did she remember later. She went to bed directly afterwards, pleading a headache, thankful that Litrik was going to the hospital in the morning and would be out all day.

She breakfasted alone and since he had already left the house she told Tuggs that she was going for a drive and presently got into the Mini and took the well-remembered road to the fairy-tale pond.

It was a sad autumn day, not raining but damp and grey, and the old woman wasn't in her garden. Fran got out of the car and knocked on the door and, bidden to enter, gave her sad news in her slowly improving Dutch.

The old woman nodded and smiled and patted her shoulder to show that she understood. She pushed a chair forward and urged Fran to sit down. *'Koffie,'* she said and trotted off to her tiny kitchen and came back presently with two cups and saucers on a tray, looking kindly into Fran's tired unhappy face. Presently she said, 'You can come here whenever you want to, Mevrouw.' And somehow that made Fran feel better; she didn't suppose that she would be in Holland much longer, but this funny little cottage was somewhere to come. She thanked the old woman and asked if she might walk to the pond.

There were damp leaves strewn all over the path now and the trees were looking woebegone, but the pond was still lovely even on such a sombre day. Fran sat down on the tree stump once more and looked at the still, grey water. She had never felt so lonely or so unhappy. She grieved for Lisa and she was saddened, too, because Litrik didn't want her or her sympathy. It was as though at the child's death, he had discarded her; she had fulfilled her part of their agreement and now he had no further interest in her... She sat up straight at her sudden astounding thought: he might not want any more to do with her, but the idea of never seeing him again struck her with sickening force. Without him life would never be the same any more. She was quite bewildered, for he behaved towards her at best as a casual friend and at worst as though he couldn't bear the sight of her. So how could she possibly love him? She reminded herself of his coldness, the faint mockery with which he looked at her, his total lack of interest in her as a person. That he had always behaved in exactly the right manner towards her when Lisa had been with them meant nothing; the happy picnics, the games of Ludo and Snakes and Ladders, the laughter and early morning teas, all of them had been to give Lisa happiness.

She watched the water coot weave in and out of the reeds and then disappear. In all fairness, she thought, when Litrik had made his astonishing proposal, he hadn't offered her friendship or even liking, only his promise that, when she returned to England, he would see that she would get a job again.

She shifted a bit more on the tree stump, feeling the chill creeping up her legs. But to be honest, she hadn't expected anything else from him, had she? And it had all seemed so simple and straightforward, hadn't it? But it wasn't any more. She had grown to love Lisa even in the short time that she had known her and as well as that she had grown to love Litrik's home; now there was nothing more she could ask of life than to stay there with him for the rest of her life and his. Only he didn't want her.

She got up and walked slowly back to where she had parked the car, waved goodbye to the old woman and drove back to the house. It was late afternoon by then; Tuggs brought her tea in the little sitting room and she sat with the dogs, thinking about Lisa and thinking of the future. She would have to stay for a little while after the funeral but there was nothing to stop her planning what she would do when she went back to England. Not to the aunts, of course; they would never understand in the first place. Sooner or later they would have to be told but not just yet. And she would try for a job in London and make a new life for herself.

Litrik came back for dinner. He asked her kindly enough if she had found the day trying, expressed relief that she had taken the car for a run and went on to talk about his work at the hospital. He didn't mention Lisa once, merely remarking as they crossed the hall to the drawing room for their coffee that he hoped that she and Nel had arranged things for Friday.

'Yes,' said Fran, 'everything is seen to.' And before she could add to that he went on, 'I've spoken to Nanny. She will take a few weeks' holiday starting on Saturday. Her home is in Friesland; Tuggs will drive her there.'

He was sitting in his chair by the fire and she thought with compassion that he looked every day of his age, his grief hidden under that bland mask of a face. She opened her mouth ready to pour out the sympathy she felt and then closed it again; they had nothing to say to each other—he had said that and she mustn't forget it. She had no idea that loving someone who wasn't even interested in you could hurt so much. They drank their coffee, not talking much, and presently he went away to his study.

It was raining when she got up in the morning and when she got downstairs Tuggs met her with the news that Litrik had gone in to the hospital at Zeist and she wasn't to expect him until the evening. 'A mercy that he is kept so busy, Mevrouw, if you'll pardon the liberty.' He gave her a worried look. 'Not a nice day for you to go out, Mevrouw.'

'No, I'll take the dogs for a walk and then I'll go over to Bloemendaal and see my cousin—I'll stay for lunch, Tuggs, but I'll be back round about tea time in case Nel wants any help. Everything is all right for tomorrow, isn't it?'

It was mid-morning by the time she got back with the dogs and had dried them and settled down in the small sitting room. Clare was in when she phoned and eager to see her; she got into her new Burberry and the smart little hat that went with it, put on some elegant shoes and drove off.

She hadn't told Clare about Lisa; that was something she would have to do during her visit with as little emotion as possible. Clare's baby was due in two months or so and she was living in a happy world of her own which it would be cruel to disturb.

She hadn't seen her cousin since the wedding although they had talked on the phone; Clare and Karel had been away staying with his parents and they wouldn't have heard of Lisa's death.

She parked the car and rang the bell and ran up the stairs to the flat, stifling a strong urge to pour out the whole unhappy business to Clare—she realised she couldn't do that; Dominee Meertens had said that only the three of them knew the true facts of the marriage... It wasn't her secret.

Clare was waiting at the open door and they hugged each other delightedly. 'Gosh, you look marvellous!' declared Fran. 'It's not too long now, is it?'

She cast off her raincoat and hat and her cousin eyed the suede outfit with envy. 'Well, look at you,' she declared, 'and those shoes—Fran, I hardly recognise you.' She gave Fran another look. 'Come in and have coffee—it's all ready, and you can tell me why you've lost weight and look as though you haven't slept for nights on end.'

Which made it easy for Fran to tell her about Lisa. 'It has upset us all,' she finished, 'and Litrik is broken-hearted—he adored her.' She paused. 'So did I.'

'What a mercy he married you,' observed Clare. 'You've got each other and that's all that matters, isn't it?' She gave Fran a long thoughtful look. 'So that's why you look so unhappy—you had me worried...'

Fran passed her cup for more coffee. She didn't want it, but it was something to do. 'And I want to know all about you and the baby—when is he due? Not long, surely?'

Clare was only too ready to talk about it and presently Fran was shown the baby's outfits and the dear little room Karel had decorated and fitted out.

'And once he is here, we shall come over and see you,' declared Clare happily. 'Will you be here for Christmas or will Litrik take you over to England? Not that it would be much fun to be with the aunts.'

'Well,' said Fran calmly, 'he's not said anything but then I hadn't expected him to; and he is very busy at the hospital—there have been several cases of legionnaire's disease and he specialises in tropical diseases and fevers, you know.'

She steered the talk back to the baby and Clare chatted happily until Fran said reluctantly that she would have to go.

'Oh, of course, Litrik gets back about tea time, I suppose, and you like to be there. Come and see me again, Fran.' Clare kissed her warmly. 'And next time you'll be your old self.'

Fran managed a laugh. 'Oh, dear, have I been such a wet blanket?'

'No, love—just unhappy and hiding it very well.'

It was a nasty afternoon turning rapidly into evening, with a cold rain falling steadily and a lot of traffic on the roads, even the country roads she took. It suited her mood; depression sat heavily upon her; the sight of Clare so happy, bubbling over with excitement about the baby, had filled her with an envy she didn't realise she possessed. It was impossible not to dream a little—to be happily married to Litrik who loved her and to have his babies. Fran, lost in her dream world, put out her right-hand indicator and turned left and was subjected to an indignant fanfare of horns.

She was surprised to find Litrik at home when she got in. She said awkwardly as he came into the hall, 'I spent the day with Clare. I didn't know you would be back before dinner.'

He took her raincoat and threw it over a chair. 'She is well, I hope?' he enquired politely, and stood aside for her to go into the drawing room. He spoke pleasantly and she did her best to follow his lead. 'Oh, fine—the baby's due in about eight weeks.'

She sat down near the fire. 'What a wretched afternoon. I came home through the side roads and everything was very gloomy.'

He had come to sit opposite to her. 'I'll explain tomorrow's arrangements, shall I? Very simple, but it helps to know something about them beforehand.'

And during the next day, which was sad and difficult, she had been grateful for the things he had told her. They had helped her to play her part without faltering, act hostess to his family and friends and hide her own grief under a calm exterior. Only when everyone had gone and they were standing in the hall as Tuggs closed the doors on the last of the family, did she say suddenly and incoherently, 'You don't mind—I'd like to go—a headache...'

He had been so kind and thoughtful, perhaps only because there were other people there, but she didn't think so—it was as though he had understood at last that she was grieving for Lisa, too. But now she couldn't bear another minute of it. She had to get away and pull herself together. She loved him so much that she was terrified of showing it in some way and her longing to comfort him was almost unbearable. He had gone through the day with a calm face, courteous to everyone who had come, but now she wondered what he would do.

He answered her incoherent excuses with impersonal kindness. 'Of course you must be tired. I'll get Nel to send up something on a tray for you later on.'

She said quickly, 'I'll come down for dinner—you'll be alone...'

'I've a good deal to do—letters to write; I'll be too busy to miss you.' He smiled as he spoke, dismissing her, and she went to her room. Even if he weren't busy he wouldn't miss her, she thought drearily.

She didn't expect to sleep but she did and in the morning she felt better. Moping and moaning weren't going to help; she would have to pick up the threads of life again and wait patiently until Litrik considered it the right moment to get the annulment. It was no use trying to alter things; she had known exactly what he had planned from the very beginning and she had agreed with him. She hadn't been in love with him then, of course, which complicated things, but that was something she must learn to get over as soon as possible.

She dressed and went down to breakfast, outwardly serene. He would be away all day, he told her in the pleasant impersonal manner which chilled her so, and he would be flying to Brussels on the following day—a deliberate arrangement to get him away from home, she felt sure. Having to keep up the pretence of their marriage now that Lisa wasn't with them any more must be irksome to him. After all, her reason for being there in the first place had gone; she had no place with him any more. She replied suitably to his news, expressed the wish that his visit would be successful and asked in her matter-of-fact way if there was anything she could do for him while he was away.

There wasn't and there wasn't any way of being sure when he would be back. An answer she had expected anyway.

They were alone in the room and he bade her goodbye in a manner which put her very much in mind of his leave taking on her wards, pausing just long enough to tell her that if necessary he could be reached at the phone number he had left on his desk in the study.

She sat at the table, listening to him talking to Tuggs in the hall and then to the sound of the receding car. Tuggs came in then to see if there was anything she wanted and she told him briskly that she would take the dogs for a walk and then drive into Zeist to buy some embroidery wools.

'And I'll stay out for lunch, Tuggs. Shall I come and see Nel now?'

She went to the kitchen for her daily talk with that lady. Until now it had been brief, for Lisa demanded all her attention, but now there was time to learn a few useful words and pick up a few hints about the housekeeping, a waste of time really since she wouldn't be there for long enough to need them, but it kept her occupied.

She walked the dogs for an hour and then drove to Zeist, to potter round the shops there, drink coffee and then fill in another hour choosing knitting patterns until she could go to the Hermitage Hotel and have lunch.

She didn't drive straight back but meandered around the country roads, losing her way several times so that the afternoon was fading when she got home. The drawing room looked inviting and the dogs were glad to see her; Tuggs brought tea and she sat down by the fire, just for the moment enjoying an illusion of content, broken by Tuggs with the afternoon post. There was a letter from her aunts—she wrote to them weekly but they wrote seldom and when they did their letters unsettled her. They had a companion housekeeper now who apparently did nothing right and expected free evenings and a weekend off once a month, during which time, if Aunt Kate was to be believed, the aunts starved, froze to death and suffered all the privations of being neglected. Fran sat with the letter on her lap when she had read it and wondered if she should go back and live there with them when she went back to England. Perhaps it was her duty; on the other hand, when she had lived with them they had found fault with her continuously and matters would not improve. Far better to go right away and start again. She began to think what she might do, resolutely refusing to dwell on a future without Litrik; her heart might be breaking but she must ignore that and no one need ever know. She was debating the advantages of a post in London in a teaching hospital against a job in Canada or New Zealand when Litrik walked in. She hadn't expected him to come home before dinner and she jerked up in her chair as the dogs went to meet him.

'I startled you. I'm sorry, Francesca.' His glance fell on the open letter in her lap. 'Letters from home?'

He had sat down on the other side of the fireplace with Muff draped over his feet and Thor sitting beside him. 'You've had a pleasant day?' he wanted to know.

'Yes, thank you. Would you like tea?'

He shook his head. 'I had a cup at the hospital.' He glanced at his watch. 'I must go again in an hour—a private patient at my rooms. Don't wait dinner for me. Perhaps you would ask Nel to leave something for me—sandwiches will do.'

She asked, 'Are you going to the hospital before you leave tomorrow? Will you want an early lunch?'

'I must leave here soon after six o'clock—I've a lecture to give in the morning. I'm catching an early plane from Schiphol.'

She said quietly, 'I see,' and then, because it was something to say, 'do you know Brussels well?'

'I have been there on various occasions.' He got up and fetched the small pile of letters on one of the tables and then sat down again. 'You don't mind if I read my post?'

'No,' said Fran and wished that she had her knitting with her. They were like two strangers who, having met for the first time, didn't like each other but felt impelled to make polite conversation. A waste of time, she thought, suddenly pettish, when we could be talking about Lisa and helping each other through this ghastly time. I could even have gone to Brussels with him...

She sat composedly, the picture of serenity, and the doctor, glancing at her over his letters, looked a second time before going back to his reading and then almost reluctantly looked at her again. He asked abruptly, 'You'll be all right while I'm away?'

That surprised her. 'Oh, yes, there are the dogs and so much to do...'

He looked a little taken aback. 'Much to do? What?'

'Well, as I said—the dogs. They like a good long walk, don't they? And then I talk to Nel about the meals and so on, and there are always letters to write and knitting to do and I can take the car to Zeist or Utrecht.'

'Do you miss your work at the hospital?' he asked abruptly.

'I didn't; perhaps I do now. You see, I've always...that is, a nurse's life is busy.'

'You don't dislike the idea of going back to it?'

'Not in the least.' Her voice was quite steady. Perhaps he was going to tell her that he'd see about the annulment. She shrank from hearing about it but at least he was talking to her.

She was to be disappointed; he put his letters aside and got up to go. 'Well, I must be off—I'll phone from Brussels before I leave there. Good night, Francesca.'

She wished him good night in a bright voice and only when she heard the car start did she get up and go upstairs to her room. She could howl her eyes out there in peace.

She felt much better after that; indeed a small well of indignation spread quite rapidly from somewhere deep inside her. She had done her best to keep her side of the bargain and he could have shown some gratitude, at least. Lisa's death had hit him hard, but it had made her very unhappy, too, and he hadn't seen that—but then he hardly ever looked at her...

She walked down to the village the next morning, put fresh roses from the garden on Lisa's grave and then had coffee with Dominee Meertens and his wife. The house was quieter now for the children were in school and they sat comfortably in the rather untidy sitting room, talking in a pleasant desultory fashion until Mevrouw Meertens asked, 'Did you not want to go with Litrik? He would have been glad of your company.'

Before Fran could answer the *dominee* said, 'Well, he would have very full days. I imagine it would hardly be worth your going, Francesca?'

She agreed and threw him a grateful glance. Perhaps she could have a real talk with him sometime and find out what Litrik proposed to do and when.

She spent the afternoon at the piano and after her solitary dinner went to bed early.

Litrik didn't telephone for three days; he would be back for dinner that evening, he told her over the phone and, after a polite enquiry as to her well being, rang off. It was unfortunate that his mother had been driven over for a brief afternoon visit and was sitting near enough for her to hear Fran's side of the conversation, businesslike yeses and noes and no endearments of any sort. When Fran had sat down again Mevrouw van Rijgen passed her cup for more tea and remarked, 'Is Litrik a difficult husband, my dear? Not that you are likely to tell me. His first marriage was so unhappy you know; he became so—so remote, and now losing Lisa has upset him badly. We had hoped that when he married you it would help him to accept the fact that she was dying and to regain his happiness.' She hesitated. 'A happy home life and children... He is very fond of children.'

Fran poured herself more tea. She said in a calm voice, 'I think it's early days for Litrik to feel better about Lisa—he loved her very much and even though he had known for months that there was no hope for her, it was still a dreadful shock. We all miss her, you know. I wish I had known her for longer.'

'Yes, well, my dear... I dare say a few weeks spent quietly here with you will help him. It has been hard to talk to him since his first marriage broke up; you are a sweet girl and gentle and I think you will succeed where the rest of us have failed.' She added abruptly, 'He can be unkind but I believe that he doesn't mean it.'

She put down her cup and got up. 'I must go home. I've enjoyed our little chat, Francesca. Give my love to Litrik when he gets back, and tell him we hope to see you both soon.'

She kissed Fran with warmth and went out to the waiting car, leaving her to ponder over their talk. Did Litrik's mother suspect that things weren't quite as they should be with a newly married couple? Not that it mattered now, very soon they would part and once she was back in England she would be forgotten in a few months' time. They would be very kind about it; an unfortunate mistake made by both of them and luckily dealt with in time before there were any children. Finally she fell to daydreaming over little Litriks and their sisters running round the house, rushing to meet a devoted Papa each evening while she stood, presently to be held close and kissed.

She dressed carefully for Litrik's return and went to sit in the drawing room with the tapestry work she had started. He came in quietly and she paused with her needle poised to say serenely, 'Hallo, Litrik. I hope you had a successful time in Brussels and a good journey back.'

It sounded very stilted in her eyes, but it was either that or jumping up and flinging herself into his arms and that wouldn't do at all.

He went to pour a drink and offered her sherry before he sat down opposite her. 'Have you been lonely?' he asked abruptly.

She answered him evasively. 'I've had a visit from your mother—she came to tea. And I went to Dominee Meertens and had coffee. The weather's been quite nice; that meant the dogs and I have been able to walk miles.'

'You haven't answered my questions.'

She took a couple of stitches very precisely. 'One doesn't have to be alone to be lonely,' she told him coolly.

'While I was away I had time to think. I've treated you badly, Francesca, and I'm sorry. You were sad and I did nothing to help you. It's been a difficult time and I made it worse for you. I'm grateful for what you have done and you did it splendidly.'

She glanced at him. 'I loved Lisa,' she said baldly.

'Yes, I know.' He bent to stroke Muff's ears and then throw an arm round Thor. 'Francesca, there is something you are entitled to know. I have told no one else and don't intend to. Lisa wasn't my daughter.' And, at Fran's sudden surprised gasp, 'No, don't say anything yet. My first wife had an affair before we married unknown to me. She was pregnant then. It wasn't until some weeks later that I found out quite by chance that she had done her best to get rid of the child without my knowledge. She failed but Lisa was born handicapped. Her mother would have nothing to do with her—rejected her completely and left us both. I swore then that Lisa would have every possible chance to live and be happy. She has been my first concern since then.'

'Why did she marry you?' whispered Fran. 'Couldn't she have married the father?'

'He had no money. I happen to be wealthy, I was also infatuated.'

'And her mother?' Fran's voice was still a shocked whisper.

'Has been dead for five years.'

'And you still love her?'

He looked at her with hard eyes. 'I never loved her—love and infatuation are two quite different things. Love to my mind, is something one reads about—a myth...'

'That's rubbish!' said Fran sharply. 'What about your parents and your sisters and Dominee Meertens and his wife and Clare and Karel? Of course it's not a myth and if you loved someone you wouldn't talk such nonsense.'

He smiled at her mockingly. 'Why, Francesca, one might almost think that you were speaking from experience.'

She saw that he considered it so ridiculous that there was no need to be serious about it. She said merely, 'I use my eyes,' and changed the subject abruptly. 'Your mother hopes to see you soon.'

'We'll go over this weekend. Was my father with her?'

Fran shook her head. 'No, he had to attend some meeting or other.'

'They like you...'

'I'm glad of that.' She chose some wool with care and threaded her needle. He went on deliberately, 'And I find that I like you, too, Francesca, though unwillingly.'

Her heart rocked against her ribs. 'Then when we part we shall be able to do so in a friendly fashion.' She gave him a considered look. 'When is that to be, Litrik?'

'I have thought about that, too—I think we must wait a little while longer.' He was staring at her so hard that she felt the colour creeping into her cheeks. She didn't look away. 'I'm quite ready to go when you want me to.' She folded her work and laid it on the table by her chair.

'There's the gong—I expect you are hungry?'

Dinner passed off well enough; Litrik when he chose could be an amusing companion. They went back to the drawing room for their coffee and Fran, not wishing to push her luck, went to bed shortly afterwards. Litrik had seemed to enjoy her company; he had confided in her, admitted that he liked her; it wasn't much, but it was better than the cold silences she had had to put up with. She would have to leave, of course, but at least not just yet. For that she was thankful. Every single minute of his company was something to treasure for the future.

CHAPTER EIGHT

A WEEK WENT BY, during which Litrik came home for lunch each day and returned in the early evening and even, on two occasions, for tea. They had gone to lunch with his parents, sustained an unexpected afternoon visit from Tante Olda and Tante Nynke, on their stately way to visit friends in Valkenburg, and had Professor van Tromp, a large quiet man who said little, to dinner. He and Litrik wandered off after dinner to the latter's study. They returned full of apologies; they had had a most interesting discussion, he explained to her, and begged her forgiveness. 'But of course, being a doctor's wife you will understand,' he ended kindly and drank the coffee she had ready for them and took his leave, inviting her at the same time to visit the hospital if she should care to do so. 'Although I dare say Litrik has been badgering you to do so already.'

As they went back into the drawing room Fran asked thoughtfully, 'Why don't you? Invite me to see round your hospitals—and your consulting rooms? Wives are supposed to take an interest in their husband's work, aren't they?' And, when he didn't answer, 'I am a little tired of this pretence and surely you must be, too. When Lisa was alive there was a reason for it.'

She was standing in the centre of the room, looking at him. 'How long does it take—an annulment, I mean?'

His voice was very even. 'A little while—we must talk about it.'

She had been feeling off colour all the evening, now her head began to ache most vilely. Perhaps because of that she snapped, 'No, we mustn't. You said that we had nothing to say to each other.' She walked to the door murmuring a good night, longing for her bed. For some reason the staircase was unending; by the time she reached the gallery above she was worn out and icy cold. She undressed quickly, her head hammering so hard now that all she could think of was getting into bed. She was sliding into its comfort when she got out again, put on her dressing-gown and went back into the gallery, making for the stairs. She felt ill, but at the same time there was something that she simply had to say to Litrik. She reached the staircase and started down it. Her head was a ball of fire, some demon was pouring ice water down her spine, her legs had no bones. Halfway down she paused; the stairs spread away from her, curiously flattened so that she wasn't certain where the next tread was. She put out a cautious foot, missed a step and tumbled headlong.

Litrik, in his study, with a pile of notes before him, ignored them, seeing instead a pair of lovely eyes in a tired face, and listening to a regrettably snappy voice telling him strongly that they had nothing to say to each other. He frowned as his thoughts were interrupted by a series of soft gentle bumps and the slithering of Fran's small person. He got up and went into the hall; it was past midnight and the house had been silent for some time.

Fran lay in an untidy heap, almost at the bottom of the staircase. She had knocked herself out, which was a pity, otherwise she would have heard—even if she hadn't believed—Litrik's, 'Fran—my dear little Fran,' uttered in a voice quite unlike his usual cool tones.

There was a reddened bump already visible on her forehead

which told its own tale. He lifted her eyelids and looked into her eyes, took her pulse, made sure that there were no broken bones, then scooped her up and carried her upstairs to her room, where he put her on the bed, took off her dressing-gown and tucked her up. Only then did he go to the bell-pull by the fireplace and give it a sharp tug. There wouldn't be anyone in the kitchen at that time of night, but the Tuggs had their sitting room only a short distance from it and the bell was loud. While he waited he went back to the bed and took another look at Fran. Her face was pale and the bump was getting bigger but that wouldn't account for her obvious high fever.

He began to examine her carefully and when Tuggs, cosily dressing-gowned, came into the room he said, 'Get my bag from the study will you, Tuggs, and then go to the kitchen and get some ice and some cloths to put in it. My wife has knocked herself out falling down the stairs, but I believe she has some kind of infection.'

Tuggs, beyond a worried 'Tut tut', wasted no time on words. He was back in no time at all with the bag and went away again without a word.

Fran's temperature was high enough to make Litrik raise his eyebrows. He studied her face carefully in an impersonal and professional manner, sure that the concussion was secondary to the sudden high fever. He got up and shaded the bedside light carefully, pulled a chair close to the bed and, when Tuggs came back, wrapped ice in the linen hand towels he had brought, and held it over her forehead. He didn't look up as Nel came quietly in to stand beside him. She spoke in a whisper and he listened patiently and shook his head, answering her softly, and presently, after an anxious peer at Fran, she went away to get the coffee he had asked for.

'And Tuggs, will you go to my study and bring up the papers on my desk—the pile in the centre in a folder.'

'You'll stay here, sir?' Tuggs hesitated. 'Me and Nel will gladly sit with Mevrouw.'

'Thank you, Tuggs, I know you would, but I'll stay just to make sure she is all right when she comes round. She will probably be sick and feel peculiar; perhaps it'll make things easier if I'm here. You both go back to bed—I'll get you on the house phone if I need you.' He glanced at the faithful Tuggs. 'Don't worry—my wife's picked up a virus infection I believe—that's how she came to fall downstairs. A few days in bed will put her right again.'

It took more than a few days. Fran came round in the early hours of the morning to see Litrik sitting by her bed, writing busily. She still had a fearful headache; indeed, the whole of her ached but her head felt clearer. He had looked up and seen her eyes open and on him and got to his feet and come to take her pulse and feel her hot forehead. 'That's better,' he told her soothingly. 'I'm going to give you something for the headache I'm quite certain you've got, and you'll go to sleep again and feel better by morning.'

He had turned her pillow and it felt blessedly cool to her poor hot head and he asked her if she wanted a drink, and offered her something in a medicine glass, and then another drink, and she had slept again, to wake in the morning feeling almost sensible once more, but disinclined to so much as turn her head on the pillow. When she saw him still sitting in the chair she muttered, 'Have you been there all night? You must go to bed—I'm quite all right now, but if you don't mind I don't think I'll get up just yet.'

His low laugh made her frown. 'You won't get up until I tell you that you may, Francesca, and I warn you that if you do you will fall flat on your face. I shall go away presently and Nel or one of the maids will be here.'

He got up and went to the door. 'I shall be home for lunch. Tuggs will take any calls. Nel will give you something to bring down the fever; drink as much as you can manage.'

He might just have finished a ward round, thought Fran drowsily.

Incredibly, it was more than a week before she crept from her bed, sat in an easy chair, and crept thankfully back again. The concussion hadn't been severe; the bump had subsided, leaving a yellow and purple bruise, but the virus had taken longer to go, and it had taken a good deal of the energy she possessed with it. But despite her small size she was strong and healthy and within a few days of getting up again she was downstairs, rather pale and a good deal thinner.

Litrik had visited her daily morning and evening, sitting down by her bed to tell her any small items of family news and read her the many letters written by his family, as well as long screeds from Clare and the brief stiff letters from the aunts, flavoured with the faint suggestion that if she chose to marry a foreigner and live on the continent, she must expect to fall a prey to unpleasant illnesses. She had chuckled weakly at this and Litrik laughed with her.

His father and mother came to visit her, as did Jebbeke and Wilma, and, since the weather was fine even if cold, she was wrapped up warmly by Nel and taken for short drives by Litrik. It was three weeks before she felt herself again, and once more went walking with the dogs and going down to the village to visit Dominee Meertens and his wife. It was on one of these visits, while his wife was out of the room with the idea of fetching the coffee, that she asked diffidently if Litrik had said anything to him about the annulment.

'Yes, he has.' The *dominee*'s booming voice had sunk to a discreet level. 'And at a suitable moment I have no doubt he will speak to you, Francesca.'

She had to be content with that; she had the sense to know that Litrik wouldn't have said anything while she was ill and she had been thankful for that, shutting her mind to her inevitable departure.

But Litrik said nothing. They began to go out and about again to friends for dinner, to the theatre and even, to her surprise, to the hospital in Utrecht, where she had a guided tour of the hospital while Litrik delivered a lecture to a hall full of students, coming to collect her in Theatre Sister's office, where he sat drinking coffee and behaving in a manner which she imagined an attentive husband might. She had been bewildered for there was really no need for him to go to such lengths.

The next afternoon she drove the Mini to see the old woman. It was a blustery day with grey clouds scudding across a cold blue sky, but the old woman, muffled in an old coat, was working in her garden. She stuck her fork in the ground when she saw Fran getting out of the car and came down the path to meet her. It took Fran a moment or two to unravel the old woman's Dutch. Her knowledge of that language was getting better by the day and she could at least make herself understood. Her companion nodded sympathetically as Fran explained her long absence, invited her to drink a cup of coffee and suggested that while it was being prepared perhaps she would like to walk to the pond. Even on such a dreary day as this, said the old woman, it was beautiful. She spoke proudly as though she owned the pond, which, reflected Fran, perhaps she did. She nodded her acceptance of the coffee and went out of the garden and along the path between the bushes and trees, mostly bare now, until she came to the pond. The old woman was right, it was beautiful, its water reflecting the stormy sky, its banks littered with fallen leaves. And the tree stump was still there; Fran sat down on it. Perhaps Lisa's happy little ghost was beside her; certainly her memory was vivid. She sat for a few minutes, grateful for the peaceful quiet all around her and presently went back to the cottage where she drank her coffee and carried on a muddled but animated conversation with her hostess.

She couldn't stay long, Litrik would be back before six o'clock and she had made a point of being home when he got in. When Lisa had been alive he had come home in time for tea if he possibly could, but now he had taken to staying at his consulting rooms each afternoon. There was, after all, no need for him to hurry home any more.

She saw very little of him; breakfast was never a protracted meal and if he was in for lunch that, too, was by no means a leisurely meal. Only in the evenings would he sit with her before dinner, talking pleasantly about nothing that mattered, making small talk at the table and then, when they had had coffee, going to his study. She saw more of him if friends or family came to dinner or they went out, but although she longed to be with him, the effort of hiding her real feelings was getting a bit too much.

She bade the old woman goodbye, promised to return in two days' time and drove home.

It was the following week, her fourth visit since she had been ill, that she arrived at the cottage to find no sign of the old woman. Her two cats were sitting on the doorstep, looking anxious, and there was no smoke coming from the chimney. Fran walked up the little path, looking around her. The garden fork was stuck in the earth beside a row of carrots, half dug, and the cats, when she reached them, looked hungry. She knocked on the door and heard nothing in the silence all around her. She knocked again and this time she did hear something, a weary rending cough.

'Bronchitis,' said Fran to the cats, her nurse's instincts taking over, and she tried the door. It opened. The cats shot past her into the tiny lobby. The little sitting room was empty and cold; she went into the kitchen and at once saw the old woman huddled on a chair by the old-fashioned pot stove, now out. She looked ill and exhausted and when she tried to speak coughed instead so that Fran begged her to save her breath. It would take too long to ask her slowly thought out questions and then puzzle out the answers. She filled a kettle at the old-fashioned stone sink, lighted the Calor gas ring and found the coffee pot. She found milk, too, in an icy little pantry, put some on to heat, and then gave the cats each a saucerful.

Between bouts of coughing the old woman drank a cupful of coffee and Fran was relieved to see a little colour creeping back into her cheeks. She sought feverishly for the Dutch for blanket and dredged it up from the back of her head with great relief. The old woman pointed a feeble hand towards the ceiling and Fran climbed the ladderlike narrow stairs and found an attic above, one corner boarded off to make a bedroom of sorts. There were blankets here; she took two and made her precarious way back down the stairs and tucked them round her patient and then set about dealing with the stove. There was an empty bucket beside it. She picked it up and went outside and round the cottage to the back where there were some broken-down sheds. There was a small pile of egg coals there, some small logs and several broken wooden boxes. Firewood, said Fran happily, and found a lethal looking axe propped against the wall with which she attacked the boxes. She wasn't very expert but she was desperate to get the house warm. Armed with her bucket of coal and the wood she went back indoors, cleaned the stove as best she could and laid the fire, following her companion's muttered instructions very carefully. The stove obliged, roaring up the flue pipe in an alarming manner until, obedient to the old woman's urgent directions, she opened this and shut that and added more coal.

It was growing dark and she lit the oil lamp on the kitchen table, washed her grimy hands and found a basin. The old woman wasn't too keen on being washed, but she looked a little better by the time Fran had sponged her face and hands and presently dozed off, waking for coughing bouts and dropping off again. 'Food,' said Fran to the cats and remembered the hens the old woman kept—she and Lisa had seen them on one of their visits scratching contentedly in a wired-in enclosure behind the cottage. They would need to be fed and the eggs collected; she had no idea how long the old woman had been ill but she began to doubt if she had been able to cope with the hens. Fran went quietly out of the house again and explored the sheds. In one of them she found a sack of what she hoped was chicken feed. She filled a dipper and made her way to the hens, who rushed to the wire as soon as they saw her and fell to with a good deal of clucking. There was an egg box behind the chicken house; she opened it cautiously and found eggs. 'Egg and milk,' said Fran, and sped back to the cottage.

Her patient was still in uneasy sleep. She got the egg and milk ready, found some stale bread in an earthen crock, warmed more milk and gave it to the cats. The kitchen was warm now and, by the lamp's light, looked quite cosy. Dusk had slipped into darkness and she drew the curtains over the one window. The old-fashioned wall clock struck seven as she did so and she was shocked at the chimes. There was no way of letting anyone know where she was; the old woman couldn't be left even for the short time it would take her to drive back to the village and try to find a phone. She would have to spend the night and hope that someone would go past the cottage in the early morning. The old lady woke and Fran coaxed some of the egg and milk down her reluctant throat, and, when she could take no more, gave the rest to the cats and went to fetch more of the egg coals. The stove smelled vilely but the warmth had revived the old woman; if she could keep her going until the morning... Fran sat down on one of the hard wooden chairs at the table, thankful that for the moment, at least, her patient was asleep.

Presently she told herself she would warm up the coffee, it would keep her awake. The cats had curled up on the blankets, cocooning their mistress, and for the moment there was nothing for her to do except think how angry Litrik would be.

In this she was mistaken. He had arrived home at his usual hour to find Tuggs looking anxious. 'It's Mevrouw, sir—always home by now and no sign of her...'

'Where did she go?' Litrik sounded calm.

'Well, that's the worry—I don't know. When Lisa was alive they used to go off together, ever so happy, some afternoons, and they always got back before five o'clock. And for the last week or so Mevrouw has driven off at just the same time and come back here soon after four o'clock.'

'And you've no idea where they—she goes?'

Tuggs shook his head.

Litrik was putting on his car coat again. 'I remember that it was mentioned one day—a secret they told me, but that was all. Do you suppose that anyone in the house has any idea?'

Tuggs slid away through the baize door into the kitchen regions and the doctor stood motionless, staring at the wall before him. Presently Tuggs came back with Bep, the elder of the two young maids who did the housework. She was a sensible girl. 'Yes,' she said, in answer to Litrik's questions, 'once, when they got back a bit later than usual and it had been raining, I helped them with their wet things and they were talking. A fairy pool they were talking of, and an old woman in a cottage.'

The doctor thanked her gravely, told Tuggs to get the car out again and went to his study, where he spread a map on his desk and studied it carefully. He found what he sought presently, picked up his bag and went out to the car where Tuggs was waiting.

'It's a long shot, Tuggs, but worth a try. Stay here, I'll phone you if I need you.' He paused. 'And if there are any messages make a careful note of them.'

Tuggs voiced the doctor's thought. 'If there's been an accident, sir, we'd have heard by now.'

Litrik nodded, got into the car and drove away. He knew the surrounding country well, he reached the crossroads and turned down the narrow lane and went slowly through the village. Half a mile further his headlights picked out the Mini parked untidily on the side of the lane.

He parked behind the Mini, leaving his lights on, took his bag from the car and went up the garden path.

There was a faint glimmer of light coming from somewhere inside and then the sound of someone coughing. He knocked on the door and when no one came, knocked again, this time loudly and at length. He was rewarded by the glimmer of light becoming stronger and then Fran's voice calling in her slow Dutch, 'Who's there?'

'Litrik—open up, Francesca.'

The door was flung open and Fran with the lamp in her hand stood gazing up at him. She said breathlessly, 'Thank God you've come! How did you know? She's ill, the old woman who lives here, and I don't know what to do...'

He crowded into the tiny lobby, kissed her fiercely, took the lamp from her and went into the kitchen, where he set the lamp on the table, took off his coat and went to look at the old woman, awake now and looking bewildered.

He treated her very gently, asked her quiet questions while he took her pulse and temperature and, without disturbing the cats, contrived to go over her chest with his stethoscope. Then he wrapped her up again, gave her a reassuring pat and turned to Fran.

'So, tell me all you know and what you've done.'

So she told him and when she had finished he nodded. 'You did well. It's bronchitis and she tells me she refuses to leave here. I'm going back to the village to find someone to come out here and look after her. I'll phone Tuggs at the same time. Everyone at the house is beside themselves about you.'

But not you, thought Fran silently, though all she said was, 'I'm sorry to have worried them. What do you want me to do?'

He smiled a little. 'What a practical girl you are. What is upstairs?'

'An attic and a bedroom boarded off. There is a second bed in the attic.'

'See if you can find any sheets and blankets and make up the beds. I'm going to give her an antibiotic now. Provided she will stay in bed for a few days I think she will recover. Is there any food in the house?'

'The eggs I fetched, some milk and stale bread. There's not much coal—it's that pressed coal dust. Oh, and nothing for the cats.'

'I'll tell Tuggs. Now come and hold this arm for me.'

The house was very quiet when he had gone. She sped up

the stairs once more and poked her nose by the light of a candle into a cupboard in the attic and found sheets and blankets and an old eiderdown. She took them all downstairs again and spread them round the stove and went back to look for the old woman's night clothes—a voluminous nightie, spotlessly clean, and a thick shawl. She found towels, too, and a jug and basin and an old-fashioned stone hot water bottle.

It took a little time to take all the bedclothes upstairs again and boil the water for the bottle but that done she set to to make up the beds, wrap the nightie round the bottle and bury it into the bedclothes. She went downstairs then and saw that Litrik had been gone for almost an hour. The old woman was awake again and coughing. Fran heated more milk and got her to take it, and was thankful to hear the car stopping in the lane.

Litrik had someone with him, a middle-aged woman with a long face and bright blue eyes, who shook her hand as he said, 'This is Juffrouw de Wit; she lives in the village on her own. I suppose one would call her a girl Friday in England. She is sensible and willing to stay until Mevrouw Honig is better. Tuggs is coming over with food and so on. Have you made up the beds?'

'Yes, but there is only one hot water bottle.'

'Tuggs is bringing one with him.' He went to bend over his patient while Juffrouw smiled widely at Fran and took off her coat and carefully removed a hard felt hat from her head. Fran thought she would have made an excellent nurse.

The two of them went upstairs then and Litrik followed with Mevrouw Honig in his arms, and left them to get their patient undressed and into her warm nightie and shawl and sitting comfortably against the pillows Fran had found. It wasn't so cold in the attic now; the chimney breast took up a good deal of the attic wall and was beginning to warm it. Mevrouw Honig coughed and sighed and dozed off, leaving Fran and Juffrouw de Wit to tidy up and go back to the kitchen. Litrik had fetched more coal and stoked up the stove. He was in his waistcoat and shirt sleeves, washing his hands at the sink, when there was a knock at the door. 'Tuggs,' he said over his shoulder. 'Let him in, please, Francesca.'

Tuggs beamed at her as he edged past, carrying a big box. 'We've all been in such a state, Mevrouw—what a relief to know you are safe and sound. Is this the kitchen?'

He put the box on the table and Fran and Juffrouw de Wit unpacked it. The contents were all that was most needed: milk and fresh bread, a simple dish of sliced meat, neatly covered, for Juffrouw de Wit, an egg custard, tea and coffee, sugar, tins of soup and a packet of scraps of things suitable for the cats. There were candles, too, and soap and a bottle of Dettol. Juffrouw looked her satisfaction and began to tidy everything away into the pantry, and Litrik put on his jacket and shrugged on his coat. He went upstairs then to take another look at his patient and when he came down gave Juffrouw de Wit the antibiotic pills which would have to be taken and his instructions as to the care of Mevrouw Honig. Fran, listening, made out that he would pay a visit on the next day.

They drove back then, Tuggs leading with Fran just behind him and Litrik last of all. They caused quite a stir going through the village.

It was nice to be fussed over as she went into the house. Nel with Bep and Corrie, the younger maid, had formed a kind of welcoming committee to take her outdoor things and exclaim over her, even though she didn't understand all they said. She went up to her room and took a look at herself in the looking-glass. Then she saw that she looked frightful; her face was grimy and her hair hung in wisps and her dress was smeared in coal dust. She washed and did her hair, changed her dress and went downstairs and found Litrik waiting for her. He handed her a glass of sherry, remarking that she looked as though she needed it, which remark, considering that she had just spent ten minutes improving her appearance, was unfortunate. She drank the sherry rather fast and it went straight to her head. She had had no tea and it was now late evening and she was famished.

She blinked away a sudden vagueness in her surroundings and Litrik, watching her, observed blandly, 'I dare say you're hungry, but would you like another sherry first?'

The look she gave him was so unhappy that he put his glass down and took her hands in his.

'Francesca—what is it? Do you not feel well? What's wrong?'

Everything was wrong; she was tired, she was hungry and she was hopelessly in love with a man who didn't care a row of pins about her. But, of course, she couldn't tell him that. 'How did you know where I was?' she asked.

He didn't appear to have noticed that she hadn't answered his questions.

'Bep remembered hearing Lisa talking to you about a cottage and a fairy pond; I know the country round here and I had a map—it wasn't difficult.'

He didn't tell her that he had sweated with fear, imagining her overcome by disaster and him unable to find her. He had been beside himself under his calm.

He let her hands go. 'There's the gong. You must be as famished as I am.'

It was long past their normal dinner hour but Nel had succeeded in offering a delicious meal. Fran listened to Litrik's easy talk about nothing much and answered when she should. It wasn't until he told her that Nanny, who hadn't come back from her holiday because of her mother's illness, was coming back on the following day that she smiled.

'Oh, I'm glad and I'm sure that Nel and the girls must have missed her. What will she do now that...?' She stopped.

'Lisa isn't here,' finished Litrik. 'Nel has plenty for her to do, so Tuggs tells me. Nel wants to see you about it—pickling and jam making and so on.'

Fran said slowly, 'There's no need to see me. I mean, Nel has been housekeeper here for years, hasn't she? And since I'll be gone...'

'Ah yes, but perhaps you would like to stay until the New Year? Have you anything in mind?'

'Well, no.' She added a little desperately, 'But I'd like to go as soon as you can arrange everything.'

He made no attempt to persuade her to say that she would stay. They went back to the drawing room and he told her, rather unnecessarily she thought, about the splendid Christmas and New Year celebrations. 'Everyone comes here,' he told her smoothly, 'we have a great tree in this room and the whole house is decorated and Nel turns out the most delicious food. Friends call and we give a party at New Year, and if it's cold enough we skate. A pity you won't be here to enjoy it all.'

She couldn't bear any more of that; she went to bed but before she went she asked, 'Do you want me to go and see Mevrouw Honig tomorrow?'

'I'll be home to lunch and I've no appointments until after four o'clock. We'll both go.'

He opened the door for her and as she went through she paused, her tongue uttering the words she had no intention of saying. 'Why did you kiss me like that?'

He didn't smile. 'An unavoidable reaction,' he observed. 'Good night, Francesca.'

In bed, curled up between fine linen sheets, she thought of Mevrouw Honig and Juffrouw de Wit and wondered what would have happened if she hadn't gone to the cottage that afternoon. It would have been nice if Litrik had said something kind about her hard work there, for it had been hard work. If she had been a dainty blond with big blue eyes and a helpless manner he would have praised her to the skies; as it was he took her for granted. She went to sleep on a wave of self-pity.

The morning was taken up with settling Nanny in again and hearing her news and then going to the kitchen to agree to Nel's suggestions about pickles and jams, and after lunch she got into the Daimler beside Litrik and was driven to the cottage.

It was one of those days when approaching winter allowed

a forgotten autumn day to take over. The sun shone and although it was chilly there was little wind. They went up the path together and Juffrouw de Wit opened the door, her long face wreathed in smiles.

They were ushered into the small front room, very clean and neat but cold since there was no fire in the stove. But fortunately Litrik said that he would see his patient at once and at the same time swept Fran into the kitchen where Juffrouw de Wit had hurried to make coffee. It was warm there and Fran sat down at the table and listened to her companion's account of the night. All was well, she was told, Mevrouw Honig had slept fairly well and the cough seemed less severe. The doctor would be pleased...

He came down the precipitous stairs presently, ducking his head to avoid knocking himself out in the doorway, and accepted coffee while he listened to Juffrouw de Wit repeating everything she had said to Fran.

He allowed himself to be cautiously optimistic, he told Fran; the old woman was better but would need several days in bed still. Then he turned his attention to Juffrouw de Wit once more, listening patiently to what she had to say, and then writing down fresh instructions.

'Is she all right for food?' asked Fran.

It seemed that someone had walked from the village that morning and brought milk and groceries with them. There was enough and to spare, declared Juffrouw de Wit.

They sat for a little while before Fran went up to see Mevrouw Honig. The antibiotic was already doing good work, the old woman was a better colour and she smiled at Fran and muttered something and Fran mustered her Dutch and wished the old woman a speedy recovery.

She and Litrik went down the garden under Juffrouw de Wit's approving eyes and as she went through the gate Fran asked, 'Would you like to see the fairy pool? I think Lisa would like that.'

He cast her a quick tender look, which she didn't see. 'I should like that.'

She led the way along the path and when the pond came into view she stopped for him to catch up with her. It was very quiet and the only movement was from the water coots on the far side of the pond.

'We always sat on that tree stump,' said Fran and two tears ran down her cheeks. She put up a gloved hand and wiped them away and blinked hard to hold back the rest of them, sniffing like a child. Litrik took a snowy handkerchief from a pocket and turned her round and mopped her face and she took it from him and blew her nose in a resolute fashion and said steadily, 'I am sorry, I didn't mean to cry. We were always happy here.' She looked up at him. 'You're not angry because we didn't share it with you?'

He stared down at her for a long moment and then shook his head. 'When I asked you to marry me it was because I wanted Lisa to have all the happiness she could before she died. You gave her that happiness; how could I possibly be angry?'

She watched a coot slide into the reeds just below them, and said sadly, 'I was happy, too...'

He asked abruptly, 'But not any more. I had wondered?'

'Well, everything is a bit uncertain, isn't it? I feel a fraud now, that is why I'd like to go.' She added politely, 'When it's convenient.' She looked around her and then back at his quiet face. 'It's been like a dream, hasn't it? But dreams end and we have to go our separate ways again.'

'You want that, Francesca?'

'Yes, oh yes, I do... You must see...'

He said very quietly, 'You want to go back to nursing—to your old life in England? If that is your wish, then I will do all I can to help you.' He turned to leave the pool. 'Dreams don't have to end,' he said.

She wasn't really listening, which was a pity; her mind was already busy with the ways and means of getting a job. Not

London—something remote, preferably in the country where she could find her way back to her old life once more. When that was done she could go to London and get a good post and make nursing her career. She sighed at the very idea and Litrik turned to look at her.

'Don't worry, Francesca, you shall go just as soon as I can arrange it. You may have to come back briefly for the annulment but I'll do all I can to make things easy for you.'

She turned to take a final look at the pool. She could hardly see it through her tears.

CHAPTER NINE

LITRIK DIDN'T COME into the house with her, but drove off straight away to Utrecht, saying he would be home shortly before dinner, so she had a solitary tea by the fire and then went in search of Nanny who had elected to repair the tapestry on one of the massive armchairs in the drawing room. She was a clever needlewoman and, as she pointed out to Fran, only too glad to make herself useful. 'Until such time as I can be a nanny again,' she added and looked hopefully at Fran.

Fran bent over the chair, hiding her red face, murmuring vaguely. These were the awkward moments Litrik hadn't troubled to consider; they cropped up all the time and each time she felt like blurting out the truth. She began, a little feverishly, to talk to Nanny about Clare and the expected baby, a successful red herring which got her through the next five minutes and out of the room, with the excuse that she must walk the dogs.

She walked for miles, thinking about Litrik's promise that she could return to England as soon as he could arrange it. He hadn't sounded in the least put out about it; perhaps he was relieved that she had brought the subject up—it would have been an awkward subject for him to broach. All the same, he might have shown some regret. She turned for home, determined to start her packing as soon as possible so that she could go immediately he had arranged her journey.

To be thwarted within half an hour of his return home. Great Aunt Olda would be celebrating her eightieth birthday in four days' time and the whole family would foregather to make it an occasion. Naturally, he pointed out, they would go. The great aunts lived to the north of Leeuwarden in the village of Rinsumaard, something over a hundred miles. He had arranged to be free on that day, they could drive up for lunch and return after dinner in the evening. And perhaps she would go into Utrecht with him and choose a suitable present.

She went with him the following morning since he wasn't due at the hospital until after lunch and spent an absorbing hour in a jeweller's shop choosing a diamond brooch for Tante Olda. Its price staggered Fran but, as Litrik pointed out, one wasn't eighty years old more than once and such an event called for something special. He took her to lunch after that, to Smits Hotel, and then drove her back home before returning to the hospital.

She suggested diffidently on their way back that she might get out the Mini and visit Mevrouw Honig and he agreed readily. 'I shall be going to see her tomorrow some time, but I'm sure she will be glad to see you. Could you find out if Juffrouw de Wit has all she wants? Anything she needs I can take with me tomorrow. And take a look at Mevrouw Honig, will you, and let me know how she is. Juffrouw de Wit is a worthy soul, but she isn't a trained nurse.'

So Fran got into the Mini and drove herself over to the cottage, to be met by Juffrouw de Wit with a most satisfactory report of her patient's progress. Certainly the old woman seemed better; beginning to eat again, said Juffrouw de Wit cheerfully, and taking her pills regularly. Fran checked her temperature and pulse and saw that her breathing was easier; the worst was over and she would be able to give Litrik a good report when he got home.

She supposed it was inevitable that she should be asked if she would accompany him the next morning to see his patient. He had private patients to see at midday and no rounds at the hospital until the afternoon. She got into the car beside him with the dogs nicely settled on the back seat, taking with her a few small luxuries Mevrouw Honig might enjoy, happy to be there beside him. He hadn't said any more about her leaving but it wouldn't be long now, she imagined. Once they had visited Tante Olda he would tell her.

Litrik was pleased with his patient's progress; another few days and she might get up. They drank coffee with Juffrouw de Wit, handed over the odds and ends Fran had brought with her, and drove back. This time there had been no suggestion of going to the pond.

Fran watched Litrik drive off from the house and went to pay her usual visit to the kitchen and then to Nanny, still industriously plying her needle, and after lunch she telephoned Mevrouw van Rijgen, doubtful about what she should wear to Aunt Olda's party.

'Bring a pretty dress with you, my dear,' counselled Mevrouw van Rijgen. 'It's only family but Tante Olda will expect us to do honour to the occasion. Something short. Litrik tells me you are driving back after the party—a pity you can't stay the night but I expect he had a full day of appointments ahead of him.' There was a faint query in her voice and Fran made haste to say that he was very busy and couldn't manage to get away for more than just the one day. She rang off and went upstairs to go through her wardrobe. She would wear the blue woollen suit and take one of her after-six dresses—the mulberry silk velvet with the long tight sleeves and the satin sash. There were high-heeled velvet slippers to match and perhaps the pearls would be lent to her again.

They left soon after breakfast on Tante Olda's birthday, taking the route through Amsterdam and Hoorn and over the Afsluitdijk so that Fran might see something of that part of

Holland. 'For,' as Litrik pointed out blandly, 'you might not have another opportunity to see our famous sea dyke. We'll drive back down the other side of the Isselmeer, but it will be dark then, of course.'

He was at his most interesting pointing out various landmarks which he thought might interest her and never once mentioning the fact that she would be going away very soon. She had hoped, when he had remarked upon her not seeing the Afsluitdijk again, that he would say something about her leaving, but it seemed that it was the last thing he was thinking of.

They stopped for coffee in Alkmaar; it had meant that he had gone into the town expressly for that purpose, but, as he pointed out, they had the time to do so and, like the Afsluitdijk, it was a place it would be a pity for her not to visit while she had the opportunity.

She drank her coffee rather silently, thinking that he seemed determined to remind her that any day now she would be gone, and at the same time he seemed equally determined not to tell her when that was to be.

They arrived at Rinsumaard just before midday, to find a big gathering already there. The aunts lived in a large, rather forbidding house on the edge of the village, it had a large garden around it and its furnishings were opulent and at the same time gloomy. Wilma, greeting Fran in the hall, whispered, 'Isn't it overpowering? All dark oak and family portraits—you ought to see the kitchens. How nice you look. Come and say hallo to the aunts. Tante Olda is having a lovely time...' She turned to Litrik who had been talking to his father. 'Have you bought something fabulous? I've never seen so many handsome presents.' She lifted her face for his kiss. 'Come on, then we can have a drink before lunch.'

Tante Olda received their congratulations and the brooch with dignity and the command that Fran should return to talk to her later on. 'I rest in the afternoon,' she observed, 'but we must have a little chat before you leave this evening. Such a pity that you have to return tonight; I only hope that Litrik is a careful driver.'

Fran assured her that he was. Very careful but fast, only she didn't say that; she wasn't a very fast driver herself but sitting beside Litrik she enjoyed the exhilarating speed.

She got separated from him after that and during luncheon, since he was sitting at the other end of the vast oval table, she could only get a glimpse of him now and then around the vast floral centrepiece. And after lunch, when the aunts and the elderly had retired for their post-prandial naps, Jebbeke and Wilma carried her off to see the gardens and then explore the house.

'It's like a museum,' said Jebbeke. 'We all hate it, but it's been in the family for years and years and it'll go to Uncle Hilwert, who doesn't want it.'

Fran agreed that it wasn't her idea of a cosy home and thought with sudden longing of Litrik's house, just as big but somehow it was a home, its rooms comfortably furnished, with firelight and lamplight and the dogs lying around and Nel and Tuggs and Nanny. She was going to miss them all—and she was going to miss Litrik for the rest of her life.

'Don't look so sad,' said Wilma, and flung a friendly arm round her shoulders. 'You and Litrik won't have to live here, nor will your children. And aren't you lucky? We are all coming to you at New Year, you know that I expect. We have a lovely time—it's a kind of tradition. When Litrik can tear himself away from his patients you must come and spend a weekend with us.'

Fran wondered what they would think of her when Litrik told them that they had decided to part. He would allow no blame to attach to herself, she knew him well enough for that, but all the same she felt guilty.

'You're looking sad again,' said Jebbeke, 'You need a cup of your English tea.' She glanced at her watch. 'It will be in the red salon.'

The red salon was exactly that: red carpet, curtains and upholstery, with a glittering chandelier overhead and stern faced ancestors staring coldly down from the red panelled walls. Several of the family were already there and Litrik crossed the room to join them as they went in.

He included all three of them in his smile, but he spoke to Fran.

'What do you think of the house, Francesca? A little overpowering isn't it? Come over to the fire and have some tea; the aunts aren't coming down until we meet for dinner.'

Tea was a pleasant interlude and presently they scattered again, the men to play billiards, the ladies to enjoy a discussion of the latest fashions, and presently they went upstairs to the various rooms allotted to them to change for the evening.

Fran found herself in a vast room, heavily furnished in the Beidermeyer style with a bathroom and dressing room leading from it. There was no sign of Litrik although his clothes had been laid out in the dressing room. She undressed and had a bath and then dressed quickly in the mulberry velvet. She was sitting at the dressing-table doing things to her face when she heard Litrik in the dressing room, and then presently in the bathroom.

She was quite ready, still sitting at the dressing-table when he tapped on the door and came in. He looked quite splendid in his black tie and her heart turned over at the sight of him and then thumped so loudly that when he came to stand beside her she was afraid that he would hear it.

'A dreadfully depressing room,' remarked Litrik, and added silkily, 'not conducive to connubial bliss.'

She was thinking up a suitable answer to this when he took the pearls out of a pocket and fastened them round her neck. His fingers were cool against her neck and businesslike. He had the earrings, too, and watched while she fastened them, staring at her reflection in the mirror so that she found it difficult to keep her composure.

'Shall we go?' he asked. 'Out of this door, I think—it will look better if we are together, will it not?'

He gave her a brief mocking smile as she went past him.

Everyone had gathered in the drawing room, with Tante Nynke arriving just a few minutes ahead of Tante Olda, who swept in with a fine sense of the dramatic, wearing black satin and a great many diamonds. There were drinks then and a slow procession into the dining room, and this time Fran was between Litrik's cousins, young and only too delighted to entertain her while they ate their way through iced melon, poached salmon, roast pheasant and a magnificent ice pudding, and all of these helped along with champagne. Fran laughed and talked and ate hardly anything, aware of Litrik's eyes upon her face from the other side of the table.

Everyone gathered in the drawing room after dinner, groups forming and dispersing and reforming while Tante Olda sat by the fire in state, talking to first one and then another of the family.

The evening was far gone when Jebbeke tapped Fran on the arm. 'Your turn,' she said lightly. 'Tante Olda wants a chat.'

Litrik had been standing nearby and he had heard his sister. He smiled and nodded at Fran as she crossed the room and sat down beside the old lady, to be looked over by a pair of very shrewd eyes.

'I'm getting tired,' observed Tante Olda, 'but I wanted to talk to you, Francesca; we have had so little opportunity to get to know each other. I do not intend to pry but there are two questions I wish to ask you, and since you are a sensible and honest girl I have no doubt that you will give me truthful answers.'

She was silent for so long that Fran decided that she had dozed off. But she hadn't.

'I am devoted to Litrik—we have always been close, he and I. As a small boy...' She fell silent again and went on in a quite different voice, 'After the disastrous fiasco of his first marriage he changed. Oh, outwardly still charming and an amusing companion, but beneath that, cold and detached, just as though he would never care for anything or anyone again—except for little Lisa, of course. For her, he was his true self. But underneath that coldness there is still the real man, warm and passionate, and you, my dear, are the one to find that man again.' She gave Fran a searching look. 'You do love him, Francesca?'

Fran's heart answered before her sensible head could frame a reply. 'Yes, I love him—I love him so much.'

The old lady nodded in satisfaction. 'You want to have his children?'

'Yes, oh yes, more than anything in the world, but...'

She was interrupted by Litrik's voice behind her. 'Sorry to break up your gossip.' He sounded lazily tolerant. 'I've just noticed the time as I was talking to Father and we really must go—I have a round in the morning.'

Fran had gone pale. How long had he been there and what had he heard?

She glanced quickly at him; his face was calm, his voice casual and his father was standing at the other end of the long room. A stealthy glance told her that Litrik couldn't have had the time to cross the room and overhear what she had said. She heaved a sigh of relief, kissed the elderly proffered cheek, thanked Tante Olda prettily and then accompanied Litrik round the room, saying goodbyes.

It was really goodbye this time, she thought sadly.

Someone had packed their things and fetched the car to the door. She had put her winter coat into the car and now Litrik wrapped her into it and they drove off to a chorus of goodbyes.

It was a cold dark night with frost sparkling on the roof tops and the fields. Litrik drove fast and almost in silence and presently she slept.

The house was warm and welcoming; they drank the coffee Nel had left out before Fran wished Litrik good night. 'I enjoyed it', she ventured a little shyly. 'You do have a nice family, Litrik.'

He gave her a mocking smile. 'Such a pity that you will never get to know them, Francesca. As you have pointed out to me, that is by your own wish.'

There was nothing for her to do but wish him good night for the second time and go up to bed.

She came down to breakfast very late the next morning and he had already gone. She spent an hour with Nel and Nanny, telling them about Tante Olda's party, and then took the dogs for a walk and, because she had slept badly, she dozed in front of the fire after lunch.

Litrik came back at tea time. She sat up as he came into the room and he said pleasantly, 'Catching up on last night's sleep?' He put an envelope on the table beside the chair. 'Your tickets, Francesca. I wasn't able to get you a flight—I've booked you on the night ferry to Harwich for the day after tomorrow.'

She had been expecting it for days and now it had come and she was too taken aback to speak. She picked up the envelope and peered inside. The tickets were there, sure enough, and she said faintly, 'Oh, thank you.'

Litrik sat down in his chair and stretched out his legs, the epitome of relaxed comfort. 'You'll get into London about midmorning, that gives you plenty of time to go on down to your aunts if you wish, or find an hotel.' He picked up the first of the pile of letters waiting for him. 'I'll see that you have sufficient money and write you a reference—that's what you wanted, isn't it?'

It was a little more than Fran could stand. Illogically she was thunderstruck at the suddenness of it all—she had just one day in which to pack her things and say goodbye to Mevrouw Honig and Dominee Meertens. And what was she to say to the staff?

She said savagely, 'How absolutely beastly of you!'

He lifted his handsome head from the letter he was reading. 'Why, my dear Francesca, you have been badgering me to let you return home for days—I'm surprised at you.'

He lowered his eyes to his letters again and she said in a choked voice, 'Well, I'd better go and start packing.'

When she left the room, Litrik rang for Tuggs and, when that faithful friend came, 'Now listen, Tuggs, there are one or two things I want you to do.' Tuggs listened carefully and went back to the kitchen and when Nel asked him what the doctor had wanted, he told her to ask no questions and she would be told no lies!

Fran, in her room, took a wistful look at the lovely clothes she had bought with Litrik's money, and began to pack the things she had brought with her. She would have to travel in the Jaeger suit for she had no coat with her but she could wear a sweater with it and hope that it wouldn't be too cold a day. Having done this she did her face and hair and went downstairs for dinner, to hold a desultory conversation with Litrik and agree with every appearance of pleasure to his suggestion that, as he intended visiting Mevrouw de Wit in the morning, she might like to go with him.

The old woman was well on the way to recovery, sitting downstairs in a chair by the fire Juffrouw de Wit had kindled in the parlour. She accepted Fran's gift of fruit and biscuits, assured her that she would soon be on her feet once more and asked her if she wanted to go to the pond.

It was after they had all had coffee that Litrik said that he would like to examine his patient and if Fran wished to go for a stroll perhaps she would like to go now. 'Ten minutes,' he said. 'I must be in Zeist by eleven o'clock.'

So she trod the well-known path once more for the last time and went to sit on the log and watch the coots and listen to the few birds. It had been a happy place with Lisa, but now it was sad; she went back before the ten minutes were up, took a brief farewell of the two ladies and got into the car. Litrik talked cheerfully about his patient during the brief drive back and left at once for the hospital, and she went to the kitchen where she told Nel and Nanny that she would be going to England on the following day. They received her news calmly, hoped that she would have a good time and plunged into the question of whether she wanted all the guestrooms opened and prepared for Christmas. Somehow she escaped answering that and took herself and the dogs for a long walk and directly after lunch went to say goodbye to the *dominee*. She was hurt and surprised at the matter-of-fact manner in which he received her news, and still more disappointed at his vague answers to her anxious questions about the annulment.

'You are anxious to leave us?' he boomed at her.

'Yes—no—that is—I can't explain...' And to her relief he said no more.

Feeling frustrated, she shook hands with him and his wife and as he went down the garden path with her she was perplexed to hear him say, 'Most satisfactory—this is something I had hoped and prayed for.'

She wanted very much to ask him what he meant—he must have been referring to Lisa. She didn't go straight back to the house, but walked on towards the lake, making and discarding plans for her future. She had a little money of her own but she would have to decide quickly where she wanted to go and then look for a job. Litrik had said that he would see that her career wouldn't suffer and she believed him; it would help a lot if she made up her mind before she left the next day, then there would be no need to write to him.

She wandered on, trying to envisage a future without him and filled with despair at the thought. But that was a waste of time and the sooner she stopped mooning after him, she told herself briskly, the better. She would tell him that she would like to work in Scotland; she wasn't fussy where but preferably in a large hospital where there was plenty of work. Her mind made up, she turned for home, pecked at her lunch and went to her room to finish her packing. That done, she spent half an hour fingering the lovely things still hanging in the closet, wondering what Litrik would do about them. They were too small for Nanny, and his sisters were big girls. Besides, they had more than enough money to buy anything they wanted. It was a pity she must leave the winter coat, it would have been a comfort on the journey.

Litrik didn't come home for tea and although he came in just before dinner, he went out again almost immediately they had finished. She sat in the drawing room knitting, her mind refusing to think any more.

He was at breakfast, wishing her good morning as usual and, before he went to the hospital, warning her to be ready to leave at eight o'clock that evening. 'I shall be back by six o'clock so will you arrange dinner for an hour earlier than usual—we can leave directly after that.'

'We?' asked Fran startled. She had expected Tuggs to drive her to Utrecht to catch the boat train.

'Naturally I shall drive you myself.'

He had gone, leaving her to spend her last day roaming round the house and the gardens. At least she would have the chance to talk to him about her plans, for the drive to the Hoek would take an hour, perhaps more. She had herself nicely in hand by the time he returned in the evening, made rather feverish small talk during dinner, said goodbye to everyone and got into the Daimler. It was a brilliant night, the wind still and with a silver moon giving sparkle to the frost, and there was not much traffic. She settled down beside Litrik and began to compose the various questions in her head. They had skirted Utrecht before she had them exactly as she wished and then she forgot every one of them as they passed a road sign.

'We're going the wrong way,' she said urgently. 'Emmeloord and Leeuwarden—the Hoek's the other way.'

'We are not going to the Hoek,' said Litrik calmly.

'I'm going to miss the boat... Why not?' She took a steadying breath. 'Where are we going?'

'To a cottage I have near Sneek.' He gave a great sigh. 'You see, my dear, I am in love with you and I cannot let you go.'

The road was straight and empty before them; he slowed the car and stopped. 'I believe that I have loved you for a long time now, perhaps since that first time when I made you cry during that lecture—afterwards I felt as though I had wounded some small creature and left it to die. Then I met you again and I knew that you were exactly the mother Lisa had wished for for so long—a mouse, she had said, and that is what you are, a small beautiful mouse with a soft voice and lovely eyes and a gentle mouth and I knew for certain then that I loved you. Only you had made it clear that for you our marriage was purely for Lisa's sake and I have tried very hard to keep to my side of our pact.'

Fran stirred in her seat. 'Could we get out?' she asked softly. 'Please?'

He went round the car and took something from the boot and opened her door and she saw that he had her coat over his arm.

'I went to look in your room—I guessed what you would do. You see how well I know you, my darling? I asked Nel to pack some of your things and put this into the car.'

He helped her into it and buttoned it up cosily under her chin and took her arm and began walking along the road. Fran looked into his face, very clear in the moonlight. 'I love you,' she said, 'but how did you know? Because you do know, don't you?' She frowned. 'You heard me and Tante Olda?'

'I eavesdropped quite shamelessly, my darling, reminding myself that all is fair in love and war. You see, I know Tante Olda very well indeed; she has this habit of asking searching questions. I know you, too, and I knew you would answer her honestly.'

'You could have told me on our way home.'

'You slept, my love. And I wanted to be sure—that's why I gave you the tickets. And you seemed pleased so that I wanted to hurt you.'

'Well, you did,' declared Fran, 'and I really can't think why I love you so very much for sometimes you are so tiresome.'

He stopped and swung her round into his arms and let out a great bellow of laughter. 'Oh, I will try so hard not to be tiresome,' he promised her and kissed her gently and then very hard and indeed, and presently he took her arm again and began walking back to the car. And as they went he stopped to kiss her once in a while. 'Love in the moonlight,' he observed, 'there is nothing quite like it.'

'Tell me,' said Fran, 'this cottage—are we going to stay there?'

'For a week—Mama's retired cook lives there and looks after it for me; Tuggs will have phoned her and told her to expect us.'

'Supposing that I had insisted on going to the Hoek?'

'I should have kidnapped you,' said Litrik, and kissed her once again.

* * * * *

Heaven Is Gentle

CHAPTER ONE

THE ROOM WAS large and well lighted, and by reason of the cheerful fire in the wide chimneypiece and the thick curtains drawn against the grey January afternoon, cosy enough. There were three persons in it; an elderly man, sitting at his ease behind a very large, extremely untidy desk, a thin, prim woman at a small table close by and a tall, broad-shouldered man sitting astride a small chair, his arms folded across its back, his square, determined chin resting on two large and well cared for hands. He was a handsome man, his dark hair silvered at the temples, and possessing a pair of formidable black brows above very dark eyes. In repose he appeared to be of an age approaching forty, but when he smiled, and he was smiling now, he looked a good deal younger.

Miss Trim paused in the reading of the names from a typed list before her and glanced at the two men. They were smoking pipes and she gave a small protesting cough which she knew would be ignored, anyhow.

'They sound like a line of chorus girls,' commented the younger of her two companions. His smile turned to an engaging grin. 'How do you like the idea of being nursed by a

Shirley Anne, or an Angela, or—what was that last one, Miss Trim? A Felicity?'

His elderly companion puffed a smoke ring and viewed it with satisfaction. 'We should have tried for a male nurse,' he mused out loud, 'but from a psychological point of view that would not have been satisfactory.'

'There are still a few names on the list, Professor Wyllie.' Miss Trim sounded faintly tart, probably because of the smoke wreathing itself around her head. She coughed again and continued to read: 'Annette Dawes, Marilyn Jones, Eliza Proudfoot, Heather Cox…'

She was interrupted. 'A moment, Miss Trim—that name again, Eliza…?'

'Miss Eliza Proudfoot, Professor van Duyl.'

'This is the one,' his deep voice with its faint trace of an accent, sounded incisive. 'With a name like that, I don't see how we can go wrong.'

He glanced at the older man, his eyebrows lifted. 'What do you say, sir?'

'You're probably right. Let's hear the details, Miss Trim.'

Before she could speak: 'Five foot ten,' murmured Professor van Duyl, 'with vital statistics to match.' He caught the secretary's disapproving eye. 'She'll need to be strong,' he reminded her blandly, 'not young any more, rather on the plain side and decidedly motherly.' He turned his smiling gaze on Professor Wyllie. 'Will you like that?'

His companion chuckled. 'I daresay she will do as well as any, provided that her qualifications are good.' He gave Miss Trim a questioning look, and she answered promptly, mentioning one of the larger London hospitals.

'She trained there,' she recited from her meticulous notes, 'and is now Ward Sister of Men's Medical. She is twenty-eight years old, unmarried, and thought very highly of by those members of the medical profession for whom she works.' She added primly, 'Shall I telephone Sir Harry Bliss, Professor? He is the consultant in charge of her ward.'

'Good lord, woman,' exploded her employer, 'you don't have to tell me that! Of course I know it's old Harry—known him man and boy, whatever that's supposed to mean. Get him on the telephone and then go away and concoct the right sort of letter to send to this young woman.'

'You wish to interview her, sir?'

'No, no. There's no time for that; if Harry says she's OK she'll do. We go to Inverpolly on the tenth; ask her to come up there whichever way she likes to by the fifteenth—expenses paid, of course. See that she gets a good idea how to reach the place and add a few trimmings—benefit to mankind and all that stuff. Oh, and warn her that she must be prepared to look after me as well if I should have an attack.'

He waved a hand at Miss Trim and she understood herself to be dismissed as she murmured suitably, thanked Professor van Duyl for opening the door for her and went back to her own office, where she set about composing a suitable letter to Miss Proudfoot, thinking as she did so that the young lady in question would need to be tough indeed if she accepted the post she was couching in such cautiously attractive terms. Conditions in the Highlands of Wester Ross at this time of year would be hard enough, working for the two men she had just left harder still. Professor Wyllie was a dear old man, but after acting as his secretary for fifteen years, she knew him inside out; he was irascible at times, wildly unpredictable, and his language when he was in a bad temper was quite unprintable. And as for Professor van Duyl—Miss Trim paused in her typing and her rather sharp features relaxed into a smile. She had met him on several occasions over the last five years or so, and while he had been unfailingly courteous and charming towards her, she sensed that here was a man with a nasty temper, nicely under control, and a very strong will behind that handsome face. As she finished her letter, she found herself hoping that Miss Proudfoot was good at managing men as well as being tough.

The subject of her thoughts, blithely unaware of the future hurtling towards her, was doing a round with Sir Harry Bliss, his registrar—one Donald Jones, a clutch of worried housemen, and the social worker, a beaky-nosed lady with a heart of gold, known throughout the hospital as Ducky. And keeping an eye on the whole bunch of them was Staff Nurse Mary Price, an amiable beanpole of a girl, much prized by Sister Proudfoot, and her willing slave as well as friend. She sidled up to her now, bent down and whispered urgently, listened in her turn, nodded and sped away.

'And where is our little Mary Price going?' enquired Sir Harry without lifting his eyes from the notes he was reading. There was a faint murmur of laughter because he prided himself on his sense of humour, but Sister Proudfoot who had heard that one a dozen times before merely handed him the patient's chart as the housemen fanned out into a respectful semi-circle around the foot of the bed. 'It's time for nurses' dinner,' she said in a composed voice.

'Implying that I am too slow on my round, Sister?' He stared down at her over his glasses.

She gave him a serene glance. 'No, sir—just stating a fact.' She smiled at him and he rumbled out a laugh. 'All right, all right—let's get on with the job, then. Let me see Mr Atkins' chest.'

She bent to the patient, a small, shapely girl with bright golden hair swept into a neat bun from which little curls escaped. Her eyes were unexpectedly hazel, richly fringed, her nose small and straight and her mouth sweetly curved. A very pretty girl, who looked years younger than her age and far too fragile for her job.

She was on her way back from a late dinner when the faithful Staff came hurrying to meet her. 'They've just telephoned from the office—Miss Smythe wants to see you at once, Sister.'

She beamed down at Eliza like a good-natured stork. 'I'll start the medicines, shall I, and get old Mr Pearce ready for X-ray.'

Eliza nodded. 'Yes, do. I wonder what I've done,' she mused. 'Do you suppose it's because I complained about the shortage of linen bags? You know we have to be careful nowadays.' She added a little vaguely, 'Unions and things.'

'But you weren't nasty,' Mary reassured her, 'you never are.'

Eliza beamed at her. 'What a great comfort you always are, Mary. We'll have a cup of tea when I get back and I'll tell you all about it.'

She turned round and sped back the way she had come, up and down corridors and a staircase or so, until she came to the Office door, where she stopped for a moment to fetch her breath before tapping on it, and in response to the green light above it, entered.

Miss Smythe, the Principal Nursing Officer, was sitting at her desk. She was a stern-faced woman, but at the moment Eliza was relieved to see that she was looking quite amiable. She waved a hand at a chair, said, 'Good afternoon, Sister Proudfoot,' waited until Eliza had sat down and began: 'I have received a letter about you, and with it a letter for yourself—from Professor Wyllie.'

Wyllie, thought Eliza, a shade uneasily, the name rang a bell; asthma research and heart complications or something of that sort, and hadn't someone told her once that he himself was a sufferer? She said cautiously:

'Yes, Miss Smythe?'

For answer her superior handed her a letter. 'I suggest that you read this for yourself, Sister, and then let me have your comments.'

Miss Trim had done her work well; the letter, while astonishing Eliza very much, could not help but flatter her. She read it to its end and then looked across at Miss Smythe. 'Well, I never!' she declared.

The lady's features relaxed into the beginnings of a smile. 'I was surprised too, Sister. It is of course a great honour, which will reflect upon St Anne's. I hope that you will consider it well and agree to go.'

'It's a long way away.'

Miss Smythe's voice was smoothly persuasive. 'Yes, but I believe that you have a car? There is no reason why you shouldn't drive yourself up there, and Professor Wyllie assures me that the whole experiment, while most important to him, will take only a few weeks. Sir Harry Bliss thinks that you should avail yourself of the opportunity, it may be of the utmost advantage to you in your career.'

Eliza frowned faintly. She had never wanted a career; somehow or other it had been thrust upon her; she had enjoyed training as a nurse, she had liked staffing afterwards and when she had been offered a Sister's post she had accepted it with pleasure, never imagining that she would still be in it five years later. She wasn't a career girl at all; she had grown up with the idea of marrying and having children of her own, but despite numerous opportunities to do this, she had always hung back at the last minute, aware, somewhere at the back of her mind, that this wasn't the right man. And now here she was, as near as not twenty-nine and Miss Smythe talking as though she was going to be a Ward Sister for ever. She sighed. 'May I have a little time to think about it? I should like to see exactly where this place is and discover precisely what it's all about. Am I to be the only woman there?'

'Yes, so I understand. That is why they wanted a somewhat older girl, and a trained nurse, of course. As a precaution, I believe; Professor Wyllie is a sufferer from asthma as well as having heart failure; his health must be safe-guarded. Over and above that, he seems to think that a woman nurse would be of more benefit to the patients. There will also be a number of technicians, the patients, of course—and a colleague of the professor's. A Dutch Professor of Medicine, highly thought of, I believe.'

Eliza dismissed him at once; he would be learned and bald and use long words in a thick accent, like the elderly brilliant friend of Sir Harry Bliss, who had discussed each patient at such length that she had had to go without her dinner.

'Let me know by this evening, Sister Proudfoot,' advised Miss Smythe, 'sooner if you can manage it—it seems that Professor Wyllie wants an answer as soon as possible.'

An observation which almost decided Eliza to refuse out of sheer perversity; she was by nature an obliging girl, but she didn't like being pushed; there were several things she wanted to know about the job, and no chance of finding out about any of them in such a short time. She walked back through the hospital, her head bowed in thought, so that when she narrowly avoided bumping into Sir Harry she was forced to stop and apologise.

'Deep in thought,' pronounced that gentleman, 'about that job my old friend Willy Wyllie has offered you, eh? Oh, I thought so—take it, girl, it will make a nice change from this place, put a bit of colour into those cheeks and a pound or two on to your bones.'

Eliza stared at him thoughtfully. 'Probably,' she agreed amiably. 'You seem to know all about it, sir, but I don't, do I? I mean the bare facts are in the letter, but where do I live while I'm there, and what about time off and how far away is it from the shops and shall I be expected to do night duty?'

'Tell you what,' said Sir Harry, 'we'll go and telephone someone this very minute and find out.'

'But I'm on duty. And you, sir, if I might remind you, are expected in Women's Medical...' She glanced at her watch. 'You were expected...' she corrected herself demurely, 'fifteen minutes ago.'

'In that case, five minutes more won't be noticed.' He swept her along with him to the consultants' room, opened the door and thrust her inside ahead of him. 'Well, really,' began Eliza, and seeing it was hopeless to say anything, watched him pick up the telephone and demand a number.

He talked for some minutes, firing questions at his unseen listener like bullets from a gun, and presently said: 'Hold on, I'll ask her.'

'Two days off a week, but probably you won't get them, three hours off a day, these to be arranged according to the day's requirements. You will have a little cottage to live in—by yourself, close to the main house. There will be an opportunity to go to the nearest town and shop if you should wish to, but it's only fair to mention that there isn't much in the way of entertainment.' He barely gave her time to absorb this sparse information before he barked: 'Well, how about it, Eliza?' He grinned at her. 'I recommended you, you can't let me down.'

She gave him a severe look. 'Did you now, sir? Miss Smythe said that I could think it over.'

'That was before you knew all these details I've gone to so much trouble to discover for you,' he wheedled. 'Come on now—it'll make a nice change.'

She gave him a sudden smile. 'All right, though I shall have to miss the hospital ball.'

He had picked up the receiver again. 'Pooh, you can go dancing any night of the week; there isn't a man in the hospital who hasn't asked you out, one way and another.' He turned away before she could reply and spoke to the patient soul at the other end of the line. 'OK, she'll come. Details later.' And when she started to protest at his high-handed methods: 'Well, why not, girl? You said you would go—you can fix the details with Miss Smythe.' He bustled her to the door. 'And now I'm late for my round, and it's your fault.'

He trod on his way, leaving her speechless with indignation.

Mary Price had tea ready, the ward under control and five minutes to spare when Eliza got back to Men's Medical. They sipped the dark, sweet brew in the peace and quiet of the office while Eliza explained briefly about the strange offer she had been made.

'Oh, take it, Sister,' begged her faithful colleague. 'We shall miss you dreadfully, but it'll only be for a week or two, and think of the fun you'll have.' Her brown eyes sparkled at the thought. 'You could go up by car.'

'Um,' said Eliza, 'so I could. Miss Smythe said that I'd been chosen from quite a long list of likely nurses. Why me, I wonder?'

'Sir Harry, of course—you said yourself that he knew all about it.' She refilled their cups. 'What are you supposed to do once you're there?'

'I'm not quite sure. It's an experiment—cardiac asthma as well as the intrinsic and extrinsic kinds—they want to prove something or other about climate and the effect of complete freedom from stress or strain.'

'Sounds interesting. When do you have to leave?'

'I have to report for duty on the fifteenth,' she peered at the calendar, 'eight days' time. We'll have to do something about the off duty, if you have a weekend before I go…'

They became immersed in the complicated jigsaw of days off, and presently, having got everything arranged to their mutual satisfaction, they left the office; Staff to supervise the return of the convalescent patients to their beds and Sister Proudfoot to cast her professional eye over the ward in general.

So that Mary might get her weekend off before she herself went away, Eliza took her own days off a couple of days later. She left the hospital after a long day's work, driving her Fiat 500, a vehicle she had acquired some five years previously and saw little hope of replacing for the next few years at least. But even though it was by now a little shabby, and the engine made strange noises from time to time, it still served her well. She turned its small nose towards the west now, and after what seemed an age of slow driving through London, reached its outskirts and at length the M3. Here at least she could travel as fast as the Fiat would allow, and even when the motorway gave way to the Winchester bypass, she maintained a steady fifty miles an hour, only once past Winchester and on the Romsey road, she slowed down a little. It was very dark, and she had wasted a long time getting out of London; she wouldn't reach Charmouth until midnight. The thought of the pleasant house where her parents lived spurred her on; they would wait up for her, they always did, and there would be hot soup and sausage rolls, warm and featherlight from the oven. Eliza, who hadn't stopped for supper, put her small foot down on the accelerator.

The road was dark and lonely once she had passed Cadnam Corner. She left the New Forest behind, skirted Ringwood and threaded her way through Wimborne, silent under the blanket of winter clouds. Dorchester was silent too—she was getting near home now, there were only the hills between her and Bridport and then down and up through Chideock and then home. Here eager thoughts ran ahead of her, so that it seemed nearer than it actually was.

The lights of the house were still on as she brought the little car to a halt at the top of the hill at the further end of the little town, it lay back from the road, flanked by neighbours, all three of them little Regency houses, bowfronted, with verandahs and roomy front gardens. She was out of the car, her case in her hand, and running up the garden path almost as soon as she had switched off the engine; the cold bit into her as she turned the old-fashioned brass knob of the door and went inside. Her mother and father were still up, as she knew they would be, sitting one each side of the open fire, dozing a little, to wake as she went into the room. She embraced them with affection; her mother, as small a woman as she was, her father, tall and thin and scholarly. 'Darlings,' she declared, 'how lovely to see you! It seems ages since I was home and I've heaps to tell you. I'll just run the car across the road.'

She flew outside again; the car park belonged to the hotel opposite but the manager never minded her using it. She tucked the Fiat away in a corner and went back indoors, to find the soup and the sausage rolls, just as she had anticipated, waiting for her. She gobbled delicately and between mouthfuls began to tell her parents about the unexpected job she had been asked to take. 'There was a list,' she explained. 'Heaven knows how they made it in the first place or why they picked on me—with a pin, most likely. I almost decided not to accept it, but Sir Harry Bliss thought it would be a good idea—and it's only for a few weeks.'

Her mother offered her another sausage roll. 'Yes, darling, I see. But isn't this place miles away from everywhere?'

'Yes. But I'm to have my own cottage to live in and I daresay I'll be too busy to want to do much when I'm not on duty.'

'There will be another nurse there?' asked her father.

She shook her head. 'No—I'm the only one and it sounds as though I shan't have much to do. A handful of volunteer patients—all men, a few technicians and the two professors; William Wyllie—he's an asthma case himself and I may have to look after him; he's quite old—well, not very old, touching seventy.'

'And the other doctor?' It was her mother this time.

'Oh, a friend of his. I daresay he'll have asthma too, he'll certainly be elderly.' She brushed the crumbs from her pretty mouth and sat back with a sigh of content. 'Now tell me all the news, my dears. Have you heard from Henry? and has Pat got over the measles?'

Henry was a younger brother, working in Brussels for the Common Market, and Pat was her small niece, her younger sister Polly's daughter, who had married several years earlier. Her mother embarked on family news, wondering as she did so why it was that this pretty little creature sitting beside her hadn't married herself, years ago. Of course she didn't look anything like her age, but thirty wasn't far off; Mrs Proudfoot belonged to the generation which considered thirty to be getting a little long in the tooth, and she worried about Eliza. The dear girl had had her chances—was still having them; she knew for a fact that at least two eligible young men had proposed to her during the last six months. And now she was off to this godforsaken spot in the Highlands where, as far as she could make out, there wasn't going to be a man under sixty.

The two days passed quickly; there was so much to do, so many friends to visit, as well as helping her mother in the nice old house and going for walks with her father, who, now that he had retired from the Civil Service, found time to indulge in his hobby of fossil gathering. Eliza, who knew nothing about fossils, obligingly accompanied him to the beach and collected what she hoped were fine specimens, and which were almost always just pebbles. All the same, they enjoyed each other's company and the fresh air gave her a glow which made her prettier than ever, so that one of the eligible young men, meeting her by chance in the main street, took the instant opportunity of proposing for a second time, an offer which she gently refused, aware that she was throwing away a good chance.

She worried about it as she drove herself back to London. Charlie King was an old friend, she had known him for years; he would make a splendid husband and he had a good job. She would, she decided, think about him seriously while she was away in Scotland; no doubt there would be time to think while she was there, and being a long way from a problem often caused it to appear in a quite different light. She put the thought away firmly for the time being and concentrated on her driving, for there had been a frost overnight, and the road was treacherous.

The next few days went rapidly, for she was busy. Mary Price had gone on her promised weekend the day after she got back and although she had two part-time staff nurses to help her, there was a good deal of extra paper work because she was going away. It was nice to see Mary back again and talk over the managing of the ward while she was away. Eliza spent her last day smoothing out all the last-minute problems, bade her patients and staff a temporary goodbye and went off duty to while away an hour with her friends in the Sisters' sitting room before going to her room to pack ready for an early start in the morning—warm clothes and not too many of them—thick sweaters and slacks, an old anorak she had brought from home and as a special concession to the faint hope of a social life, a long mohair skirt and cashmere top in a pleasing shade of old rose.

She left really early the following morning, her friends' good wishes ringing in her ears, instructions as to how to reach her destination written neatly on the pad beside the map on the seat beside her. She planned to take two, perhaps three days to get to Inverpolly, for although the Fiat always did its best, it wasn't capable of sustained speed; besides, the weather, cold and blustery now, might worsen and hold her up. She had three clear days in hand and she didn't suppose anyone would mind if she arrived a little sooner than that.

She made good progress. She had intended to spend the night at York, but she found that she had several hours in hand when she reached that city. She had an early tea and pressed on to Darlington and then turned on to the Penrith road where she decided to spend the night at the George. She was well ahead of her schedule and she felt rather pleased with herself, everything had been much easier than she had expected. She ate a good supper and went early to bed.

It was raining when she left, quite early, the next morning. By the time she had got to Carlisle, it was a steady downpour and from the look of the sky, was likely to continue so for hours, but it was a bare two hundred miles to Fort William, though there were another hundred and sixty miles after that, probably more, it was so difficult to tell from the map, but she felt relaxed now, eager to keep on for as long as possible, perhaps even complete the journey. She had thought at first that she would take the road to Inverness, but the map showed another, winding road round the lochs, she had almost decided to try it when she reached Fort William for a quick, late lunch, studying the map meanwhile. But it would have to be Inverness, she decided, the coast road looked decidedly complicated, and there was a ferry which might not be running at this time of year. She would push on; it was only three o'clock and roughly speaking, only another hundred and thirty miles to go. Even allowing for the early dark, she had two hours of driving and she was used to driving at night. She took another look at the map and saw that she didn't need to go to Inverness at all; there was a side road which would bring her out on the road to Bonar Bridge.

It was dark when she got there and she wanted her tea, but she was too near the end of her journey to spare the time now; only another thirty miles or so to go. But she hadn't gone half that distance before she regretted her wild enthusiasm; it was a lonely road she was travelling along now and after a little while there were no villages at all and almost no traffic. To try to find the remote lodge where Professor Wyllie was working would be madness; fortunately she remembered that there was a village with an impossible name just outside the National Park of Inverpolly, she could spend the night there. She reflected rather crossly now because she was tired and thirsty and just the smallest bit nervous that it was an impossible place to reach, and if she hadn't had a car what would they have done about getting her there? Being learned men, wrapped up in their work, they had probably not given it a thought. The road appeared to be going nowhere in particular. Perhaps she was lost, and that was her own fault, of course; she should have realised that parts of the Scottish Highlands really were remote from the rest of the world. Eliza glanced at the speedometer; she had come quite a distance and passed nothing at all; she must be on the wrong road and told herself not to be a fool, for there had been no other road to take. It was then she saw the signpost. Inchnadamph, one mile.

The hotel was pleasant; warm and friendly too, although by now she was so tired that a barn would have been heaven. They gave her a large, old-fashioned room and fed her like a queen because there was only a handful of guests and they had already dined. She met them briefly when she went to have her coffee in the lounge, and then, hardly able to keep her eyes open, retired to her comfortable bed. A good sleep, she promised herself, and after breakfast she would drive the last few miles of her journey.

It was raining when she started off again, but she wasn't tired any more and she had had an enormous breakfast; even the friendly warning that the road, once she was through Lochinver, was narrow and not very good couldn't damp her good spirits; it was daylight now and she had hours of time in which to find the lodge.

They were right about the road, she discovered that quickly enough, although she found the village of Inverkirkaig easily enough. The lodge was a couple of miles further on, said her instructions; there was a track on the left of the road which would lead her to the house. But the instructions hadn't mentioned the winding, muddy road though, going steadily and steeply uphill until she began to wonder if the Fiat would make it. But she reached the track at last and turned carefully into it. It was, in fact, nothing more than a way beaten by car wheels through rough ground; the little car bounced and squelched from one pothole to the next, while the trees on either side dripped mournfully on to it. The rain had increased its intensity too. Eliza could barely see before her, but when at last she turned a corner, she saw the lodge in front of her, a depressing enough sight in the rain, and as far as she could see as she drew up before its shabby door, badly in need of a paint. She got out and banged the iron knocker; the place was a disgrace. Possibly the two professors, blind to everything but their work, had noticed nothing. That was the worst of elderly gentlemen with single-track minds. There was a movement behind the door. She edged a little nearer out of the rain and waited for it to be opened.

CHAPTER TWO

SHE HAD EXPECTED SOMEONE—a woman from the village she had just passed through, perhaps—as faded and neglected as the house to open the door, not this enormous, elegant man with his dark crusader's face, dressed, her quick eye noted, with all the care of a man about to stroll down St James' to his club, instead of roughing it in this back-of-beyond spot. The owner of the place? A visitor?

She became aware that the rain was trickling down the back of her neck and she frowned. 'I'm the nurse,' she stated baldly, since it seemed there were no niceties of introduction. 'Perhaps you'll be kind enough to let Professor Wyllie know that I'm here.'

The tall man made no move, indeed he blocked the whole of the doorway with his bulk; for one awful moment Eliza wondered if she had come to the wrong place and added anxiously: 'Professor Wyllie is here, isn't he?'

He nodded, and now she could see that his dark eyes were gleaming with laughter. 'Miss Eliza Proudfoot,' he said slowly, not addressing her really; merely confirming his own thoughts. 'Five foot ten and buxom...'

She stared at him in amazement. 'I beg your pardon?' Her voice was acid—forgivable enough; she wanted to get in out of the rain and a cup of coffee would be welcome. She added crossly: 'I'm getting wet.'

She was plucked inside as though she had been a wet kitten. 'Forgive me.' His voice was politely concerned, but she could sense his amusement too. 'Is that your car?'

'Yes.'

He stared down at her. 'Such a pretty girl, and such a pretty voice too, though decidedly acidulated at the moment.'

He paid her the compliment and took it away again with a lazy charm which infuriated her. 'Are you the owner of this place?' she wanted to know.

He looked faintly surprised. 'As a matter of fact, I am.'

'Then perhaps you will tell me where I can find Professor Wyllie, since you seem unwilling to take me to him.' She added nastily: 'My case is in the car.'

He chuckled at that and opened the door again, so that she immediately felt forced to exclaim: 'You can't go out like that—you'll ruin that good suit!'

He looked down at his large person. 'The only one I have,' he murmured apologetically.

'Well, then... Professor Wyllie?'

He turned without a word and led her down the hall, past a rather nice staircase which needed a good dust, and opened a door. The room was a study, overflowing with books and papers, and sitting in the middle of it all was an elderly gentleman, who looked up as they went in, peering at them over his half glasses with guileless blue eyes.

'Miss Eliza Proudfoot,' announced the large man blandly, and now there was no hiding the amusement in his voice.

'God bless my soul!' exclaimed Mr Wyllie, and took off his glasses and polished them.

Eliza took a few steps towards the desk at which he sat. She was fast coming to the conclusion that either she was dealing with eccentrics, or the whole affair was some colossal mistake. But she had been dealing with men of every age and sort, and ill at that, for a number of years now; she said in a matter-of-fact voice: 'You weren't expecting me.'

She had addressed the older man, but it was the man who had admitted her who answered. 'Oh, indeed we were, although I must admit at the same time that we weren't expecting—er—quite you.'

She gave him a cool look, she wasn't sure that she liked him. 'That's no answer,' she pointed out, and then suddenly seeing his point, cried out: 'Oh, I'm the wrong nurse, is that it? Five foot ten and buxom…but I really am Eliza Proudfoot.'

'What was old Harry about?' demanded Professor Wyllie of no one in particular. 'Why, you're far too small to be of any use, and no one will make me believe that you're almost twenty-nine.'

She winced; no girl likes to have her age bandied about once she is over twenty-one. 'I'm very strong, and I've been in charge of Men's Medical at St Anne's for more than five years, and if you are acquainted with Sir Harry Bliss you'll know that if he said I could do the job, then there's no more to be said.'

'We don't know about being motherly yet, but she's tough,' remarked the large man. He was sitting on the edge of the desk, one well-shod, enormous foot swinging gently.

She shot him an annoyed glance and walked deliberately across the room to stand before him. It was a little disconcerting when he rose politely to his feet, so that she was forced to crane her neck in order to see his face. 'You have done nothing but make remarks about me since you opened the door,' her voice was crisp and, she hoped, reasonable, 'and I can't think why you are trying to frighten me away—because you are, aren't you? But since you only own the house—and you should be ashamed to have let it lapse into such a neglected state,' she admonished him in passing, 'I really can't see why you should interfere with my appointment. I've come to work for Professor Wyllie, not you.'

The dark face broke into a slow smile. 'My dear young lady, I must correct you; you have come to work for me too.' He held out a hand that looked as though it had never seen hard work in its life. 'I quite neglected to introduce myself—Professor Christian van Duyl.'

Eliza allowed her hand to be wrung while she recovered from her surprise. She was still framing a suitable answer to this bombshell when he gave her back her hand and started for the door.

'I'll see about your luggage and put the car away,' he told her, 'while you and Professor Wyllie have a chat.' He turned to the door. 'You would like some coffee, Miss Proudfoot?'

She nodded and then looked at the elderly gentleman behind the desk. He was smiling, a friendly smile, she was glad to see. 'Excuse me getting up, girl... I shall call you Eliza if I may—which means that I grow abominably lazy. You came up by car?'

She sat down in the chair he had indicated. 'Yes,' and she couldn't refrain from asking innocently, 'How else does one get here?'

He grinned. 'Helicopter?'

'If I had known that this place was so remote, I might have thought of that.'

He was studying her quietly. 'It's beautiful here in the autumn and late spring.'

'Surely the climate is all wrong for asthma cases?'

He chuckled. 'That's part of the exercise. Professor van Duyl and I have established that the stress and strain of modern life are just as much deciding factors in bringing on attacks as the wrong climate—now we need to prove that. We have ten volunteer patients with us—five Dutch, five English, and we intend to test our theory. If it holds water, then it gives us a lead, however slender, in the treatment of the wretched complaint.'

'Why did you want a nurse, sir?'

'We want the patients to feel secure—it is remarkable what a nurse's uniform will do on that score, and you will have work to do—general duties,' he looked vague—'and of course you will need to deal with any attacks which may crop up—one or two of the men are cardiac cases, but we will go into all that later. They warned you, I hope, that I'm an asthmatic myself with a touch of cardiac failure—I daresay you will be a lot busier than you think.'

He looked up as the door opened and Professor van Duyl came in, followed by a stocky, middle-aged man bearing a tray set neatly with a large coffee pot, milk, sugar and a selection of mugs. He set it down on a table which Professor van Duyl swept free of papers and books, smiled paternally at her, and disappeared discreetly. She wondered who he was, but as no one volunteered this information, she supposed him to be one of the staff, then forgot him as she poured the coffee.

She learned a good deal during the next hour; she liked Professor Wyllie, even though he did get carried away with his subject from time to time, leaving her a little out of her depth, and as for Professor van Duyl, he treated her with a tolerant amusement which annoyed her very much, while at the same time telling her all she would need to know. It was he who outlined her duties, gave her working hours and explained that the ten patients were housed very comfortably in a Nissen hut, left over from the war, and now suitably heated and furnished to supply a degree of comfort for its inmates.

'Professor Wyllie and I sleep in this house, and so do those who work with us. We are connected by telephone to both the Nissen hut and your cottage, and although we hope that this will not be necessary, we should expect you to come immediately should you be asked for, day or night.'

She nodded; it seemed fair enough. 'Is there someone on duty with the patients during the night?' she wanted to know.

'No—we believe there to be no need. They have but to telephone for help, neither will it be necessary for you to remain on duty all day; they are all of them up patients—indeed, if they were home, they would be working.' He looked at Professor Wyllie. 'Is there anything else you want to talk to Miss Proudfoot about?' he asked. 'Would it be a good idea if she were to go over to the cottage and settle in before lunch? You will need her all the afternoon, I take it—she will have to be taken through the case notes.'

Professor Wyllie nodded agreement. 'A good idea—take her over, Christian, will you? Hub knows she's here, he'll be on the lookout presumably. Sheets and things,' he added vaguely. For a moment he looked quite worried so that Eliza felt constrained to say in a rallying voice: 'I shall be quite all right, sir. I'll see you later.'

She walked beside the Dutchman down the hall and out of the door into a light drizzle of rain, casting round in her mind for a topic of conversation to bridge the silence between them, but she could think of nothing, and her companion strode along, deep in his own thoughts, so that she saw that any idea she might have about entertaining him with small talk was quite superfluous. They went round the side of the house and took a narrow muddy path which was overgrown with coarse grass and shrubs. There was a sharp bend in it after only a few yards, and the cottage stood before them. It was very small; a gardener's house, or perhaps a gamekeeper, she thought, looking at its low front door and the small square windows on either side of it.

Her companion produced a key, opened the door and stood aside for her to enter. It gave directly on to the sitting room, a surprisingly cheerful little apartment, with a window at the back and three doors leading from it. Professor van Duyl gave her no time to do more than glance around her, however, but went past her to open one of the doors.

'Bedroom,' he explained briefly, 'bathroom next door, kitchen here.' He swept open the third door. 'You will eat with us, of course, although when you have your free days you may do as you wish. There's a sitting room up at the house which you are welcome to use—there's television there and books enough. Breakfast at eight, lunch at one—we don't have tea, but Hub will fix that for you. Supper at eight, but that will depend on how the day has gone.' He turned to go. 'Hub will bring your case along in a minute and light the fire for you.' He eyed her levelly. 'And don't get the idea that this a nice easy job—you'll not only have the patients to see to but a good deal of paper work as well, and remember that you will be at our beck and call whether you're off duty or not.'

Eliza eyed him coldly in her turn. 'Charming! I'm not quite sure what you expected, but I'm not up to your expectations, am I? Well, I didn't expect you and you're not up to mine—I expected a nice old gentleman like Professor Wyllie, so at least we understand each other, don't we, Professor?' She walked towards the bedroom, saying over her shoulder:

'I'll see you at lunch. Thank you for bringing me over.'

She didn't see the little gleam of appreciation in his dark eyes as he went. The door shut gently behind him and she dismissed him from her mind and began to explore her temporary home. It was indeed very small but extremely cosy, the furniture was simple and uncluttered and someone had put a bowl of hyacinths on the little table by one of the two easy chairs. There were nice thick curtains at the windows, she noticed with satisfaction, and a reading lamp as well as a funny old-fashioned lamp hanging from the ceiling. The bedroom was nice too, even smaller than the sitting room and furnished simply with a narrow bed, a chest of drawers and a mirror, with a shelf by the bed and a stool in one corner. There was no wardrobe or cupboard, though; presumably she would have to hang everything on the hooks behind the bedroom door. The kitchen was a mere slip of a place but adequately fitted out; she wouldn't need to cook much, anyway, but it would be pleasant to make tea or coffee in the evenings before she went to bed. She was roused from her inspection by the rattle of the door knocker and when she called 'come in', the same elderly man who had brought the coffee tray came in with her case. He smiled at her, took it into the bedroom and then went to put a match to the fire laid ready in the tiny grate.

'I can do that,' exclaimed Eliza, and when he turned to shake his head at her: 'You're Hub, aren't you? Are you Mr Hub, or is that your Christian name, and are you one of the staff?'

When he answered her she could hear that he wasn't English, although he spoke fluently enough. 'Yes, I'm Hub, miss—if you will just call me that—I'm one of the staff, as you say.' He added a log to the small blaze he had started and got to his feet. 'You will find tea and sugar and some other groceries in the kitchen cupboard, miss, and if you need anything, will you ask me and I will see that you get it.'

She thanked him and he went away; he was a kind of quartermaster, she supposed, seeing to food and drink and household supplies for all of them; she couldn't imagine either of the professors bothering their clever heads about such things.

She remembered suddenly that she had promised that she would telephone her mother when she arrived; she would just have time before she went to lunch. She picked up the receiver, not quite believing that there would be anyone there to answer her, but someone did—a man's voice with a strong Cockney accent, assuring her that he would get the number she wanted right away.

Her mother had a great many questions to ask; Eliza talked until five to one, and then wasn't finished. With a promise to write that evening, she rang off, ran a comb through her hair, looked at her face in the mirror without doing anything to it because there wasn't time and went back to the house.

Lunch, she discovered to her surprise, was a formal meal, taken in a comfortably furnished room at a table laid with care with good glass and china and well laundered table linen. There was another man there, of middle height and a little stout, pleasant-faced and in his late forties, she guessed. He was introduced as John Peters, the pharmacist and a Doctor of Science, and although he greeted her pleasantly if somewhat absentmindedly, he had little to say for himself. It was the two professors who sustained the conversation; a pleasant miscellany of this and that, gradually drawing her into the talk as they sampled the excellent saddle of lamb, followed by an apricot upside-down pudding as light as air. Eliza had a second helping and wondered who did the cooking.

They had their coffee round the table, served by Hub, and she had only just finished pouring it when Professor van Duyl remarked smoothly:

'We should warn you that we start work tomorrow and are unlikely to take our lunch in such comfortable leisure. Indeed, I doubt if we shall meet until the evening—other than at our work, of course. You see, each attack which a patient may have must be recorded, timed and treated—and there are ten patients.' He smiled at her across the wide table, his head a little on one side, for all the world, she thought indignantly, as though he were warning her that she was there strictly for work and nothing else. The indignation showed on her face, for his smile became mocking and the black eyebrows rose.

'You have had very little time to unpack,' he observed with chilling civility, 'if you like to return to the cottage and come to the office at—let me see...' he glanced at Professor Wyllie, who nodded his head, 'half past two, when you will meet the rest of the people who are here before seeing the patients. This evening we can get together over the case notes and explain exactly what has to be done. You have your uniform with you?'

She was a little surprised. 'Yes, of course.'

'Good. May I suggest that you put it on before joining us this afternoon?'

'Very wise,' muttered Professor Wyllie, and when she looked at him enquiringly, added hastily: 'Yes, well...h'm' and added for no reason at all: 'You have a raincoat with you too, I trust? The weather in these parts can be bad at this time of year.' He coughed. 'You're a very pretty girl.'

She went back to the cottage after that, poked up the fire and unpacked her few things, then rather resentfully changed into uniform. As she fastened the silver buckle of her petersham belt around her slim waist, she tried to sort out her impressions; so her day had been arranged for her—her free time was presumably to be taken when Professor van Duyl was gracious enough to let her have any. A very arrogant type, she told herself, used to having his own way and bossing everyone around. Well, he had better not try to boss her! She caught up the thick ankle-length cape she had had the foresight to bring with her, huddled into it, and went back to the study. Professor Wyllie was sitting in his chair, his eyes closed, snoring quite loudly. She was debating whether she should go out again and knock really loudly, or sit down and wait for him to wake up, when Professor van Duyl's voice, speaking softly from somewhere close behind her, made her jump. 'He will wake presently, Miss Proudfoot—sit down, won't you?'

But first she turned round to have a look; he was standing quite close with a sheaf of papers in his hand and a pair of spectacles perched on his splendid nose; his dark eyes looked even darker because of them.

She sat, saying nothing, and jumped again when he said: 'You are very small and—er—slight, Sister.' He made it sound as though it were a regrettable error on her part.

She didn't turn round this time. 'Oh, so that's why you don't like me.'

He made an exasperated sound. 'My dear good girl, I have no personal feelings about you; just as long as you do your job properly while you are here.'

Eliza tossed her pretty head. 'You really are...' She spoke in a hissing whisper so that the nice old man behind the desk shouldn't be disturbed, but he chose that moment to open his eyes, and although he smiled at her with evident pleasure, she thought how tired he looked. She was on the point of saying so, with a recommendation to go to bed early that evening, but he spoke first.

'Christian, you have the notes sorted out? Good. We'll deal with those presently.' He got up. 'Now, Eliza, if you will come with us.'

He led the way from the room with Eliza behind him and Professor van Duyl shadowing her from behind. They went first to a small, rather poky room where Mr Peters was busy with his pills and phials.

'Each patient has his own box,' he told Eliza, 'clearly marked. Syringes and needles here,' he indicated two deep enamel trays, 'injection tray here—for emergency, you understand. Kidney dishes and so on along this shelf. I'll have them all marked by this evening. I'm on the telephone and you can reach me whenever you want. If I'm not here, young Grimshaw will help you.'

He nodded towards a pleasant-faced young man crammed in a corner, checking stock, and he and Eliza exchanged a smile and a 'Hi', before she was led away to what must, at one time, have been the drawing room of the house. It had several tables and desks in it now and a small switchboard. 'Harry,' said Professor Wyllie, waving a friendly hand, 'sees to the telephone—house and outside line. Bert here does the typing and reports and so on and sees to the post.' He crossed the room and opened another door. 'And this is Doctor Berrevoets, our Path Lab man—does the microscopic work, works out trial injections and all that. He's Dutch, of course.'

Unmistakably so, with a face like a Rembrandt painting, all crags and lines, with pale blue eyes and fringe of grey hair encircling a large head. He made some friendly remark to Eliza, and his English, although fluent, was decidedly foreign. She thought him rather nice, but they didn't stay long with him, but went back the way they had come while Professor Wyllie explained that they all slept in the house and that should she ever need help of any kind, any one of them would be only too glad to assist her. He flung open another door as he spoke. 'The kitchen,' he was vague again; obviously it was a department which had no interest for him at all. Hub was there, pressing a pair of trousers on the corner of the kitchen table, and another man with a cheerful face was standing at the sink, peeling potatoes. Eliza smiled at Hub, whom she already regarded as an old friend, and walked over to the sink.

'Did you cook lunch?' she wanted to know.

He had a rich Norfolk accent as well as a cheerful face. 'I did, miss—was it to your liking?'

'Super. Are you a Cordon Bleu or something like that?'

He grinned. 'No such luck, miss, but I'm glad you liked it.'

Outside in the dusty hall again, Professor van Duyl said blandly: 'Well, now that you have the staff eating out of your hand, Sister, we might settle to work.'

She didn't even bother to answer this unkind observation. 'Who does the housework?' she enquired, and was pleased to see the uncertainty on their learned faces. 'Who washes up and makes the beds and dusts and runs the place?'

They looked at each other and Professor van Duyl said seriously: 'You see that size has nothing to do with it, after all. Motherly, we said, did we not?'

His elderly colleague reminded him wickedly, 'No looks, and not young.'

Eliza listened composedly. 'So I'm not what you expected? But excepting for my size, I am, you know. I can be motherly when necessary and I—I'm not young.' She swallowed bravely. 'You are both quite well aware that I am getting on for twenty-nine.'

Professor Wyllie took her hand and patted it. 'My dear child, we are two rude, middle-aged men who should know better. You will suit us admirably, of that I am quite sure.'

He trotted away down the hall, taking her with him. 'Now, as a concession to you, we will have a cup of tea before visiting the patients.'

Hub must have known about the tea, for he appeared a moment later with a tray of tea things. 'Only biscuits this afternoon,' he apologised in his quaint but fluent English, 'but Fred will make scones for you tomorrow, miss.'

Eliza thanked him and poured the tea, and looking up, caught Professor van Duyl's eyes staring blackly at her; they gleamed with inimical amusement and for some reason she felt a twinge of disappointment that he hadn't added his own apologies to those of his elder colleague.

The Nissen hut was quite close to the house, hidden behind a thick, overgrown hedge of laurel. It looked dreary enough from the outside, but once through its door she saw how mistaken she had been, for it had been divided into ten cubicles, with a common sitting room at the end, and near the door, shower rooms, and opposite those a small office, which it appeared was for her use. She would be there, explained Professor van Duyl, from eight in the morning until one o'clock, take her free time until half past four and then return on duty until eight in the evening.

'The hours will be elastic, of course,' he told her smoothly, 'it may not be necessary for you to remain for such long periods as these and we hope that there will be no need for you to be called at night.'

She looked away from him. What had she taken on, in heaven's name? And not a word about days off—she would want to know about that, but now hardly seemed to be the time to ask.

She met the patients next; they were sitting round in the common room reading and playing cards and talking, and although they all wore the rather anxious expression anyone with asthma develops over the years, they were remarkably cheerful. She was introduced to them one by one, filing their names away in her sharp, well-trained mind while she glanced around her, taking in the undoubted comfort of the room. Warm curtains here, too and a log fire in the hearth, TV in one corner and well stocked bookshelves and comfortable chairs arranged on the wooden floor with its scattering of bright rugs.

'Any improvements you can suggest?' asked Professor Wyllie in a perfunctory tone, obviously not expecting an answer.

'Yes,' she said instantly. 'Someone—there must be a local woman—to come and clean each day. I could write my name in the dust on the stairs,' she added severely. 'The Nissen hut's all right, I suppose the patients do the simple chores so that you can exclude any allergies.'

Both gentlemen were looking at her with attention tinged with respect.

'Quite right,' it was the Dutchman who answered her. 'They aren't to come into the house. For a certain period each day they will take exercise out of doors, under supervision, and naturally they will be subjected to normal house conditions.' He smiled with a charm which made her blink. 'I am afraid that we have been so engrossed in getting our scheme under way for our ten cases that we rather overlooked other things. I'll see if Hub can find someone to come up and clean as you suggest.' He added politely: 'Do you wish for domestic help in the cottage?'

Eliza gave him a scornful look. 'Heavens, no—it won't take me more than half an hour each day.'

As they went back to the study she reflected that it might be rather fun after all, but she was allowed no leisure for her own thoughts, but plunged into the details of the carefully drawn up timetable.

As the time slid by, Eliza saw that she was going to be busier than she had first supposed. Only ten patients, it was true, and those all up and able to look after themselves, but if one or more of them had an attack, he would need nursing; besides that, each one of them had to be checked meticulously, TPR taken twice a day, observed, charted, exercised and fed the correct diet. There would be exercises too, and a walk each day. She asked intelligent questions of Professor van Duyl and quite forgot that she didn't like him in the deepening interest she felt for the scheme. It was later, when the last case had been assessed, discussed and tidily put away in its folder, that Professor Wyllie said:

'There's me, you know. They did tell you?'

She nodded. 'Yes, sir.'

'Good. I'm not much use if I start an attack, I can tell you—you'll have to act sharpish if it gets too bad. Got a nasty left ventricular failure that doesn't stand up too well...'

She answered him with quiet confidence. 'Don't worry, Professor, I'll keep a sharp eye on you. Do you carry anything around with you or do I have to fetch it from Doctor Peters?'

'Got it with me, Eliza—waistcoat pocket; usually manage to get at it myself before it gets too bad.'

'You're not part of the experiment?' she asked.

'Lord, no. Couldn't be bothered—besides, I'm a bit past such things.' He laughed quite cheerfully although his blue eyes were wistful.

'Come, come,' she said in the half-wheedling, half-bracing tones she might have used towards one of her own patients, quite forgetting that this nice old man was an important and learned member of his profession and not merely someone who needed his morale boosted. 'That's no way to talk, and you a doctor, too.'

'Motherly,' murmured Professor van Duyl, and she detected the faint trace of a sneer in his voice. 'Is there anything else you wish to know, Sister?'

He was dismissing her and she resented it, but she got to her feet.

'Not at present, thanks. I should like to go back to my office—if I may?' She didn't look at him but at Professor Wyllie, who dismissed her with a wave of his hand and 'Dinner at eight o'clock, Eliza.'

The rest of the day she spent with the patients, getting to know them, and when their supper was brought over from the house she served it, just as she would have done if she had been on her own ward at St Anne's. It was almost eight o'clock by the time she got back to the cottage, to find that someone had been in to mend the fire and turn on the table lamp. She tidied herself perfunctorily because she was getting tired, and huddled in her cloak once more, picked up her torch and went up to the house.

The dining room seemed full of men with glasses in their hands. They stopped talking when she went in and stared as Professor van Duyl crossed the room towards her. She eyed him warily, expecting some nasty remark about being late, but she couldn't have been more mistaken; he was the perfect host. She was given a glass of sherry, established beside him, and presently found herself surrounded by most of the men in the room. She had already met them all that afternoon, but there were three missing, someone told her; Harry, the telephonist, who was on duty, Hub and Fred the cook. They would, they assured her, take it in turns to man the switchboard each evening, and what did she think of the local scenery and did she know that there wasn't a shop for miles around, and how long had she been a nurse?

She answered them all readily enough, but presently excused herself and made her way over to the fireplace, where Professor Wyllie was sitting in a large chair, talking to Doctor Peters, who smiled at Eliza nicely as he strolled away. She perched herself on a stool in front of the old man.

'I wanted to tell you that I think I'm going to like this job very much. I spent an hour or so in the hut—what a nice lot of men they are, and so keen to cooperate. It's all rather different from Men's Medical, though. I hope I'll do.' She looked at him a little anxiously.

'Of course you'll do, girl—couldn't have chosen better myself.'

Her lovely eyes widened. 'But I thought it was you...'

He chuckled. 'Let me explain.' And he did. 'So you see, Christian was a little taken aback when you arrived. He was so certain that Eliza Proudfoot would live up to her name—a worthy woman with no looks worth mentioning and—er—mature.'

'Motherly, buxom and tough,' murmured Eliza.

'Exactly. And instead of that he opens the door on to a fairy creature who looks incapable of rolling a bandage.'

'Is that why he doesn't like me?'

The innocent blue eyes became even more so. 'Does he not? He hasn't said so; indeed, he agreed with me that you will suit us admirably—a nice sharp mind and the intelligence to use it, and not afraid to speak out.' He chuckled gently, then went on seriously. 'I must explain that Christian is engaged to be married to a very...' he hesitated, 'high-minded girl—never puts a foot wrong, the perfect wife, I should imagine, and very good-looking if you like her kind of looks.' He glanced at her. 'That's why he chose you, you see. We had a list of names; yours was the only...' he paused again. 'Well, girl, it's a plain sort of name isn't it? but if you will forgive me for saying so, it hardly matches your delightful person. It was a shock to him.'

'Well, that's all right,' Eliza declared in a matter-of-fact voice. 'He was a shock to me and I don't like him either, though of course I'll work for him just as though I did.'

'Honest girl.' He got to his feet. 'Now, let us eat our dinner and you shall tell me all the latest news about St Anne's.'

Dinner was a gay affair because she sat beside Professor Wyllie and Professor van Duyl was at the other end, at the foot of the table. Although she tried not to, every now and then she glanced at him and caught his eyes upon her in an unfriendly stare, his dark face unsmiling. It spurred her on to make special efforts to amuse her companions at table, and by the time they were drinking their coffee, the laughter around her was evident of her success. But she didn't allow this pleasant state of affairs to swamp her common sense; at exactly the right moment she bade everyone a quiet good night and beat an unassuming retreat. But not a solitary one; Professor van Duyl got to the door—despite the fact that he had been at the other end of the room—a fraction of a second ahead of her, and not only opened it but accompanied her through it. She paused just long enough to catch up her cloak and torch from a chair.

'Thank you, sir,' her voice was pleasantly friendly, if cool, 'I have a torch with me. Good night.'

He took it from her, gently, and opened the house door. It was pitch dark outside and cold, and she felt thankful that it wasn't raining, for her cap, a muslin trifle, lavishly frilled, would have been ruined. As they turned the corner of the house she slowed her pace. 'I'm going over to the hut to say good night,' she informed him. 'I said that I would.'

He made no answer, merely changed his direction, and when they reached the hut, opened the door for her and followed her inside.

The men were glad to see her; they were, to her surprise, glad to see her companion too. He seemed a different man all at once—almost, one might say, the life and soul of the party, and his manner towards herself changed too; he was careful to let them all see that she was now a member of the team, to be relied upon, trusted and treated with respect; she was grateful to him for that. It struck her then that whether she liked him or not, she was going to enjoy working for him.

They stayed for half an hour while Eliza made sure that they were all comfortable for the night; that they understood what they were to do if any one of them started to wheeze. 'I'll be over before I go to breakfast in the morning,' she assured them. 'Good night, everyone.'

They left the hut followed by a chorus of good nights and walked in silence to the cottage, and Professor van Duyl unlocked the door for her.

'Someone came in while I was away and made up the fire,' she told him. 'It was kind of them.'

'Hub—I asked him to. I have a key which I keep in my possession, and I hope that you will do the same.'

'Of course. Good night, Professor.' The little lamp on the

coffee table cast a rosy glow over her, so that she looked prettier than ever.

He said austerely, 'And you will be good enough to lock your door when you are in the cottage, Miss Proudfoot.'

'Well, of course I shall—at night time, at any rate.'

'During the day also.'

'But that's a bit silly!' She watched his mouth thin with annoyance.

'Miss Proudfoot, I am seldom silly. You will do as you are told.'

'Oh, pooh!' she exclaimed crossly, and without saying good night, went into the cottage and shut the door. She had been in the room perhaps fifteen seconds when she heard the faint tapping on the back window of the sitting room. A branch, she told herself firmly, then remembered that when she had looked out of the window during the afternoon, there had been no tree within tapping distance. It came again, urgent and persistent. She ran to the door and flung it open, and in a voice a little shrill with fright, called: 'Oh, please come back! There's something—someone...'

CHAPTER THREE

EITHER HE HAD not gone away immediately or he had been walking very slowly; he was there, reassuringly large and calm, before Eliza could fetch another breath.

'The back window—someone's tapping. I'm afraid to look.'

He had an irritating way of not answering when she spoke to him, she thought, as she watched him cross the small room in two strides and fling back the curtains. She shut her eyes tightly as he did so; she might be a splendid nurse, a most capable ward Sister and a girl of spirit, but she wasn't as brave as all that. She heard the Professor laugh softly, and opened them again. He had the window open and was lifting a small, bedraggled cat over the sill, a tabby cat, badly in need of a good grooming, with round eyes and an anxious look. She was across the room and had it in her arms before she spoke: 'Oh, what a prize idiot I am! You poor little beast, I never thought...' She looked at the Professor, who was standing, his hands in his pockets, watching her. 'I'm sorry,' she told him, 'calling you back like that—it's a bad start, isn't it, behaving like a coward.'

He didn't laugh, but said quite gently: 'You're not a coward.' He was going to say more than that, she felt sure, but for some reason he didn't; only as his eyes fell on the little cat: 'Shall I take her up to the kitchen with me? Fred and Hub will look after her.'

'Oh, please don't, I'd love to keep her—that's if you don't mind. She'll be someone to talk to.' She had no idea how wistful she sounded. 'She's very thin...' She looked at the small creature for a minute and then back to her companion's impassive face. 'She's going to have kittens,' she stated.

'So I noticed. You will need a box and some old blanket, and she looks in need of a meal. Don't give her too much to begin with—warm milk if you have any.' He put a hand on the door. 'I'll get a box and something to put inside it—I'll be back very shortly.' At the door he turned. 'Lock the door, Miss Proudfoot.'

It was an order, and rather to her surprise Eliza obeyed it without a murmur.

She warmed some milk, the cat tucked under her arm, and gave it to the starving little beast, who lapped it up and mewed for more. Before she could give it there was a knock on the door and when she opened it, the Professor came in, saying as he did so: 'It is foolish of you to open the door without enquiring who is there, Miss Proudfoot. Don't do it again.'

'I shall begin to feel that I'm on Devil's Island if you go on like this,' she told him roundly, but he only smiled slightly.

'I'm responsible for you. Here is a box and the old blanket and Hub sent this—chicken from dinner—I'll cut it very small, for she mustn't eat too much at a time. She drank her milk?'

'Yes.' Eliza was arranging the box near the fire. 'She wanted more.'

He was in the kitchen at the table; she could see him through the open door, bending his great height over the chicken. For no reason at all, she found herself wondering about the girl he was going to marry. High-minded, Professor Wyllie had said. The perfect wife and good-looking to boot; he must have picked her with care—a girl who would never irritate him or forget how important he was, and who wouldn't expect him to run around at night rescuing cats. She set the little beast in the box and called:

'I'll finish that, sir. It was kind of you to fetch it. I'll let her have a little and then she can go to sleep.'

He came back from the kitchen with a saucer of chicken, cut very small, and stood looking down at her. 'By all means give her some, but I should wait until she has had the kittens.' He put the saucer down, threw another log on the fire and pulled up a chair. 'Are you going to stay there on the floor, or would you like a chair?' And when Eliza said she would stay where she was, he sat himself down and stretched his legs out to the blaze. Apparently he intended to remain.

'I'm not frightened of being alone,' she told him.

His dark face was transformed by a charming smile, 'I know you're not,' he assured her, 'but this creature's in a poor state, she might want a little help.'

They sat in silence for a few minutes, and Eliza, peeping at him, saw that he had closed his eyes. They opened immediately at a faint mew from the cat, though, and caught her looking at him, so that she had to look away quickly. There was a black and white kitten in the box. 'Ah, Primus,' declared Eliza, glad of something to talk about. 'Do you suppose she belongs to someone? That village I came through on the way here—she could have come from there.'

'Perhaps, but I doubt if anyone would want her back; she has obviously been on her own for some time. Here's Secundus.' A small tabby had arrived, squeaking loudly. 'I doubt if there will be any more.'

He was right. They sat watching the pathetic little mother, now content and purring, for another ten minutes or so until Eliza asked: 'Should she have something to eat now? The chicken?'

He offered the saucer, and its contents were scoffed with incredible rapidity, as was a second saucer of milk. The cat licked appreciative whiskers and curled herself up tidily, the kittens tucked up against her.

'She's purring again,' said Eliza with satisfaction. 'Isn't that super?' She got to her feet and the Professor got up too, remarking as he went:

'We met only today, and yet it seems as though...' He didn't finish what he had begun to say but bade her a brusque good night, and she was left to puzzle about it, and wonder why he had looked, all of a sudden, so very annoyed. Just as she had decided that he was rather nice after all. As she got ready for bed she found herself envying—in a vague way—the girl he was going to marry.

She got up early the next morning so that she might tidy the cottage and tend to the little cat's needs. The little creature would need a name; Eliza tried out several, but they didn't sound right, but when she gave it a final stroke and called it, for lack of inspiration, Cat, it responded with such pleasure that she gave it that name then and there.

Up at the house as she passed the kitchen, Hub came out to meet her. 'The little cat, miss,' he asked, after a polite good morning, 'shall I feed her for you during the morning?'

She was glad to have that little problem solved for her. 'Oh, Hub, if you would—I left the window open so that she could go in and out, and the kittens are well tucked up. I'll give her a good meal at midday. There are two kittens.'

'So the Professor told me, miss.' He smiled at her in a fatherly fashion and went to open the dining room door for her.

There were several people there at various stages of breakfast, but neither of the professors were at table. Eliza exchanged good mornings, ate a good breakfast with the speed of long custom and went over to the hut. It was only just half past seven and still barely light, but it was her first day; there would be plenty to do and she was bound to be a little slow.

The patients were already up, and mindful of her instructions, she took temperatures, noted what sort of a night they had had and served their breakfast. She had only just finished this when Professor van Duyl came in, wished her an austere good morning and sat down at the breakfast table with his patients, where he stayed for several minutes, talking in Dutch or English as the occasion demanded and drinking the coffee she had thoughtfully poured for him. He went away presently, and when she went to her office she found him there, sitting on a corner of the desk, scrutinising the charts. He didn't look up as she went in, but after a few minutes, asked: 'The cat is well?'

She began to write up the diets, sitting at the desk within inches of him. 'Yes, thank you. I'm going to call her Cat—isn't it fortunate that the men all suffer from extrinsic asthma and not the allergy kind?'

His mouth curved faintly. 'Very, otherwise we would have to have found her a new home.' He looked at his watch and got up go. 'You are confident of the day's routine, Sister?'

She nodded silently, feeling snubbed, and when he had gone, sat down herself, to tidy the desk and read through the notes she had made. The purpose of the whole experiment, Professor Wyllie had told her during the previous afternoon, was to see if something could be done to ease the lot of the asthmatic patient, who, unlike his fellow sufferer, needed no dust or cat fur or pollen to start him off wheezing, only an emotion. One of the men in the group, he had told her, needed only a good laugh to start an attack, and several started to wheeze only when they were confronted with some circumstance which upset them. 'We want to keep them here for a month,' he explained, 'give them a strict, healthy routine to live by with little or no chance of them encountering the causes of their asthma as possible. Build up their mental resistance, as it were. Of course we're bound to have the odd setback—Mijnheer Kok, for example, who starts to wheeze the moment he sets eyes on his mother-in-law, I have known him to go into *status asthmaticus* at the sight of a letter from her. But this research may help a little towards preventing what is a distressing condition.'

And probably he was quite right, she thought, gathering the papers tidily together before going to see if her ten charges were ready for their prescribed walk. At least it wasn't raining; indeed, there had been a touch of frost during the night; a walk would be pleasant. Eliza got her cape and stood looking down at her feet, encased in sensible enough shoes but hardly the thing for a walk in the Scottish Highlands. She was wondering what to do about them when Hub appeared silently at the open door.

'Miss?' He held out a pair of Wellington boots and a pair of knitted gloves. Both were too big but very acceptable. She thanked him nicely, to be told that it had been Professor van Duyl's orders, and would she remember not to go any further than the stream at the end of the rough track behind the house. 'And the post will be here when you get back, miss,' said Hub as he turned to go. 'I have also visited the little cat.'

She enjoyed the walk, going from one group to the next as they went, getting to know them, watching them carefully, taking care to temper the pace so that they wouldn't be overtired. There were pulses to take when they got back, hot mid-morning drinks to give out and the charts to write up carefully; it was surprising how quickly the morning flew by.

And she had a letter too, from her mother. She read it over her coffee, smiling a little because her mother so obviously thought of her job as being rather more orthodox than it was. The men's dinner came over at midday; she served them out, made sure that it was eaten, and afterwards gently chivvied the men to their beds for their rest period. She was free now to go to her own lunch, leaving careful instructions as to where she would be before she did so.

But first she had to go and see Cat. Someone had been there before her; the fire was freshly lighted, a guard set before it, and the little cat with her kittens established in the box within the circle of its warmth. She had been fed too, Eliza noted, that would be Hub again. She stroked her protégée, did her hair and face with speed and went up to the house.

Only Professor Wyllie was there in the dining room. He greeted her cheerfully, explaining that lunch was a moveable feast and that she would have to put up with his company. 'Most of them have eaten,' he told her, 'and Christian has gone down to the village to fetch a woman who might do for the cleaning. Perhaps you would see her presently and tell us what you think—better still, engage her if she suits you.'

Eliza helped herself to an appetizing macaroni cheese. 'Of course. How marvellous to get anyone—however did you manage it?'

'Not me—Christian; went down to make enquiries this morning early—said he'd better get someone before you flew off the handle again.' He chuckled richly and Eliza choked indignantly. 'I never flew...well, perhaps just a bit; the stairs are very dusty,' she pointed out severely.

They didn't talk much, but the long silences were companionable; she liked Professor Wyllie and she suspected that he didn't always feel as fit as he would like people to believe. He was puffing a little and he looked pinched. She said diffidently: 'Professor Wyllie, will you be sure and let me know if there's anything I can do for you at any time?'

The blue eyes were very direct. 'I will, thank you, Eliza. I dare say you will have me on your hands sooner or later. Are you quite comfortable in your cottage? And what's all this about a cat and kittens?'

The rest of the meal passed pleasantly enough; Eliza was on the point of leaving the dining room when the door opened and Professor van Duyl came in. He said without preamble: 'There you are. I have a Mrs MacRae here—I've put her in the sitting room—you had better see if she'll suit you.'

He sounded quite bad-tempered about it and she had half a mind to say so, but there seemed little point; he didn't like her and she would have to accept that fact. A faint flicker of regret about that caused her to shake her head and frown as she went out of the room.

The sitting room was quite nice but hopelessly neglected. No one used it—the two professors and possibly Doctor Peters and Doctor Berrevoets used the study, and there was another smaller room down the hall where the rest of the team went. Mrs MacRae was sitting on the very edge of a chair, registering disapproval, and Eliza could hardly blame her. Someone with a frivolous turn of mind had written: 'Dust me,' on the mirror and there were cobwebs on the walls, and yet it could be a charming room; the furniture was old-fashioned but good and comfortable too. If the carpet were once cleared of dust, and its red serge curtains shaken and brushed and a few flowers here and there... She smiled at Mrs MacRae and said: 'Good afternoon. I'm Eliza Proudfoot, the nurse looking after the patients here. The professor asked me to see you.' She paused hopefully, but all Mrs MacRae said was 'Aye.'

'It's quite a nice house,' said Eliza, trying again, 'but you can see how neglected it is—it was the first thing I noticed, and if I had the time I would give it a good clean, but my days are pretty full. I wondered if you...?'

'Aye,' said Mrs MacRae again, and much emboldened by this monosyllable, Eliza asked: 'When could you come? Just an hour or two each day...'

'The noo. Twa, three hours.'

'Oh, super!' She watched while Mrs MacRae, a small, sandy-haired body with the most beautiful blue eyes in the plainest of faces, opened the large plastic bag on her lap. From it she drew an overall, a cotton head-square and a pair of carpet slippers.

'I say, may I help you?' Eliza felt drawn to the little woman, perhaps because it would be so delightful to have another woman about the place even if only for a few hours a day.

'Aye.' Her companion eyed her uniform. 'Ye'll need a pinny.'

Eliza nodded. There was an apron hanging in the kitchen at the cottage and she could cover her hair with a scarf. 'Where shall we start?' she asked with enthusiasm.

'Upstairs. Is there a broom and such?'

'I'll find everything,' promised Eliza, and flew away.

She was back within minutes, swathed in the apron, her hair tucked away under the scarf, bearing a variety of household appliances. They went upstairs without waste of time and opened the first door they came to—Professor Wyllie's room, the bed neatly made, it was true, but otherwise sorely neglected. Mrs MacRae tut-tutted, gave directions and set to work with Eliza a willing helper. They were bearing the sheepskin rugs downstairs to the garden behind the house when they encountered Professor van Duyl. He flattened himself against the wall to let them pass and when Eliza was level with him remarked nastily: 'You are one of those people who keep a dog and bark yourself, Sister Proudfoot.' He eyed her coldly. 'You are also extremely dirty.'

She paused, and a cloud of dust rose from the rugs she was carrying. 'Pooh,' she declared roundly, 'and you've got the wrong proverb. 'You mean: "Many hands make light work".'

She gave him a cold look, her lovely face quite undimmed by the layer of dust upon it, and went on down the stairs, out to the rough grass which must, at some time or other, have been a beautiful lawn. They brushed and beat and shook the mats until they reached the perfection both ladies found desirable and bore them back upstairs, and Eliza, who had been uncommonly hard on her rugs, felt much better, although she would have preferred to have banged and thumped Professor van Duyl instead of the sheepskins.

They hung the curtains once more, polished the furniture and stood back to admire their handiwork. The room looked quite different; she doubted if Professor Wyllie would notice anything, but they at least had the satisfaction of knowing that it was shining and spotless.

'Come and have a cup of tea with me,' suggested Eliza. 'You can come as you are and put your things on in the cottage. There's half an hour to spare.' She hardly waited for Mrs MacRae's 'Aye,' but ran downstairs to get back to the cottage and put the kettle on. As she drew level with the kitchen door, however, it opened and Hub stepped out into the hall.

'Fred took the liberty of making some scones,' he said in his fatherly way. 'There's a nice fire burning and the teapot's warming.'

She took the covered plate he was offering her. 'Oh, Hub, you are a dear—and Fred, bless you both, we shall enjoy them. I'll come and thank Fred later.'

The cottage looked homely and welcoming and Cat got out of her box and came to meet her. Eliza gave her a saucer of milk, put the kettle on, took off her apron and scarf, and washed her face and hands; presently she would take a shower before she went on duty, but now there was no time. She was uncovering the plate which Hub had given her, to discover little cakes as well as scones, when Mrs MacRae arrived.

They made an excellent tea, although there wasn't much time. 'How will you get home?' Eliza wanted to know.

'The Professor, in his car. I'll come tomorrow, same time.'

Eliza wondered if he found it annoying to have to drive to and fro each day as she helped her guest tidy herself, and when she was ready, she went with her to the house, to return the plate and thank Fred. Hub was there too and she thanked him for a second time and he accepted her thanks with dignity, thinking privately that it was a pity he couldn't tell her that it was Professor van Duyl who had gone to the kitchen and told him to see that Miss Proudfoot had a good tea provided each day—it would be more than his job was worth to even hint at it, which was a pity, seeing that the pair of them had started off on the wrong foot.

Eliza, who had privately hoped that she might have seen Professor van Duyl when she went up to the house, didn't see him again that day. His elder colleague came down to the hut to talk to his patients during the evening, making copious notes as he did so, and when she went off duty and went up to the house for supper, it was to find no sign of the Dutchman, but Harry was there, sitting opposite her. He called across the table: 'Watcher, sister,' and when she answered him and wanted to know what he was doing, away from his telephone, he told her: "Is Nibs is doing a stint at the switchboard—turns 'is 'and ter anything, 'e does, that man. 'Ow's tricks, Sister?'

She told him readily enough, musing the while over the punctilious way in which everyone addressed her as Sister. It made her feel a little elderly and aloof, and she guessed that it was Professor van Duyl who had instigated it. The conversation became general and lively enough over the excellent supper, only from time to time she found herself glancing down the table to where he should have been sitting, and wasn't, and although she assured herself that it was a great deal nicer without his dark gaze meeting hers each time she raised her head, she was conscious of disappointment.

Sitting by the dying fire in the cottage after her good night round in the hut, she found herself thinking about him again—an ill-tempered, arrogant man, she told Cat, given to wanting his own way. 'I hope,' she observed to the small creature, 'that this paragon of a girl he is going to marry will keep him in his place.'

Cat yawned and took no notice at all, and Eliza said a little crossly:

'Oh, of course you wouldn't agree—he rescued you, didn't he?' She cast the animal a smouldering glance and went to bed.

The ringing of the internal telephone, placed strategically by her bed, wakened her, and when she answered it with a quick 'Yes?' it was one of the Dutchmen, Mijnheer Kok, who wheezed out an agonised 'Sister...'

'I'm coming,' she told him, and hung up. She was in her slacks and an old guernsey, pulled over her nightie, within seconds, with the socks she had charmed out of Hub on her feet and her length of hair tied back with an end of ribbon. The torch and her Wellingtons were by the door; she shoved her feet into their roominess, shone the torch on Cat to make sure that she and the kittens were still safe and sound, and let herself out into the dark. The cold bit her as she turned the key in the lock and slipped it into her pocket; it was almost three o'clock in the morning and freezing.

Mijnheer Kok was sitting up in his bed, gasping in air and then struggling to let it out again, and there was no need, even if he had had the breath, to tell Eliza what was the matter. She nodded at him reassuringly as she switched on the oxygen, took his pulse and then went to the telephone in the office. Professor van Duyl answered her. He listened in silence while she made her brief urgent report, said: 'I'll be with you in a couple of minutes,' and rang off. She was standing by her patient, adjusting the oxygen flow, when she became aware of him, in a tremendously thick sweater and slacks, standing beside her.

'How long?' he asked, and smiled reassuringly at Mijnheer Kok.

'I was called at five minutes to three. I've not asked him any questions.'

He nodded, aware as she was that poor Mijnheer Kok had no breath for conversation. 'OK,' he handed her an ampoule, 'give him adrenaline 1:1000—0.5 stat.'

Eliza did as she was told, listening to him talking in his own language to Mijnheer Kok. His voice sounded different; there was no coldness in it now; it was unhurried and calm as he took the man's pulse and rolled up his pyjama sleeve, and there was a warmth in it she hadn't heard before. She gave the injection slowly and then picked up the chart to record it while they waited for it to take effect. Only poor Mijnheer Kok showed no signs of improvement; the prescribed half hour dragged by and there was nothing to do but maintain a calm front and see that the oxygen was at its correct volume, but the moment the thirty minutes were up, at a nod from the Professor she drew up another injection and gave that. It was obvious that this wasn't going to help either; another half hour had almost gone when he said: 'I'm going to give aminophylline—0.25 should do it. A syringe, please, Sister, and ten ml. of sterile water.'

She prepared it and watched while he found a vein and injected it and this time the improvement was dramatic. Mijnheer Kok's labouring chest gradually quieted itself, his breathing became slower and his colour almost normal, and after a little while he smiled at them. Eliza arranged him more comfortably on his pillows and began to tidy up, leaving everything to hand in case it should be needed again. The Professor was talking quietly to his patient, and presently she heard him give a low laugh. 'Kok had a dream about his mother-in-law,' he explained. 'He woke up thinking about her and started wheezing at the very idea. We'll put him on phenobarbitone for a day or two and something last thing to abort any further paroxysm.' He looked intently at his patient. 'He's tired out, he'll sleep now.' He looked at his watch. 'I'll stay the rest of the night in the office.'

Eliza didn't look at him as she straightened the blankets. 'That won't be necessary, thank you, sir. I'll stay, that's what I'm here for.'

'True,' he agreed coolly, 'but if you don't get another hour or two's sleep there will be no one in a fit state to look after the other nine men later.' He gave her a quick detached look and added, 'That's an order, Sister Proudfoot.'

She didn't answer but went obediently to the door, and he added quickly:

'Wait—Kok is asleep and will remain so. I'll walk over to the cottage with you.'

'I'm quite all right, thank you, I'm not nerv...' She could have bitten out her tongue the moment she had said it; only last night she had behaved like a frightened child. But all he said was, in the mildest of voices, 'I know that. All the same, you will allow me to take you back.' He turned back to the sleeping man for a moment, then followed her out of the cubicle.

'I'll just make sure the rest of them are sleeping,' she whispered, and went softly from one man to the other before rejoining him.

It took less than a minute to reach the cottage; he took the key from her and opened the door and switched on the light before standing on one side to allow her to enter. Cat stretched in her box, made a pleasant welcoming sound and walked to meet them, leaving the kittens in a sleeping heap. She passed Eliza with a mere flick of her tail and went to wreathe her small body round the Professor's long legs.

'Ungrateful wretch!' exclaimed Eliza. 'I'm the one who feeds you and gives you a home.' She yawned unaffectedly like a small girl and turned to wish her companion a good night—not that there was much night left by now. Bed, with a hot water bottle and possibly a hot drink. The idea of the Professor sitting over in the hut pricked her conscience. 'Look,' she said quickly, 'let me go back—you'll be so tired.'

A strange look came over his face. He said slowly: 'That is kind of you, but I shall be quite all right. It will be better if you do your full duty tomorrow, you are more necessary than I.'

Bed making, she thought, and seeing that the men were warmly clad and weren't too hot and did their breathing exercises, and all the other small, necessary chores. He was right, of course. 'Well, would you like a hot drink? Have you time?'

He had picked up Cat and was stroking her small, large-eared head.

'That would be nice, thank you.'

'Well, sit down. There's still a little warmth in the ashes—the kettle won't take long.'

She left him to go into the kitchen and make tea, and presently came back with a tray and a tin of biscuits beside. When she had poured him a cup and given Cat a saucer of milk she took a sip from her own cup and asked: 'Hell be all right now?'

'Kok? I think it unlikely that he will have another attack in the immediate future, if he does we must try him with Prednisolone—we don't want *status asthmaticus*, do we? Tranquillisers may help. We'll try for a day or so and I'll talk to him—if I can convince him that his stay here, away from everyone, will contribute to the lessening of his attacks, we might manage to control them to a certain extent.'

'Inject him, as it were, with an anti-emotion.'

His dark eyes snapped. 'You understand. I have tried it once or twice in Holland with success and Professor Wyllie has done the same thing over here. This is the field of psychology, of course, but we both feel strongly that the family doctor or a specialist with whom the patient is familiar is more suited to such work.'

'Have you a practice?'

He hesitated slightly. 'Yes—in Nijmegen.' He got up, towering over her in the small room. 'I must go back to Kok.' His voice, which had been warmly friendly, had become indifferent again; he was all of a sudden anxious to be gone. 'Thank you, Sister.'

His glance raked her and a smile tugged at the corner of his mouth and she knew why. Anyone looking less like a hospital Sister would be hard to find. The guernsey was on its last legs, her slacks were stuffed into the Wellingtons and her hair, escaped from its hastily tied ribbon, hung curly and untidy, around her face. She said with tremendous dignity:

'Don't mention it, sir. Thank you for coming over.' She ushered him to the door, wished him a brisk good night and shut the door smartly behind him. As she cleared away the tea tray and filled her hot water bottle, she told Cat exactly what she thought of him. 'And if he wants to snub me whenever I open my mouth,' she explained to the listening animal, 'then he shan't have the chance!'

As from that very day, she decided, huddling into bed and shivering a little, she would give him no opportunity to talk. No more cups of tea and certainly no more light chat about his work in Holland. She would say 'Yes, sir,' and 'No, sir,' and keep out of his way. As she drifted off into sleep she realized that she was sorry about this, but she was far too tired to go into her feelings more deeply.

CHAPTER FOUR

SHE WAS UP at her usual time in the morning, and after attending to Cat's small wants, went over to the hut. It was early still, and she had quite forgotten her resolution to keep out of Professor van Duyl's way; it was something of a shock to find him still there, sitting by Kok's bed. He had been writing, for there were a number of closely written sheets scattered round his chair, but now he was sitting doing nothing, his dark features rendered darker still by reason of the stubble on his chin and the deep lines of tiredness running between his handsome nose and mouth. That his thoughts were far away was evident; perhaps with the girl he was going to marry. Eliza frowned as she thought it—she was allowing her mind to dwell too much on him and his affairs. She wished him a good morning in a cool voice and offered to make him a cup of tea, which he refused with a curtness which verged upon rudeness.

'Let him sleep,' he told her, nodding towards Kok. 'If he wakes before I get back, give him a light breakfast. I shall return before you go with the men for the morning exercise.'

And he did, freshly shaved, the tired lines miraculously gone, and as immaculate as though he had enjoyed a good night's sleep and all the time in the world in which to dress. She wondered how he did it—and presumably he had had his breakfast too.

Beyond telling him that she had left coffee warming on the hot plate in the day room, she said nothing. Mr Kok was still sleeping quietly, the men were ready to go out; Eliza put on her cape and boots and went with them.

She helped Mrs MacRae again that afternoon; after all, there was a great deal to do, more than one person could manage, though once they had turned the house out thoroughly, a daily clean through, which Mrs MacRae would be able to manage on her own, would suffice. She followed the stalwart little woman upstairs once more and into a bedroom, as dusty as the first one had been but considerably tidier, only on a small table drawn up under a window there was a hotchpotch of papers, closely written notes, and open books. Professor van Duyl's room, Eliza guessed, and had the guess confirmed by the sight of a framed photograph of a young woman, placed, she couldn't help but notice, where it could be seen from every corner of the room. She had no chance to look at it immediately, but later, when Mrs MacRae had gone downstairs with the rugs, leaving her to get on with the polishing, she took the photograph to the window so that she might study it. Professor Wyllie had been right; here was a very handsome young woman, with classical features and wearing the air of one who would never allow anyone or anything to upset her calm. Insipid, nonetheless decided Eliza, despite the fact that she had the appearance of a person who was always right and took care to tell you so.

She didn't know what made her look over her shoulder. The Professor was standing in the doorway watching her, his face sombre with some emotion she had no time to guess at. She turned round to face him, still clutching the photograph, her face pink, and she found that when she came to speak that she had lost most of her breath.

'You don't mind?... You must think me very inquisitive... She's so very good-looking.'

He glared down his splendid nose. 'Since you have taken upon yourself the work of a housemaid as well as that of nurse, and have access to my room, it would appear useless for me to mind.'

She fidgeted under the chilly voice and the even chillier look; surely there was no need to be so scathing? She decided to ignore it. 'But she is very good-looking,' she persisted. 'Is she your fiancée?'

She thought he wasn't going to answer. 'Yes. Tell me, Sister Proudfoot, have you no prospects of marriage?'

It seemed a funny way of putting it, and the tone of his voice suggested that she must be lacking in something or other. She said quite sharply: 'Of course I have—but I've never met a man I wanted to marry.'

A lie, she realized that even as she uttered it. Of course she had met him; he was here, staring down at her through the glasses he had seen fit to put on, fiercely frowning at her through them and behaving as though he couldn't stand the sight of her. She felt bewildered at the suddenness of her discovery and looked back at him, her pretty mouth a little open.

'You stare, Sister.' His voice had an edge to it; it caused her to close it with a snap and pulled her tumbling wits together. It seemed to her extraordinary that he hadn't seen...that he could be unaware of the strength of the feelings bottled up inside her and screaming to give utterance... She must look the same as usual; the thought was capped by his: 'You are as dirty and untidy as you were yesterday. Must you really do this work? You ask for someone to clean the house and then you do most of it yourself?'

At least her thoughts were diverted. She explained carefully about there being too much work for Mrs MacRae, and added: 'Once we've done it all thoroughly, she'll be able to manage nicely on her own. And I don't mind.'

He smiled, a thin, half-sneering smile which made her wince. 'That is beside the point. You were not asked to do housework; if you choose to do it, that is entirely your own affair and certainly not my business.'

He turned on his heel and walked away, and although she saw him later at supper, he had nothing to say to her.

The days slid past until they made a week. Eliza had the routine nicely organised now; she knew the men and their small fads and fancies, she knew, instinctively, when any one of them was verging on an attack. With the first look of apprehension and the first wheeze, she pounced with the ephedrine or the isoprenaline, summoned one of the professors, and had the sufferer nicely propped up in a chair by the time someone arrived, ready to be talked out of further wheezes, and if that were not possible, ready for whatever treatment was ordered. The men had come to trust her as well as like her, and seeing how they had improved and become relaxed under the strict régime in which they lived, she spent more time with them than was strictly required of her.

By the end of the week, too, the house cleaning had been finished; she was no longer needed, Mrs MacRae told her, adding thanks for the help she had received, but she still came each day and had a cup of tea with Eliza in the cottage, not talking much, but pleased to be there. And Cat had fattened up nicely, fed by the entire community; she found that she had time to herself now—an hour or two each afternoon, and once or twice Professor Wyllie had come down to the hut after tea and sent her off duty, declaring that if he needed her he could get her quickly enough. She spent pleasant hours by the fire, with Cat and her kittens at her feet, writing letters and reading, and one evening, because she had felt like it, she had changed into a high-necked jersey dress in a pleasing shade of brown, and taken pains with her hair and face; it had been gratifying to feel the little stir it had created amongst the rest of the staff, only Professor van Duyl had looked at her as though she had no right to be there.

And about him, she had come to terms with herself; he didn't like her and he was going to marry another girl; these two facts alone made it amply clear that even if she had set out to engage his interest, she would have had no chance, and the alternative was clear; to go on as she was going now for another three weeks or so, and then, after that, to forget him. It was a little difficult to keep to this resolve, but she felt that she was doing rather well; she was certainly learning to keep out of his way, and unless he was in the hut, that wasn't too difficult, and in the hut they were both on the job and things were different.

The weather was beginning to change; the rain had given way to light frost and occasional clear skies, but the wind seemed to increase each day. Eliza sat in her cottage, listening to it whistling and sighing, and wondered what it would be like if it should blow a gale, and well into the second week the rain returned and combining with the wind, made it impossible for the men to go out, so that other forms of exercise had to be devised—mild drill, deep breathing and steady marching round the cleared day room took up an hour or more of each morning, with Mr Grimshaw acting as instructor and Eliza keeping a close eye on pulses and respirations. It made a nice change.

It was after two days of this weather that she wakened in the night to hear the rain pelting down, and when she went outside in the morning, it was to find a waterlogged path and pools of water in all the hollows. It rained again during the morning, a steady downpour from a black sky which turned with frightening suddenness to a torrential downpour. Eliza, mindful of her patients' aptitude to wheeze if they became worried or anxious, settled them round the table with a Monopoly board, pulled the curtains against the disturbing world outside, and went to join them. It was almost dinner time for the men; presumably someone would telephone from the house and tell her what to do about it, for it was certainly no weather in which to go out.

Professor van Duyl didn't share her views, however. He appeared not five minutes later, in oilskins and a sou'wester, his feet in Wellingtons, all of which he discarded, together with a couple of large cans.

'Stew,' he explained laconically, 'potatoes in the other one.' He went back to the oilskins and fished around in one of its pockets, to produce two cardboard cartons. 'Eggs—Fred is sure you can make omelettes.'

He carried the whole lot to the other end of the room where the hot plate was and without another word went to take her place at the table while Eliza put the cans to heat and went in search of a bowl and a frying pan, thanking heaven silently that omelettes were something she was rather good at.

They laid the table between them presently, and when the Professor gave himself a plate, she filled it with stew before taking some for herself and sitting down to eat it quickly so that she might get started on the omelettes. It was a laborious business, what with only having a small bowl and a fork to do the beating, but she managed well enough, with the men laughing and joking and assuring her that she was a marvellous cook, and when they had all finished, she carried everything out to the sink beside the office and did the washing up with more helpers than she really needed. Only the Professor didn't come near her; he went into the office, and she could hear him talking on the telephone in his own language and longed to know who it was.

The rain ceased abruptly and he went away to fetch Mrs MacRae, warning her to walk carefully when she went over to the cottage, a walk she hardly relished, but the men were comfortably tucked up for the afternoon and there was nothing for her to do; she put on her cape and boots and went outside, where she found it still raining although the sky had become lighter and it seemed to her that the wind had gathered strength. The path to the cottage was water-logged and outside the front door it was trickling slowly down the hill, but inside it was warm and dry. It was nice to find the fire alight and Cat's dinner— the tastiest bits from the kitchen—left on the table. She fed her, changed into slacks and a sweater and turned on her small radio. Gales, said a voice, and heavy rain and more gales; those living in certain areas should beware of flooding. She poked the fire to a greater warmth, kicked off her shoes and toasted her feet as she started on a letter home. She had written half of it when she became aware of Cat's strange behaviour; she had got out of her box and was carrying a kitten off to the bedroom. Presently she came back and took the second one too, and Eliza, intrigued, got up quietly and followed her. All three of them were in the centre of the bed and Cat was making anxious noises.

'Well, whatever's the matter with you?' enquired Eliza. 'Surely it's warm enough by the fire? And you can't be hungry; you've only just had your dinner.'

But Cat was looking anxious, so Eliza went back to her chair—but on the way something stopped her. There was water seeping in under the door—just a gentle ooze, spreading lazily, so that it lapped first the door mat and then crept round its edges to inch its way over the brick floor towards the rush matting which covered the greater part of it. Eliza went to the door and had a look, taking the precaution of putting on her boots first, which was a good thing; the path outside was no longer a path but a small, swift-running river, channelling its way through the rough ground on its way downhill. As she stared, another surge of water washed under the door; no wonder Cat had removed herself and her kittens so prudently.

'You might have told me!' cried Eliza, whipping the doormat out of the way, rolling back the matting and starting to move the furniture away from that end of the room. The water was coming in steadily now and she stood uncertainly for a few moments, watching it. But standing and looking at it wouldn't help and it might not get any worse; she could at least get rid of what she'd got. She fetched the large old-fashioned broom from the kitchen and opened the door again, defiantly sweeping the water out as fast as it came in. She was still engaged in this unrewarding task when Professor van Duyl arrived, wading down the path, a broad plank of wood over one shoulder. He brushed past her, put the plank down and started to take off his oilskins.

'Beastly weather,' he observed mildly, a remark which set her off laughing, so that she stopped work with the broom and the water she had swept out came creeping in again.

'What's that for?' she asked, nodding at the board.

'To stop the water coming in, of course. But you'll need to get all this out of the place first.'

She handed him the broom. 'You're bigger than I am—you sweep, I'll start mopping up.'

A look of surprise swept over his face, followed by amusement.

'You can use a broom, I suppose?' she wanted to know. She put it into his hand, and not stopping to see whether he could or not, went back into the kitchen to find a bucket and floor-cloth.

The little room looked a mess and it was hard to know where to begin, but at least her companion was making headway against the flood. He shot the worst of it through the door, flung down the broom and rammed the plank across the door, put on his gear once more and went outside to stand in the water, patiently wedging stones against it to hold it firm.

Eliza picked up the broom and put it tidily away, then got down on her knees. The bricks were covered in a thin film of mud with puddles in the crevices, and it was a dirty job; she mopped and squeezed and changed the filthy water, and presently, his job done outside, the Professor joined her. He was a little awkward at it to begin with, but before long he was going as fast as she was. They wrung the last muddy drops from their cloths and she said kindly: 'You're quite good at it—you must have had a very sensible mother.'

He blinked rapidly. 'Er—yes, though I can't remember...'

'Well, I don't suppose you can,' she interrupted impatiently. 'What I mean is, she brought you up to be handy about the house—boys should be able to make themselves useful.'

He said yes meekly and offered to empty the bucket while she boiled the kettle. 'For the floor will have to be scrubbed before the mat goes back,' she explained, 'but you can have some hot water first and wash. There's hot water in the shower, but it's difficult to get at unless you don't mind getting wet all over.'

He said nothing to this, only waited until she had filled her bucket with hot soapy water, then took it from her and went back into the sitting room, where he patiently mopped the floor dry as she scrubbed it. With two of them it didn't take long. They left it to dry out and went back to the kitchen, where they cleared away the mess and washed at the kitchen sink. 'Where's Cat?' asked the Professor suddenly.

'On my bed—with the kittens, of course. She took them there just before I saw the water coming in—wasn't she clever? Is the house flooded too?'

'No. It stands on a rise, you know, and so does the hut, you're the only one—the entire manpower in the place was poised to come and rescue you. I said I'd take a look and let them know if I needed more help.'

She was drying her hands on a muddy towel, her face rosy with her efforts, her hair slipping from its pins. 'How kind of them all, and thank you for coming. I should have been all right, but it's so much quicker with two. Would you like a cup of tea?'

She ushered him back into the sitting room and told him to make himself comfortable. 'Though you might put a log or two on the fire first,' she suggested. 'It's only biscuits, I'm afraid. Hub always has a plate of cakes or scones ready for me in the afternoons—he's really very kind. Did you know him before you came here?'

A peculiar expression crossed the Professor's fine features. He stooped to poke the fire and throw on another log. 'Yes—he's a very good chap.' He strolled back to the kitchen. 'Do you want Cat brought back?'

She spooned the tea into a well warmed pot and added the boiling water.

'Well, what do you think? Will she feel safe, do you suppose?' She turned to look at him enquiringly. 'It won't do it again, will it?'

'I doubt it. It was the burn at the top of the ridge which overflowed, I imagine, and most of it will have gone down the other side of the hill—this was only an outlet for the surplus.'

He carried the tray to the fire and put it on the table by one of the chairs. 'This is very pleasant,' he observed, and sounded faintly surprised as he said it. Not quite his way of life, thought Eliza shrewdly, she doubted if he had ever in his life before taken tea in his socks and muddy slacks and sweater, with an equally grubby hostess to pour out for him. She tucked her stockinged feet out of sight and lifted the teapot.

It seemed strange that they should be sitting together, talking amicably about this and that, just as though they were old friends, when probably the next time they met he would flatten her with some nasty chilling remark. It would have been fun to have asked him about his life in Holland and especially about the girl he was going to marry, even if it would be turning the knife in the wound, but at least she would know something about him, something to remember...now she could only guess. She ventured: 'Is Nijmegen a big city?'

His dark eyes flickered over her face and then looked away. 'Not very. Two hundred thousand people, perhaps. Charlemagne lived there. Once upon a time it was an imperial city of the Hanseatic Empire. The country around is charming and we have a splendid park and an open-air theatre.' He fell silent; apparently these few sparse facts were deemed sufficient to stay her curiosity. She had her mouth open to ask more questions when he asked abruptly: 'And you, Eliza, where do you live?'

He had never called her by name before. She had always disliked it very much, but he had made it sound pretty. She sighed, not knowing it, and said: 'In a small town called Charnmouth, in Dorset. It's really only one main street with a handful of turnings off it. It's close to the sea though, and the coast is very grand, you know, cliffs and a pebbly shore, though there's some sand too. People come in the summer, but not very many, and in the winter it's quiet and very peaceful.' She sighed again, this time with a tinge of homesickness.

'Your parents?' he prompted.

'The house is in the main street at the top of the town, where the road turns round to go to Lyme Regis. My father's retired now—he was in the Civil Service—he collects fossils; there are heaps on the beach, but I never know them from stones. My mother's just as useless at it.'

He smiled. 'You go home often? In your little car, perhaps?'

'Yes—once a month for a long weekend and for almost all of my holidays.' She paused, seeing her home in her mind's eye. 'It's quite different from the country round here.'

'You like it here?'

'Very much, now that the house is cleaned, and once the weather clears a little, I intend to go walking.'

He put down his cup. 'If you do, I suggest that you take a companion, at least for the first time. It is easy enough to get lost around here; there are no roads to speak of, and very few lodges like this one—Glencanisp Forest stretches for several miles, and although Canisp and Suilven are several miles away, there is plenty of rough hilly country in which to go astray.'

'You know this part of the Highlands?'

He stood up. 'I've been here before.'

Their pleasant little truce was over. He had become all at once distant, even impatient to be gone. She got up too, looking absurdly small without her shoes, and accompanied him to the door. The floor was quite dry again, and a still fast-moving riverlet outside rushed past the board, leaving the cottage dry. He stepped over it and turned to look down on her. 'Thanks for the tea.'

Eliza stared back at him, craning her neck. 'I enjoyed it,' she told him, and smiled delightfully. She was quite unprepared for his sudden swoop. 'My God, so did I,' he said, so softly that she barely heard him, and kissed her hard.

He strode off without another word, leaving her to shut the door and wash the tea things. 'Well, he may be a learned professor,' she told Cat, 'but he certainly knows how to kiss!' She stacked the cups and saucers dreamily, trying to reconcile that kiss with the austere calm of the girl in the photograph. Did she come alive under it, Eliza wondered, as she herself had done, or did that chilly calm remain unmoved? She hoped not, for the Professor's sake. And could that be the reason for his cold ill-humour? she wondered.

She went back on duty presently, to find that the rain had ceased at last, and although the paths were still awash, the worst of the flooding was over. Doctor Berrevoets came over that evening to take blood samples, so that she was kept moderately busy until supper time, and once in the dining room she was bombarded with enquiries as to how she had fared that afternoon. She gave a lighthearted account of it all, saying almost nothing about Professor van Duyl, who wasn't there anyway. He came in late, greeted everyone quietly, wished her a pleasant good evening, just as though he hadn't seen her for a long time and didn't much mind if he didn't see her again, and sat down to eat his supper. It was young Grimshaw who walked over to the hut with her after the meal and stayed while she saw to the men for the night. She wished him a friendly goodnight at the cottage door and locked herself in as he squelched away up the path to the house. Even with Cat and the kittens, it seemed lonely in the room. Eliza sat in her chair and closed her eyes and tried to imagine that the Professor was sitting opposite her, but it was of no use. She got up and started to undress, telling herself impatiently that she was being a fool; a bracing opinion which did nothing to prevent her from bursting into tears.

CHAPTER FIVE

PERHAPS IT WAS because Professor van Duyl persisted in treating her, during the next few days, with a chilling politeness which forbade any but the most necessary conversation being held between them, that she decided to spend her next free afternoon exploring. It was a pity that the very day she had had this idea, she had already committed herself to an afternoon of table tennis with young Grimshaw; a pleasant enough way in which to spend an hour or two, but William seemed very young; she found herself comparing him with Christian van Duyl, an exercise which did nothing to improve her mood. She let William win and went back to a solitary tea with no one for company but Cat and the kittens, for Mrs MacRae had gone home early.

By the following afternoon, after a morning of snubs from the Professor, she was ripe for rebellion. It was a cold day, the sky grey and strangely quiet—a little frightening, she had to admit to herself as she changed into slacks and a thick sweater and crammed her anorak on top. If it hadn't been for the wretched man vexing her so much, she would never have dreamed of going. She fed Cat, tied a scarf over her hair, and set off, waving to Mijnheer Kok, who was looking out of his window as she went past the hut. It was colder than she had thought, and the sky, now that she was in the open and could see it properly, was full of wind clouds and getting darker by the minute. Common sense told her to turn round and go straight back to the warmth of the cottage, but the memory of Christian van Duyl's face, darkly disapproving, acted as a spur to her ill-judged plan. She reached the stream, still swollen from the rain, crossed it safely and began to climb steadily, up the narrow, ill-marked path which would lead her to the edge of the forest. Looking back, she could still see the Lodge; there were one or two lights burning already and they gave her some degree of comfort as she looked at them before continuing her climb. It really was extraordinarily quiet; the sort of quiet before a storm, she thought uneasily, and once again the Professor's dark face, imprinted indelibly beneath her eyelids, prevented her from turning back.

She went on steadily, stopping to look around her from time to time, secretly glad to see that the Lodge was still in sight, but it wouldn't be for much longer; the pewter-coloured sky was covering itself with racing clouds, so low that already some of the higher ground was out of sight, and there was a sudden roaring in the air which made her stop and look about her once more in bewilderment. Wind—a great gale of it—sprang up at the wink of an eye and filling the world with noise, tearing at the shrubs and trees, whistling in and out of the nooks and crannies.

Eliza took shelter under an overhanging ledge of rock, waiting for it to pass, only it didn't—it gathered strength, and the low clouds came even lower so that she was almost immediately enveloped in them. It was like being in a thick fog; she stayed where she was, fighting panic, for suddenly the world was blotted out and she didn't dare to move. The path she had been climbing had been safe enough if one could see where one was going, but now she could slip so easily, or step over the edge and fall down the rock-strewn slopes; besides, now that she could see nothing at all, she hadn't the faintest idea where the Lodge lay; downhill, that she knew, but it would be an easy thing to walk past it in this strange blank world and as far as she remembered from the map, there were no villages in that direction, only Inverkirkaig, and that was on the coast, on the road which ran through the valley. She would have to stay where she was and hope for the weather to improve.

But it didn't, it became a good deal worse; the wind, which had been bad enough, became a demoniacal monster screaming and wailing round her, so that there was no other sound, and now it brought with it short flurries of soft snow. It settled remorselessly on her so that the faster she brushed it away, the faster it blanketed her. She pressed her small person closer to the rock, for at least the overhanging ledge gave her some protection, telling herself that she was in no danger, just wet and cold and longing for a cup of tea. She was frightened too, although she didn't choose to admit that even to herself, but half-remembered tales of people getting lost in blizzards kept crowding into her head and it was difficult not to dwell on the vast area of rough, unlived-in country around her. She was, she reminded herself bracingly, only a short distance from the Lodge. The moment the snow stopped she would be able to see its lights. She gave a small scream as a tearing, rending sound close by, louder even than the wind, warned her that a tree had been blown down, but not, thank heaven, below her—the idea of negotiating a fallen tree on the way back held no appeal.

She had lost all count of time by now; she could think only of the warm little cottage with Cat purring contentedly as they shared their tea. Rather belatedly she wished that she had told someone where she was going. True, Mijnheer Kok had seen her, but he was hardly likely to say anything, and unless someone visited the hut that evening she might quite well not be missed until supper time, for the patients might suppose her to have the rest of the day free. She frowned; probably by now it was long past her usual time to return to duty. There would be no one to check the men's pulses or take their temperatures—and supposing one of them started to wheeze? The thought was so disquieting that she left the rock face and took a step or two on to the path, only to discover that it would be impossible for her to go anywhere or do anything; the wind would bowl her over for a start. She retreated, pressing herself against the rock once more, stamping her feet to keep the circulation going and almost jumping out of her skin when another tree came crashing down, bringing with it a shower of earth and stones and grass flying through the dark. There was no point in pretending that she wasn't frightened any more; she was scared stiff, and if she stayed where she was she would be frozen solid, and no one would ever find her.

She was wrong. 'Little fool!' shouted the Professor in such a tremendous voice that he outmatched the wind. He had come upon her with a suddenness to take her breath, which was a good thing, for she had none left to scream with and she would undoubtedly have screamed. All she managed was a thread of a voice: 'Oh, Christian—I've been so frightened!' Even as she said it she thought what a splendid opportunity it was for him to deliver her a lecture, only he didn't; he took her in his arms and held her close, huge and warm and safe in his sheepskin jacket. She had never felt so secure. Nor so happy. She shouted into his shoulder: 'How did you know I was here?'

'I watched you from my window. As soon as you are a little warmer, we will go back.'

She shivered violently. 'I can't...there's a thick mist...you can't see.'

'I know the way, it's perfectly safe.' His voice, though raised against the wind, sounded completely matter-of-fact, and because of that she made a great effort to pull herself together. 'I'm quite warm,' she told him, 'and I'm ready when you are.'

He grunted, took her hand in his and started down the path with Eliza a little behind him. It wasn't quite dark now that they were out from under the ledge, but the mist was just as thick, eddying violently to and fro at the mercy of the wind, but she kept her eyes on his vague dark shape inches away from her nose and stumbled along, slipping and sliding on the loose stones, expecting every moment that she would step into nothingness but knowing in her heart that Christian would never let that happen.

It was like walking through eternity; she was on the point of screaming to him that she couldn't bear another moment of it when she felt round smooth stones under her boots and realized that they were crossing the stream. The stepping stones, although large and flat, were awash with water; she could feel its iciness through her thick boots—it would be very cold if she were to slip. She shuddered strongly and felt his hand tighten reassuringly on hers.

The rough track back to the lodge was gloriously familiar under her feet and Christian had his torch out now, lighting their way, for here, lower down, the mist wasn't quite so thick. He pulled her close beside him as he stopped outside the cottage and held out his hand for the key. Eliza gave it to him silently and he opened the door, pushed her gently inside and closed it again, leaving her standing there in the cosy little room, wet and shivering and quite bewildered. She shed her clothes, had a hot shower and dressed quickly. She was due, she saw to her amazement, on duty in ten minutes—what had seemed like forever up there on the side of the hills had been only the matter of an hour.

She fed Cat, made herself some tea and sat down to drink it before the fire. The Professor had been angry, of course, that was why he hadn't spoken or given her a chance to thank him. It was just as well that she hadn't been able to see his face—had he not called her a little fool?—and yet he had held her so gently. She would have to find him at supper time and thank him, even if it meant a telling off from him, and it would, and what was more, she was honest enough to admit that she would deserve every word of it. She poured more tea, thinking dolefully that if she had wanted to annoy him deliberately she had certainly succeeded.

None of the patients knew of her afternoon's adventure, only Mijnheer Kok remarked that she couldn't have got very far in such a violent storm. She went about her evening duties outwardly as composed as usual, but inside she was in a tumult; for one thing, she hadn't quite recovered from her fright, and for another she was trying to compose a suitable speech of thanks to offer Professor van Duyl when she next saw him.

But there was little opportunity; supper was a haphazard affair, for the gale had blown down the telephone wires connecting the hut to the house, and there was a good deal of coming and going and shouting for tools and torches. Only the two professors and Doctor Berrevoets and Doctor Peters were at the table, and Doctor Peters, who never had much to say for himself anyway, did no more than smile at Eliza and murmur something she didn't catch, leaving the learned gentlemen at either end of the table to carry on any conversation, and that constantly interrupted. It was Professor Wyllie who did most of the talking, making mild little quips about her disastrous walk, pithy remarks about the abominable weather, and a rather rambling discourse about electronics, which as far as she could make out had nothing to do with anyone present. Professor van Duyl, beyond the briefest of comments when his colleague paused for breath, remained silent, although he paid meticulous attention to her wants. They were having coffee when she plucked up sufficient courage to ask him if he would spare her five minutes of his time.

His glance was brief and wholly impersonal. 'Certainly, Sister. In the study, perhaps?'

But Professor Wyllie had a better idea. 'No, you two stay here, we have a small problem to solve and we shall need the desk.'

So they were left to themselves and Eliza, glancing nervously at her companion, thought that he looked bored as well as impatient, a view confirmed the moment the door had been shut.

'And what can I do for you, Sister Proudfoot? I also have several matters to attend to...'

She said quite crossly: 'No doubt. I shan't keep you a moment longer than I need to, but I must thank you for saving me this afternoon; I think that I should have died out there if you hadn't come. I—I would have thanked you sooner, but you didn't give me the chance.'

'I wonder why you went in the first place?' he enquired in a surprisingly mild voice. 'I remember telling you most distinctly not to go too far away on your own—or are you so pig-headed a young woman that you decided that you knew best? Not so young either,' he added suavely.

Eliza had braced herself to take his reprimand with suitable meekness, but now she forgot all about that. 'Don't you know that it's rude to say things like that?' she demanded in a strong voice. 'How dare you remind me that I'm—I'm...'

'Past your first youth?' He was laughing at her. 'My dear good girl, much you would care what opinion I have of you, you must be well aware that you could pass for an eighteen-year-old girl.'

She forgot for the moment that they were quarrelling. 'Oh, do you really think so?' she asked him. 'Other people have said that to me sometimes, but I've never really believed them.'

'By other people I presume you mean other men, and should I be flattered that you believe me?'

'Oh, yes,' she answered him seriously. 'You see, you don't like me, so it's not flattery.'

He stared at her, his eyes very black. 'What a child you are!'

She frowned. 'Don't be silly, you've just been reminding me that I'm getting on a bit.'

'Age has nothing to do with it,' he told her, and his voice had become austere, 'but you will oblige me, Eliza, by not trailing off on your own in that irresponsible fashion. Supposing no one had seen you?'

'Why were you watching me?'

She thought he was never going to answer. 'I was standing by my window,' he said at length. His voice became quite level and brisk. 'And now if you have nothing more to say, I will see you back to the cottage.'

She was on her feet and making for the door, where she paused long enough to exclaim: 'Anyone would think that you were trying to make me dislike you even more than I do already—and I don't want your company.' Two palpable lies uttered with such fierceness that they sounded true.

He took no notice of her at all; by the time Eliza had caught up her cloak from the chair in the hall, he was beside her, opening the door and ushering her out into the cold dark, his torch casting a cheerful beam on the sodden path beneath their feet. And at the cottage door, when he had unlocked it and given the key back into her hand, he stood aside to let her go in and went on standing there, letting in large quantities of icy wind and swirling mist. Despite his size and self-assurance, he looked lonely. Risking a snub, she asked: 'Shall we bury the hatchet long enough for me to make us some tea?'

His sombre face broke into a smile whose charm sent her heart thudding. 'I do like a sporting enemy,' he told her, then came in and shut the door. She left him to mend the fire while she went to put the kettle on, thinking as she did so that she would give anything in the world for him not to think of her as his enemy. She carried the tray back to the sitting room and found him by the fire, with Cat and the kittens, wrapped in their blanket, in a somnolent heap on his knee. Eliza filled a mug and put it handy for him. 'Do you have cats of your own?' she asked.

'Two, and Magda, my housekeeper, has one of her own. I have a dog too, an Alsatian.'

Eliza sipped her tea. 'We had a black retriever, but he died last year—of old age. Father would like another dog, but he and Mother can't bear the thought of it just yet. I like animals round the house, don't you?'

'Indeed yes, I intended to have a second dog, but Estelle, my fiancée, doesn't care for animals, so it hardly seems fair to add to those I already have.'

She remembered Estelle's calm photographed face; no, she wouldn't like animals. She wouldn't be unkind to them, just indifferent. In fact, thought Eliza, the girl wouldn't like anything which made a mess or needed looking after—not even children. Her home would be perfection itself, with not a cushion out of place and all the meals cooked to a high standard, and poor Christian would have no legitimate target for his bad temper, because that calm would never be shaken. They weren't suited, the pair of them. The thought struck her blindingly that not only did she love Christian more than anyone else in the world, but if she could bring it about, she would marry him herself.

'I wonder what you are thinking.' Professor van Duyl's voice was quiet, but she jumped all the same and said almost guiltily: 'Oh, nothing—nothing at all. Is the project here going well?'

'So far, yes. All ten men are showing a much greater resistance to asthmatic attacks—even Kok. I have discussed this problem of his mother-in-law every day and for the last two days there has been no single wheeze. It's not conclusive, of course, but I feel that we shall have proved that there is a way to tackle the problem, given time and more knowledge.'

Eliza poured them each more tea. 'Professor Wyllie has kept very well.'

'Yes, though I should warn you that when he gets an attack it is usually severe, and he is a very bad patient.'

'I should be too.' She remembered something. 'Do you suppose that I might have a half day or a morning off one day soon—just as long as it's before we go? I want to buy a present for Mrs MacRae.'

'You will drive yourself?' He sounded only politely interested. 'I don't see why not—arrangements can be made. Ullapool is the nearest shopping town; there is a road of sorts which joins the main road between Ledmore and Ullapool, it's narrow and has a poor surface, but I don't imagine that will deter you.'

Eliza didn't answer; she didn't relish the idea of driving the Fiat miles and miles along a difficult road, probably full of S-bends, gradients like the back stairs and fearful potholes, but she had no notion of letting him know that. Perhaps she could telephone and get something suitable sent out, but what? She had no idea, and Mrs MacRae, when delicately sounded, had been as informative as a clam. She would have to go to Ullapool and pray for fine weather.

There was no need for her prayers, however; two days later Professor Wyllie, pottering in to breakfast just as she was finishing hers in company with Doctor Berrevoets and Doctor Peters, told her that young Grimshaw would keep an eye on the patients for the day and she was free to go to Ullapool as soon as she wished. 'But be back by teatime,' he begged her, 'so that you can take over for the usual evening duties.'

Eliza looked out of the window; Professor Wyllie had spoken with all the satisfied benevolence of one conferring a great treat, but it was hardly a day on which she would have chosen to go careering round unknown country in the little Fiat; the sky was grey and there was a light drizzle falling, and although the wind had moderated from gale force to a steady blow, it was unpleasant enough. With her unpleasant little adventure still fresh in her memory, she said doubtfully: 'Well, thank you, sir, but...'

'Christian has to go to Ullapool to collect some stuff we need, you can go with him.' He looked at his watch. 'He said to tell you in ten minutes' time at the front door.'

She said indignantly: 'But I'm going with the Fiat, he told me about the road—I...'

'He's changed his mind—and so have I. Eliza, this is no weather for you to go traipsing round on your own in that crackpot little car of yours.' He sounded quite testy.

'It brought me up from London,' she reminded him stubbornly.

'For which we are all deeply thankful. Go and get a coat on, child—you mustn't keep Christian waiting.'

She was tempted to dispute this high-handed remark, but instead she excused herself nicely and made her way over to the cottage, where she reassured Cat, changed rapidly into a skirt and sweater, topped them with her matching tweed coat, tied a scarf over her hair, caught up handbag and gloves, and flew up to the Lodge, all within the space of the ten minutes allotted to her. She stopped by the kitchen as she went through the hall to ask Hub to keep an eye on Cat.

'Indeed I will, miss.' He was his usual paternal self. 'And I'll see that there's a nice fire burning, too—and is there anything else I can do?'

'No, thanks, Hub, you're an angel. Do you want anything from Ullapool?'

'Well, miss, me and Fred are partial to toffees, if you should have the time.'

'Of course. 'Bye for now.' She skipped through the hall, noticing as she went how nice the stairs looked now that they shone with polish, and out the front door. There was a Range Rover parked on the muddy sweep before the door with Christian behind its wheel. He got out when he saw her, wished her good morning and opened the car door for her to get in. As he settled himself beside her, she said with a trace of resentment: 'I could have quite well gone on my own.'

He was at his most bland. 'But of course—if the weather had been good.'

'But you told me—you even explained about the road.'

'Ah, yes.' The blandness had a silky note now. 'Do you not feel, Eliza, that surprise when dealing with the enemy is of the utmost importance?'

If she hadn't loved him so much, she would have been furious, but all she felt was sadness that he was so determined not to like her. She agreed with him so soberly that he asked: 'Not sulking about it, I hope?'

Her voice was nicely composed. 'Of course not. I think I'm glad not to be going on my own. Is the road very awful?'

'Not too bad, and this goes anywhere.' He patted the wheel under his gloved hands as he drove down the track from the Lodge and on to the road which would lead them eventually to the main road to Ullapool.

Perhaps the bad road didn't seem so bad in the Range Rover; in the Fiat it would have been unspeakable. She sat contentedly beside him, looking at the different landmarks he pointed out as they went along. Even on such a dull grey morning as this was, the country was beautiful in a wild and grand fashion, and when they reached the road running beside Loch Lurgain, with Stac Polly towering on one side and the steel grey water on the other, she begged him to stop. 'I may never come this way again,' she pointed out, 'and it's quite breathtaking. Are there no villages at all?'

He shook his head. 'None. You could have come this way when you travelled up from London, you know, for it's quite a few miles further going round through Inchnadamph, even though it is a much better road. This one is lonely, especially after dark.'

They were standing together, watching the water. The wind was rustling through the rough grass and the bare trees, and made little waves on the loch. The drizzle had ceased now and the mountains on the other side of the water loomed forbiddingly. Eliza asked idly: 'Do you find it strange here? Isn't Holland flat?'

'Very, and of course it's hard to find an area as large as this where there is literally no one—the odd shepherd, I suppose, and foresters, but one seldom sees them.'

'Do you come here often?'

'I haven't been for several years. I came regularly at one time.'

'But it's so beautiful—and grand, too. You should bring your fiancée here.'

'She doesn't care for this type of country.' So that was why he didn't come any more. She sensed his withdrawal again and wondered about it. Surely it would have been natural enough for a man to talk about the girl he was going to marry, even if his listener wasn't amongst his friends—after all, they had worked together for three weeks now and although they quarrelled almost every time they met, they had a certain respect for each other's work. The idea that he didn't love Estelle returned with full force, but she pushed it resolutely to the back of her mind, and said lightly: 'I daresay I should dislike Holland.' She was thunderstruck when he said in a bitter voice: 'Because you dislike me, I suppose?' His mouth curled in a sneer. 'How illogical women are!'

'I am not...' she began, and then added lamely, 'It's so silly to quarrel.'

'Isn't bickering a better term? And since we seem unable to enjoy a pleasant conversation, we might as well go on.'

She fumed silently as he drove on; of all the unfair remarks, and she had only been trying to be friendly! Perhaps she had asked too many questions—well, that was easily remedied; she closed her pretty mouth firmly and stayed silent, an attitude which lost much of its value because he showed no disposition to talk anyway. It wasn't until they were approaching Ullapool that he said: 'My business will take about an hour. I suggest that we meet for coffee and then you can finish your shopping before lunch—there will be time for that before we need to go back.'

Eliza was still smarting from his unkind remarks. 'I should prefer to be on my own,' she told him haughtily. 'If you will tell me at what time we shall be returning I'll meet you then.'

Christian shrugged enormous shoulders. 'Just as you like.' His voice was annoyingly nonchalant. 'Three o'clock, then.'

They were in the main street by now and he drew up half way down it. 'Here,' he added, and scarcely looked at her as she got out. She walked away briskly, feeling hard done by, although she had to admit that it had been largely her fault; she could have had coffee with him at least. She took out her shopping list and studied it. She would find somewhere to have coffee, buy the small necessities on her list, and after lunch, look around for something suitable for Mrs MacRae. But the hotel she came upon was closed until the season started and she could see no café, so she gave up the idea of coffee, did her shopping and found her way easily enough to the shores of the loch. The water was still wild from the recent storms, the wind was blowing strongly still. Eliza enjoyed the exercise and felt her appetite sharpen. It prompted her to make for the centre of the town again; there must be a restaurant somewhere where she could get a meal; the hotels she had passed on her walk were all closed, but probably she hadn't explored enough. She was on the point of crossing the road to turn into the main street once more when she became aware of the man standing beside her.

'And what's a pretty little girl like you doing in this godforsaken hole?'

The voice was jovial, but the face, when she looked at it in some surprise, was thin and ratlike, and she disliked the smile. She didn't bother to answer him, but crossed the road, only to have him cross it with her and lay a hand on her arm as they reached the other side. 'What about a meal, girlie?'

She frowned at being called girlie. 'I don't know you,' she told him icily, 'and I don't want to. Kindly leave me alone.' She made to pass him, but his hand tightened. 'Not so fast, my dear...' He winced as she kicked him smartly on the shin and then burst into a roar of laughter.

'You little vixen,' he declared. 'I like a bit of spirit.'

There was no one in sight at all; just round the corner there were shops and people, but here, on the deserted road by the loch, there was no one. Which made it all the more remarkable that Christian should be suddenly there, between them. The ratfaced man was pushed away with one hand, while Eliza felt the other catch her comfortably round the waist.

'Get out,' said the Professor very quietly, 'and fast. I am a man of violent temper.' He didn't bother to watch the man turn and hurry away, but took his arm from Eliza's waist and tucked it under her arm and walked her away too, in the opposite direction.

'You see what comes of being pig-headed?' he demanded of her in a furious voice. 'Miss High-and-Mighty has to go off on her own and sulk. You deserve the unwelcome attentions of all the rat-faced commercial travellers you meet!'

Eliza had been buoyed up by indignation, fright and then the sudden relief and delight at Christian's opportune arrival, but now the desire to have a good cry had overcome those feelings. She trotted along beside her irate companion, who was walking much too fast for her, and the tears rolled silently down her cheeks. Perhaps it was the fact that she hadn't made her usual spirited rejoinder to any remark of his which made him glance down at her. He stopped so suddenly that she almost fell over, and swung her round to face him, his hands on her shoulders.

'Eliza,' and he sounded quite shocked, 'my dear girl, you're crying!'

She found her voice. 'Well, so would you if you were me.' She sniffed. 'You're quite beastly—anyone would think that I went out looking for r-rat-faced men, and all I wanted was my d-dinner.'

He made a small sound which might have been a laugh. 'Eliza, I'm sorry—I was worse than the rat-faced man, wasn't I? I think I was angry and didn't stop to think what I was saying.'

He wiped her tears away in a kindly, detached way and said: 'Better now? There's a small inn along here where we can get a meal, come along.'

It was close by, a whitewashed, low-built pub, very neat as to windows, its solid door freshly painted. Eliza, who would have liked to have finished her crying in peace, found herself ushered into its bar and then out of it again into the snuggery at the back, where there was a brisk fire burning and a small table covered with a checked tablecloth and laid for a meal. The Professor came to a halt in this comfortable apartment, unbuttoned her coat and took it from her and offered her a seat by the fire.

'Stay there,' he told her. 'I'll be back.'

He was as good as his word; she barely had the time to peer at her tear-stained face in her compact mirror before he was back again with two glasses. He handed one to her. 'Brandy,' he offered, 'it will do you good.'

'I never drink brandy.'

'I should hope not. But this is a medicinal dose, ordered by a doctor, so drink up.'

It would be useless to argue, so Eliza drank and felt its warmth at once; it also gave her the feeling that life wasn't so bad after all, and when Christian suggested that she might like to go and tidy her hair and do her face, she agreed quite meekly, and when she got back, very neat about the head and with a slightly heightened colour, the landlord was at the table with a loaded tray, and instead of going back to the fire she was invited to sit at table. She took her place opposite her companion, smiling a little uncertainly at him.

'Is it convenient?—for me to have lunch here, I mean. It doesn't look as though they...'

'I telephoned this morning before we left. There's nothing much open during the winter here, but this place will always give us lunch if we warn them.'

'Oh, I'm eating yours, then.'

'You're eating your own, Eliza. I ordered for both of us.'

She had no answer but to drink her soup, glad of something to do. It was delicious, as was the fish which followed it. By the time they had reached the mouth-watering steamed pudding set before them, she was relaxed enough to reply to his easy talk of this and that, and the Riesling they were drinking, continuing the good work the brandy had begun, made her feel quite her old self, sufficiently so, indeed, to allow her to thank him for coming to her aid. 'That's three times,' she pointed out seriously, 'if you don't count Cat. I've been rather a nuisance to you.'

He didn't answer but asked her instead if he might accompany her in her search for a present for Mrs MacRae. Eliza accepted happily; he might disapprove of her, but just now and again he seemed to forget that he didn't like her and they were like old friends.

She found what she wanted for Mrs MacRae, a quilted dressing gown in a cheerful pink. 'For,' she pointed out matter-of-factly to the Professor, 'it's no good buying her tweed or woollies—I mean, coals to Newcastle, isn't it? although there are some lovely things in that handicrafts shop across the street, but they make them in her village, don't they?' She nodded her pretty head at him. 'She needs something impractical because she's such a practical person, you see. I thought I'd get her the largest box of chocolates I can find.'

But here her companion had something to say. 'May I suggest that I send down to London and get a really glamorous box?'

'Oh, lovely—embossed velvet and ribbons and simply enormous and quite quite useless, she'll love it. That would be simply marvellous.'

She didn't see him smile as they crossed the road to examine the contents of the handicrafts shop window. 'You like these tweeds?' he wanted to know.

She nodded. 'They're heavenly—look at that red one—like holly, and that green checked one on the corner. You should buy some for your fiancée, you only need a yard for a skirt.'

She was sorry immediately she had spoken, for he said in a cold voice: 'Estelle doesn't care for tweed. She has an excellent and sophisticated taste in clothes.'

Eliza cast an involuntary glance at her own small person, so sensibly tweed-clad. There was nothing sophisticated about her, she was afraid. She glanced up and met the Professor's eye and lifted her chin at the intentness of his look; probably he was comparing her with his precious Estelle. 'I must find a sweet shop,' she said abruptly. 'I promised that I'd buy Hub and Fred some toffees.'

He gave a rumble of laughter. 'I'm surprised you didn't come armed with a list of odds and ends from the patients too. Here's a shop, let us buy these toffees and make for home. I believe the weather is breaking up again.'

'But it's been raining on and off all day,' she pointed out.

'Oh, rain—that's to be expected. But the wind's rising.'

He was right; by the time they had reached the road by the loch the gale was upon them, beating round the Range Rover, sweeping the rain in torrents against the windscreen. Eliza, profoundly thankful that she wasn't driving the Fiat, sat quietly beside Christian, who didn't seem to mind the weather in the least, although keeping the car on the narrow road was a task she didn't envy him. Once or twice she was tempted to beg him to stop and wait until the worst was over, but it would be dark soon. Besides, he might think that she was frightened, and she wasn't—not with him, so she clenched her teeth tightly and made no sound, not even when the car lurched into a deeper pothole than most and she thought they were stuck. But they weren't. Christian, muttering darkly in his own language, reversed, then roared forward into the rain-sodden gloom.

Hardly an enjoyable trip, Eliza thought as he brought the car to a halt at the Lodge front door, and yet it had been wonderful; she had been with him for hours and even if she hadn't been sure before, she knew now that there wasn't another man like him—not for her, anyway.

The sweep was a sea of muddy water once more; he came round the bonnet and opened her door and lifted her out to dump her gently in the porch.

'Go down to the cottage through the house,' he advised her. 'I'll bring the parcels.'

She did as she was told and found the little place warm and lighted and a tea tray laid ready. Cat sat up, purring loudly as she went in, and she paused only long enough to take off her coat before fetching a saucer of milk. She would put the kettle on, she told Cat, and when Christian came they would have a cup of tea; there were little cakes on the tray and she would make some buttered toast, he would be hungry... But when he came, five minutes later, he gave her a bleak refusal when she suggested it, only putting the parcels on the table for her, and pausing briefly to speak to Cat and the kittens. At the door he halted, though, when Eliza said in a level little voice, 'Thank you for my lunch and for driving me, Professor. It was a lovely day.'

He turned right round and looked at her frowningly. She still had her headscarf on; it was wet and bedraggled and there were a number of damp curls hanging untidily round her face, which no longer showed any signs of make-up. He said almost angrily, 'A lovely day,' and then, as though the words were being dragged out of him, 'And a lovely girl.'

CHAPTER SIX

ELIZA DRANK HER tea thoughtfully. She wasn't a conceited girl, but the Professor's words, wrung from him, she felt sure, most unwillingly, had given her food for contemplation; she was well aware that she was a very pretty girl and that men reacted quite naturally to this, but the Professor wasn't quite the same as most of the men she knew; for one thing he was engaged to be married, and for another, he hadn't shown any signs of liking her when they had met. Indeed, she wasn't certain that he liked her even now, although she was aware that she had made an impression upon him, reluctantly received on his part. She poured more tea and fell to thinking about Estelle. It was perhaps a little unsporting to try and take him away from the highly bred, slightly bored girl in the photograph, but Eliza was quite sure that Estelle wasn't the right girl for him. She wondered if he had discovered that for himself by now. Men, she thought bitterly, could be so very blind, but it was no good wasting time on speculation. There was only a little over a week left before she would return to St Anne's, not very long a time in which to capture a man's attention and his heart as well, but at least she would have a good try.

She tidied away the tea things and changed into uniform, talking to Cat while she did so, and then, well wrapped against the weather, went over to the hut. It was disappointing that she didn't see Professor van Duyl again that evening.

Indeed, she hardly saw him at all during the next few days. True, he came down to the hut when a patient showed signs of starting an attack, and on routine visits, but Eliza was never alone with him. She suspected him of contriving that, and it could only mean one of two things; either he disliked her so much that he avoided her at all costs, or he realized the danger in getting to know her better. She liked to think it was the second reason, and despite the shortness of the time left to her, took heart, especially as a short conversation she had with him at the lunch table confirmed her suspicions about his feelings for his fiancée.

They had been discussing the breaking up of the scheme, now five days away, and she had brought up, rather anxiously, the question of Cat. 'I think I shall take her with me,' she told Professor Wyllie. 'She and the kittens can travel in the car and I'll have to put them into a cats' home near the hospital until I go home.'

The old man smiled at her. 'Your parents won't object to three pets?'

She hesitated. 'Well, perhaps at first. I'll try and find good homes for Primus and Secundus as soon as I can.'

'Supposing I were to take them to my home?' suggested Professor van Duyl suddenly. 'They will be company for the kitchen cat as well as my own.'

Eliza turned to him impulsively. 'Oh, that would be nice, they could all live together then.' She remembered something. 'But it wouldn't do—you said that—that you didn't want any more animals.'

'I'? His look was bland. He drank the rest of his coffee and sat back in his chair as people began to leave the table and when she made to get up too: 'No, you are off duty, are you not, therefore in no hurry for a few moments. Why did you say that?'

'Well, you did say only a little while ago that you weren't going to have any more animals at your home because your fiancée didn't much care for them. Besides, three cats—and you've got three cats and a dog already, you might not have room, and they'll cost quite a lot to feed.'

A curious expression passed over his face. 'Oh, I think I can fit them in, and I must persuade Estelle to accept them. After all, we shall not marry for a month or two; Cat and her kittens will have had time to learn their way around the house.'

Eliza felt doubtful. 'Yes, but you see, if your fiancée doesn't like them, she might want them to live outside. You have got a garden?' she added anxiously.

He smiled a little. 'Oh, yes. But I will take care to see that that doesn't happen.' He went on with a sudden fierceness: 'I have the impression that you are prepared to dislike Estelle, Sister Proudfoot. I must remind you that she is a well-balanced and intelligent young woman, not in the least impulsive, and I have never known her deviate from her own very high standards of conduct.'

'She sounds like a crushing bore,' said Eliza before she could stop herself and then gasped: 'Oh, Christian, I'm sorry! I—I never meant…'

He had gone a little white around his mouth and his eyes were so dark that they might have been black. 'How dare you? And I beg of you, make no excuses. I have no idea why you should make such a vulgar remark about someone of whom you know nothing.' He got up and went and stood by the still smouldering fire, his back towards her. 'And you of all people,' he went on, more fiercely than ever, 'an impulsive, aggravating young woman who should know better.'

Eliza had got to her feet too. She said in a tight voice, 'I'm not making excuses, I can merely repeat that I'm sorry and very ashamed of myself.' At the door she couldn't resist adding: 'That should make you feel very happy.'

And later, at the end of the day, when she was back in her cottage after an afternoon and evening of avoiding Christian at all costs, she remembered, as she undressed in a storm of angry tears, that she had called him Christian. 'I'm an utter fool,' she told Cat, 'a jealous, meddlesome fool. I deserve his contempt and now I've got it.'

Cat yawned cosily, made a small comforting sound and curled up round her kittens. 'I shall miss you,' Eliza told her as she put out the light, 'but it's nice to think of you with him—and he did say he'd take care of you, so he will.' She lay awake for a long time, trying to imagine what his home was like; comfortable for certain, for he was a successful man in his profession. He dressed well and his clothes were superbly cut and she was sure that his shirts were of silk. Her thoughts sidetracked; how did he manage to present such a pristine appearance to the world with no laundry in sight; had he paid Mrs MacRae extravagant sums to press his trousers and iron his shirts, or perhaps he did them himself? The idea was so absurd that she giggled rather forlornly and at last went to sleep.

The remaining days passed all too quickly, and then it was the last day and the farewell tea-party for Mrs MacRae. Fred had excelled himself with the making of an iced cake, and Christian, true to his word, presented her with one of the largest, most extravagant boxes of chocolates Eliza had ever seen, and as well as that a bulky envelope the contents of which she guessed was money. Her own gift she had already given, and when she had seen Mrs MacRae's plain face light up as she had unwrapped it, she was glad that she had chosen something so pink and pretty. 'It'll wash and dry like a rag,' she told Mrs MacRae, 'so you can wear it every day if you want to.'

Mrs MacRae's 'Aye,' was ecstatic.

And Eliza herself had had an unexpected present too—from the patients; a small painting, done by a local artist, showing the Lodge and the surrounding countryside. 'So that you will not forget us,' Mijnheer Kok, voted spokesman, had said with such sincerity that the tears had pricked her eyelids.

But now all that was over and they were on their way; the Range Rover in front with the four doctors, herself following in the Fiat and Hub driving a minibus with the patients and the remainder of the staff. They were to spend the night in Edinburgh, some two hundred and fifty miles away, and luckily the weather had cleared so that this time, in early daylight and with someone ahead to guide her, Eliza enjoyed the journey.

She had decided on a policy of avoiding Christian, which was perhaps a little pointless, for he was quite obviously doing the same, but it was the only way of finding out if he had any interest in her at all. She stayed with the patients when they stopped on the road for meals, and that evening at the hotel she joined them at dinner too, leaving the occupants of the Rover to share a table and entertain themselves, something which they did rather successfully, she reflected, listening to the gusts of laughter. She told Cat about it as she got ready for bed in the pleasant room at the hotel, for Cat, after being fed and suitably dealt with by Hub, had been delegated to her for the night. She sat in her box, quite unworried by the excitements of the journey, the kittens curled close to her, and watched Eliza with her round eyes, making gentle little sounds by way of answer.

'Do you suppose I'm barking up the wrong tree, Cat?' Eliza demanded as she got into bed, but all Cat did was to purr.

The Dutch contingent parted from them in the morning, to fly to Holland under the rather absent-minded guardianship of Doctor Berrevoets. Eliza, shaking them each by the hand and wishing them goodbye, hoped fervently that none of them would begin to wheeze, for she very much doubted if he knew what would be expected of him, although she had seen Christian in earnest conversation with him before they left. The remainder of the party pushed on to Nottingham, and Eliza, eating her dinner with the five English patients who were left, brooded on the fact that she and Professor van Duyl hadn't spoken to each other for the entire day, beyond a chilly good morning and such social niceties as offering cups of tea and passing the salt. And the next day was the last on which she would see him, for half way between Northampton and Luton they would part company, she to travel on to London, the rest of them to go their various ways and the two professors to go across country to the small village near Halstead where Professor Wyllie lived. Presumably Christian would go back to his home from there; if she had been on better terms with him she might have asked, and she didn't like to bother Professor Wyllie who was looking tired and ill, although he had refused to admit that he was either when she taxed him with it. Eliza wished him goodbye after breakfast and he made her a nice little speech before she went to find everyone else and wish them goodbye too. She would miss Hub; she lingered with him, talking about Cat rather wistfully, putting off the moment when she would have to bid goodbye to Christian. She had failed dismally and she had been quite wrong; he didn't care a cent for her—worse, he was indifferent. She shook Hub's hand, tickled Cat under her now plump chin, and turned to go.

'The Professor is in the coffee room,' Hub said quietly. 'He came looking for you, miss, but you were with the men. He was afraid of missing you and asked me to mention it—indeed, he said I was to be sure and tell you.'

She thanked him in a voice which didn't quite conceal her feelings and went back to the hotel. She hadn't noticed the coffee room when they had arrived the night before, but it didn't matter, as it turned out, for Christian was waiting for her. 'In here, Sister Proudfoot,' he invited, and held the door wide.

He shut it firmly behind her and said without preamble: 'We have been avoiding each other.'

'Yes. You wanted that, didn't you?'

His dark eyes gleamed at that, but she didn't see because

for some reason he had put on his glasses. But his next remark surprised her.

'No, I didn't want it, Eliza.' He sighed in an exasperated sort of way. 'My dear good girl, you must know that you are a very attractive woman—I find you more than that; an amusing companion, kind and thoughtful, high-spirited, tender-hearted—absurdly so—fiercely independent and yet needing to be taken care of.' He frowned fiercely at her. 'In fact, you have disrupted my calm life. I am thankful that after today we shan't meet again. You have caused enough havoc.'

She wondered, in a detached way, what he would say if she told him that she hadn't really tried…now, if she had made up her mind the moment she had first met him and had had the whole four weeks… She said coldly: 'You make yourself very plain, but I must point out that if you loved your fiancée you wouldn't have even noticed me, and as for disrupting your life I've done no such thing—and you said it, not I. Anyway, you'll forget me the moment I'm out of sight.'

There was a good deal she would have liked to have said, but suddenly the tears crowded into her throat, making it impossible. She walked to the door, but he got there first.

'You're wrong,' he sounded goaded. 'I'll not forget you, Eliza,' and kissed her with a ferocity which took her breath, opened the door and pushed her into the foyer. She heard the door close behind her, but she didn't look round. The Fiat was outside, there was nothing to keep her any longer. Eliza got in, waved unseeingly at the little group standing by the bus, and drove away.

Her mind was a numb thing for the first ten miles or so. She went steadily down the M1, not thinking at all, but presently the numbness wore off, leaving pain and bewilderment. Christian had said that he was thankful that he would never see her again, and yet he had kissed her like a man who wanted to see her again very much. Her head began to ache with all the might-have-beens, and even while she told herself it was useless to dwell on regrets, they crept back into her mind, popping out to plague her.

She was no distance from London now and there seemed no point in getting to St Anne's too early in the afternoon. She turned off the motorway at St Albans and had lunch—a waste of money, as it turned out, for she had no appetite, but it had whiled away an hour, and since she still had time to spare she didn't go back to the motorway, but took a secondary road into London, taking her time now so that it was five o'clock by the time she had put the car away, taken her case up to her room and had a cup of tea, and that finished she tidied herself without much interest and went down to the Office. Miss Smythe would want to see her, she supposed; besides, there was the question of days off. She had had none at all at Inverpolly, and she hadn't bothered about them, but now there were eight days to come to her. She would go home, she decided as she made her way through the hospital, then come back and get down to work. It looked as though she was going to be a career girl after all.

She found Miss Smythe still on duty and looking as near agitated as such a dignified being could permit. She wasted very little time on returning Eliza's polite greeting, but exclaimed: 'How fortunate, Sister Proudfoot, that you should come at this very moment. I have just this minute received an urgent telephone call from Professor Wyllie's house. He has been taken ill—heart, as you know, and a nasty turn of asthma. He asks that you should go there immediately and look after him until he has recovered.' She looked at Eliza with a certain smugness. 'He thinks very highly of you.'

Eliza stared at her, hardly believing her ears. 'But, Miss Smythe, I've only just arrived—I've not unpacked...'

Miss Smythe didn't seem to have heard her. 'An hour?' she enquired smoothly. 'Is that long enough for you to get some things together, Sister? Someone called—er—Hub is coming to fetch you.'

'But I don't know where Professor Wyllie lives. Besides, I...'

She was ruthlessly cut short. 'North Essex, or is it Suffolk, I'm not certain, but what does it matter?' Miss Smythe dismissed the geographical details with a commanding wave of the hand.

'I've eight days off due to me,' Eliza stated, feeling as hopeless as a bridge player with no trumps.

Miss Smythe tutted. 'Men,' she observed succinctly, 'so thoughtless—so unable to cope.'

Eliza remembered her unfortunate experience in the gale and the mist; Christian had coped very nicely then, as he had with Cat and the flooded cottage—even the rat-faced man.

'Well, Sister?' Miss Smythe's voice was brisk and brought her back to the present with a rush.

'Very well,' Eliza said meekly, 'though I can't think why Professor Wyllie should want me there.'

'You are a good nurse,' her superior smiled with brief kindness. 'You have the gift of never allowing your patients to doubt that they will recover. They like that.'

Eliza was ready by six o'clock; she had even had time to go along to Men's Medical and talk to Mary Price, who managed to give her a potted resumé of the month's happenings together with news of staff changes, a new houseman, and the added information that she was going steady with the Surgical Registrar. Eliza made appropriate replies, expressed delight at Mary's matrimonial prospects, gave a brief report of her own life at Inverpolly, and raced back to her room to get her newly packed case.

Hub was waiting for her in the Range Rover, which somehow looked out of place in the heart of London, but she accorded it the briefest of attention. 'I never expected to see you again, Hub,' she exclaimed as she climbed in beside him. 'You must tell me what's happened.' She turned to smile at him.

He smiled back at her and manoeuvred the car out of the forecourt into the busy street.

'Professor Wyllie didn't feel very well—you noticed, didn't

you, miss? He had a bad turn just after we got to his home. Luckily I had dropped the last of the others off at Cambridge and got back very soon after the two professors. I was sent at once to fetch you—if you would come.'

'You mean Professor Wyllie sent for me?'

'He asked for you, miss.'

So Christian had gone; presumably Hub would go back to Holland to wherever he lived as soon as he had delivered her safely.

He drove well, making light of the snarled-up city traffic, and once clear of it, driving fast. Christian drove fast, too, she remembered wistfully, and buried the thought. 'You know the way,' she commented after a while.

'Yes, miss—I've been this way several times.'

He had avoided the busy Chelmsford road and had gone through Fyfield and Great Bardfield and turned off there for Sible Hedingham, to turn off once more into a narrow country lane, its low hedges picked out by the Range Rover's powerful lights. There was nothing to see in the dark, and presently Eliza said: 'A bit lonely isn't it?'

'Yes, miss—there's the church and some houses round the next bend, Professor Wyllie's house is just beyond them. Very nice it is too in the summer.'

She wanted to ask him how it was he knew so much about the old professor's home, but didn't like to; she wasn't quite sure who he was to begin with and although he had always answered her questions he had never volunteered any information about himself. 'You do live in Holland, don't you?' she ventured.

'Oh, yes, miss. Here is the village.'

They swept round a small village green with the dim outlines of the houses surrounding it, and on past the church before turning in through an open white-painted gate, to pull up before the door through whose transom light was streaming.

The door was opened by Miss Trim, looking worried. She said: 'How do you do, Miss Proudfoot. I hope you're not too inconvenienced by this,' because she was the sort of person who would consider it unthinkable not to observe the civilities of everyday life however trying the circumstances. And when Eliza murmured suitably: 'I'm Miss Trim, Professor Wyllie's secretary. I live in the village, but it seemed right that I should remain here until you arrived.' Her eyes focused over Eliza's shoulder. 'Hub, would you be so kind as to take me home?'

He put Eliza's case down in the lobby. 'Of course, Miss Trim. Shall I just let someone know that Sister Proudfoot is here?'

'I'll do that and fetch my coat at the same time.' She turned to Eliza. 'If you would come with me? There's a housekeeper here—she has prepared a room and has a meal ready. She's a very competent woman.'

They crossed the square hall together and Eliza asked: 'How is the professor?'

'Rather poorly, I'm afraid. The doctor came a short time ago and consulted... In here.'

She opened the door at the back of the hall as she spoke and ushered Eliza inside. The room was pleasantly warm, large and well lighted. There was a large, untidy desk at one end of it and Christian was sitting at it. Eliza heard Miss Trim wish them both good night before she went away, closing the door quietly behind her.

Eliza found her breath and said the first thing to enter her whirling head. 'Oh, hullo—how very awkward, meeting like this again. A—a kind of anticlimax.'

He had got up from his chair. 'I don't think I should call it that,' he answered quietly. He seemed larger than ever, standing there. Perhaps he had grown since she had seen him last, she thought absurdly. She shut her eyes and opened them again because she felt peculiar, and found him beside her. 'You're tired and hungry,' he stated in the kind, detached voice of his profession. 'Sit down.' He pushed her gently into a chair and went to a cupboard in the wall and came back with a glass in his hand.

'Professor Wyllie wants to see you, otherwise I'd send you

straight to bed. Drink this; it will get you up the stairs at least. Presently you shall have a meal.'

Eliza sipped and her head cleared a little. She got up carefully. 'I'm quite all right now. Is Professor Wyllie very ill?'

They were walking to the door and she hardly noticed his hand under her elbow. 'Yes, but he'll pull through, especially if he has you to look after him.'

They went upstairs and into a large room filled with heavy furniture. The old man was sitting up in bed, propped against a great many pillows, his eyes closed. Eliza had never seen him look like that before, tired to death and not bothering any more, but as she looked at him he opened his eyes and winked at her.

'Good girl,' he managed. 'Knew you'd come. Now I'll do.'

She went over to the bed and took his hand. 'Of course you'll do,' she told him hearteningly. 'Now go to sleep, there's a dear.'

They waited while he dropped off again and then went back downstairs where Christian handed her over to Mrs Moore, the housekeeper, a small, round woman who looked upset and excited as well. 'You come with me, Sister,' she breathed in a hushed voice, 'I've a nice hot supper for you.'

Professor van Duyl turned away. 'I'll be in the study when you're ready.' He spoke carelessly, already crossing the hall, away from her.

Eliza ate her supper, too tired to know what she was eating, listening to Mrs Moore's hushed voice recounting the dramatic events of the evening, and longing for her bed. But it was more than likely that she would be expected to sit with Professor Wyllie—someone would have to be there; Mrs Moore, though a nice woman, was obviously useless from a nursing point of view and there didn't seem to be any one else around but Christian and Hub, and he had gone down to the village. Eliza drank the last of the coffee and went back to the study, to receive explicit details of the patient from his colleague and instructions to go to bed at once, so that she might get up at four o'clock the next morning and take over the care of the patient.

'Yes, but who's to look after him during the night?' she wanted to know.

'I shall. Before you go we will run over the treatment...'

She sat down beside him and went carefully through the notes on the desk; the treatment and the drugs and the possibilities of things going wrong. 'A pity he can't tolerate the cortisones,' remarked the Professor. 'His heart condition rules that out—neither dare we use atrophine. He's on aminophyline injections at present—Doctor Trent, the local GP, agrees with me that they will be the most helpful in this case. Diuretics and a low salt diet, of course. I gave him morphine, as you see in the notes, very soon after the attack started. It should carry him through the greater part of the night and by the time you come on duty we can re-assess his condition.'

Eliza got to her feet, swallowed a yawn and in a voice which she strove to make unconcerned, asked: 'Are you staying until Professor Wyllie is better?'

'I had intended to return to Holland tonight; I shall stay for another twenty-four hours, longer if there is any need, but I have certain commitments...' he paused. 'Doctor Trent is a very good man.' He got up too and came round the desk. 'Rest assured, Eliza, that I shan't go if I'm needed here—Professor Wyllie and I are very old friends.' He opened the door for her. 'Mrs Moore will show you your room—have you an alarm clock with you?'

'Yes, thank you. Good night, sir.'

'You called me Christian.' His voice was faintly amused, and because she didn't know what to answer she said nothing at all, but crossed the hall to where Mrs Moore, very much on the alert, was waiting for her.

Her room was pleasant enough, although rather over furnished with mid-Victorian furniture, but the bed was a splendid one and Mrs Moore had warmed it thoroughly. Eliza undressed rapidly, had a quick bath and curled up in its comfort.

It seemed a bare ten minutes before the alarm went off. She dressed in the dazed, disciplined way night nurses quickly learn, put up her hair into an uncaring bun, left her face without make-up, and crept along the landing to her patient's room, looking, did she but know it, like a small girl dressed up in a nurse's uniform. Perhaps the same idea crossed Professor van Duyl's mind as she went in, for he got out of his chair with the hint of a smile. But there was nothing childlike about her manner. Eliza took his report with grave attention, asked a couple of pertinent questions, made sure that she knew where she could lay hands on the drugs and syringes should she need them urgently, checked the patient's pulse as he lay sleeping, agreed to waken Christian should she deem it necessary, and prepared to take up her duty.

'There's tea in the thermos,' said the Professor from the door. 'I'll be back to relieve you for breakfast.'

'That won't be necessary,' she said at once. 'I can have some coffee or something when I get Professor Wyllie whatever he wants.'

'I'm quite sure you can, nevertheless I shall be here to relieve you for breakfast. Good night.'

Her patient wakened two hours later, declaring himself to be quite recovered and promptly began to wheeze. 'Now, now,' said Eliza in a motherly voice, 'that's enough of that,' and had him propped up and an injection given before he had a chance to argue, then waited quietly until the wheezing had died down before she began to ready her patient for the day. 'Like a cup of tea?' she asked as she charted his TPR.

'What is the time, girl? Could we not have a cup together?'

'Of course—I'll go and get it, and don't you dare move until I get back.'

He grinned tiredly at her, but he wasn't looking so exhausted now; provided that he rested for a few days, he would be his own self again; not quite as fit as before, perhaps, but able to resume his usual life. He wasn't a man to take kindly to invalidism and the fact that he would have to slow down a little because of his heart wouldn't prevent him doing exactly what he wanted. He was a stubborn man, but Eliza rather liked him for that as well as admiring his courage; not many men of his age and in his condition would have risked going into the wilds of Scotland, miles from a hospital—though he'd had Christian, she conceded as she put on the kettle and assembled a tea tray; if she had been in like case and Christian had been there, however remote the spot, she would have felt quite safe too.

The Professor arrived at exactly half past eight, looking, as he had done once before, wide awake, well fed and immaculate. Eliza wondered how he did it and catching sight of her own reflection in the vast mirror of the dressing table, deplored her own rather hagged appearance. No make-up, she moaned silently, and hair in wisps, but her tired face, even without make-up, was still delightfully pretty, and hair in wisps, when it curled, didn't matter at all. Christian gave her a long, keen look as he came in and she frowned back at him because it could only mean that he found her just as untidy as she felt, but she forgot that instantly because there was the brief report to give him before she went down to breakfast.

'And after breakfast,' he said, seeing her to the door, 'you will go for a brisk walk, and be good enough to return here at eleven o'clock.'

She opened her mouth to argue this point, but he said swiftly: 'No, don't, it's such a waste of time,' and flashed her a sudden smile which transformed him from a severe-faced doctor into a delightful man whom she loved desperately.

She not only went for a brisk walk after a substantial breakfast, she had a bath, did her face with great care, her hair as well, and presented herself, as fresh as the proverbial daisy, at exactly eleven o'clock. Her patient was asleep.

'We'll leave him,' counselled the Professor. 'He needs a good rest. See that he has a light meal when he wakes and keep him as quiet as possible—he's pulled round nicely. Given a week of taking things easy he should be almost as good as new.'

'No need to keep him in bed?'

He shook his head. 'Not after the next day or so, but you will have to be firm with him, he can be stubborn. I don't imagine that he will have another attack, but use the oxygen if you need to and I've written up his drugs. Get him out of bed for half an hour if he feels like it.' He strolled away. 'I'll be around if you want me and Doctor Trent will be calling this afternoon.'

Time crawled by. Professor Wyllie slept, opened his eyes to take stock of her, smiled, and slept again. Just after two o'clock he wakened properly, demanded to get out of bed, eat his lunch and put through a few telephone calls.

Eliza dealt with him firmly. 'Lunch first,' she told him, 'then you may get up for half an hour exactly. The telephoning can wait until Doctor Trent has seen you.'

'Monster!' declared her patient. 'No one would think, looking at you…'

'It's a great asset and the secret of my success,' she told him lightly, and went downstairs to get his lunch tray.

Mrs Moore was in the kitchen and a tray was ready on the table with soup heating on the stove and an egg custard ready on its dish. She made haste to pour coffee for Eliza the moment she opened the kitchen door with a sympathetic: 'You poor thing, you've not had a bite to eat.'

'That's OK, but the coffee's lovely,' said Eliza gratefully. 'Oh, you've got Cat here.'

'That's right, Hub brought them here while he packs up, he and Professor van Duyl are going this afternoon. He thought the little creatures would be better here under my eye, no chance of getting scared or trying to run away.'

Eliza took the tray upstairs, her thoughts busy. Christian had mentioned that he might be leaving today, but she hadn't really believed him because she hadn't wanted to, but now it seemed likely that she wouldn't see him again; there was no sign of him around the house; he had forgotten about her lunch—perhaps he had already gone. And Hub? He hadn't gone yet. Were they travelling together? she wondered. She wasn't sure about Hub;

she supposed he was someone the professor knew well. Perhaps he worked in a hospital, so they would probably join forces for the journey? By plane? By boat? She had no idea, and no time to indulge in speculation.

She stood over Professor Wyllie while he ate his lunch, got him out of bed with care, sat him in a large, high-backed chair and made his bed for him, all the while talking gently about nothing much so that he wouldn't sit and think about himself. She was on the point of getting him back into bed again when the door opened and Christian and a youngish man whom she took to be Doctor Trent came in, both to become immediately absorbed in their older colleague. It was ten minutes or more before they had concluded their examination, greatly hindered by their patient's forcefully expressed opinions.

'You're on the mend, sir,' pronounced Christian, 'but you must rest for several days—Sister Proudfoot will see to that.'

'She's a tartar,' muttered Professor Wyllie, and chuckled at her, standing like a statue at the foot of his bed. All three gentlemen looked at her, Doctor Trent in open admiration, her patient with an air of mischief, and Professor van Duyl with no expression on his handsome face at all.

She looked back at them, her eyebrows slightly raised. 'Shall I come back presently, sir?' she asked.

The old man chuckled again. 'Not much of you,' he commented weakly, 'but what there is is good sound stuff. You stay here, girl, and give us a chance to stare at you; we don't often get the chance of seeing such a pretty girl.'

Eliza accepted this speech with composure. 'You've been out of bed a great deal longer than half an hour,' she pointed out, and proceeded to pop him back into bed, helped by Doctor Trent.

Professor van Duyl didn't lift a finger, merely enquired: 'He ate his lunch, Sister?'

'Every crumb.' Perhaps it was something in her voice which made him look sharply at her. 'Your own lunch—I had entirely overlooked it—you've had none.'

She agreed with him, feeling suddenly hollow. 'But don't worry,' she begged him, 'Mrs. Moore gave me a cup of coffee when I went down for the tray.'

'You'll go now, please. I shall remain here until you return—is half an hour sufficient? I am very sorry; I had a number of calls to make to Holland...'

She forgave him with a smile. Estelle, of course, whether he loved her or not. Presumably he would go and see her the moment he got back home. She ran downstairs, her head full of unhappy little pictures of the two of them meeting once more, and perhaps she had been mistaken after all and Estelle wasn't in the least like her photograph. Perhaps, just for Christian, she would come alive and warm and loving, perhaps she herself had allowed her imagination to run away with her because she had so wanted him to fall in love with her—and he hadn't.

She ate a hurried meal with Mrs Moore fussing round her, then went back on duty to find the doctors ready to leave. Doctor Trent wished her goodbye in a friendly fashion and said he would be back again in the morning and that she was to call him if she was worried. Christian wished her goodbye too, so casually that she barely murmured in reply, not realizing that this really was goodbye, for when she went down to get Professor Wyllie his tea, it was to hear he and Hub had gone and Cat and her kittens with them. Mrs Moore, a little curious, gave her a note from Hub, regretting not having seen her to wish her goodbye and promising that he would take good care of Cat and her offspring. Eliza read it twice as though there might be something in it she had missed, then took the tray upstairs, feeling lost.

She went through the rest of the day like a well-trained automaton, not believing that Christian could have gone away like that with no more than a careless word. It was a good thing that as the hours passed, her patient gathered strength and became quite irascible, making peppery remarks which she knew he didn't mean and requiring a good deal of soothing before she could settle him for the night and give him his sleeping pill, sitting prudently by his bed until she was quite sure that he was sound asleep, before going to her own room, where, unlike her patient, she didn't sleep a wink.

CHAPTER SEVEN

ELIZA HAD GIVEN the Professor his breakfast the next morning, and had her own, when she decided to take a quick walk around the garden before going back to her patient. Snuggled into her cape, she went out of the front door and round the side of the house to the sizeable garden at the back, stopping to peep in the garage as she passed it. The Fiat was there; she stood and stared at it in amazement, then hurried back to the kitchen. 'Mrs Moore,' she asked, 'do you know how my car got here?'

'Why, bless you, Sister, Professor van Duyl asked Hub to go for it yesterday—didn't he tell you?' She shook her head. 'Forgetful, that's what he is, forgot your nice hot lunch too, didn't he? Shocking, I call it. If he wasn't such a nice sort of man and so clever with it, I'd be real vexed—sitting in that study, he was, for hours yesterday, ringing up Holland in that funny language of his.'

Estelle again. Eliza thanked Mrs Moore and went back to Professor Wyllie—she might be very pretty, even a little helpless looking, but she had plenty of sound common sense; she banished Christian from her thoughts, a difficult task made easier by her patient, who, as the day proceeded, became increasingly testy. A good sign, said Doctor Trent, commenting favourably on his condition. He was to be kept at rest for a few more days, he decided, and left Eliza to the difficult job of keeping the irritable old gentleman happy. They played chess each day, a game at which she was barely passable, whereas her companion was very good indeed. But this in a way was most satisfactory, because it led to him giving her lessons, which passed the time nicely and kept him quiet, and in a few days, when he was allowed to go downstairs, Eliza cunningly offered to help him with his correspondence, which kept them both well occupied for hours on end. He had insisted, on the very first day after Christian's departure, on having the telephone plugged in by the bedside and had used it incessantly, but never as far as she knew, in order to talk to him. But he was a bad patient, and once she was out of the room there was no knowing what he did, but even though he was so trying she liked him; he had a ready sense of fun even when he wasn't feeling too well, and a mind which she envied.

They talked a good deal together, and because a restful atmosphere was so essential to him, she paid a rare visit to the village shop and purchased a traycloth and embroidery silks. She knew of no one who used such a thing, but that didn't matter. She sat with him, her pretty head bent over the fine stitches, and led him to talk of this and that, and when he became tired or bored, put her work away and got out the chessboard, or suggested in a no-nonsense voice that he needed a nap, and if she found her days dull, she gave no sign.

Soon, she supposed, she would be plunged back into the busy life of the hospital wards again and then she would be able to forget the last month for good. She grew a little quiet and thinner too, and when she telephoned her mother to explain where she was, that lady, her sharp maternal ears tuned in to every inflection of her children's voices, wanted to know what was wrong, so that Eliza had to invent a sudden cold and a lack of days off in order to lull her mother's unease.

As the Professor got better she was able to go out for longer walks, leaving the faithful Miss Trim with instructions as to what to do in an emergency, but an emergency didn't occur. Professor Wyllie continued to improve, and at the end of a week, Eliza came upon him and Doctor Trent with their heads together, deep in conversation, and the looks they cast at her were so guilty that she had no hesitation in demanding what they were cooking up between them.

'A little holiday,' explained her patient in a wheedling tone, and: 'It would do him good,' added Doctor Trent.

'Where will you go?'

'We, dear girl. Doctor Trent and—er—other advice we have sought insist that you should accompany me. Quite a short trip and just what I need to revive my interest in things. Christian van Duyl is preparing an article about our findings and would like my help. We could stay very quietly at his home.' His blue eyes studied her, as innocent as a child's. 'You could drive me in your funny little car.'

She had resolutely not thought of Christian for a whole week and it had half killed her; it was unfair that after all her efforts to forget him, he should be pushed pell-mell back into her life once more.

'It sounds just the thing for you,' she agreed, carefully noncommittal, 'but I think I must go back to St Anne's.'

'Why?'

'Well, I've been away for more than five weeks.'

'You told me yourself that you had a splendid staff nurse—they can manage quite well without you for another week or so.' He pulled down the corners of his mouth. 'I'm very upset, girl, and it's most unkind of you—now I can't go.'

'Another nurse?' she suggested, knowing that she had already lost the fight.

'No. You or no one. Go back to your precious ward and leave me here to moulder away...'

Eliza exchanged a glance with Doctor Trent, whose eyes implored her silently. 'I wouldn't do it for anyone else,' she said at length, 'but since you ask me so nicely, I see I have no choice.'

He ignored her mild sarcasm. 'Dear girl,' he beamed at her, 'what a treasure you are! I promise you that I'll be an exemplary patient, your word shall be law and I'll not wheeze once.'

She laughed then. 'I'll hold you to that, Professor, only do you feel up to arranging things with St Anne's, or do you want me to do something about it?'

'Leave it to me,' interposed Doctor Trent. 'I'll see to the details—would you like our salary paid before you go? What arrangements are usual?'

'I don't know, I don't think it's usual at all for hospital staff to be lent out, but I would like some money before I go. May I leave it to you, Doctor Trent?'

'Clothes?' asked Professor Wyllie unexpectedly.

'Well, yes—I've almost nothing with me, could I whip up to London and get a few things?'

Doctor Trent was once more helpful. 'Why not? If you could manage to get there and back tomorrow afternoon—directly after lunch, perhaps? I've a day off and will be delighted to spend the afternoon here—we're due for another game of chess, anyway.'

It was as though fate, having played her a dirty trick, was bent on compensating her for it, though she doubted whether the delight of seeing Christian again would balance the misery of parting from him and forgetting him for a second time.

She drove herself up to London the following afternoon, her thoughts in such a muddle of excitement and nervousness that it was with difficulty that she forced herself to think about clothes. Nothing much, she decided; it was still cold and wet and she didn't suppose she would go out a great deal. She packed a couple of woollen dresses and changed into a tweed suit that she had only just bought, and exchanged her topcoat for the one hanging in the wardrobe. It was a nice mixture of peat brown and green, with a green lining which matched the suit, and

Eliza searched her drawers until she found a handful of woollies which would go with this outfit; she almost decided to take the mohair skirt and cashmere top, but decided against it; it was quite unlikely that she would go out in the evening and the two dresses would do for any small social occasion.

When she had finished there was still time for her to go to Men's Medical and see Mary for a few minutes before a brief, businesslike interview with Miss Smythe, who seemed quite undisturbed at the prospect of her continued absence. 'Another week or two won't matter, Sister,' she said comfortably. 'Doctor Trent telephoned me yesterday concerning your extended stay with Professor Wyllie; as far as the hospital is concerned it's perfectly in order, and I have your cheque here; he wished me to arrange that for you. Perhaps you will let me know how things go on. The Professor is far too important a person in the medical world not to command any small service which we may be able to give him.'

She smiled complacently, just as though, thought Eliza peevishly, she was the one rendering the service. She drove back to the Professor's house a little put out, feeling in some inexplicable way that she was being pushed around by unseen forces. 'I'm nothing but a pawn,' she told herself as she parked the Fiat and went indoors, then found her ill-humour evaporating because her patient was so glad to see her back again and Mrs Moore had prepared a delicious tea for her. She had it in the sitting room while the two men finished their game, and as she munched her way through Mrs Moore's scones she speculated about Christian; for now that she was to meet him again there was no point in not thinking about him.

Supposing that when she got to his home, she found—as she suspected she might—that Estelle was quite unsuitable for him, should she do something about it? Would she be justified? Christian might not like her, but he was—had been—attracted to her; he might, just might be glad to see her again, after all. She finished the scones, polished off a slice of cherry cake and bore the tray back to the kitchen, her mind in a fine muddle, her confusion considerably increased by the delight she felt at seeing him again.

They left four days later with Professor Wyllie packed in snugly beside her, hedged about with all the safeguards necessary for the journey. They were to travel to Harwich and go aboard the night ferry; the efficient Miss Trim had dealt with everything, and now, released from her overwhelming ability and Mrs Moore's excited chatter, they were as happy as two children setting out on a treat, although Eliza, still a prey to her mixed feelings, wasn't sure if the trip would turn out to be a treat or a trial. Time would tell, she told herself, taking refuge in clichés, and did her best to enter into her companions's high spirits.

They had a surprisingly smooth crossing and the Professor at least slept the night through, and if he noticed that Eliza was rather hollow-eyed when they met for an early breakfast, he said nothing, only chatted interestingly about Holland. 'You'll like the country around Nijmegen,' he told her, 'wooded here and there and far more character to it than the rest of the country. Christian lives outside the city—it's on the German border, you know, but his home is on the Dutch side and very rural.'

She tried to speak casually. 'What is the village called?'

'Well, there isn't a village, just a hamlet. The nearest village is Horssen and that's no size at all. But with a car, of course, it's an easy matter to get to Nijmegen in ten minutes or so.'

'Isn't that inconvenient for his practice?'

Her companion blinked rapidly behind his spectacles. 'Shouldn't think so; he's got a car, you know.' For some reason he laughed and didn't tell her why.

It was an easy drive from the Hoek once she had negotiated the nightmare of Rotterdam and come out safely on to the E96 on the other side. She found the motorway dull enough, and her companion agreed with her, pointing out that the real Holland lay in the small towns and villages they bypassed on their hundred-mile journey, but when they stopped for coffee, two miles on the further side of Gorinchem, they found a small café close to the River Waal, and sat watching the long barges making their slow way up and down its busy waters. The little houses around them were peaceful under the winter sky and across the water there were windmills turning.

They went on again presently, back to the motorway, until they crossed the river at Tiel and took a more peaceful road. 'For there is no need to go all the way into Nijmegen,' explained Professor Wyllie. 'We can get to Christian's home from this end—keep on this road as far as Druten and I'll tell you where to go when we're there—it's through the place, the first turning on your right.'

The country was pretty now, even in winter, with the river coming into view every now and then and wooded land between the fields. Eliza drove through Druten and obedient to her companion's direction, turned off the road into a country lane bordered by grassland at first, then gradually becoming screened with shrubs and trees.

'Next turning on your left,' counselled the Professor. 'Look for two pillars with creatures on top of them.'

A strange sort of road, thought Eliza, as she nosed the little car between the two tall red brick columns, and caught a glimpse of dragon-like creatures crowning their tops as they went past. 'How far?' she wanted to know. 'It's a narrow road…'

Her companion grunted as she took a bend a little too fast, bringing into a view a large and splendid house.

'Oh, a research centre,' she declared. 'I suppose Professor van Duyl has his headquarters here.'

'You might say that, I suppose. Stop at the front door, girl.'

There was a sweep of steps to climb—slowly, because of the Professor's wheezing, so that by the time they had reached the imposing door it had been opened—by Hub.

He greeted them in his usual manner, but he looked different; at Inverpolly he had been used to wearing what most of the men wore, a thick sweater and corduroy or tweed slacks, but now he was nattily attired in a black jacket, pinstripe trousers, very white linen and a bow tie. He took the Professor's outstretched hand and shook it and when Eliza proffered hers, shook that too, bowing just a little as he did so. Probably a Dutch custom, thought Eliza. 'I had no idea that you worked here too,' she observed with interest, but beyond smiling and nodding he said nothing but ushered them into the lobby and from thence into the hall.

It was vast and lofty, with a magnificent staircase leading to a half landing and then winging away on either side to a remote upstairs. There were tapestries on the walls and the furniture, Eliza observed, was very grand. A showplace, owned by some hard-up member of the Dutch aristocracy and rented to the medical profession, although it looked like a stately home. At any moment, she felt sure, a door would open and a guide would appear and start to intone the beauties of her surroundings. And indeed a door did open, but not to admit a guide; it was Christian who crossed the expanse of marble floor with the assured air of the polite host. Anyone would think that he owned the place, she thought, watching him. He looked handsomer than ever and was, as usual, faultlessly turned out. She was suddenly glad that she was wearing the new tweed outfit and the Rayne's shoes she hadn't been able to afford...

He had reached them by now, shaking Professor Wyllie by the hand, welcoming him. 'You are wonderfully recovered,' he observed, and turned to look at Eliza, 'due no doubt to our redoubtable Miss Proudfoot.'

She stared at his face; his dark eyes were alight with laughter. And what had he to laugh about? she wondered uneasily. She could feel her heart thumping away under the new tweeds like a demented thing; whether meeting her again amused him or not, she was overjoyed to see him; she knew now that however hard she tried she would never be able to forget him. She said quietly: 'How do you do, Professor,' and offered a hand, mindful of the Dutch custom of shaking hands on all and every occasion, and Christian was Dutch as well as being back in his own country.

He took the hand and didn't let it go. 'Welcome to my home, Eliza,' he said, and now she knew why he had looked so amused.

Her eyes rounded with astonishment. She declared: 'Your home? all this?' she waved her free hand at the magnificence around them and choked a little. 'And I gave you a broom to clean out the cottage, and you mopped the floor!'

'Rather well, I thought.'

She wriggled her hand a little and his grip tightened. 'And Hub? Does he live here too?'

'Of course—he orders my house for me; he's my right-hand man—a paragon amongst men and a lifelong friend as well.' He laughed a little. 'I think that in England you would call him the butler, but to us he is much more than that.'

'Oh, yes, I know.' Eliza looked at Professor Wyllie, standing beside her, oozing benevolence, his blue eyes missing nothing. 'You didn't tell me,' she accused him gently.

'No need, girl—why should I? What's it to you, anyway?'

A forthright statement which left her without words, so that Christian came to her rescue with a suggestion that she might like to go to her room, nodding at Hub as he spoke. 'We lunch at half past twelve and my mother is most anxious to meet you.'

Hub, who had disappeared, returned, trailing in his wake a tall angular girl who answered to the name of Nel, and led Eliza up the great staircase, to take the left-hand wing which opened on to a wide corridor where she opened a door and waved Eliza smilingly inside. Left alone, Eliza saw that her case was already there, quite dwarfed by its surroundings, for the room reflected the magnificence of the hall. If Christian had hoped to impress her he had succeeded very well. She wandered round, picking up delicate silver, bric-à-brac and china, smelling at the bowl of flowers, fingering the books which someone had thoughtfully placed at the bedside, examining the window hangings and the bedspread on the bed with its important carved headboard. It was all quite beautiful and not quite to be believed. She turned away from its satinwood and pastel brocades and went to the window, which afforded a view of a large formal garden, which even at this dreary time of year looked pleasant, with its sunken pond and statues and straight paths and clipped hedges, but the sight of it did nothing to quieten her thoughts. She went back to the dressing table and tidied herself for lunch, and presently, outwardly serene, but inwardly scared to death, she went downstairs.

Hub was in the hall; she suspected that he had been waiting for her, for he came to her at once. 'In here, miss,' he advised her, with a kind of benevolent encouragement, just as though he knew that she was nervous, and threw open a handsome pair of doors.

She had expected another vast room, hung with brocade and family portraits and furnished with chairs, which, while extremely handsome to look at, would be most uncomfortable in which to sit, but it was nothing like that at all—a smallish room, glowing with colour and chintz-covered chairs, with a bright fire in the steel grate and under her feet a rich carpet, inches thick, all combining to give an air of great cosiness. There seemed to be a great many people, but only at first glance, for as Christian came towards her from the group around the fire, she saw that there were only five other people in the room besides the two of them. Professor Wyllie, of course, and not surprisingly, Doctor Berrevoets and Doctor Peters. And an elderly lady, not much taller than herself and still pretty.

The fifth person was a young woman, tall and rather angular, whom Eliza had no difficulty in recognising. Here then was Estelle, exactly like her photograph, excepting that it hadn't revealed her extreme slimness. No shape at all, Eliza summed up, but good-looking in a mediaeval kind of way, expensively dressed too, though what was the use of gorgeous clothes if there were no curves for them to cling to? Eliza, who had some quite satisfactory curves of her own, felt more cheerful as she murmured at Christian and was introduced to his mother. She liked the little lady immediately; she had her son's dark eyes, but there the resemblance ended; he must take after his father, she glanced at the portrait hanging above her hostess's head and knew that she was right; there was the stare, the good looks, the powerful nose with its winged nostrils. She answered Mevrouw van Duyl's gentle questions, put in excellent English, and at the touch of Christian's hand went to meet Estelle.

She had been right; now that she was close to her and actually talking, Estelle seemed more mediaeval than at first. She had a long straight nose and pale blue eyes, large and thickly lashed, but they held no expression except well-bred interest—perhaps they would light up when she was alone with Christian. Eliza's own eyes sparkled at the very idea so that Doctor Peters, standing by Estelle, was constrained to remark upon her evident good health. After that she went to talk to Doctor Berrevoets, and found herself beside him at lunch, taken in a room which could have housed half a dozen tables of the size at which they sat. She ate her way through the delicious meal, answering composedly when spoken to, but not contributing to the conversation, for somehow Estelle, without saying a word, had managed to convey to her the fact that she was the nurse and only there because they were all too well-mannered to dwell on the fact that she was paid wages and was hardly out of the same drawer, socially speaking. So silly, Eliza chided herself silently, to mind what Estelle thought about her. She wished that she was a little nearer Mevrouw van Duyl, who, although she treated her with the utmost kindness, was separated from her by a vast expanse of white table-cloth—and one couldn't shout.

She got up from the table with relief and overriding her patient's ill-tempered remarks about being bullied, led him away to his room for a much-needed nap. She didn't go downstairs again; her room was warm and comfortable and there were books to read. Someone had been in and unpacked while she had been at lunch and after a few minutes' idle reading she found her writing case and sat down to compose a letter; her parents would be interested to hear about the house and its treasures. She had almost finished it when there was a knock on the door and Estelle came in.

'Christian thought that you might like to walk in the garden,' she said in her precise English. 'If we put on coats and scarves it will be pleasant enough.'

Eliza got her coat and found a scarf; she didn't want to go walking with Estelle, but on the other hand it might give her the chance to find out more about her—there must be something which attracted Christian, and she had to admit that she had been prejudiced against her, and now would be the time to find out what Estelle was really like.

They went out of the side door which led them straight to the formal garden, and Eliza began to ask, rather feverishly, a great many questions about it; she suspected that she and Estelle would have very little in common and gardens were usually a safe topic.

Estelle talked intelligently but without much interest. They stayed out of doors for half an hour, and at the end of that time Eliza had confirmed her suspicion that the girl was a bore— nice enough, she supposed, friendly even, but she showed no emotion about anything; Eliza had unconsciously put that to the test, for, seeing a mole emerging from his hill, she had squealed with delight and would have stayed motionless for minutes in the hope that he might reappear, only a glance at her companion's face showed only too plainly that to Estelle, moles were of no interest at all, moreover there was no need to become vulgarly excited about them.

Feeling quite subdued, Eliza followed her back into the house, this time through a conservatory full of spring flowers over which she would have liked to linger. But she was given no opportunity to do this, being taken into a handsome room with a good deal of gilding on its walls and a great many chairs and little tables, where Mevrouw van Duyl was sitting by the fire. She looked up and smiled as they went in and said kindly: 'There you are, my dears—you are not too cold, I hope? Tomorrow, Eliza—I may call you that?—I will take you round the house if you are interested. It is a great awkward place, but quite beautiful—at least we think so, although it is far too big for the two of us.'

Estelle had seated herself on the other side of the chimneypiece. 'You forget, Mevrouw van Duyl, that when Christian and I are married, I shall be living here too.' She spoke gently, but Eliza saw the older lady wince and frown, though the face she turned to her was quite placid. 'Sit down, Eliza,' she was bidden, 'and tell me about yourself, for Christian has hardly mentioned you and I had not the least idea that you were so young and pretty.'

Eliza, aware that Estelle was listening to this challenging remark even though she had picked up a magazine, excused herself. 'I should like that, Mevrouw van Duyl, but perhaps another time? It's time I got Professor Wyllie on his feet again; if I let him sleep too long, he gets cross.'

Her hostess smiled. 'Of course, Eliza. I forget that you are a nurse—you do not look like one, you see, and somehow, from the little Christian said of you, I imagined you to be middle-aged and plain.'

All three of them laughed and Eliza hoped that her merriment sounded real, for it was nothing of the sort. Going upstairs to the Professor's room presently it struck her that however unsuitable Estelle was, she couldn't carry out her intention of bringing the match to an end and marrying Christian herself; she hadn't known then that he was the owner of this vast house and living in the lap of luxury; he might be a hard-working doctor and a successful one too, but he didn't belong to her world, but Estelle did and that was why he had chosen her to be his wife. She would make him a very good wife, but whether she would make him happy was a moot point. She was very quiet as she got her patient out of bed and tidied up the room. He was still a little irritable and his pulse was too high, but she knew better than to dissuade him from doing what he wished with the rest of the day. A long chat with the other men, he told her with glee; it would be most interesting, and she should hear all about it later. 'And I'll have my tea up here,' he decided. 'Ring that bell and ask for it, Eliza, and have a cup with me.'

She was only too glad to do so, for she had been dreading going back to the drawing room; a chat with Mevrouw van Duyl would have been nice, but an hour of Estelle's company, trying to find something to talk about, wasn't tempting.

They had their tea and presently, when he had gone downstairs, she went back to her room, finished her letter and then, uncertain of the evening ahead, bathed and changed into one of the woollen dresses, dove grey with a high white collar and little cuffs. It was a very plain dress, save for the silk bow under her chin, but it was suitable for after six in a quiet sort of way, and anyway, she wasn't quite sure of her status; was she a guest, or was she to be considered as Professor Wyllie's nurse? There was a difference, quite a large one; when she saw him again she would have to ask him.

She spent time on her face and hair because she had nothing else to do—indeed, she took her hair down again and started brushing it out with the idea of trying another style. The knock on the door was unexpected, but Hub's anxious face and urgent voice brought her to her feet at once.

'It's Professor Wyllie, miss—if you would go to the library right away.'

She had taken the precaution of bringing the portable oxygen with her as well as the drugs he might need and syringes and needles; she had laid them out ready on a linenfold dower chest standing at the foot of the bed; now she snatched them up and was flying downstairs almost before Hub had finished speaking.

She knew where the library was; Estelle had pointed it out to her as they had left the house that afternoon. She opened the door and walked in. Professor Wyllie was sitting in a large armchair, having what she could see was a nasty attack. Christian was bending over him, loosening his tie, while the other two doctors stood nearby, looking helpless. She skipped past them, offered her neat little parcel of phials and syringes to Christian, got the oxygen started and applied it to Professor Wyllie's anxious face. 'Better in a moment,' she assured him soothingly. 'We're going to get you out of that jacket.' She turned round to engage help from Doctor Peters and thus missed the look on Christian's face; when she did have time to look at him, he was gravely checking the injection before plunging it into his colleague's arm. The result was dramatic; within a few minutes the old man was breathing easily once more and giving testy instructions as to what would be done next, to none of which Christian paid the least attention.

'Bed for you, sir,' he ordered in a quiet voice which brooked no refusal. 'Eliza, go ahead and see that it's ready, would you?' He went to the door with her and as he opened it, murmured: 'You weren't going to bed, by any chance?'

She had forgotten that her hair was hanging loose and that her feet were still in the pink quilted mules someone or other had given her for Christmas. Under his amused gaze she went a delicate pink. 'Of course not!' she snapped, and whisked past him.

She had the bed ready by the time they had borne the protesting Professor upstairs, and with Christian's help, got him into it. 'Would you stay five minutes?' she asked, and flew to her own room to get into the uniform she had brought with her; at least her evening was settled for her now.

And Christian, when he saw her in her cap and apron once more, said nothing—probably he had expected it, or welcomed it as a solution of a delicate problem, for she felt sure that whatever he felt about it, Estelle, in the nicest possible way, would have pointed out to him that she was a nurse, not a guest.

But she had reckoned without her host. The dinner gong had

hardly ceased to sound when there was a knock on the door and Hub came in.

'You are to go down to dinner, miss,' he told her, looking paternally at her. 'I will stay with the Professor and let you know if anything should occur.'

She glanced at the sleeping figure on the bed. 'Oh, Hub, that's very good of you, but I'd much rather stay up here—if I could have something on a tray?' She smiled at him. 'That's if no one would mind.'

'But I do mind very much.' Christian had followed Hub into the room. 'You will give us the pleasure of your company downstairs, Eliza.' He came across the room to her and took her arm. 'You know as well as I do that Professor Wyllie will be perfectly all right again; a day in bed and he will be as he usually is, and Hub knows exactly what he must do in an emergency.'

'Yes—but I'm the Professor's nurse, that's why I came. Besides, I'm in uniform.'

He smiled at her and her heart rocked. 'And very nice too, though I found your previous outfit most eye-catching.' He had walked her across the room and out of the door, which Hub closed silently behind them.

'Oh, please, I really would rather not...'

He took no notice at all, only said strangely: 'I wish we were back at Inverpolly,' and bent to kiss her swiftly, then, still holding her arm, went down the stairs beside her, silent now, just as she was, for surprise had taken her tongue.

CHAPTER EIGHT

ELIZA WAS GLAD, when she saw Estelle, that she had got back into uniform again, for the little grey wool dress would have been entirely eclipsed by that young lady's long crêpe gown, an expensive garment, thought Eliza, running an experienced female eye over it, beautifully cut but far too low in the neck for those regrettable salt-cellars. If Estelle didn't put on a few pounds soon, she would be skinny by the time she was forty. Eliza, in her mind's eye, knew just how she would look, but perhaps Christian liked thin women. Her thoughts shied away from him; it was no time to reflect upon his kiss. Instead, she made small talk with Doctor Berrevoets and drank her sherry before going to talk to Mevrouw van Duyl, who carried on with the small talk in her kindly way while her dark eyes took stock of Eliza, and presently they held the same amused gleam which showed from time to time in her son's eyes. Eliza didn't see that, but presently when they were on the point of going to the dining room, he left Estelle's side and lingered a moment with his parent.

'What gives you that delightfully satisfied expression, Mama? You look like the cat who discovered the cream.'

She patted his arm and gave him a wide smile. 'Dear boy,' she said, and then: 'Talking of cats—I'm sure Eliza would love to go and see that quaint little animal you brought back with you. Such a dear girl, and you never told me how very pretty she was. Perhaps you could take her to see the little animals after dinner, and I daresay you would like a little talk, too.'

It was her son's turn to smile. 'Dear Mama,' he spoke very mildly, 'how you must have delighted Father with your little plots!'

'Yes, dear—and you are so like him.' She looked suddenly downcast. 'It was only one of my silly notions, a—a daydream.'

He looked at her with fondness. 'Yes, dearest, but do not allow yourself to forget that Estelle and I plan to marry within the next few months.'

'No, Christian, I never forget that. Such a pleasant girl, and so capable, sometimes it seems to me that she had already taken over the running of this house when she comes to stay—of course she does it beautifully.'

His mouth hardened. 'Quite so, Mama. Now, since everyone is waiting…'

Eliza sat next to Doctor Berrevoets with Christian, at the head of the table, on her other side, but it was quickly apparent to her that conversation between them was to be limited to platitudes, uttered at sufficiently frequent intervals to escape sheer neglect. It was Estelle, on his other side, who received the lion's share of his attention, although what she said to interest him, in Eliza's opinion, could have been put on a postage stamp and room to spare, nor was his attention in the least loverlike—she noted that while inclining her neatly capped head towards Doctor Berrevoets, listening to his dissertation on butterflies. The study of them was his hobby and he was delighted to find such a ready listener. She knew nothing of the pretty creatures, although she could recognise a Red Admiral or a Cabbage White, but she gave him almost all of her attention, the remaining bit of it being focused on Christian and Estelle: she could see no sign of any deep feeling between them. True, Christian was hardly a man to demonstrate his affections in public, but no one, least of all herself who was so in love with him, could have failed to mistake the look of a man in love. And there was no such look, she was quite sure of that, and as for Estelle, if she had any feelings at all, she was keeping them well concealed.

It was a pity that he wasn't an ordinary GP with not much money and an ordinary house; then she would have done her best to rescue him from a marriage which she was certain would be disastrous, but that was impossible now. Estelle, for all her tepid nature, had all the attributes required of her; she would be an excellent hostess, know all the right people, never lose her temper and know exactly what to do even in the most awkward situation. She would never let him down, she would certainly not expect him to rescue her off mountains because she would never be fool enough to go there in the first place, neither would she given him a broom and tell him to sweep... Eliza caught Doctor Berrevoets' eye, fixed expectantly on her, and she hadn't the slightest idea what he had been saying.

'You're quite right,' said Christian, speaking across her, coming to her rescue with all the ease of an accomplished host. 'Very few people realise that the female Blue Butterfly is in fact brown. Personally, I find the Holly Blue particularly lovely.'

'Ah, yes,' said Doctor Berrevoets happily, '*Celastrina Argiolus*, quite charming. I was just telling Eliza that when she goes home she must use her eyes.'

'Indeed, yes.' Christian's voice was bland, as was his face. 'I have observed, though, that she does that to good effect.' He smiled at her and she glared at him, a futile gesture quite lost on him. 'And that reminds me, my mother is sure that you will want to see Cat and the kittens, they have settled in very nicely; my own cats have quite taken to her and so has the kitchen cat. She has a basket in my study—perhaps you would like to see her presently?'

'Oh, please. I did wonder...but there hasn't been much opportunity to ask. But I knew they'd be comfortable here.'

They went back to the drawing room for their coffee after that, and this time Eliza found herself sitting beside Mevrouw van Duyl, but not for long; Christian joined them within a few minutes. 'Estelle and I are going to take Eliza to see Cat,' he told his mother, and Eliza watched the two pairs of eyes, so dark and alike, meet and wondered why he should give his mother a faintly mocking smile.

Cat remembered her and offered a small head for a caress. She looked sleek and content, quite another animal from the poor bedraggled thing Christian had hauled into the cottage, and Eliza told her so, picking her up to cuddle her, while the kittens, their eyes open now, stared unblinkingly up at her.

'Oh, aren't they sweet?' She was down on her knees now, tickling their chins. 'You'd never think, looking at her now, that she'd been half starved—and so wet!' She chuckled. 'Do you remember how frightened I was when she tapped on the window?' She laughed up at Christian and found him looking at her, his face alight and warm.

'You certainly sounded terrified.' He was sitting on his heels beside her now and Cat was wreathing herself round him. 'She's turned into a charming little creature.'

'There are already three cats in the house as well as a dog,' Estelle, standing behind them, pointed out in a reasonable voice. 'Surely we might find good homes for them?'

'They have a good home here.' Christian's voice was quiet, but Eliza sensed his impatience at the remark.

She put the kittens down and got to her feet. 'I don't suppose they'll bother anyone,' she offered placatingly, 'I mean, they quickly learn where they're allowed to go and who...' She stopped awkwardly and Estelle took her up, still in an agreeable voice.

'You make me sound a hard-hearted person.'

'Oh, I'm sorry, I didn't mean that at all. I know you'll be very kind to them.'

'Certainly I shall, as long as they stay in their right place. I have never been able to understand sentimentality in the treatment of animals.' Estelle sat down in a high-backed chair, looking complacent, and went on: 'It will be my duty as mistress of this house to see that all its occupants are properly cared for, a duty for which I feel myself eminently suited.' She closed her eyes as she spoke—and a good thing too, for Eliza was regarding her open-mouthed and Christian's face had the look of a man who is teetering on the edge of a very high cliff. By the time she had opened her eyes again they had normal expressions on their faces and she continued: 'I discovered a book the other day, a child's book by someone called Beatrix Potter.' She wrinkled her patrician nose in faint disgust. 'Animals, dressed like people! I must say that I found it most extraordinary.'

'In Dutch? How marvellous—I had no idea they were translated into Dutch.' Eliza was quite carried away with the idea. 'The Flopsy Bunnies and Jemima Puddleduck...'

'Mrs Tiggywinkle and Tom Kitten,' said Christian.

'You know them too? I was brought up on them, I think they were the first books I learned to read.'

'My favourite bedtime reading,' remembered the Professor, 'my mother has them still.' They smiled at each other, sharing pleasant memories, and Estelle said sharply: 'Should we not go back to our guests, Christian? I am sure Eliza wishes to go back to her patient.'

There was the faintest hint of annoyance in her voice, and Eliza said at once, 'Yes, I do. Thank you for letting me visit Cat, it's nice to see her happy.' She got herself to the door. 'Good night. Would you please say good night to the rest of them for me?'

She was through the door and half way up the staircase before they followed her out of the study; she was too far away to hear what they were saying, but Christian sounded annoyed.

The Professor was dozing lightly and Hub came quietly to meet her.

'There was no need for you to come back yet, miss; Professor van Duyl said that I was to stay until you came up to bed.'

'How kind, Hub, but there are one or two things I want to do. I've been to see Cat and the kittens.'

'Settled down very well, if I might say so, miss. Professor van Duyl took care of that, very anxious he was to have the little beasts comfortable. Sits in his study, he does, working, and they sit there with him—them and Willy the dog. Very fond of him he is too.'

'The Alsatian—I've not seen him, Hub.'

'Well, miss, Juffrouw van der Daal doesn't like him overmuch, so he's in the kitchen now. The Professor takes him out as usual of course, and he was in the library with the gentlemen this afternoon, but you wouldn't have noticed him under the desk. When we're on our own he has the run of the house.'

Eliza heard the wistfulness in his voice. 'I hope I see him before I go back, Hub.'

'I'm sure you will, miss. Would the Professor like a light supper presently?'

'Oh, yes, please. Shall I come down for it?'

He looked shocked. 'Oh, no, miss. Someone will bring it up, and perhaps you would ring when you want the tray removed. Soup? A morsel of fish? And I believe Cook has some excellent water ices.'

'Oh, yes—I had some at dinner, they were delicious. That would do very well, Hub, I'm not sure what the Professor should drink, though. Tonic water's a bit dull, isn't it?'

'A little fresh fruit juice, perhaps?' And when she nodded, he smiled paternally and went quietly away. He was a dear, she thought, as she went to sit by the bed and picked up her embroidery and began to stitch so that when her patient woke up he wouldn't think that she was just sitting there waiting impatiently for him to open his eyes.

He wakened very shortly afterwards, irritable and inclined to snap her head off, but the arrival of supper caused him to brighten considerably. Only her offer of the fruit juice sent him into a fit of the sulks, which she was doing her best to weather when the door opened and Christian came in. He had a bottle in one hand and glasses in the other.

'Ah, just in time, I see. I met Hub in the hall and he told me that he had just served fruit juice with your supper, something which I felt should be remedied at once.'

He put the glasses down on a small table, a delicate trifle of rosewood inlaid with mother-of-pearl, and set to work on the bottle's cork.

Professor Wyllie, all at once sunny-tempered as a happy baby, watched him, and Eliza watched him too. He dominated the room, just as he did any company and any room without making any conscious effort to do so. For some reason that simple fact made her feel that all was right with her world, although common sense told her that this was not so. The next few days weren't going to be particularly happy ones, Estelle didn't like her and although good manners would prevent her from saying so out loud, she would make sure that Eliza would never forget that she was the nurse and not a guest.

'I shall come up here tomorrow, sir,' observed Christian easily. 'We can just as easily work on that article with you here in bed as downstairs.' He glanced at Eliza. 'A pity you don't type, dear girl.'

'I do.'

'Splendid. You can keep an eye on our patient and type the thing for us.' He handed them each a glass. 'Your health, sir.'

The elder man beamed. 'A splendid idea, though a little boring for Eliza.'

The dark eyes were fixed on her face and she made haste to stare down into her glass. 'Then we must recompense her, must we not? A drive round the countryside, perhaps, or a trip to Nijmegen. Which would you prefer, Eliza?'

'I really don't mind. Besides, it would take up your time—there must be other things...'

'There are. What do you think of the champagne?'

'It's very nice,' she told him sedately, and heard the old man laugh.

'Heidsieck Monopole—Diamant Bleu 1961. Am I right, Christian?'

'You are.' He had gone to sit down, disposing his length in a comfortable fashion which suggested that he had come to stay. Eliza put down her glass and picked up her needlework once more. She feared that the champagne would go to her head; they had, after all, had wine with their dinner; she thought it was a burgundy, but she wasn't sure. As though he had read her thoughts, Christian continued, 'We had a Corton Charlemagne 1966 at dinner—a splendid white burgundy, don't you agree?—you shall sample it when you come down.'

'There was no need for champagne, dear boy.' The Professor was chumping away at his fish, in a splendid good humour.

'You're wrong. I'm celebrating something.'

'May we know?' Professor Wyllie asked the question and Eliza echoed it silently. They had decided the date of the wedding, they would be married immediately...her thoughts ran riot. Why had she ever come, she must have been mad... Her fragmental ideas were swept tidily away by his answer.

'No. No one knows.' He got to his feet slowly. 'I'll wish you both good night.'

The room seemed empty when he had gone, and very quiet. Eliza went on stitching, making conversation with her patient, and when he had finished his supper, suggested that he might like a game of cards. 'Or better still, there's a table here for chess or draughts.'

They played a mild game or so of draughts and Eliza, busy with her thoughts, allowed him to win before getting him ready for bed; arranging his pillows how he liked them, setting the bell close at hand, and turning out all but a small table lamp. 'I'm not in the least tired,' she lied cheerfully to him, 'and there's a book I want to dip into—do you mind if I bring it in here for half an hour?'

He smiled at her very nicely. 'What a dear child you are! Afraid that I'm going to start another wheeze? I promise you I won't, but I shall enjoy your company. Get the book by all means.'

He was already sleepy and when she returned from her room he had his eyes closed, to open them once to bid her good night. 'You're a great comfort to me, Eliza,' he told her.

She had taken off her cap and put on her pink sippers again. The house was very quiet, but then in a house of that size, she reminded herself, it would be hard to hear voices from downstairs. She moved her chair cautiously a little nearer the lamp and opened John Donne.

She didn't hear Christian come in; something made her look up to see him standing there, just inside the door, watching her. He crossed the room with surprising lightness considering his size and bent down to whisper: 'Why are you not in bed?'

'Well,' her voice was a mere thread of sound, 'I wanted to be quite sure.'

He didn't answer her but took the book from her hand and studied. She had been reading *The Broken Heart* and he stared down at the page before handing it back to her and then, his mouth very close to her ear: 'Beatrix Potter—and now John Donne.'

'I have a very catholic taste,' she assured him seriously.

'But not, I hope, a broken heart?'

She returned his piercing look steadily, her mouth firmly closed against the things she wished to say to him and could not; she shook her head instead and crossed her fingers unseen because although she hadn't said a word, it was the same as telling a lie.

'Strange,' his whisper was fierce in her ear. 'I imagined that you had.'

Eliza didn't look up; her eyes were fixed on John Donne lying in her lap. They focused on the end of the poem: 'My ragges of heart can like, wish and adore, but after one such love, can love no more.' Donne had hit the nail on the head; her heart wasn't just broken, it was in rags too.

'And what do you think of Estelle?' The whisper had become silky.

She spoke to the book. 'She is charming—and very handsome.'

'She will be a splendid hostess, don't you think? and run my home, sit on local committees and be the Lady Bountiful, as would be expected of my wife—the kind of wife I thought I wanted, Eliza. My mother will have time on her hands, will she not? I hadn't realized quite how much. Estelle has money too—she won't need my millions.'

Eliza's startled eyes flew to his face. 'Not millions—money millions?'

He grinned. 'Indeed I'm afraid so—in guldens, of course, in England I am merely a wealthy man.'

He wasn't joking. Eliza swallowed and said woodenly, 'Well, you have a large house to maintain.'

He shrugged. 'Perhaps you don't approve?'

'Why ever not? It's a beautiful house and the things in it are beautiful too. It would be terrible if you couldn't look after it all.'

He fetched a chair and set it down opposite her and bestrode it, his arms folded across its back. 'Did you notice Estelle's ring?'

How silly men were; didn't they know that a girl always noticed things like that within the first few seconds? 'It's magnificent.'

He shook his head. 'Diamonds in a modern setting, but Estelle wanted it. The family betrothal ring is old-fashioned; rose diamonds and rubies set in gold—all the wives have worn it and there are earrings to match, given to each successive bride as a wedding gift. Estelle wants earrings to match her ring.'

'I expect they will look very nice,' Eliza whispered in a tepid voice, and then, carried away by curiosity, went on: 'What are you celebrating?'

Christian fixed her with a dark look. 'Ah, so you're interested, are you? That at least is something. I shan't tell you.' He grinned again and suddenly unable to bear the conversation any longer she got up. 'I think if you don't mind, I might go to bed now.'

He stood up too. 'Do that, Eliza, but before you go to sleep, lie in your bed and remember everything I have said. Don't bother to recall your part of the conversation; most of it wasn't true, anyway.'

He opened the door for her after she had taken a quick peep at the sleeping form in the bed and wished her a whispered good night, but for some stupid reason she wanted to cry. She nodded her head at him instead, her eyes very wide to hold back the tears.

She was up early, in fact she was dressed when Nel came in with her morning tea. Eliza took her cup to the window and stood looking out on to the garden, bleak in the half darkness of the grey morning, and when she had finished it she went quietly along to Professor Wyllie's room. He was awake, bright-eyed and refreshed after a good night's sleep, and was all for getting up straight away. Fortunately Hub arrived with his morning tea and with it a message for Eliza. 'Would you care to join Professor van Duyl downstairs, miss? He thought you might enjoy a quick walk with him and Willy.'

One of the conclusions Eliza had come to during the night had been that of not seeing more of Christian than she must; instantly forgotten as she settled Professor Wyllie against the pillows, begged him to be good and ran to her room to fetch her cloak.

Christian was in the hall with Willy sitting patiently beside him. She was wished a good morning, introduced to the great beast and ushered down a narrow passage to a side door. 'I saw your light,' explained the Professor as they went through it into the chilly day and turned away from the house, down a flagstoned path between shrubs and trees. At the end of it there was a wall with a little wooden door and when they emerged on the other side Eliza saw that they were in a small park. 'Is this yours too?' she wanted to know.

'Yes.' He was walking along at a great rate, so that she was forced to skip a step or two to keep up. Willy was already out of sight and after a minute or two she asked: 'Do you have a surgery here?'

'No, though everyone hereabouts knows that I'm always available if I'm home. I have a room in one of the cottages in the village and go there three times a week, but my consulting rooms are in Nijmegen. I go there every day, but not today.'

'You work in the hospital there as well?'

'Oh, yes.' He had slowed his stride and taken her arm. 'I've beds at the hospitals in Appeldorn and Arnhem, and a couple in Utrecht.'

'But you can have very little leisure.' Somehow she had never suspected that he was so wrapped up in his work.

'I like it that way.' Something in his voice stopped her asking any more questions, so she said instead: 'Willy's a wonderful dog,' and whistled to him so that he came tearing across the grass towards her. She bent to scratch his ears. 'Does he go everywhere with you?'

'Yes. He sits under my desk during surgery hours and guards the car while I'm on my visits.'

'He must miss you very much when you're away from home.'

'He does, though my mother dotes on him.' They had come to another wall, with a little wicket gate in it which he opened. 'We can go through here and walk round to the other end and come in through the front drive,' he told her. 'And now tell me, what are your plans?'

'Plans? I haven't any. I'll go back to St Anne's, to my job on

Men's Medical, as soon as Professor Wyllie is well enough—that will be within a few days, I suppose.'

'Eager to get back?' His voice was blandly enquiring and she made haste to say: 'Of course not,' and then, in case he began to ask awkward questions: 'Is it colder here than in England during the winter?'

His mouth twitched very slightly. 'Yes, on the whole I think it is,' and he launched into a lengthy discourse about atmospheric pressures, isobars and meteorologist's forecasts which set her head reeling. It lasted until they were walking up the drive, and only ceased as they reached the bend in the drive where the house came so magnificently into view. 'Like it?' he asked her.

'It's super. When I saw it for the first time, it took my breath. It must be wonderful to live here—to make it your home.'

'It is.' He whistled to Willy, who joined them at once, walking soberly at his master's heels. 'We'll go in through the kitchen entrance so that Willy can be dried off.'

She went with him round to the back of the house and across a cobbled courtyard to a low wooden door, and then along a brick-floored passage and so to the kitchen, a large room with a great many doors and occupied by a number of people bustling about. Cat and the kittens were in their basket before the Aga stove and Willy, barely giving Hub time to rub him down, went to settle himself beside her. Eliza said good morning to the watching faces and saw them all smiling, and when Christian said something to them in Dutch they answered him cheerfully. They looked happy and contented and were obviously on good terms with him. It would be nice, she mused, to own a house such as this one and have these cheerful people to work for you in it.

They were back in the hall, climbing the staircase, when she observed:

'You have a lot of people working here.'

He said casually: 'Oh, yes—they live here too; it is their home.'

And she remembered how, when she had first known him, she had thought him to be arrogant and ill-tempered and uncaring of other people. He wasn't; he minded about these people who so obviously liked and respected him; probably they loved the place as much as he did.

They parted on the landing, richly carpeted and hung with portraits on its silk-panelled walls. 'Breakfast in half an hour,' he told her with a friendly smile, and opened Professor Wyllie's door for her.

It surprised her to find everyone in the breakfast room when she at last found it; no one had mentioned that there was such a place and she had gone to the dining room and found it deserted, its table, its mahogany gleaming, devoid of cloth and cutlery. She went back into the hall, supposing that she would have to listen at all the doors until she heard voices, when Hub came from the kitchen and with an apology, opened a door for her. It made matters worse to find that those seated at table were already half way through their meal, and Estelle's gentle good morning, coupled with her swift glance at the clock, was hard to bear.

Eliza sat down and addressed herself to her hostess. 'I'm sorry I'm late,' she explained. 'I didn't know that breakfast was in this room, I went to the dining room.'

The dark eyes twinkled kindly. 'It is I who should be sorry, Eliza, for not telling you. In any case breakfast is eaten when we wish to eat it, there is no strict time for it.'

A remark which put her at her ease, although she could see that Estelle didn't agree with that at all. Probably when she was mistress of the house, everyone would have to be in their places on the dot. She peeped at Christian, sitting immersed in his post and the newspapers; with all her heart she longed for him to become suddenly poor so that Estelle wouldn't marry him after all. No, that wouldn't do, for the girl had money of her own, he had said so. It would have to be the house, taken from him by some dramatic stroke of misfortune—because that was why Estelle had said she would marry him, Eliza guessed; no girl in her senses would miss such an opportunity of becoming its mistress—a thunderbolt, perhaps, or a long-lost heir who returned from the dead to claim his rightful heritage... Her colourful imagination ran riot and was only checked when Christian addressed her. 'Will ten o'clock suit you, Eliza?'

She said: 'Yes, Professor,' in a meek voice and went on with her dreaming. No, he couldn't give up the house; he loved it, and it was quite unchristian of her to wish that Estelle could drop dead. She sighed, so loudly that several pairs of eyes were turned upon her, and decided that there was nothing for it but this marriage, which would make three of them unhappy for the rest of their lives—no, four; Mevrouw van Duyl didn't like Estelle either.

The morning passed quickly—too quickly, for Eliza enjoyed herself. The Professor was feeling quite himself again and was in a good mood, sitting cosily in a great armchair not too near the fire, arguing happily about the article they were writing, crossing out a great deal of the notes and filling in whole pages in his terrible spidery writing, and she, sitting at a table hastily set up in one corner of the room, typed what she was given. It was when they paused for coffee that he wanted to know what Estelle was doing.

'I hope she isn't annoyed with me, taking you away in this fashion,' he observed to Christian, looking quite unrepentant.

'She's gone out with Peters.' Christian's voice was casual. 'They share a consuming interest in Roman remains—I believe they intend to stay out for lunch.'

'But, my dear boy, you will see almost nothing of her. You go to your rooms tomorrow, don't you?'

'Yes—I've several patients lined up, I believe. Which reminds me to ask Eliza if she would like a lift into Nijmegen in the morning. I have to be back here after lunch, for I have a patient coming here to see me in the afternoon.'

'Of course she's dying to go,' said Professor Wyllie, giving her no chance to speak for herself. 'Besides, she must have off duty and all that.' He held out his cup for more coffee. 'I have letters to write and must have peace and quiet.'

Eliza handed him back his filled cup and said indignantly: 'Well, really, anyone would think I wore army boots and weighed half a ton! And you know quite well,' she went on, warming to her theme, 'that when you say you want to be quiet I hardly breathe.'

'All the more reason why you should go with Christian. You will be allowed to breathe—though to do you justice, girl, you are as light as a fairy on your feet, and twice as pretty.'

She didn't answer this piece of blatant flattery, but finished her coffee, and avoiding Christian's eye, went back to her typing.

They had finished the first draft by lunchtime and Eliza went downstairs to eat that meal with Mevrouw van Duyl and Doctor Berrevoets, who was leaving that afternoon, and of course, Christian. It was far nicer without Estelle, she considered, for everyone was light-hearted and talked a little nonsense, and Willy sat beside his master as he usually did. Afterwards she went back to her patient and coaxed him to lie down on his bed for a nap until tea time, when he was to get up and go downstairs for an hour or two. She was free now, she supposed; she was wondering what to do with her time when Nel came upstairs with a note from Mevrouw van Duyl, asking her if she would spend an hour with her in the small sitting room, so Eliza, glad of something to do, repaired downstairs. The room looked bright and welcoming, with its flickering fire and a lamp or two to brighten the gloom of the winter afternoon. She sat down a little shyly opposite her hostess.

'It was kind of you to ask me to come down,' she said.

'But, my dear, I have been wanting to do so, for I have had no chance to talk to you and I am full of curiosity. Perhaps you do not mind if today we talk like this, and later you shall be shown the house.' She nodded her small, silvery head. 'I wish to know about you,' she stated simply, a remark she instantly qualified by asking a string of questions about Eliza's work, her family and her likes and dislikes. Eliza answered her willingly enough—there was no point in doing otherwise; she had nothing to hide and the elder lady's interest was kindly. And presently she received her reward for her forbearance, for Mevrouw van Duyl embarked on a monologue about her son.

'He's thirty-seven,' she confided, 'and I have wished for years that he would marry, for I am not so young as I was and there is a good deal to do here, and it seems that I am to have my wish.' She paused to sigh and Eliza felt sorry for her because her wish had turned sour on her. 'Christian works too hard,' she went on presently, 'for he has a great number of patients as well as work in the hospitals. He is very good at his work, you understand, my dear, and he loves it, just as he loves his home.' She sighed and Eliza said quickly: 'I suppose he's at his surgery this afternoon?'

'Oh, no, my dear. He went down to the village to see some of the old people there—those without families to help them, you know. He arranges for them to have help when that is the case and goes regularly to visit them. Willy has gone with him, and that means that they will go for a walk on the heath before they come home.'

'I love Willy—he must be a wonderful companion.'

'He is, we're excellent friends, he and I. Christian told me about Cat and how you found her—such a dear little creature and such pretty kittens. They will have a good home here, of that you may be sure. Christian will see to that.' She glanced at Eliza, who waited for her to go on, for it seemed as though she had more to say on the subject, but after a brief pause she went on to talk of other things and no more was said about her son. Eliza, listening to her hostess rambling on gently about this and that, thought what a dear little lady she was; Estelle couldn't know what a marvellous mother-in-law she was getting.

Half an hour later she got up to go, for the Professor would have to be wakened, tidied for his tea and shepherded downstairs. In the hall she met Estelle and Doctor Peters, returned from their outing. They were standing hand in hand and when they saw her, sprang guiltily apart, although to her eye they both seemed in high spirits; that was, as high-spirited as they were able to be. Eliza eyed them with some puzzlement—she quite liked Doctor Peters, although they had seldom had much to say to each other. He was what she described to herself as a worthy man and boring, but perhaps he and Estelle, both bores, didn't bore each other? It was an interesting point. She called a casual hullo to them as she went upstairs, then forgot about them because Professor Wyllie was ringing his bell.

She cast a professional eye over him, handed him his hairbrushes, found him a clean handkerchief and escorted him downstairs, where the rest of the party were assembled for their tea. Christian was there too, with Willy sitting very close to his master's chair. Eliza patted the noble animal's head as she slipped past to sit a little apart, happy to see the interest focused on Professor Wyllie, who, now that he felt almost well again, was showing the better side of his nature—indeed, he cornered the conversation, making Mevrouw van Duyl laugh a good deal. Everyone else laughed too, of course, but Eliza couldn't help noticing that Doctor Peters and Estelle were a little distrait, and Christian said almost nothing at all, although his eyes seldom left his fiancée's face.

She was on the point of uttering some polite excuse and slipping away to her room when Estelle suddenly suggested that they should go to the Rijn Hotel that evening. 'Such a lovely view of the river while we dine,' she pointed out with more animation than she had hitherto shown, 'and we can dance afterwards—besides, I have that new organza dress I'm longing to wear.'

She smiled round at everyone, sure that they would fall in with her wishes, and when her eyes lighted on Eliza, she added with exactly the right degree of politeness: 'And you too, of course, Eliza.'

Gathered into the general invitation with casual good manners, Eliza swallowed resentment and then stifled regret as she refused. There was nothing approximating to an evening dress amongst her few clothes hanging in the vast wall closet in her bedroom. She made polite excuses rather vaguely and went back to her room, saying that she had some typing to finish. She didn't see Christian again until several hours later, when she bumped into him in the long passage running from the conservatory to the front of the house. He looked splendid in his dinner jacket, but she didn't pause to take a better look, only murmured something or other and made to slip past him. Instead of which she found herself halted within an inch or so of his white shirt front, while a large hand clamped her shoulder fast.

'So—Eliza Proudfoot doesn't care to come out for the evening.' His voice was silky. 'Are we too frivolous for you, or is it that you don't care for our company?'

She studied the immaculate expanse of white before her eyes. 'Neither, Professor, it's just that I have the rest of the article to type, and besides that,' she hurried on, aware that he would dismiss that as a flimsy excuse, 'I have notes to write up and letters...if you don't mind, I should like to catch up on them. After all, I'm here to work.'

She took a cautious step backwards as she spoke and he stood on one side to let her pass with the casual courtesy which he might have accorded a stranger. Eliza made herself smile in his direction as she went past, and being an honest girl, spent the greater part of her lonely evening carefully typing what was left to be done, making out the charts Professor Wyllie had wanted and writing a number of quite unnecessary letters. And all the time she was doing this, a small, persistent portion of her mind was dwelling on the delights of the evening she was missing. But she couldn't have gone; she had glimpsed Estelle before they had all left, eye-catching in a lovely stained glass window dress which must have cost a small fortune. Even if she had had the pink skirt and the Marks and Spencer's top with her, she couldn't have completed with pure silk organza cut by an expert.

She told herself, once more, that the less she saw of Christian the better, quite forgetting that she was going to Nijmegen with him in the morning. Here, in this great house with its costly furnishing, he was different—no, not different, just unapproachable, someone who treated her with kindness and consideration but who was nevertheless dead set on marrying a wife who would be entirely suitable. Her fretful mind glossed over his strange whispered conversation of the previous evening, though she went on, talking out loud, because there was no fear of anyone hearing her. 'He's not in love with her at all, only she's the kind of wife he took it for granted he would marry.' She sighed, put away her writing case, and went to bed.

She prevailed on Professor Wyllie to remain in bed for his breakfast on the following morning, for although he was delighted with himself after his evening out, he was still tired. His pulse was up a little too; it would make a splendid excuse not to go with Christian, but in this she was forestalled by Professor Wyllie, who, when she mentioned the fact mildly, instantly commanded her to go, reminding her cunningly that he was far more likely to have a bad turn if he were crossed in his wishes. Eliza went down to her own breakfast torn between pleasure at the thought of spending some time with Christian, and a wish to carry out her resolution not to see so much of him. She was a little late for breakfast, loitering down the great staircase while she pondered about it.

Everyone was already seated at table; Mevrouw van Duyl, reading her post and drinking coffee, looked up to wish her a friendly good morning. Estelle was smoking a cigarette in a long holder and listening to a low-voiced monologue from Doctor Peters, and the master of the house sat at the head of the table, making inroads into his toast and marmalade and looking as black as thunder. He barely glanced at her as she sat down, and the atmosphere at his end of the table was so frosty that she made haste to drink some coffee, crumble a piece of toast and take herself off again.

Mevrouw waited until Eliza had left the room for some moments before remarking: 'Eliza looks tired.'

'Probably she got carried away with her typing and stayed up too late. She should have come with us,' ground out her son savagely.

Estelle put down her coffee cup with a little laugh. 'How ridiculously blind men can be,' she said with tolerant kindness. 'I daresay she did no work at all, poor little thing. How could she have come with us? She had no suitable clothes.'

He looked thunderstruck, then: 'Why didn't you lend her something of yours—heaven knows you've enough and to spare.'

She turned a mildly annoyed face to his. 'My dear Christian, lend her something of mine? You must be even more blind than I imagined. Eliza is small and just a little plump and, forgive me, not very distinguished. She would have looked ridiculous in any one of my gowns.'

She bridled smilingly under the dark eyes which raked her, ignoring his ferocious look. 'After all, she is the nurse, isn't she, not one of our guests. She would hardly bring evening clothes with her even if she had them. In any case, I don't suppose she knew anything about your way of life.'

There was no expression on his face when he answered her. 'No, Eliza had no idea of how I lived, but I must remind you that she is just as much a guest in my house as you are, Estelle. And in passing, I wasn't aware that you had invited her. I believe that inviting my friends to my home is still very much my own affair.' He got up from the table and went to kiss his mother. On the way to the door he said quite pleasantly:

'Let me put you right on something; I like small women, just a little plump, and with no urge to be distinguished.'

This remark had the effect of putting a satisfied gleam into his parent's eye, while Estelle, composed as always, turned to Doctor Peters and said in a low voice: 'He is so changed, I feel that I no longer need to consider him...'

Eliza was in Professor Wyllie's room, pottering around and wondering what she should do. Christian had said nothing about her going with him, and he had been in a nasty, cold temper; if she kept out of the way, he might go without her, and when they met later she could pretend that she had forgotten the whole arrangement. Better still, he might have forgotten about it too.

She was mistaken, for he came into the room at that very moment, wished his colleague a good morning and told her in a perfectly ordinary voice to get her coat and not keep him waiting. And something in his face caused her to obey him meekly without uttering a single word of dissent.

CHAPTER NINE

THE DRIVE TO Nijmegen was short and undertaken in silence. Eliza sat beside Christian in the Bentley convertible she had never seen before and which was still taking her breath at its subdued magnificence, and wondered what she was supposed to do. Would he put her down at some convenient spot in the city, and was she to make her own way back? Or would she be expected to meet him later? She was still mulling over these problems when they reached the city's outskirts, and by the time she had paused for a minute or two in her thinking to look around her, he had drawn up before a narrow house, one of a row, in a quiet, tree-lined street with a canal running down its centre. Presumably this was to be the convenient spot. She undid her safety belt and put a hand on the door handle, but not quickly enough, for he was out of his own seat and had opened her door while she was still trying to turn its handle. 'What time do you want me to be ready?' she asked in a bright little voice.

'Come inside and see my rooms,' he invited without answering her question. 'I'd like you to meet Ina, my secretary and right hand.'

Eliza felt an absurd jealousy of this paragon as they crossed the brick pavement and entered a narrow doorway. The house was used by several doctors, she saw, their names displayed on well-polished brass plates on the wall. Christian had the ground floor; he flung open a door and waved her into a pleasant room, empty save for a middle-aged woman in a white overall sitting at a desk under the window. She got up and smiled at them as they went in and spoke to him in Dutch, then when he introduced her to Eliza, switched over to English, her mild blue eyes studying her as she talked. She broke off in a few moments, however, to speak to Christian again, who answered her briefly, took Eliza by the arm and led her to a door at the back of the room. 'My first patient is due in ten minutes, just time to see the rest of the place.'

But in his consulting room he made no effort to show her anything, but stood looking out of the window at the quiet street below. 'I'll be ready by half past eleven,' he told her, 'then I have a hospital round to do—say an hour. Would you like to come with me? I'll get someone to show you round while I'm on the wards. I thought we might have lunch before we go back home.'

She was surprised and it showed in her face. 'Oh, how nice! I didn't expect...that is, I thought you would just pick me up when you'd finished.'

He smiled at her and she looked away quickly, because although she had steeled herself against his bad temper, she hadn't expected that he would look at her like that, disarming her completely.

'If you want to look round the shops—there are some rather nice ones—and come back here at about a quarter past eleven? So that we can all have coffee. You would like to have lunch with me, Eliza?'

She felt reckless under the dark-eyed, intent look. 'Yes, very much, thank you. Would you tell me the name of this street in case I miss my way?'

He wrote the address down and gave it to her. 'Have you enough money?' he asked her matter-of-factly.

'Yes, oh, yes, thanks. I don't want to buy a great deal—presents, that's all.'

He nodded and opened the door for her, and she crossed the waiting room which already held his first two patients, exchanging smiles with Ina as she went out.

She found the shopping streets easily enough and spent an hour buying cigars for her father, and for her mother a brooch, a garnet set in a gold circle, and then wandered round, to stare at the Town Hall and its statues and peer at the old houses with their quaint gables, but she didn't go far because she was afraid of being late for Christian. As it was she was exactly on time, and the three of them drank their coffee together in the waiting room. She spoke little because she could see that Christian had instructions and notes to give to Ina, who scrawled away in shorthand and yet had time to ask kindly of Eliza if she had enjoyed her tour of the shops. They left her to clear up presently, and went out to the car, and for want of anything else to talk about Eliza made the observation that the Bentley was quite super.

Christian had eased it into the thin stream of traffic. 'I'm glad you like her. She's a beauty to handle and much roomier than the Porsche 911s I sometimes use. My mother has a little car of her own—a small Mercedes—and she's a splendid driver, though I like Hub to be with her if I'm not there.' He turned into a narrow street, going slowly. 'My mother likes you.'

Eliza said readily: 'And I like your mother; she's kind and sweet,' and then, afraid that it sounded as though she had deliberately left Estelle out of it, she added: 'Estelle is very nice too.' Perhaps she had offended him, for he made no answer. It was a relief when he turned into a large paved courtyard and stopped outside the hospital entrance.

He was met at the door by two house doctors and a pretty girl in nurse's uniform whom he introduced as Lottie. 'She will take you round the place,' he explained. 'Be back here within the hour, will you?'

He was gone, striding along the corridor without a backward glance; Eliza suspected that he had already forgotten her. Lottie, though, seemed to know a good deal about her and her English was excellent. 'I am *Hoofd Zuster* of the Medical Floor,' she told Eliza, 'and you are that also, are you not? We will therefore go first to that part of the hospital.'

She led the way down the same corridor as Christian had taken and the pair of them wandered happily in and out of small, modern wards, each patient with his or her own intercom and a nurses' station in each broad corridor. It was all well planned, light and airy, and the nurses looked exactly like the nurses in Eliza's own hospital, and when she remarked on this, they had an interesting exchange of views about caps and uniforms and whether it was best to live in or out. They became so engrossed that they had to hurry through the Surgical Wing, the Children's Unit and the Theatre Block, where they paused again to compare notes on the Intensive Care Unit, and only a glance at the clock prevented them from continuing this absorbing chat and caused them to hurry back to the entrance, to arrive just as Christian appeared in the corridor. Lottie went over to him and spoke laughingly, then said in English: 'We have had so much to talk about, you must please allow Eliza to come again, for there is a great deal she has yet to see.'

He looked interested. 'I'll see that she does,' he promised without saying how that would be arranged, so that Eliza guessed that he was just being polite, for as far as she could see, she would only be in Holland for a few more days. Professor Wyllie had finished his article and even allowing for a day or two's holiday, he must surely be thinking of returning soon. She got back into the car and when he was beside her thanked him for arranging the visit. 'Lottie was so sweet,' she told him, 'and I really enjoyed it.'

He started the car. 'Yes, she's very popular and the senior Sister on the Medical side. You liked the hospital?'

There was plenty to talk about as he drove through the city

and out on to the motorway towards Arnhem, but presently Eliza broke off in mid-sentence to say: 'We didn't come this way this morning.'

'No. We're going to a place on the Rhine for lunch. The view is charming and I've booked a window table so that we can watch the barges going up and down the river.' He turned to smile at her. 'We'll go home on one of the quieter roads and cross the river at Ochten instead of going through Nijmegen again.'

The hotel was rather splendid and its restaurant even more so. Eliza was glad that she wearing the good tweed coat and had put on the prettier of her two dresses, a pleasing garment of green and brown which matched her eyes. She saw Christian's look of approval as they sat down, and glowed under it. But he said nothing, only called her attention to the promised view and asked her what she would like to drink. She chose Dubonnet and then, under his guidance, decided on *Croquettes de Turbot Sauce Homard* followed by a *Soufflé aux Pêches*. She wasn't quite sure what this might be—a pancake with peaches didn't seem quite exquisite enough for their surroundings, but the turbot was delicious, washed down with a Chablis which her companion assured her would make the meal all the more enjoyable. He was quite right; by the time the dessert arrived, she was feeling very much at ease with him. It was like being back at Inverpolly; they had quarrelled often enough while they were there, but there had been times when they had been good friends, just as they were now. She beamed across the table at him. 'This is quite super, you know. What a lot I shall have to tell everyone when I get back!'

She eyed the confection on her plate and saw that it was very worthy of its opulent surroundings—peaches, Kirsch, apricot sauce and piles of whipped cream. She ate it with pleasure and no self-conscious remarks about putting on weight, while Christian ate his cheese and biscuits and watched her with a gleam in his eyes which she failed to see. They drank their coffee, still talking with the enthusiasm of two people who have discovered each other for the first time and then, quite reluctantly, went back to the car.

Perhaps it was the Chablis which emboldened her to ask: 'Why were you so cross yesterday when I said I wouldn't go out to dinner?'

'I thought, mistakenly, that you didn't want to come.'

'Who told you that I did?' she wanted to know suspiciously.

'Estelle—at least, she felt sure that you did and refused because you had no dress to wear, although she didn't say this until breakfast this morning.'

'She said that?' Eliza's voice was a little shrill with indignation. 'Well...' words failed her. After a few minutes she said: 'She was quite right, actually.'

He said gravely: 'Yes, I supposed she was, but I'm ashamed that I didn't think of it at the time; I was only ready to believe that you merely wished to vex me.'

They were going quite slowly along a country road, well away from Nijmegen. Eliza looked at the quiet fields sliding past, wondering how to answer that, and said finally: 'No, I had no wish to do that, it's just that I do vex you sometimes, don't I, without meaning to—or most of the time anyway.' She missed his little smile as she went on: 'Thank you for my outing, it was kind of you.'

'My pleasure. Besides, I wanted to take you to that particular restaurant, for it's as pleasant by day as it is in the evening.'

Enlightenment was painful. 'That's where you all went last night?' She didn't wait for him to answer, because she was sure that it was so. 'You took me there because of what Estelle said.' Her voice trembled with outraged pride. 'She didn't ask you to take me?'

'Of course not.' His surprise was comfortingly genuine.

'You invited me out of pity...' She stammered a little, her pretty face quite pink.

He drew into the side of the road and switched off the engine and turned to face her. 'No. If you remember I asked you to come with me to Nijmegen yesterday morning and I had already formed the intention of taking you out to lunch. Why are you so annoyed?'

It was difficult to put into words; in the end she gave up and said in a rather mumbling voice: 'I'm not.' There was really nothing she could add, she decided, and added with the air of someone making polite conversation:

'When is Professor Wyllie going home?'

If he found the change of conversation a little unexpected he gave no sign. 'The day after tomorrow, I believe.'

So that, thought Eliza, was that. She had achieved nothing; Christian would marry Estelle and be unhappy ever after, which was very silly, because it was evident to any female eye that Estelle rather liked Doctor Peters, who definitely liked her... What a stupid situation, when all it needed was one person to speak the truth. And now it was too late. She bit her lip with vexation, knowing that her hands were tied and even if she had succeeded in charming him away from Estelle there would always be the vexed question as to whether she had wanted him for his money. Perhaps it was better like this. She said overbrightly: 'Don't you have to get back for your patient?'

He had been watching her while she thought; now he laughed softly as he started the car, and she wondered why. She made stilted conversation for the rest of the short journey and once indoors, flew upstairs with a murmured excuse that she had things to do. She heard him chuckling to himself as she reached the landing.

She didn't see him again until dinner time, and then everyone else was there too. She had already told Professor Wyllie about her outing; Mevrouw van Duyl was the only other person who wanted to know if she had enjoyed herself; Estelle and Doctor Peters were too engrossed in planning another trip to more Roman remains to do more than wish her a civil good evening, and Christian, when he joined them, was a charming host and that was all. What he was really thinking behind that bland face was anyone's guess.

Eliza tackled Professor Wyllie about their return before he went to bed that night; she had made one or two efforts to speak to him in the drawing room after dinner and had been frustrated; the old man had gone off with Christian after half an hour or so and not returned until almost eleven o'clock, leaving her to keep Mevrouw van Duyl company while the other two continued making their plans for the next day. Eliza waited until her patient had made his good nights, then did the same and followed him upstairs.

'Professor van Duyl tells me that you are going back to England the day after tomorrow,' she began without beating about the bush. 'You didn't say anything to me, though. When exactly do you want to leave, because I'll need to take a look at the car. Are we going back the way we came?'

He mumbled something about not being sure and then observed testily that he wasn't in the mood to be plagued with a lot of planning at that hour of night. 'Time enough tomorrow,' he told her, and sent her off to bed.

Eliza wakened early, and unable to sleep again got up and looked out of the window. It was early February now and still winter, yet the garden carried a hint of spring in the morning half-light from a clear sky which promised sunshine later. And as she looked, Christian came round the house, striding across the lawn, Willy beside him. Presently, she knew, he would be going to his surgery and the hospital, and she thought wistfully that it would have been nice to have gone with him again. If Professor Wyllie chose to leave early the following morning, she wouldn't see much more of Christian. It was a saddening thought, but she threw it off, got dressed and finding Professor Wyllie asleep, went downstairs to find Hub, who willingly enough allowed her to visit Cat, who had just enjoyed a good breakfast and was lying back while the kittens enjoyed theirs. The little beast blinked at her and purred, looking the picture of content, and Eliza said: 'She's sweet, isn't she, Hub? I suppose Willy has gone with his master?'

'Yes, miss, half an hour ago. Would you like your breakfast now?'

She breakfasted alone, for it was still early, wondering as she ate at what hour the servants got up; the whole place shone and sparkled already and there was a cheerful coming and going of people, half of whom she hadn't yet seen. It was fantastic, in this day and age, to come across a house so well run and so well staffed.

She was on her way upstairs again when she remembered something and ran down again to ask Hub, in the hall sorting the post: 'Does Professor van Duyl really own the Lodge at Inverpolly?'

He had acquired his master's calm way of never looking surprised. 'Yes, miss. He hasn't been there very often in the last few years, though, but only yesterday he was telling me that the place is to be decorated and refurbished.'

She longed to ask more questions, but didn't like to. Christian had told her that Estelle didn't like the Scottish Highlands, or had she changed her mind since his return? It seemed unlikely. Eliza recalled the lonely place with something like homesickness as she went slowly up the staircase again.

She spent a wretched morning, typing notes from Professor Wyllie's spidery hand, for as he explained to her, there would probably be a second article in the course of time and Christian might as well be given some of the data he might require before they left. But she was finished by lunchtime and went downstairs to find Mevrouw van Duyl and Professor Wyllie drinking sherry together.

'Estelle and Doctor Peters are out,' explained her hostess in a dry voice. 'Probably they have decided to return later in the day.' She looked at Eliza with bright-eyed intentness. 'Go and take that uniform off, child, and then come and have lunch; I'm sure you don't need to be a nurse any longer. Why not go for a walk this afternoon? Just in the park, perhaps? There is a charming lake beyond the trees.'

Eliza went and put on the grey dress and did her hair very tidily, so that only a very few curls escaped the pins. The sherry she had had lent a sparkle to her eyes and the two elderly people waiting for her smiled indulgently at her as she joined them. The three of them had an enjoyable meal together, and presently, when they had had their coffee, she left them sitting by the fire in the small sitting room and went to fetch her coat.

It was cold outside but pleasant in the thin sunshine. Eliza buried her chin in the folds of her head-scarf, stuck her gloved hands into her coat pockets and started off briskly, down the formal garden, through the door in the wall, and into the park beyond. She cut across the grass here towards the group of trees which concealed the pond, and had just reached the first of them and glimpsed the water when she heard voices. Estelle and Doctor Peters, standing very close together and only a few yards from her—and Estelle was speaking in a high, clear voice which penetrated the thicket with remarkable clarity, what was more, she was speaking in English. 'It was a great mistake in the first place,' she was assuring her companion. 'I see now that we are not compatible, he and I...' She turned her head as Eliza trod on a twig. 'Why are you standing there?' she asked coldly.

'Because I came out for a walk, and how can I help but hear you when you choose to talk like a tragedy queen?' asked Eliza snappishly. 'And I'm glad to hear that you've realised at last that you and Christian don't suit—I hope you'll have the sense to break it off and leave him free to make his own plans...'

Estelle had taken a step towards her, but now she stopped abruptly, her blue eyes wide.

'So kind,' said Christian to the back of Eliza's head, 'of you to allow me to arrange my own future, although I have my doubts about it.'

He walked past her petrified form to where Estelle was standing, remembering to nod to Doctor Peters. 'I came looking for you,' he told her blandly. 'I thought it was time that we had a talk.' His eyes rested for a moment on Doctor Peters. 'But it seems that most of my talking has been done for me.' He held out a hand. 'I take it that we are no longer to be married—but friends just the same, I hope.'

Estelle's face took on a slightly frustrated look; she wasn't being allowed to squeeze a single dramatic moment from the scene, although she made the most of removing the ring from her finger, forestalled however by Christian's cheerful: 'No, no—keep it, do. I never liked it, you know. You shall have the earrings for a wedding present.' He turned away, leaving her breathing heavily with annoyance, caught Eliza by the arm and dragged her along with him.

'Musn't stay there,' he told her briskly. 'Leave them in peace to discuss their Roman remains—there's nothing they like better.'

He didn't speak again and Eliza hurried along beside him, still held firmly by the elbow so that even if she could have thought of something to say, she wouldn't have had the breath to spare. They gained the side door at last and she muttered: 'I'm going upstairs…'

'No, you're not,' his voice was mild but decisive. He turned down another passage and opened the door into the covered verandah which ran along the back of the house. It was almost warm here in the winter sunshine. Eliza, freed at last of his compelling hand, went and stood at its wrought iron railing, looking down on to the small garden below, where early daffodils were beginning to show amongst the crocus and the grape hyacinths. In the distance she could see Estelle and Doctor Peters, still a long way away, emerging from the trees.

'So you decided that Estelle wasn't suitable for me and set about putting an end to our engagement, Eliza?' Christian's voice was bland, the voice he used when he didn't want anyone to know what his real feelings were.

She said: 'I don't know how you knew that. Yes,' without looking round.

'And may I ask if you intend to interfere with any future plans I may have—marriage-wise?'

She shook her head. 'No. I was going to, you know. You see I knew that Estelle wasn't the right wife for you and I knew you didn't love her; it would never have done at all. I-I meant to marry you myself.' She swallowed back tears at the mere thought and went on in a matter-of-fact way: 'But that was before I knew that you had all this—I thought you were just a doctor.'

'I am just a doctor, Eliza.'

'Oh, no, you're not. You—we don't belong to the same world and it's no good saying different. My mother and father—I'm proud of them, but they're not...'

'I found them delightful.'

She whirled round to face him, forgetful of the tears on her cheeks. 'When? How did you find...?'

'I went to visit them. You see, when I got back home I realised that Estelle and I—I went down to meet your parents, Eliza, and I liked them immensely and I hope they liked me.'

'It doesn't make any difference.' She had turned her back on him again, remembering the tears. 'This house and the park—why, I've never seen so many people about the place—just to look after you.'

'Regrettable, perhaps, but they depend on me, you see, just as they depended on my father and his father before him.' He smiled a little at the back of her head. 'I pay them,' he pointed out mildly. 'Besides, when I marry they will have my wife to look after and in the course of time, a bunch of high-spirited children.'

She found herself asking: 'High-spirited? How do you know that?'

'I have always considered you to be that, my darling; children normally have some, at least, of the characteristics of their mother.' He smiled again. 'Tell me, how did you know that I didn't love Estelle?'

He had called her his darling, or had she dreamt it? 'You kissed me—that day the cottage was flooded. I don't think that a man who loved a girl enough to want to marry her would kiss another girl in that fashion.' She wiped her tears away with one hand. 'Oh, dear, and I made you sweep the floor.'

'An experience I thoroughly enjoyed. We must make sure that our sons learn the rudiments of house cleaning.'

Eliza said in a choking voice: 'Oh, please—I've been very silly, but at least I've been honest about it, only please don't make a joke of it.'

'Turn around, Eliza, and look at me.' He was leaning against the verandah wall, his hands in his pockets. 'Am I joking?' he asked gently, and when she looked at him she could see that he wasn't, so that her mouth curved in a smile. 'I'm most unsuitable,' she told him, 'I...'

She was given no chance to say any more; he had left the wall and his arms were holding her close. 'I see no alternative,' he told her softly, 'and I find you most suitable. Indeed, I cannot imagine my life without you, my little love.'

He bent to kiss her, and presently, when she had her breath again, she observed into his shoulder: 'I find it very strange, for you didn't like me at first, did you?'

'Now what gave you that idea? I liked you all too much; I found Estelle dwindling away to a cardboard figure which had nothing to do with me and I knew then that she never had, though I tried very hard to believe that that was not so. But you drew me like a magnet—it was as though I had my feet on a path which led to you and no one and nothing else. "When a man finds his way, Heaven is gentle"—someone wrote that, I don't know who, but it's true; I found my way just in time, didn't I, dear heart?'

He kissed her again, taking his time, and Eliza stirred in his arms and said, half laughing: 'Oh, Christian, they can see us.'

Estelle and Doctor Peters had come into the garden below them, but Christian took no notice of her, but kissed her once more. Only then did he remark: 'Good, perhaps it will encourage them to do the same. They shall come to our wedding—it might put the idea of their marrying each other into their heads.'

'I'm still waiting to be asked,' she reminded him a little tartly.

'Ah, yes, I was coming to that, my darling. Come into the study. There will be no one—only Cat and Willy and the kittens—to disturb us there, and I will ask you to marry me in a manner which you will never forget as long as you live.'

She reached up to kiss him. 'That sounds very satisfactory. I'll come and hear what you have to say,' said Eliza.

* * * * *

Ring In A Teacup

CHAPTER ONE

THE SUN, already warmer than it should have been for nine o'clock on an August morning, poured through the high, uncurtained windows of the lecture hall at St Norbert's Hospital, highlighting the rows of uniformed figures, sitting according to status, their differently coloured uniform dresses making a cheerful splash of colour against the drab paintwork, their white caps constantly bobbing to and fro as they enjoyed a good gossip before their lecture began—all but the two front rows; the night nurses sat there, silently resentful of having to attend a lecture when they should have been on their way to hot baths, unending cups of tea, yesterday's paper kindly saved by a patient, and finally, blissful bed.

And in the middle of the front row sat student nurse Lucy Prendergast, a small slip of a girl, with mousy hair, pleasing though not pretty features and enormous green eyes, her one claim to beauty. But as she happened to be fast asleep, their devastating glory wasn't in evidence, indeed she looked downright plain; a night of non-stop work on Children's had done nothing to improve her looks.

She would probably have gone on sleeping, sitting bolt upright on her hard chair, if her neighbours hadn't dug her in the ribs and begged her to stir herself as a small procession of Senior Sister Tutor, her two assistants and a clerk to make notes, trod firmly across the platform and seated themselves and a moment later, nicely timed, the lecturer, whose profound utterances the night nurses had been kept from their beds to hear, came in.

There was an immediate hush and then a gentle sigh from the rows of upturned faces; it had been taken for granted that he would be elderly, pompous, bald and mumbling, but he was none of these things—he was very tall, extremely broad, and possessed of the kind of good looks so often written about and so seldom seen; moreover he was exquisitely dressed and when he replied to their concerted 'good morning, sir,' his voice was deep, slow and made all the more interesting by reason of its slight foreign accent.

His audience, settling in their seats, sat back to drink in every word and take a good look at him at the same time—all except Nurse Prendergast, who hadn't even bothered to open her eyes properly. True, she had risen to her feet when everyone else did, because her good friends on either side of her had dragged her to them, but seated again she dropped off at once and continued to sleep peacefully throughout the lecture, unheeding of the deep voice just above her head, explaining all the finer points of angiitis obliterans and its treatment, and her friends, sharing the quite erroneous idea that the occupants of the first two rows were quite safe from the eyes of the lecturer on the platform, for they believed that he always looked above their heads into the body of the hall, allowed her to sleep on. Everything would have been just fine if he hadn't started asking questions, picking members of his audience at random. When he asked: 'And the result of these tests would be...' his eyes, roaming along the rows of attentive faces before him, came to rest upon Lucy's gently nodding head.

A ferocious gleam came into his eyes; she could have been

looking down into her lap, but he was willing to bet with himself that she wasn't.

'The nurse in the centre of the first row,' he added softly.

Lucy, dug savagely in the ribs by her nervous friends, opened her eyes wide and looked straight at him. She was bemused by sleep and had no idea what he had said or what she was supposed to say herself. She stared up at the handsome, bland face above her; she had never seen eyes glitter, but the cold blue ones boring into hers were glittering all right. A wash of bright pink crept slowly over her tired face, but it was a flush of temper rather than a blush of shame; she was peevish from lack of sleep and her resentment was stronger than anything else just at that moment. She said in a clear, controlled voice: 'I didn't hear what you were saying, sir—I was asleep.'

His expression didn't alter, although she had the feeling that he was laughing silently. She added politely, 'I'm sorry, sir,' and sighed with relief as his gaze swept over her head to be caught and held by the eager efforts of a girl Lucy couldn't stand at any price—Martha Inskip, the know-all of her set; always ready with the right answers to Sister Tutor's questions, always the one to get the highest marks in written papers, and yet quite incapable of making a patient comfortable in bed— The lecturer said almost wearily: 'Yes, Nurse?' and then listened impassively to her perfect answer to the question Lucy had so regrettably not heard.

He asked more questions after that, but never once did he glance at Lucy, wide-awake now and brooding unhappily about Sister Tutor's reactions. Reactions which reared their ugly heads as the lecture came to a close with the formal leavetaking of the lecturer as he stalked off the platform with Sister Tutor and her attendants trailing him. Her severe back was barely out of sight before the orderly lines of nurses broke up into groups and began to make their way back to their various destinations. Lucy was well down the corridor leading to the maze of passages which would take her to the Nurses' Home when a breathless nurse caught up with her. 'Sister Tutor wants you,' she said urgently, 'in the ante-room.'

Lucy didn't say a word; she had been pushing her luck and now there was nothing to do about it; she hadn't really believed that she would get off scot free. She crossed the lecture hall and went through the door by the platform into the little room used by the lecturers. There were only two people in it, Sister Tutor and the lecturer, and the former said at once in a voice which held disapproval: 'I will leave you to apologise to Doctor der Linssen, Nurse Prendergast,' and sailed out of the room.

The doctor stood where he was, looking at her. Presently he asked: 'Your name is Prendergast?' and when she nodded: 'A peculiar name.' Which so incensed her that she said snappily: 'I did say I was sorry.'

'Oh, yes, indeed. Rest assured that it was not I who insisted on you returning.'

He looked irritable and tired. She said kindly: 'I expect your pride's hurt, but it doesn't need to be; everyone thought you were smashing, and I would have gone to sleep even if you'd been Michael Caine or Kojak.'

A kind of spasm shook the doctor's patrician features, but he said merely: 'You are on night duty, Miss—er—Prendergast.' It wasn't a question.

'Yes. The children's ward—always so busy and just unspeakable last night, and then I had a huge breakfast and it's fatal to sit down afterwards,' and when he made no reply added in a motherly way: 'I expect you're quite nice at home with your wife and children.'

'I have not as yet either wife or children.' He sounded outraged. 'You speak as though you were a securely married mother of a large family. Are you married, Miss Prendergast?'

'Me? no—I'd be Mrs if I were, and who'd want to marry me? But I've got brothers and sisters, and we had such fun when we were children.'

His voice was icy. 'You lack respect, young lady, and you

are impertinent. You should not be nursing, you should be one of those interfering females who go around telling other people how to lead their lives and assuring them that happiness is just around the corner.'

She tried not to blush, but she couldn't stop herself; she was engulfed in a red glow, but she looked him in the eye. 'I don't blame you for getting your own back,' she added a sir this time. 'Now we're equal, aren't we?'

She didn't wait to be dismissed but flew through the door as though she had the devil at her heels, back the way she had come, almost bursting with rage and dislike of him; it took several cups of tea and half an hour in a very hot bath reading the *Daily Mirror* before she was sufficiently calmed down to go to bed and sleep at last.

Lucy forgot the whole regrettable business in no time at all; she was rushed off her feet on duty and when she was free she slept soundly like the healthy girl she was, and if, just once or twice, she remembered the good-looking lecturer, she pushed him to the back of her mind; she was no daydreamer—besides, he hadn't liked her.

She had expected a lecture from Sister Tutor, but no word had been said; probably, thought Lucy, she considered that she had been sufficiently rebuked for her behaviour.

She went home for her nights off at the end of the following week, a quite long journey which she could only afford once a month. The small village outside Beaminster, which wasn't much more than a village itself, was buried in the Dorset hills; it meant going by train to Crewkerne where she was met by her father, Rector of Dedminster and the hamlets of Lodcombe and Twistover, in the shaky old Ford used by every member of the family if they happened to be at home.

Her father met her at the station, an elderly man with mild blue eyes who had passed on his very ordinary features to her; except for the green eyes, of course, and no one in the family knew where they had come from. He led her out to the car, and after a good deal of poking around coaxed it to start, but once they were bowling sedately towards Beaminster, he embarked on a gentle dissertation about the parish, the delightful weather and the various odds and ends of news about her mother and brothers and sisters.

Lucy listened with pleasure; he was so restful after the rush and hurry of hospital life, and he was so kind. She had a fleeting memory of the lecturer, who hadn't been kind at all, and then shook her head angrily to get rid of his image, with its handsome features and pale hair.

The Rectory was a large rambling place, very inconvenient; all passages and odd stairs and small rooms leading from the enormous kitchen, which in an earlier time must have housed a horde of servants. Lucy darted through the back door and found her mother at the kitchen table, hulling strawberries—a beautiful woman still, even with five grown-up children, four of whom had inherited her striking good looks, leaving Lucy to be the plain one in the family, although as her mother pointed out often enough, no one else had emerald green eyes.

Lucy perched on the table and gobbled up strawberries while she answered her mother's questions; they were usually the same, only couched in carefully disguised ways: had Lucy met any nice young men? had she been out? and if by some small chance she had, the young man had to be described down to the last coat button, even though Lucy pointed out that in most cases he was already engaged or had merely asked her out in order to pave the way to an introduction to one of her friends. She had little to tell this time; she was going to save the lecturer for later.

'Lovely to be home,' she observed contentedly. 'Who's here?'

'Kitty and Jerry and Paul, dear. Emma's got her hands full with the twins—they've got the measles.'

Emma was the eldest and married, and both her brothers were engaged, while Kitty was the very new wife of a BOAC pilot, on a visit while he went on a course.

'Good,' said Lucy. 'What's for dinner?'

Her parent gave her a loving look; Lucy, so small and slim, had the appetite of a large horse and never put on an ounce.

'Roast beef, darling, and it's almost ready.'

It was over Mrs Prendergast's splendidly cooked meal that Lucy told them all about her unfortunate lapse during the lecture.

'Was he good-looking?' Kitty wanted to know.

'Oh, very, and very large too—not just tall but wide as well; he towered, if you know what I mean, and cold blue eyes that looked through me and the sort of hair that could be either very fair or grey.' She paused to consider. 'Oh, and he had one of those deep, rather gritty voices.'

Her mother, portioning out trifle, gave her a quick glance. 'But you didn't like him, love?'

Lucy, strictly brought up as behoved a parson's daughter, answered truthfully and without embarrassment.

'Well, actually, I did—he was smashing. Now if it had been Kitty or Emma...they'd have known what to do, and anyway, he wouldn't have minded them; they're both so pretty.' She sighed. 'But he didn't like me, and why should he, for heaven's sake? Snoring through his rolling periods!'

'Looks are not everything, Lucilla,' observed her father mildly, who hadn't really been listening and had only caught the bit about being pretty. 'Perhaps a suitable regret for your rudeness in falling asleep, nicely phrased, would have earned his good opinion.'

Lucy said 'Yes, Father,' meekly, privately of the opinion that it wouldn't have made a scrap of difference if she had gone down on her knees to the wretched man. It was her mother who remarked gently: 'Yes, dear, but you must remember that Lucy has always been an honest child; she spoke her mind and I can't blame her. She should never have had to attend his lecture in the first place.'

'Then she wouldn't have seen this magnificent specimen of manhood,' said Jerry, reaching for the cheese.

'Not sweet on him, are you, Sis?' asked Paul slyly, and Lucy being Lucy took his question seriously.

'Oh, no—chalk and cheese, you know. I expect he eats his lunch at Claridges when he's not giving learned advice to someone or other and making pots of money with private patients.'

'You're being flippant, my dear.' Her father smiled at her.

'Yes, Father. I'm sure he's a very clever man and probably quite nice to the people he likes—anyway, I shan't see him again, shall I?' She spoke cheerfully, conscious of a vague regret. She had, after all, only seen one facet of the man, all the others might be something quite different.

She spent her nights off doing all the things she liked doing most; gardening, picking fruit and flowers, driving her father round his sprawling parishes and tootling round the lanes on small errands for her mother, and not lonely at all, for although the boys were away all day, working for a local farmer during the long vacation, Kitty was home and in the evenings after tea they all gathered in the garden to play croquet or just sit and talk. The days went too quickly, and although she returned to the hospital cheerfully enough it was a sobering thought that when she next returned in a month's time, it would be September and autumn.

Once a month wasn't enough, she decided as she climbed the plain, uncarpeted stairs in the Nurses' Home, but really she couldn't afford more and her parents had enough on their plate while the boys were at university. In less than a year she would qualify and get a job nearer home and spend all her days off there. She unpacked her case and went in search of any of her friends who might be around. Angela from Women's Surgical was in the kitchenette making tea; they shared the pot and gossiped comfortably until it was time to change into uniform and go on duty for the night.

The nights passed rapidly. Children's was always full, as

fast as one cot was emptied and its small occupant sent triumphantly home, another small creature took its place. Broken bones, hernias, intussusceptions, minor burns, she tended them all with unending patience and a gentleness which turned her small plain face to beauty.

It was two weeks later, when she was on nights off again, that Lucy saw Mr der Linssen. This time she was standing at a zebra crossing in Knightsbridge, having spent her morning with her small nose pressed to the fashionable shop windows there, and among the cars which pulled up was a Panther 4.2 convertible with him in the driving seat. There was a girl beside him; exactly right for the car, too, elegant and dark and haughty. Mr der Linssen, waiting for the tiresome pedestrians to cross the street, allowed his gaze to rest on Lucy, but as no muscle of his face altered, she concluded that he hadn't recognised her. A not unremarkable thing; she was hardly outstanding in the crowd struggling to the opposite pavement—mousy hair and last year's summer dress hardly added up to the spectacular.

But the next time they met was quite another kettle of fish. Lucy had crossed the busy street outside the hospital to purchase fish and chips for such of the night nurses who had been out that morning and now found themselves too famished to go to their beds without something to eat. True, they hadn't been far, only to the Royal College of Surgeons to view its somewhat gruesome exhibits, under Sister Tutor's eagle eye, but they had walked there and back, very neat in their uniforms and caps, and now their appetites had been sharpened, and Lucy, judged to be the most appropriate of them to fetch the food because she was the only one who didn't put her hair into rollers before she went to bed, had nipped smartly across between the buses and cars and vans, purchased mouth-watering pieces of cod in batter and a large parcel of chips, and was on the point of nipping back again when a small boy darted past her and ran into the street, looking neither left nor right as he went.

There were cars and buses coming both ways and a taxi so

close that only a miracle would stop it. Lucy plunged after him with no very clear idea as to what she was going to do. She was aware of the taxi right on top of her, the squealing of brakes as the oncoming cars skidded to a halt, then she had plucked the boy from under the taxi's wheels, lurched away and with him and the fish and chips clasped to her bosom, tripped over, caught by the taxi's bumper.

She wasn't knocked out; she could hear the boy yelling from somewhere underneath her and there was a fishy smell from her parcels as they squashed flat under her weight. The next moment she was being helped to her feet.

'Well, well,' observed Mr der Linssen mildly, 'you again.' He added quite unnecessarily: 'You smell of fish.'

She looked at him in a woolly fashion and then at the willing helpers lifting the boy up carefully. He was screaming his head off and Mr der Linssen said: 'Hang on, I'll just take a look.'

It gave her a moment to pull herself together, something which she badly needed to do—a nice burst of tears, which would have done her a lot of good, had to be squashed. She stood up straight, a deplorable figure, smeared with pieces of fish and mangled chips, her uniform filthy and torn and her cap crooked. The Panther, she saw at once, was right beside the taxi, and the same girl was sitting in it. Doctor der Linssen, with the boy in his arms, was speaking to her now. The girl hardly glanced at the boy, only nodded in a rather bored way and then looked at Lucy with a mocking little smile, but that didn't matter, because she was surrounded by people now, patting her on the shoulder, telling her that she was a brave girl and asking if she were hurt; she had no chance to answer any of them because Mr der Linssen, with the boy still bawling in his arms, marched her into Casualty without further ado, said in an authoritative way: 'I don't think this boy's hurt, but he'll need a good going over,' laid him on an examination couch and turned his attention to Lucy. 'You had a nasty thump from that bumper—where was it exactly?' and when she didn't answer at once: 'There's no need to be mealy-mouthed about it—your behind, I take it—better get undressed and get someone to look at it...'

'I wasn't being mealy-mouthed,' said Lucy pettishly, 'I was trying to decide exactly which spot hurt most.'

He smiled in what she considered to be an unpleasant manner. 'Undress anyway, and I'll get someone along to see to it. It was only a glancing blow, but you're such a scrap of a thing you're probably badly bruised.' To her utter astonishment he added: 'For whom were the fish and chips? If you'll let me know I'll see that they get a fresh supply—you've got most of what you bought smeared over you.'

She said quite humbly: 'Thank you, that would be kind. They were for the night nurses on the surgical wards...eight cod pieces and fifty pence worth of chips. They're waiting for them before they go to bed—over in the Home.' She added: 'I'm sorry I haven't any more money with me—I'll leave it in an envelope at the Lodge for you, sir.'

He only smiled, pushed her gently into one of the bays and pulled the curtains and turned to speak to Casualty Sister. Lucy couldn't hear what he was saying and she didn't care. The couch looked very inviting and she was suddenly so sleepy that even her aching back didn't matter. She took off her uniform and her shoes and stretched herself out on its hard leather surface, muffled to the eyes with the cosy red blanket lying at its foot. She was asleep within minutes.

She woke reluctantly to Casualty Sister's voice, begging her to rouse herself. 'Bed for you, Nurse Prendergast,' said that lady cheerfully, 'and someone will have another look at you tomorrow and decide if you're fit for duty then. Bad bruising and a few abrasions, but nothing else. Mr der Linssen examined you with Mr Trevett; you couldn't have had better men.' She added kindly: 'There's a porter waiting with a chair, he'll take you over to the home—Home Sister's waiting to help you into a nice hot bath and give you something to eat—after that you can sleep your head off.'

'Yes, Sister. Why did Mr der Linssen need to examine me?'

Sister was helping her to her reluctant feet. 'Well, dear, he was here—and since he'd been on the spot, as it were, he felt it his duty...by the way, I was to tell you that the food was delivered, whatever that means, and the police have taken eye-witness accounts and they'll come and see you later.' She smiled hugely. 'Little heroine, aren't you?'

'Is the boy all right, Sister?'

'He's in Children's, under observation, but nothing much wrong with him, I gather. And now if you're ready, Nurse.'

Lucy was off for two days and despite the stiffness and bruising, she hadn't enjoyed herself so much for some time. The Principal Nursing Officer paid her a stately visit, praised her for her quick action in saving the boy and added that the hospital was proud of her, and Lucy, sitting gingerly on a sore spot, listened meekly; she much preferred Home Sister's visits, for that lady was a cosy middle-aged woman who had had children of her own and knew about tempting appetites and sending in pots of tea when Lucy's numerous friends called in to see her. Indeed, her room was the focal point of a good deal of noise and laughter and a good deal of joking, too, about Mr der Linssen's unexpected appearance.

He had disappeared again, of course. Lucy was visited by Mr Trevett, but there was no sign of his colleague, nor was he mentioned; and a good thing too, she thought. On neither of the occasions upon which they had met had she exactly shone. She dismissed him from her mind because, as she told herself sensibly, there was no point in doing anything else.

She was forcibly reminded of him later that day when Home Sister came in with a great sheaf of summer flowers, beautifully ribboned. She handed it to Lucy with a comfortable: 'Well, Nurse, whatever you may think about consultants, here's one who appreciates you.'

She smiled nicely without mockery or envy. It was super, thought Lucy, that the hospital still believed in the old-fashioned

Home Sister and hadn't had her displaced by some official, who, not being a nurse, had no personal interest in her charges.

There was a card with the flowers. The message upon it was austere: 'To Miss Prendergast with kind regards, Fraam der Linssen.'

Lucy studied it carefully. It was a kind gesture even if rather on the cold side. And what a very peculiar name!

It was decided that instead of going on night duty the next day, Lucy should have her nights off with the addition of two days' sick leave. She didn't feel in the least sick, but she was still sore, and parts of her person were all colours of the rainbow and Authority having decreed it, who was she to dispute their ruling?

Her family welcomed her warmly, but beyond commending her for conduct which he, good man that he was, took for granted, her father had little to say about her rescue of the little boy. Her brothers teased her affectionately, but it was her mother who said: 'Your father is so proud of you, darling, and so are the boys, but you know what boys are.' They smiled at each other. 'I'm proud of you too—you're such a small creature and you could have been mown down.' Mrs Prendergast smiled again, rather mistily. 'That nice man who stopped and took you both into the hospital wrote me a letter—I've got it here; I thought you might like to see it—a Dutch name, too. I suppose he was just passing...'

'He's the lecturer—you remember, Mother? When I fell asleep.'

Her mother giggled. 'Darling—I didn't know, do tell me all about it.'

Lucy did, and now that it was all over and done with she laughed just as much as her mother over the fish and chips.

'But what a nice man to get you another lot—he sounds a poppet.'

Lucy said that probably he was, although she didn't believe that Mr der Linssen was quite the type one would describe as a poppet. Poppets were plump and cosy and good-natured, and he was none of these. She read his letter, sitting on the kitchen table eating the bits of pastry left over from the pie her mother was making, and had to admit that it was a very nice one, although she didn't believe the bit where he wrote that he admired her for bravery. He hadn't admired her in the least, on the contrary he had complained that she smelt of fish...but the flowers had been lovely even if he'd been doing the polite thing; probably his secretary had bought them. She folded the letter up carefully. 'He sent me some flowers,' she told her mother, 'but I expect he only did it because he thought he should.'

Her mother put the pie in the oven. 'I expect so, too, darling,' she said carefully casual.

Lucy was still sitting there, swinging her rather nice legs, when her father came in to join them. 'Never let it be said,' he observed earnestly, 'that virtue has no reward. You remember my friend Theodul de Groot? I've just received a telephone call from him; he's in London attending some medical seminar or other, and asks particularly after you, Lucy. Indeed he wished to know if you have any holiday due and if so would you like to pay him a visit. Mies liked you when you met seven—eight? years ago and you're of a similar age. I daresay she's lonely now that her mother is dead. Do you have any holiday, my dear?'

'Yes,' said Lucy very fast, 'two weeks due and I'm to take them at the end of next week—that's when I come off night duty.'

'Splendid—he'll be in London for a few days yet, but he's anxious to come and see us. I'm sure he will be willing to stay until you're free and take you back with him.'

'You would like to go, love?' asked her mother.

'Oh, rather—it'll be super! I loved it when I went before, but that's ages ago—I was at school. Does Doctor de Groot still practise?'

'Oh, yes. He has a large practice in Amsterdam still, mostly poor patients, I believe, but he has a splendid reputation in the city and numbers a great many prominent men among his friends.'

'And Mies? I haven't heard from her for ages.'

'She helps her father—receptionist and so on, I gather. But I'm sure she'll have plenty of free time to spend with you.'

'Wouldn't it be strange if you met that lecturer while you were there?' Mrs Prendergast's tone was artless.

'Well, I shan't. I should think he lived in London, wouldn't you?' Lucy ran her finger round the remains of custard in a dish and licked it carefully. 'I wonder what clothes I should take?'

The rest of her nights off were spent in pleasurable planning and she went back happily enough to finish her night duty, her bruises now an unpleasant yellow. The four nights went quickly enough now that she had something to look forward to, even though they were busier than ever, what with a clutch of very ill babies to be dealt with hourly and watched over with care, and two toddlers who kept the night hours as noisy as the day with their cries of rage because they wanted to go home.

Lucy had just finished the ten o'clock feeds on her last night, and was trying to soothe a very small, very angry baby, when Mr Henderson, the Surgical Registrar, came into the ward, and with him Mr der Linssen. At the sight of them the baby yelled even louder, as red in the face and as peppery as an ill-tempered colonel, so that Lucy, holding him with one hand over her shoulder while she straightened the cot with the other, looked round to see what was putting the infant into an even worse rage.

'Mr der Linssen wants a word with you, Nurse Prendergast,' said the Registrar importantly, and she frowned at him; he was a short, pompous man who always made the babies cry, not because he was unkind to them but because he disliked having them sick up on his coat and sometimes worse than that, and they must have known it. 'Put him back in the cot, Nurse.'

She had no intention of doing anything of the sort, but Mr der Linssen stretched out a long arm and took the infant from her, settling him against one great shoulder, where, to her great annoyance, it stopped bawling at once, hiccoughed loudly and went to sleep, its head tucked against the superfine wool of his jacket. Lucy, annoyed that the baby should put her in a bad light, hoped fervently that it would dribble all over him.

'Babies like me,' observed Mr der Linssen smugly, and then: 'I hear from Mr Trevett that you are going to your home tomorrow. I have to drive to Bristol—I'll give you a lift.'

She eyed him frostily. 'How kind, but I'm going by train.' She added: 'Beaminster's rather out of your way.'

'A part of England I have always wished to see,' he assured her airily. 'Will ten o'clock suit you?' He smiled most engagingly. 'You may sleep the whole way if you wish.'

In other words, she thought ungraciously, he couldn't care less whether I'm there or not, and then went pink as he went on: 'I should much prefer you to stay awake, but never let it be said that I'm an unreasonable man.'

He handed the baby back and it instantly started screaming its head off again. 'Ten o'clock?' he repeated. It wasn't a question, just a statement of fact.

Lucy was already tired and to tell the truth the prospect of a long train journey on top of a busy night wasn't all that enthralling. 'Oh, very well,' she said ungraciously, and had a moment's amusement at the Registrar's face.

Mr der Linssen's handsome features didn't alter. He nodded calmly and went away.

CHAPTER TWO

LUCY SAT STIFFLY in the comfort of the Panther as Mr der Linssen cut a swathe through the London traffic and drove due west. It seemed that he was as good at driving a car as he was at soothing a baby and just as patient; through the number of hold-ups they were caught up in he sat quietly, neither tapping an impatient tattoo with his long, well-manicured fingers, nor muttering under his breath; in fact, beyond wishing her a cheerful good morning when she had presented herself, punctual but inimical, at the hospital entrance, he hadn't spoken. She was wondering about that when he observed suddenly: 'Still feeling cross? No need; I am at times ill-tempered, arrogant and inconsiderate, but I do not bear malice and nor—as I suspect you are thinking—am I heaping coals of fire upon your mousy head because you dropped off during one of my lectures... It was a good lecture too.'

And how did she answer that? thought Lucy, and need he have reminded her that her hair was mousy? She almost exploded when he added kindly: 'Even if it is mousy it is always clean and shining. Don't ever give it one of those rinses—my young sister did and ended up with bright red streaks in all the wrong places.'

'Have you got a sister?' she was surprised into asking.

'Lord, yes, and years younger than I am. You sound surprised.'

He was working his way towards the M3 and she looked out at the river as they crossed Putney Bridge and swept on towards Richmond. She said slowly, not wishing to offend him even though she didn't think she liked him at all: 'Well, I am, a bit... I mean when one gets—gets older one talks about a wife and children...'

'But I have neither, as I have already told you. You mean perhaps that I am middle-aged. Well, I suppose I am; nudging forty is hardly youth.'

'The prime of life,' said Lucy. 'I'm twenty-three, but women get older much quicker than men do.'

He drove gently through the suburbs. 'That I cannot believe, what with hairdressers and beauty parlours and an endless succession of new clothes.'

Probably he had girl-friends who enjoyed these aids to youth and beauty, reflected Lucy; it wasn't much use telling him that student nurses did their own hair, sleeping in rollers which kept them awake half the night in the pursuit of beauty, and as for boutiques and up-to-the-minute clothes, they either made their own or shopped at Marks & Spencer or C. & A.

She said politely: 'I expect you're right' and then made a banal remark about the weather and presently, when they reached the motorway and were doing a steady seventy, she closed her eyes and went to sleep.

She woke up just before midday to find that they were already on the outskirts of Sherborne and to her disjointed apologies he rejoined casually: 'You needed a nap. We'll have coffee—is there anywhere quiet and easy to park?'

She directed him to an old timbered building opposite the Abbey where they drank coffee and ate old-fashioned currant buns, and nicely refreshed with her sleep and the food, Lucy told him about the little town. 'We don't come here often,' she observed. 'Crewkerne is nearer, and anyway we can always go into Beaminster.'

'And that is a country town?' he asked idly.

'Well, it's a large village, I suppose.'

He smiled. 'Then let us go and inspect this village, shall we? Unless you could eat another bun?'

She assured him that she had had enough and feeling quite friendly towards him, she climbed back into the car and as he turned back into the main street to take the road to Crewkerne she apologised again, only to have the little glow of friendliness doused by his casual: 'You are making too much of a brief doze, Lucy. I did tell you that you could sleep all the way if you wished to.' He made it worse by adding: 'I'm only giving you a lift, you know, you don't have to feel bound to entertain me.'

A remark which annoyed her so much that she had to bite her tongue to stop it from uttering the pert retort which instantly came to her mind. She wouldn't speak to him, she decided, and then had to when he asked: 'Just where do I turn off?'

They arrived at the Rectory shortly before two o'clock and she invited him, rather frostily, to meet her family, not for a moment supposing that he would wish to do so, so she was surprised when he said readily enough that he would be delighted.

She led the way up the short drive and opened the door wider; it was already ajar, for her father believed that he should always be available at any time. There was a delicious smell coming from the kitchen and when Lucy called: 'Mother?' her parent called: 'Home already, darling? Come in here—I'm dishing up.'

'Just a minute,' said Lucy to her companion, and left him standing in the hall while she joined her mother. It was astonishing what a lot she could explain in a few seconds; she left Mrs Prendergast in no doubt as to what she was to say to her visitor. 'And tell Father,' whispered Lucy urgently, 'he's not to know that I'm going to Holland.' She added in an artificially high voice: 'Do come and meet Mr der Linssen, Mother, he's been so kind…'

The subject of their conversation was standing where she had left him, looking amused, but he greeted Mrs Prendergast charmingly and then made small talk with Lucy in the sitting room while her mother went in search of the Rector. That gentleman, duly primed by his wife, kissed his youngest daughter with affection, looking faintly puzzled, and then turned his attention to his guest. 'A drink?' he suggested hospitably, 'and of course you will stay to lunch.'

Mr der Linssen shot a sidelong glance at Lucy's face and his eyes gleamed with amusement at its expression. 'There is nothing I should have liked better,' he said pleasantly, 'but I have an appointment and dare not stay.' He shot a look under his lids at Lucy as he spoke and saw relief on her face.

Her mother saw it too: 'Then another time, Mr der Linssen— we should be so glad to give you lunch and the other children would love to meet you.'

'You have a large family, Mrs Prendergast?'

She beamed at him. 'Five—Lucy's the youngest.'

The Rector chuckled. 'And the plainest, poor child—she takes after me.'

Lucy went bright pink. Really, her father was a darling but said all the wrong things sometimes, and it gave Mr der Linssen the chance to look amused again. She gave him a glassy stare while he shook hands with her parents and wished him an austere goodbye and added thanks cold enough to freeze his bones. Not that he appeared to notice; his goodbye to her was casual and friendly, he even wished her a pleasant holiday.

She didn't go to the door to see him off and when her mother came indoors she tried to look nonchalant under that lady's searching look. 'Darling,' said her mother, 'did you have to be quite so terse with the poor man? Such a nice smile too. He must have been famished.'

Lucy's mousy brows drew together in a frown. 'Oh, lord—

I didn't think—we did stop in Sherborne for coffee and buns, though.'

'My dear,' observed her mother gently, 'he is a very large man, I hardly feel that coffee and buns would fill him up.' She swept her daughter into the kitchen and began to dish up dinner. 'And why isn't he to know that you're going to Holland?' she enquired mildly.

Lucy, dishing up roast potatoes, felt herself blushing again and scowled. 'Well, if I'd told him, he might have thought... that is, it would have looked as though... Oh, dear, that sounds conceited, but I don't mean it to be, Mother.'

'You don't want to be beholden to him, darling,' suggested her mother helpfully.

Lucy sighed, relieved that her mother understood. 'Yes, that's it.' She took a potato out of the dish and nibbled at it. 'Is it just the three of us?'

'Yes, love—the others will come in this evening, I hope—the boys just for the night to see your godfather. Kitty's visiting Agnes'—Agnes was a bosom friend in Yeovil—'but she'll be back for supper and Emma will come over for an hour while Will minds the twins.'

'Oh, good—then I'll have time to pack after dinner.'

She hadn't many clothes and those that she had weren't very exciting; she went through her wardrobe with a dissatisfied frown, casting aside so much that she was forced to do it all over again otherwise she would have had nothing to take with her. In the end she settled for a jersey dress and jacket, a swimsuit in case it was warm enough to swim, a tweed skirt she really rather hated because she had had it for a couple of years now, slacks and a variety of shirts and sweaters. It was September now and it could turn chilly and she would look a fool in thin clothes. She had two evening dresses, neither of them of the kind to turn a man's head, even for a moment. It was a pity that both her sisters were tall shapely girls. She rummaged round some more and came upon a cotton skirt, very full and rose-patterned; it might do for an evening, if they were to go out, and there was a silk blouse somewhere—she had almost thrown it away because she was so heartily sick of it, but it would do at a pinch, she supposed. She packed without much pleasure and when her mother put her head round the door to see how she was getting on, assured her that she had plenty of clothes; she was only going for a fortnight, anyway. She added her raincoat and a handful of headscarves and went to look at her shoes. Not much there, she reflected; her good black patent and the matching handbag, some worthy walking shoes which she might need and some rather fetching strapped shoes which would do very well for the evenings. She added a dressing gown, undies and slippers to the pile on the bed and then, because she could hear a car driving up to the Rectory, decided to pack them later with her other things; that would be her father's friend, Doctor de Groot.

She had forgotten how nice he was; elderly and stooping a little with twinkling blue eyes and a marked accent. Her holiday was going to be fun after all; she sat in the midst of her family and beamed at everyone.

They set off the next morning, and it didn't take Lucy long to discover that the journey wasn't going to be a dull one. Doctor de Groot, once in the driver's seat of his Mercedes, turned from a mild, elderly man with a rather pedantic manner into a speed fiend, who swore—luckily in his own language—at every little hold-up, every traffic light against him and any car which dared to overtake him. By the time they reached Dover, she had reason to be glad that she was by nature a calm girl, otherwise she might have been having hysterics. They had to wait in the queue for the Hovercraft too, a circumstance which caused her companion to drum on the wheel, mutter a good deal and generally fidget around, so that it was a relief when they went on board. Once there and out of his car, he reverted to the mild elderly gentleman again, which was a mercy, for they hadn't stopped on the journey and his solicitous attention was very welcome. Lucy retired to the ladies' and did her hair and her face, then returned to her seat to find that he had ordered coffee and sandwiches. It took quite a lot of self-control not to wolf them and then help herself to his as well.

They seemed to be in Calais in no time at all and Lucy, fortified with the sandwiches, strapped herself into her seat and hoped for the best. Not a very good best, actually, for Doctor de Groot was, if anything, slightly more maniacal on his own side of the Channel, and now, of course, they were driving on the other side of the road. They were to go along the coast, he explained, and cross over into Holland at the border town of Sluis, a journey of almost two hundred and thirty miles all told. 'We shall be home for supper,' he told her. 'We don't need to stop for tea, do we?'

It seemed a long way, but at the speed they were going she reflected that it wouldn't take all that long. Doctor de Groot blandly ignored the speed signs and tore along the straight roads at a steady eighty miles an hour, only slowing for towns and villages. He had had to go more slowly in France and Belgium, of course, for there weren't many empty stretches of road, but once in Holland, on the motorway, he put his foot down and kept it there.

It seemed no time at all before they were in the outskirts of Amsterdam, but all the same Lucy was glad to see the staid blocks of flats on either side of them. She was tired and hungry and at the back of her mind was a longing to be at home in her mother's kitchen, getting the supper. But she forgot that almost as soon as she had thought it; the flats might look rather dull from the outside, but their lighted windows with the curtains undrawn gave glimpses of cosy interiors. She wondered what it would be like to live like that, boxed up in a big city with no fields at the back door, no garden even. Hateful, and yet in the older part of the city there were lovely steepled houses, old and narrow with important front doors which opened on to hidden splendours which the passer-by never saw. To live in one of those, she conceded, would be a delight.

She caught glimpses of them now as they neared the heart of the city and crossed the circular *grachten* encircling it, each one looking like a Dutch old master. She craned her neck to see them better but remembered to recognise the turning her companion must take to his own home, which delighted him. 'So you remember a little of our city, Lucy?' he asked, well pleased. 'It is beautiful, is it not? You shall explore...'

'Oh, lovely,' declared Lucy, and really meant it. The hair-raising trip from Calais, worse if possible than the drive to Dover from her home, was worth every heart-stopping moment. She could forget it, anyway; she would be going back by boat at the end of her visit and probably Doctor de Groot would be too busy to drive her around. Perhaps Mies had a car...

They were nearing the end of their journey now, the Churchilllaan where Doctor de Groot had a flat, and as it came into view she could see that it hadn't changed at all. It was on the ground floor, surrounded by green lawns and an ornamental canal with ducks on it and flowering shrubs, but no garden of its own. The doctor drew up untidily before the entrance, helped her out and pressed the button which would allow the occupants of the flat to open the front door. 'I have a key,' he explained, 'but Mies likes to know when I am home.'

The entrance was rather impressive, with panelled walls and rather peculiar murals, a staircase wound itself up the side of one wall and there were two lifts facing the door, but the doctor's front door was one of two leading from the foyer and Mies, warned of their coming, was already there.

Mies, unlike her surroundings, had changed quite a lot. Lucy hadn't see her for almost eight years and now, a year younger than she, at twenty-two Mies was quite something—ash-blonde hair, cut short and curling, big blue eyes and a stunning figure. Lucy, not an envious girl by nature, flung herself at her friend with a yelp of delight. 'You're gorgeous!' she declared. 'Who'd have thought it eight years ago—you're a raving beauty, Mies!'

Mies looked pleased. 'You think, yes?' She returned Lucy's hug and then stood back to study her.

'No need,' observed Lucy a little wryly. 'I've not changed, you see.'

Mies made a little face. 'Perhaps not, but your figure is O.K. and your eyes are *extraordinaire*.'

'Green,' said Lucy flatly as she followed the doctor and Mies into the flat.

'You have the same room,' said Mies, 'so that you feel you are at home.' She smiled warmly as she led the way across the wide hall and down a short passage. The flat was a large one, its rooms lofty and well furnished. As far as Lucy could remember, it hadn't changed in the least. She unpacked in her pretty little bedroom and went along to the dining room for supper, a meal they ate without haste, catching up on news and reminding each other of all the things they had done when she had stayed there before.

'I work,' explained Mies, 'for Papa, but now I take a holiday and we go out, Lucy. I have not a car...' she shot a vexed look at her father as she spoke, 'but there are bicycles. You can still use a *fiets*?'

'Oh, rather, though I daresay I'll be scared to death in Amsterdam.'

The doctor glanced up. 'I think that maybe I will take a few hours off and we will take you for a little trip, Lucy. Into the country, perhaps?'

'Sounds smashing,' agreed Lucy happily, 'but just pottering suits me, you know.'

'We will also potter,' declared Mies seriously, 'and you will speak English to me, Lucy, for I am now with rust.' She shrugged her shoulders. 'I speak only a very little and I forget.'

'You'll remember every word in a couple of days,' observed

Lucy comfortably. 'I wish I could speak Dutch even half as well.'

Mies poured their after supper coffee. 'Truly? Then we will also speak Dutch and you will learn quickly.'

They spent the rest of the evening telling each other what they did and whether they liked it or not while the doctor retired to his study to read his post. 'I shall marry,' declared Mies, 'it is nice to work for Papa but not for too long, I think. I have many friends but no one that I wish to marry.' She paused. 'At least I think so.'

Lucy thought how nice it must be; so pretty that one could pick and choose instead of just waiting and hoping that one day some man would come along and want to marry one. True, she was only twenty-three, but the years went fast and there were any number of pretty girls growing up all the time. Probably she would have to settle for someone who had been crossed in love and wanted to make a second choice, or a widower with troublesome children, looking for a sensible woman to mind them; probably no one would ask her at all. A sudden and quite surprising memory flashed through her head of Mr der Linssen and with it a kind of nameless wish that he could have fallen for her—even for a day or two, she conceded; it would have done her ego no end of good.

'You dream?' enquired Mies.

Lucy shook her head. 'What sort of a man are you going to marry?' she asked.

The subject kept them happily talking until bedtime.

Lucy spent the next two days renewing her acquaintance with Amsterdam; the actual city hadn't changed, she discovered, only the Kalverstraat was full of modern shops now, crowding out the small, expensive ones she remembered, but de Bijenkorf was still there and so was Vroom and Dreesman, and C. & A. The pair of them wandered happily from shop to shop, buying nothing at all and drinking coffee in one of the small coffee bars which were all over the place. They spent a long time in

Krause en Vogelzang too, looking at wildly expensive undies and clothes which Mies had made up her mind she would have if she got married. 'Papa gives me a salary,' she explained, 'but it isn't much,' she mentioned a sum which was almost twice Lucy's salary—'but when I decide to marry then he will give me all the money I want. I shall have beautiful clothes and the finest linen for my house.' She smiled brilliantly at Lucy. 'And you, your papa will do that for you also?'

'Oh, rather,' agreed Lucy promptly, telling herself that it wasn't really a fib; he would if he had the money. Mies was an only child and it was a little hard for her to understand that not everyone lived in the comfort she had had all her life.

'You shall come to the wedding,' said Mies, tucking an arm into Lucy's, 'and there you will meet a very suitable husband.' She gave the arm a tug. 'Let us drink more coffee before we return home.'

It was during dinner that Doctor de Groot suggested that Lucy might like to see the clinic he had set up in a street off the Haarlemmerdijk. 'Not my own, of course,' he explained, 'but I have the widest support from the Health Service and work closely with the hospital authorities.'

'Every day?' asked Lucy.

'On four days a week, afternoon and evenings. I have my own surgery each morning—you remember it, close by?'

'That's where I work,' interrupted Mies. 'Papa doesn't like me to go to the clinic, only to visit. I shall come with you tomorrow. Shall we go with you, Papa, or take a taxi?'

'Supposing you come in the afternoon? I shall be home for lunch and I can drive you both there, then you can take a taxi home when you are ready.'

The weather had changed in the morning, the bright autumn sunshine had been nudged away by a nippy little wind and billowing clouds. The two girls spent the morning going through Mies' wardrobe while the daily maid did the housework and made the beds and presently brought them coffee.

She prepared most of their lunch too; Lucy, used to giving a hand round the house, felt guilty at doing nothing at all, but Mies, when consulted, had looked quite surprised. 'But of course you do nothing,' she exclaimed, 'Anneke is paid for her work and would not like to be helped, but if you wish we will arrange the table.'

The doctor was a little late for lunch so that they had to hurry over it rather. Lucy, getting into her raincoat and changing her light shoes for her sensible ones, paused only long enough to dab powder on her unpretentious nose, snatch up her shoulder bag and run back into the hall where he was waiting. They had to wait for Mies, who wasn't the hurrying sort so that he became a little impatient and Lucy hoped that he wouldn't try and make up time driving through the city, but perhaps he was careful in Amsterdam.

He wasn't; he drove like a demented Jehu, spilling out Dutch oaths through clenched teeth and taking hair's-breadth risks between trams and buses, but as Mies sat without turning a hair, Lucy concluded that she must do the same. She had never been so pleased to see anything as their destination when he finally scraped to a halt in a narrow street, lined with grey warehouses and old-fashioned blocks of flats. The clinic was old-fashioned enough too on the outside, but once through its door and down the long narrow passage it was transformed into something very modern indeed; a waiting room on the left; a brightly painted apartment with plenty of chairs, coffee machine, papers and magazines on several well-placed tables and a cheerful elderly woman sitting behind a desk in one corner, introduced by the doctor as Mevrouw Valker. And back in the passage again, the end door revealed another wide passage with several doors leading from it; consulting rooms, treatment rooms, an X-ray department, cloakrooms and a small changing room for the staff.

'Very nice,' declared Lucy, poking her inquisitive nose round every door. 'Do you specialise or is it general?'

'I suppose one might say general, although we deal largely

with Raynaud's disease and thromboangiitis obliterans—inflammation of the blood vessels—a distressing condition, probably you have never encountered it, Lucy.'

She said, quite truthfully, that no, she hadn't, and forbore to mention that she had slept through a masterly lecture upon it, and because she still found the memory of it disquieting, changed the subject quickly. The first patients began to arrive presently and she and Mies retired to an empty consulting room, so that Mies could explain exactly how the clinic was run. 'Of course, Papa receives an honorarium, but it is not very much, you understand, and there are many doctors who come here also to give advice and help him too and they receive nothing at all, for they do not wish it—the experience is great.' She added in a burst of honesty: 'Papa is very clever, but not as clever as some of the doctors and surgeons who come here to see the patients.'

'Do they pay?' Lucy wanted to know.

'There are those who do; those who cannot are treated free. It—how do you say?—evens up.'

Lucy was peering in the well-equipped cupboards. 'You don't work here?'

'No—it is not a very nice part of the city and Papa does not like me to walk here alone. When we wish to go we shall telephone for a taxi.'

Lucy, who had traipsed some pretty grotty streets round St Norbert's, suggested that as there would be two of them they would be safe enough, but Mies wasn't going to agree, she could see that, so she contented herself with asking if there was any more to see.

'I think that you have seen all,' said Mies, and turned round as her father put his head round the door. 'Tell Mevrouw Valker to keep the boy van Berends back—she can send the patient after him.' He spoke in English, for he was far too polite to speak Dutch in front of Lucy, and Mies said at once: 'Certainly, Papa. I'll go now.'

The two girls went into the passage together and Mies disappeared into the waiting room, leaving Lucy to dawdle towards the entrance for lack of anything better to do. She was almost at the door when it opened.

'Well, well, the parson's daughter!' exclaimed Mr der Linssen as he shut it behind him.

'Well, you've no reason to make it sound as though I were exhibit A at an old-tyme exhibition,' snapped Lucy, her temper fired by the faint mockery with which he was regarding her.

He gave a shout of laughter. 'And you haven't lost that tongue of yours either,' he commented. 'Always ready with an answer, aren't you?'

He took off his car coat and hung it any old how on a peg on the wall. 'How did you get here?'

Very much on her dignity she told him. 'And how did you get here?' she asked in a chilly little voice.

He frowned her down. 'I hardly think...' he began, and then broke off to exclaim: 'Mies—more beautiful than ever! Why haven't I seen you lately?'

Mies had come out of the waiting room and now, with every appearance of delight, had skipped down the passage to fling herself at him. 'Fraam, how nice to see you! You are always so busy...and here is my good friend Lucy Prendergast.'

He bent and kissed her lovely face. 'Yes, we've met in England.' He turned round and kissed Lucy too in an absent-minded manner. 'I've just one check to make. Wait and I'll give you a lift back.'

He had gone while Lucy was still getting her breath back.

Mies took her arm and led her back to the room they had been in. 'Now that is splendid, that you know Fraam. Is he not handsome? And he is also rich and not yet married, even though he has all the girls to choose from.' She giggled. 'I think that I shall marry him; I am a little in love with him, you know, although he is old, and he is devoted to me. Would we not make a nice pair?'

Lucy eyed her friend. 'Yes, as a matter of fact, you would,

and you're a doctor's daughter, too, you know what to expect if you marry him.'

'That is true, but you must understand that he is not a house doctor, he is consultant surgeon with many hospitals and travels to other countries. He has a practice of course in the best part of Amsterdam, but he works in many of the clinics also. He has a large house, too.'

'It sounds just right,' observed Lucy. 'You wouldn't want to marry a poor man, would you?'

Mies looked horrified. 'Oh, no, I could not. And you, Lucy? You would also wish to marry a man with money?'

She was saved from answering by the entrance of a young man. He was tall and thin and studious-looking, with fair hair, steady blue eyes and a ready smile. He spoke to Mies in Dutch and she answered him in what Lucy considered to be a very offhand way before switching to English.

'This is Willem de Vries, Lucy—he is a doctor also and works at the Grotehof Ziekenhuis. He comes here to work with Papa.' She added carelessly: 'I have known him for ever.'

Willem looked shy and Lucy made haste to say how glad she was to meet him and added a few rather inane remarks because the atmosphere seemed a little strained. 'Did you go to school together?' she asked chattily, and just as he was on the point of replying, Mies said quickly: 'Yes, we did. Willem, should you not be working?'

He nodded and then asked hesitantly: 'We'll see each other soon?' and had to be content with her brief, 'I expect so. You can take us to a *bioscoop* one evening if you want to.'

After he had gone there was a short silence while Lucy tried to think of something casual to say, but it was Mies who spoke first. 'Willem is a dull person. I have known him all my life, and besides, he does not kiss and laugh like Fraam.'

'I thought he looked rather a dear. How old is he?'

'Twenty-six. Fraam is going to be forty soon.'

'Poor old Fraam,' said Lucy naughtily, and then caught her breath when he said from the door behind her:

'Your concern for my advanced age does you credit, Miss Prendergast.'

She turned round and looked at him; of course she would be Miss Prendergast from now on because she had had the nerve to call him Fraam, a liberty he would repay four-fold, she had no doubt. She said with an airiness she didn't quite feel: 'Hullo. Listeners never hear any good of themselves,' and added: 'Mr der Linssen.'

His smile was frosty. 'But you are quite right, Miss Prendergast. It is a pity that we do not all have the gift of dropping off when we do not wish to listen, though.'

Her green eyes sparked temper. 'What a very unfair thing to say—you know quite well that I'd been up all night!'

Mies was staring at them both in turn. 'Don't you like each other?' she asked in an interested way.

'That remains to be seen,' observed Mr der Linssen, and he smiled in what Lucy considered to be a nasty fashion. 'Our acquaintance is so far of the very slightest.'

'Oh, well,' declared Mies a little pettishly, 'you will have to become friends, for it is most disagreeable when two people meet and do not speak.' Her tone changed to charming beguilement. 'Fraam, do you go to the hospital dance next Saturday? Would you not like to take me?' She added quickly: 'Willem can take Lucy.'

Lucy, watching his handsome, bland features, waited for him to say 'Poor Willem,' but he didn't, only laughed and said: 'Of course I would like to take you, *schat*, but I have already promised to take Eloise. Besides, surely Willem had already asked you?'

Mies hunched a shoulder. 'Oh, him. Of course he has asked me, but he cannot always have what he wants. And now I must find someone for Lucy.'

They both looked at her thoughtfully, just as though, she

fumed silently, I had a wart on my nose or cross-eyes. Out loud she said in a cool voice: 'Oh, is there to be a dance? Well, don't bother about me, Mies, I don't particularly want to go—I'm not all that keen on dancing.'

And that was a wicked lie, if ever there was one; she loved it, what was more, she was very good at it too; once on the dance floor she became a graceful creature, never putting a foot wrong, her almost plain face pink and animated, her green eyes flashing with pleasure. She need not have spoken. Mies said firmly: 'But of course you will come, it is the greatest pleasure, and if you cannot dance then there are always people who do not wish to do so. Professors...'

Mr der Linssen allowed a small sound to escape his lips. 'There are some most interesting professors,' he agreed gravely, 'and now if you two are ready, shall I drive you back?'

'Which car have you?' demanded Mies.

'The Panther.'

She nodded in a satisfied manner. 'Fraam has three cars,' she explained to Lucy, 'the Panther, and a Rolls-Royce Camargue, which I prefer, and also a silly little car, a Mini, handy for town but not very comfortable. Oh, and I forget that he has a Range Rover somewhere in England.'

'I have a bicycle too,' supplied Mr der Linssen, 'and I use it sometimes.' He glanced at Lucy, goggling at such a superfluity of cars. 'It helps to keep old age at bay,' he told her as he opened the door.

Lucy sat in the back as he drove them home, listening to Mies chattering away, no longer needing to speak English, and from the amused chuckles uttered by her companion, they were enjoying themselves. Let them, brooded Lucy, and when they reached the flat, she thanked him in a severe voice for the lift and stood silently while Mies giggled and chattered for another five minutes. Presently, though, he said in English: 'I must go—I have work to do. No, I will not come in for a drink. What would Eloise say if she knew that I was spending so much time with you?' He kissed her on her cheek and looked across at Lucy who had taken a step backwards. She wished she hadn't when she saw the mocking amusement on his face. 'Goodnight, Miss Prendergast.'

She mumbled in reply and then had to explain to Mies why he kept calling her Miss Prendergast. 'You see, I'm only a student nurse and he's a consultant and so it's not quite the thing to call him Fraam, and now he's put out because I did and that's his way of letting me know that I've been too—too familiar.'

Mies shrieked with laughter. 'Lucy, you are so sweet and so *oudewetse*—old-fashioned, you say?' She tucked an arm under Lucy's. 'Let us have coffee and discuss the dance.'

'I really meant it—that I'd rather not go. Anyway, I don't think I've anything to wear.'

Mies didn't believe her and together they inspected the two dresses Lucy had brought with her. 'They are most *deftig*,' said Mies politely. 'You shall wear this one.' She spread out the green jersey dress Lucy had held up for her inspection. It was very plain, but the colour went well with her eyes and its cut was so simple that it hardly mattered that it was two years old. 'And if you do not dance,' went on Mies, unconsciously cruel, 'no one will notice what you're wearing. I will be sure and introduce you to a great many people who will like to talk to you.'

It sounded as though it was going to be an awful evening, but there would be no difficulty in avoiding Mr der Linssen; there would be a great crush of people, and besides, he would be wholly taken up with his Eloise.

Lucy, in bed, allowed her thoughts to dwell on the enchanting prospect of turning beautiful overnight, and clad in something quite stunning in silk chiffon, taking the entire company at the dance by storm. She would take the hateful Fraam by storm too and when he wanted to dance with her she would turn her back, or perhaps an icy stare would be better?

She slid from her ridiculous daydreaming into sleep.

CHAPTER THREE

LUCY DRESSED VERY carefully for the dance, and the result, she considered, when she surveyed herself in the looking glass, wasn't too bad. Her mousy hair she had brushed until it shone and then piled in a topknot of sausage curls on the top of her head. It had taken a long time to do, but she was clever at dressing hair although she could seldom be bothered to do it. Her face she had done the best she could with and excitement had given her a pretty colour, so that her eyes seemed more brilliant than ever. And as for the dress, it would do. The colour was pretty and the silk jersey fell in graceful folds, but it was one of thousands like it, and another woman would take it for what it was, something off the peg from a large store; all the same, it would pass in a crowd. She fastened the old-fashioned silver locket on its heavy chain and clasped the thick silver bracelet her father had given her when she was twenty-one, caught up the silver kid purse which matched her sandals and went along to Mies' room to fetch the cloak she was to borrow.

Mies looked like the front cover of *Vogue*; her dress, blue and pleated finely, certainly had never seen anything as ordinary as a peg; it swirled around her, its neckline daringly low, its full skirt sweeping the floor. She whirled round for Lucy to see and asked: 'I look good, yes?' She was so pleased with her own appearance that she had time only to comment: 'You look nice, Lucy,' before plunging into the important matter of deciding which shoes she should wear. Lucy, arranging Mies' brown velvet cape round her shoulders, fought a rising envy, feeling ashamed of it; if it wasn't for Mies and her father she wouldn't be going to a big dance where, she assured herself, she had every intention of enjoying herself.

They were a little late getting there and the entrance hall of the hospital was full of people on their way to leave their wraps, stopping to greet friends as they went. Doctor de Groot took them both by the arm and made his way through the crowd and said with the air of a man determined to do his duty that he would stay just where he was while they got rid of their cloaks and when they rejoined him, he offered them each an arm and told them gallantly, if not truthfully in Lucy's case, that they were the two prettiest girls there.

The dance was being held in the lecture hall and a rather noisy band was already on the decorated platform while the hall itself, transformed for the occasion by quantities of flowers and streamers, was comfortably filled with dancers. Mies was pounced upon by Willem the moment they entered, leaving Doctor de Groot to dance with Lucy. He was a poor dancer and she spent most of her time avoiding his feet, and as he was waltzing to a rather spirited rumba, she was hard put to it to fit her steps to his; it hardly augured a jolly evening, she reflected, and then reminded herself that at least she was on the floor and not trying to look unconcerned propped up against a wall.

The band blared itself to a halt and she found herself standing beside Doctor de Groot, and staring at Mr der Linssen who still had an arm round a willowy girl with improbable golden hair worn in a fashionable frizz and wearing a gown with a plunging neckline which Lucy privately considered quite unsuitable to her bony chest. The sight of it made her feel dowdy;

her own dress was cut, she had been quick to see, with a much too modest neckline. If she had had a pair of scissors handy, she felt reckless enough to slice the front of it to match the other dresses around her; at least she wasn't bony even if she was small and slim.

She exchanged polite good evenings and was relieved when Mies joined them with the devoted Willem in tow, to kiss Mr der Linssen and shriek something at his companion who shrieked back. She then turned to Lucy to exclaim: 'Is it not the greatest fun? You have danced with Papa? Now I will find you someone to talk to,' she included everyone: 'Lucy does not wish to dance...'

It was Willem who ignored that; as the band struck up once more he smiled at her: 'But with me, once, please?'

It was one of the latest pop tunes; Lucy gave a little nod and followed Willem on to the almost empty floor; perhaps she wouldn't have any more partners for the rest of the evening, but at least she was going to enjoy this. She dipped and twirled and pivoted in her silver sandals, oblivious of the astonished stares from the little group she had just left. It was Mies who said in an amazed voice: 'But she said that she didn't like to dance!'

'She is a mouse of a girl and dowdy,' observed the tall girl, 'but one must say that she can dance.'

Mr der Linssen turned to look at her. 'Is she dowdy?' he asked in an interested voice. 'She seems to me to be quite nicely dressed.'

The two girls looked at him pityingly. 'Fraam, can you not see that it is a dress of two years ago at least which she wears?'

'I can't say that I do.' He sounded bored. 'Shall we join in?'

Lucy had no lack of partners after that. Willem, for all his shyness, had a great many friends; she waltzed and foxtrotted and quickstepped and went to supper with Willem and a party of young men and girls, and if their table was a good deal noisier than any of the others the looks they got were mostly of frank envy, for they were enjoying themselves with a wholeheartedness which was completely unselfconscious.

And after supper, as she was repairing the curly topknot and powdering her nose with Mies, that young lady remarked: 'You dance so well, Lucy, I am surprised, but I am also glad that you enjoy yourself,' she added with unconscious wisdom: 'You see, it has nothing to do with your dress.'

Lucy beamed at her. 'Oh, my dear, if I were wearing a dress like yours I'd be well away—just as you are.'

'But I am not away, I am here.'

'Ah, yes—well, it's a way of saying you're a thundering success.'

'Thundering?'

'Enormous,' explained Lucy patiently. 'Doesn't Willem dance well?'

Mies shrugged. 'Perhaps—I have danced with him so often that I no longer notice.' Her eyes brightened. 'But Fraam—now, he can dance too.'

'Who's the beanpole he's with…the thin girl?'

'That is his current girl-friend. He has many friends but never a close one—that is, girls, you understand.'

They started down the corridor which would take them back to the dance. 'Well, he seems pretty close with you, love,' declared Lucy comfortably.

'I worked on it,' confided her friend, 'but you see I have known him for a long time, just like Willem, and he doesn't—doesn't see me, if you know what I mean.'

'I know just what you mean,' said Lucy.

But apparently Mr der Linssen had seen her, for a little later he cut a polite swathe through the group of young people with whom Lucy was standing, said, equally politely: 'Our dance, I believe, Lucy,' and swung her on to the floor before she could utter whatever she might have uttered if she had had the chance.

After a few surprised moments she said to the pearl stud in

his shirt front: 'I suppose you're dancing with me because it's the polite thing to do.'

'I seldom do the polite thing, Miss Prendergast. I wanted to dance with you—you are by far the best dancer here, you know, and I shall be sadly out of fashion if I can't say that I have danced at least once with you.'

For some reason she felt like bursting into tears. After a moment she said in a tight little voice: 'Well, now you have, and I'd like to stop dancing with you, if you don't mind. You're—you're mocking me and in a minute you will have spoilt my evening.'

They were passing one of the doors leading to a corridor outside and he had danced her through it before she could say anything more. 'I'm not mocking you,' he said quietly, 'and if it sounded like it, then I'm sorry. Perhaps we don't always see quite eye to eye, Lucy, but you're not the kind of girl to be mocked, by me or anyone. I'll tell you something else since we're—er—letting our hair down. You look very nice. Oh, I know that your dress isn't the newest fashion, but it's a good deal more becoming than some that are here tonight.' He added: 'I am so afraid that something will slip,' so that she laughed without meaning to. And: 'That's better,' he observed. 'Shall we finish our dance?'

Which they did and as he danced just as well as she did, Lucy enjoyed every minute of it, but at the end he took her back to Doctor de Groot and she didn't speak to him again. She saw him continuously, dancing most of the time with the tall beauty and several times with Mies, but he didn't look at her even, and when eventually the affair finished and they came face to face in the entrance, his goodnight was said without a smile and carelessly as though she had been a chance partner whom he had managed to remember.

On Monday Doctor de Groot's receptionist, whom Mies helped for the greater part of each day, was ill so that Mies had to go to work, which left Lucy on her own. Not that she minded; she had presents to buy before she went home at the end of the week, and besides, she wanted to roam through the city, taking her own time and going where she fancied.

It was raining on Monday, so she did her shopping, going up Kalverstraat and Leidsestraat doing more looking than buying and enjoying every moment of it. She had a snack lunch at one of the cafés she and Mies had already visited and then, quite uncaring of the heavy rain, wandered off down Nieuwe Spiegelstraat to gaze into the antique dealers' windows there. She got back very wet but entirely satisfied with her day and since Mies would have to work for at least one more day, she planned another outing as she got ready for bed that night.

This time she ignored the shops and main streets and went off down any small street which took her eye, and there were many of them; most of them bisected by a narrow canal bordered by trees and a narrow cobbled road, the lovely houses reflected in the water. She became quite lost presently, but since she had the whole day before her, that didn't worry her, the sun was shining and the sky was a lovely clear blue even though the wind had a chilly nip in it.

It was while she was leaning over a small arched bridge, admiring the patrician houses on either side of the water, that somebody came to a halt beside her. Willem, smiling his nice smile and wishing her a polite good day.

'Well,' said Lucy, 'fancy seeing you here—not that I'm not glad to see you—I'm hopelessly lost.'

'Lost?' he sounded surprised. 'But I thought...' he hesitated and then went on shyly: 'I thought you might be visiting Mr der Linssen, he lives in that large double-fronted house in the centre there.'

He nodded towards a dignified town house with an important front door, wide windows and a wrought iron railing guarding the double steps leading up to its imposing entrance.

Lucy looked her fill. 'My, my—it looks just like him, too.'

Willem gave her a reproachful look. 'It is a magnificent house.'

'And I'm sure he's a magnificent man and a splendid surgeon,' said Lucy hastily. 'I just meant it looked grand and—well, aloof, if you see what I mean.'

Willem saw, all the same he embarked on a short eulogy about Mr der Linssen. Obviously he was an admirer, fired by a strong urge to follow in his footsteps. Lucy listened with half an ear while she studied the house and wondered what it was like inside. Austere? Dark panelling and red leather? Swedish modern? She would never know. She sighed and Willem said instantly: 'I am free until three o'clock. Would you perhaps have a small lunch with me?'

'Oh, nice—I was just wondering where I should go next. Are we a long way away from the main streets?'

He shook his head. 'No, not if we take short cuts.' He waited patiently while she took another long, lingering look—too lingering, for before she turned away the front door opened and Mr der Linssen came out of his house. He looked, she had to admit, very handsome and very stylish; his tailor's bill must be enormous. She turned away, but not quickly enough; he had seen them, although beyond giving them a hard stare he gave no sign of doing so. Probably he thought she was snooping, just to see where he lived. She went a little pink and marched away so quickly that Willem, for all his long legs, had to hurry to keep up with her.

'You're going the wrong way,' he told her mildly. 'We could have stayed and spoken to Mr der Linssen.'

'Why? He didn't look as though he wanted to know us,' and when she saw the shocked look on his face: 'I'm sorry, but that's what I think—he...at least, I think he doesn't like me.'

Willem gave her a puzzled look. 'Why not? He's nice to everyone, unless he has good reason to be otherwise.'

'Oh, well, we can't all like each other, can we?' She smiled at him. 'Let's have that lunch, shall we?'

They ate toasted sandwiches and drank coffee in a little coffee shop just off the Kalverstraat and presently the talk turned to Mies. It was Willem who brought her into the conversation and Lucy followed his lead because it was quite obvious to her that he wanted to talk about her.

'She's so pretty,' said Willem, 'but she's known me for years and I'm just a friend.' He looked stricken. 'She doesn't even see me sometimes.'

'Just because you are a friend,' explained Lucy. 'Now if something were to happen—if you fell for another girl perhaps, or lost your temper with Mies—I mean really lose it, Willem, or weren't available when she wanted you, then she would look at you.'

He looked surprised. 'Oh, would she? But I haven't got a bad temper; I just can't feel angry with her, and if she asked me to do something for her I'd never be able to refuse...'

'Then you're going to fall for a girl,' said Lucy. 'How about me?'

Willem's mild eyes popped. 'But I haven't...'

'Don't be silly, of course you haven't, but can't you pretend just a bit? Just enough to make her notice?'

'Well, do you think it would work? And wouldn't you mind?'

'Lord, no,' she spoke cheerfully, aware of an unhappy feeling somewhere deep inside her. 'It might work—only I'm only here for five more days, you know. You'll have to start right away.' She paused to think. 'I'll just mention that I've spent the afternoon with you and this evening you can ring me up...'

'What about?'

'Oh, anything, just so long as you do it—recite a poem or something. Then I'll say that you're taking me out tomorrow.'

'But I can't—I'm on duty.'

She sighed. 'Willem, you have to—to play-act a bit, never mind if you're on duty—so what? Mies won't know, will she? If you're off in the evening you can come round and take me out for a drink; ask her too and then pay attention to me, if you see what I mean.'

Willem was a dear but not very quick-witted. 'Yes, but then Mies will think…'

'Just what you want her to think—treat her like an old, old friend.'

'She is an old…' He caught Lucy's exasperated eye. 'Oh, well, yes, I see what you mean. All right.'

They parted presently, Willem to his duty in the hospital, Lucy to return to the flat, brooding over what she would say and hoping that it would work. And she supposed that she would have to apologise to Mr der Linssen when she had the chance.

That chance came long before she expected it. The flat was empty when she got to it, Mies was still at the surgery with her father and the housekeeper was out shopping so that when the door bell rang Lucy, armed with the list of likely callers which Mies had thoughtfully drawn up for her, went to answer it. It could be clothes back from the cleaners, the man to see to the fridge, the piano tuner… She opened the door, confident that she was quite able to deal with all or any one of them. Only it wasn't anyone on her list; it was Mr der Linssen standing there, looking rather nice until he saw who she was and his face iced over. She wished that his blue eyes weren't so hard as she wished him a rather faint good afternoon and added in a small voice: 'I'm afraid there's no one else here but me.'

He looked over her shoulder at nothing in particular. 'In that case perhaps I may come in and leave a note for Doctor de Groot.' He spoke so politely that she almost smiled at him and then turned it off just in time as he observed: 'Don't let me keep you from whatever you are doing.'

'I'm not doing anything—I've only just got back…' It seemed the right moment to explain the afternoon's little episode. 'You must have thought me very rude this afternoon, staring at your house like that, only I didn't know it was yours. I'd got lost and then Willem came along and explained where I was and told me where you lived. I could see that you were annoyed.'

'Indeed?' He had paused in his writing of the note to look at her and his eyebrows asked such an obvious question that she felt bound to go on.

'Well, yes—you didn't take any notice of us at all, did you? It was just as though you didn't see me.'

'Your powers of observation are excellent, Miss Prendergast. You were quite right, I do my utmost not to see you, although since we seem to bump into each other far too frequently, I find it becomes increasingly difficult.' He handed her the note. 'Perhaps you will give this to Doctor de Groot when he returns.'

She took it in a nerveless hand and said something she hadn't meant to say at all. 'Are you going to marry that girl—the beautiful one you danced with?'

He looked so thunderous that she took a step backwards. 'If I do, it will be entirely your fault,' he flung at her, and made for the door.

Anyone else would have left it prudently there, but not Lucy. She asked: 'Why do you say that? If you dislike me as much as all that I can't see that it makes any difference whom you marry.' She added kindly: 'There's no need to get so worked up about it, I'm sure you can marry just whom you like and I should think she would do very nicely...' A sudden thought caused her to pause. 'Perhaps you're in love with Mies? Of course, I never thought of that—she likes you very much, you know, but Willem gets in her way, but that's all right because he's rather taken to me, so if you had any ideas about keeping away from her because of him, you don't need to...'

He was at the door and she couldn't see his face. 'What a remarkable imagination you have! Have you nothing better to do with your time?'

'I'm on holiday,' she pointed out. 'You look very put out, if you could spare the time to go home and take a couple of aspirin and lie down for half an hour...' Her words were drowned in his shout of laughter as he went out and banged the door after him.

An ill-tempered man, she reflected as she went along to the kitchen to put the kettle on, and really she should dislike him, but she didn't. She hadn't forgotten how gentle he had been with the small boy outside St Norbert's and in an offhand sort of way, he'd been gentle with her too. She wondered what he would look like if he smiled and his blue eyes lost their icy stare. She would never know, of course. Whenever she met him she said or did something to annoy him. Somehow the thought depressed her, and even the pot of strong tea she made herself did little to cheer her up.

Mies came in presently, rather cross and tired, which was perhaps why she only shrugged her shoulders when Lucy told her about her meeting with Willem. And when he telephoned later and Lucy told her that he had asked her out for the following evening, all she said was: 'Nothing could be better; there is a film I wish to see and I shall ask Fraam to take me.' She had a lot to say about Fraam that evening, although none of it, when Lucy thought about it later, amounted to anything at all, and she harped on her feelings about him; she would marry him at once, she had declared rather dramatically, and when Lucy had asked prosaically if he had asked her yet, had said peevishly that he would do so at any time. It seemed strange to Lucy that he wasn't aware of Mies' feelings, but perhaps Mies was concealing them—clever of her, for Mr der Linssen didn't strike her as the kind of man who wanted a girl to fall into his lap like an apple off a tree. She supposed they would make a very happy couple, although at the back of her mind was the unvoiced opinion that Mies was too young for him—not in years, that didn't matter, but in her outlook on life, and it was going to be hard on poor Willem. Lucy curled up in a ball and closed her eyes. Her last sleepy thought was of the lovely old house where Mr der Linssen lived; she would dearly love to see inside it.

And so she did, but hardly in the manner in which she would have wished. It was a house which asked for elegance; well-groomed hair, a nicely made-up face, good shoes and as smart an outfit as one could muster, so it was irritating at the least to discover herself inside its great door in slacks, a raincoat which was well-worn to say the least of it and a headscarf sopping with rain.

She had popped out directly after breakfast to buy the fruit which Mies had forgotten to order the day before, and as the greengrocer's shop was in a nearby main street, she took a short cut—a narrow dim *steeg* bounded by high brick walls, with here and there a narrow door, tight closed. It was really no more than an alley and infrequently used, but now, as she turned into it, she had seen a group of boys bending over something on the ground. They had looked round at the sound of her footsteps and then got to their feet and raced off, their very backs so eloquent of wrongdoing that she had broken into a run, for they had left something lying there... A cat, a miserable scrawny tabby cat with a cord tightly drawn round its elderly neck. She had dropped to her knees on the wet, filthy cobbles and tried frantically to loosen the knot. She needed a knife or scissors and she had neither; she picked the beast up and ran again, this time towards the busy street she could see at the end of the *steeg*. It was only as she emerged on to it that she paused momentarily—a shop or a passer-by, someone with a pocket knife... The pavement seemed full of women and the nearest shop was yards away. Lucy was on the point of making for it when she heard her name called. At the kerb was a Mini and in it Mr der Linssen, holding the door open. She had scrambled in and demanded a knife with what breath she had left and he, with a brief glance which took in the situation, had drawn away from the kerb back into the stream of traffic. 'I can't stop here—there are lights ahead—it's only a few yards, let's pray they're red.'

They were. He had whipped out a pocket knife and carefully cut the cord and was ready to drive on as the queue of cars started up again. Lucy looked at the cat; it looked in a poor way and she said frantically: 'Oh, please, take me to a vet...'

'We'll take him home, it's close by.' Mr der Linssen had sounded kind and assured. 'If he's survived so far, he's still got a chance. Let him stay quiet in the meantime, he needs to get some air into his lungs.'

And when they had reached his house, he took the cat from her and ushered her in through the door and into a long narrow hall with panelled walls and an elaborate plaster ceiling and silky carpets on its black and white paved floor, only she hadn't really noticed them then, she had been so anxious about the cat. She hadn't noticed either that she was dripping all over his lovely carpets, her hair sleeked to her head and her scarf awash on top of it. She had been dimly aware that a stout middle-aged man had appeared silently and helped her off with her raincoat and taken the deplorable scarf with a gentle smile and had hurried to open a door, one of several leading from the hall. A large light room because of its high windows, furnished with a great desk with a severe chair behind it and several more comfortable ones scattered around. There were shelves of books too and a thick carpet under her feet as she hurried along behind Mr der Linssen.

He had settled the cat carefully on a small table and bent to examine it while she stood by, hardly daring to look. Presently he had unbent himself. 'Starved,' he had observed, 'woefully neglected and one or two tender spots, but no broken bones or cuts and as far as I can tell, the cord didn't have time to do too much damage.'

And Lucy, to her shame, had allowed two tears to spill over and run down her cheeks. She went hot with mortification when she remembered that, although he had pretended not to see them, turning away to ring the bell and when the same stout man appeared soft-footed, giving some instructions in his own language. Only then had he turned round again so that she had had the time to wipe the tears away. 'Rest and food,' he observed cheerfully, 'and in a few days' time he'll be on his feet again. What are we going to call him?'

'You mean you'll keep him? Give him a home?'

'Why not? My housekeeper has a cat, they'll be company for each other and Daisy won't mind.'

'Daisy?' She had been aware of a strange feeling at his words; could Daisy be the lovely girl who had been at the dance?

'My golden Labrador. Ah, here is Jaap with the milk.'

The cat's nose twitched and it put out a very small amount of tongue, but that was all; lapping seemed beyond it. Lucy had dipped a finger in the creamy warmth and offered it and after a minute the tongue had appeared again and this time it licked her finger eagerly, even if slowly. It had taken quite a time to get the milk into the cat and by then it had been tired with the effort. Mr der Linssen, sitting on the side of his desk, watching, had simply said: 'Good, two-hourly feeds for a day or so, I think,' and had nodded in a satisfied manner when Jaap appeared with a box, cosily lined with an old blanket. Lucy had watched the little animal carefully laid in it and borne away and in answer to her questioning look, Mr der Linssen had said: 'To the kitchen—it's warm there and there are plenty of people to keep an eye on it. I'll find time to see a friend of mine who's a vet and ask him to give the beast a going over.'

He had come to stand in front of her and there seemed a great deal of him. 'Thank you very much, I'm so grateful.' She looked down at her sensible shoes, muddied and wet. The damage she must have done to those carpets!

'Well,' said Mr der Linssen easily, 'I think we've earned a cup of coffee, don't you?'

Lucy looked at him, noticing now that he was in slacks and a sweater and needed a shave. 'You've been at the hospital. Oh, you must be tired. I—I won't have any coffee, thank you, I was going shopping for Mies.' The name reminded her of their previous conversation and she flushed uncomfortably. But he had chosen to forget, it seemed, for he had spoken pleasantly.

'Only since four o'clock. I'm wide-awake but famished. Do keep me company while I have my breakfast, in any case your raincoat won't be dry yet.'

So she had gone with him to a charming little room at the back of the house. It overlooked a small paved yard surrounded with roses and even in the light of the grey morning outside, it was cosy; mahogany shining with polishing and a rich brocaded wall hanging, ruby red, almost obscured by the paintings hung upon it. He had sat her down at a circular table and poured coffee for her, just as though he hadn't heard her refusing it. And she was glad enough to drink it, it gave her something to do while he made his breakfast, talking the while of this and that and nothing in particular. Presently, when he had finished, she said rather shyly that she should go and he had agreed at once. Remembering that she felt a little hurt, but stupidly so, she told herself. There was no reason why he should wish for her company; he had been helpful and kind and courteous, but probably he had had just about enough of her by then. But he had taken her to see the cat before she went; sleeping quietly before the Aga in the enormous, magnificently equipped kitchen in the basement, and then he had excused himself because he had patients to see and Jaap had shown her out with a courtesy which had restored her self-esteem.

She had thought about the whole episode quite a lot during the day. The house, what she had seen of it, was every bit as lovely as she had imagined it would be and considering that Mr der Linssen had no time for her, he had been rather a dear. She hoped that she would hear about the cat—perhaps Mies could find out for her. She ate her solitary lunch and then wrote a letter, forgetting that she would more than likely be home before it got there, but she couldn't settle to anything. She supposed that seeing the house had excited her; she had been so curious about it…

Mies came home presently with the news that the receptionist would be back in the morning so that she would be free once more, and they fell to planning the day. 'And we'll get Willem to take us to the *bioscoop*,' declared Mies, and then said a little crossly: 'Oh, well, isn't he taking you this evening? I forgot. Not that I care, I see too much of him, he is always under my feet.'

So Lucy felt a little guilty as she and Willem, who was free after all, walked down Churchilllaan to the nearest bus stop. Mies might not love Willem, but she had got used to him being around; he had been her slave, more or less, for years, and anyway, she had said that she wanted to marry Fraam. It was all rather muddled, thought Lucy, waiting beside Willem to cross the street. There wasn't much traffic about, for the weather was still wet and chilly; she watched the cars idly. Mr der Linssen's Panther de Ville or the Rolls for that matter, or failing those, his Mini would be preferable to a bus ride. The Rolls slid past as she thought it, with him at the wheel and Mies beside him. Mies didn't see her, but he did. His smile was cool and she looked away quickly to see if Willem had seen them too. He hadn't, and a good thing too, she decided. Bad enough for her evening to be spoilt, although she wasn't quite clear as to why it should be. There was certainly no reason for Willem to have his evening spoilt too.

CHAPTER FOUR

AT BREAKFAST THE next morning Mies monopolised the conversation. She had, quite by accident, she explained airily, met Fraam when she went out to post letters and he had taken her to the hospital to pick up some notes he had wanted before bringing her home. It was only after a lengthy description of this that she asked nonchalantly if Lucy had enjoyed herself.

Lucy answered cautiously. It was a little difficult; she had promised to help Willem to capture Mies' attention and she fancied that Mies wasn't best pleased that he had taken her out, but, on the other hand, if Mies was really in love with Mr der Linssen and he with her, surely they should be allowed to stay that way? And in that case what about Willem?

'Willem is nice to go out with,' she observed, aware that it was a silly remark. 'I expect you go out with him quite a lot.'

Mies shrugged. 'When there is no one else.'

'He wondered,' persisted Lucy, 'if we might all go out this evening—just for a drink somewhere.'

She was a little surprised at Mies' ready agreement. 'Only it must be dinner too,' she insisted. 'We will go to 't Binnenhofje, the three of us—Papa has an engagement and will not be home; it will be convenient to go out.'

'It sounds lovely,' agreed Lucy, 'but didn't you tell me it was wildly expensive? I mean, Willem...'

'Do not worry about Willem, he has plenty of money, his family are not poor. I will telephone him and tell him to book a table for eight o'clock.'

'I don't think I've anything to wear,' said Lucy worriedly.

'The patterned skirt and the pink blouse,' Mies decided for her, 'and I—I shall wear my grey crêpe.' She got up as she spoke. 'I shall telephone now.'

And she came back presently with the news that Willem would be delighted to take them out and would call for them in good time. 'And now what shall we do with our day?' enquired Mies. 'You have bought presents already? Then we go down to the hospital; there is something I have to deliver for Papa—a specimen.'

Lucy didn't mind what she did; she enjoyed each day as it came, although she did make the tentative suggestion that they might go to the clinic just once more before she went home.

'But why?' asked Mies. 'You have seen it.'

'Yes, but I found it very interesting.'

'Well, there is no time,' said Mies positively. 'Today is Friday and on Saturday you go home. Why do you want to go?'

'I said—it's interesting, but it doesn't matter, Mies. I've had a simply super time, you've been a dear—you must come and stay with us...'

'If I am still unmarried,' said Mies demurely. 'And now we go out. We can take a bus and walk the rest of the way.'

Lucy agreed readily although at the back of her mind was the vague idea that she wanted to see Mr der Linssen just once more before she left Amsterdam. She wasn't sure why, perhaps to make sure that he was as taken with Mies as she was—apparently—with him. But now it seemed unlikely that she would see him again, not to speak to, that was. Possibly she would attend another of his lectures in the future and watch him standing on the lecture hall platform, holding forth learnedly about something or other. Pray heaven she wouldn't be on night duty.

It was another wet day; she put on her raincoat and the sensible shoes, wondering about the cat. She could of course telephone Mr der Linssen's house and find out. She tied a scarf under her determined little chin and joined Mies in the hall.

The bus was packed and they had to stand all the way so that the short walk at the end of it was welcome even though it was wet. The hospital looked gloomy as they approached it and it wasn't much better inside. Lucy, told to stay in the entrance hall while Mies went along to the Path. Lab., wandered round its sombre walls. Mies was being a long time; Lucy had gone round the vast echoing place several times, perhaps she had some other errand or had met someone. Willem, or Mr der Linssen? And had it been arranged beforehand? she wondered. She paused to stare up at a plaque on the wall. She couldn't understand a word of it, but probably it extolled the talents and virtues of some dead and gone medical man.

Advancing footsteps and voices made her turn round in time to see Mr der Linssen coming down the central staircase, hedged about by a number of people, rather like a planet with attendant satellites. He passed her within a foot or so, giving her a distant nod as he went and then stopped, spoke to the man beside him and came back to her, leaving the others to go on. He wasted no time in unnecessary greetings but: 'You return to England tomorrow, do you not?'

She nodded, studying him; he looked different in his long white coat; she liked him better in slacks and a sweater... 'How's the cat?' she asked.

'Making a good recovery. He has the appetite of a wolf but a remarkably placid disposition.'

'He's no trouble?' she asked anxiously. 'You really are going to keep him?'

He frowned. 'I told you that I would give him a home. Have you any reason to doubt my word?'

Very touchy. Lucy made a vigorous denial, then sought to lighten the conversation. 'Mies is here—she went to the Path. Lab.'

Mr der Linssen nodded carelessly. 'She comes frequently with specimens from her father's clinic.' He seemed to have nothing to say and Lucy wondered just why he had stopped to speak to her. She tried again. 'I expect you're very busy...'

'Offering me a chance to escape, Miss Prendergast?' His voice was silky. 'But you would agree with me that not to say goodbye to you would be lacking in good manners?'

This wasn't a conversation, she thought crossly, it was questions and answers, and how on earth did she answer that? She said carefully: 'Well, I'm glad you stopped to say goodbye, and considering, it was kind of you to do so.'

'Considering what?'

She looked up at him and glimpsed an expression on his face she had never seen before. It had gone before she could decide what it was, to be replaced by a polite blandness. And that told her nothing at all.

She said in a serious voice: 'You said once that you tried not to see me but somehow we keep meeting—it's silly really, because we don't even live in the same country. I was surprised to see you at the clinic—I never thought...but I've tried to keep out of your way.'

'Have you indeed? I wonder...' His bleep interrupted him and she heard his annoyed mutter. She was taken completely by surprise when he bent and kissed her fiercely before striding away to the porter's lodge across the hall and picking up the telephone there. He was racing up the staircase without so much as a glance in her direction, and all within seconds. Lucy was still wondering why he had kissed her when Mies arrived.

'Was I a long time?' She looked smug. 'I met Fraam.'

Lucy, accompanying her out of the hospital entrance, forbore from saying that she had met him too. For the last time, she reminded herself.

She wondered, as she dressed that evening, if their dinner party was going to be a success; three wasn't an ideal number, Mies could surely have found another man. Lucy, determined to do justice to the occasion even if she was going to be the odd one out, took time to roll her hair into elaborate curls again. And it was worth the effort, for the hair-do added importance to her pink blouse and patterned skirt. Not that it mattered, since there would be no one to see. She wondered too how Willem would behave; was he going to carry on pretending that he was gone on her or would he devote himself to Mies?

She took a last look at herself in the looking glass and went along to borrow the brown cloak again, for she had nothing else.

Mies looked lovely, but then she always did. The grey crêpe was soft and clinging and feminine and, unlike the gown she had worn to the dance, demure. Lucy, admiring it, thought that it might please Willem mightily.

It did. When he arrived at the flat he could hardly take his eyes off Mies, and he certainly didn't notice her marked coldness towards him. And if he's going to drool all over her all the evening, he'll never get anywhere, thought Lucy crossly, and then told herself that she was silly to bother, she wouldn't see them again for a long time, and by then they would either have married or have forgotten each other.

Binnenhofje was a smart place. Lucy immediately knew herself to be a trifle old-fashioned in her dress the moment they were inside its door. The younger women were wearing rather way-out dresses and the older ones were elegantly turned out in the kind of simple dress which cost a great deal of money. True, there were one or two tourists there, easily recognisable in their uncrushable manmade fibres, but all the same, she felt like a maiden aunt. She corrected herself; like the parson's daughter. Which naturally put her in mind of Mr der Linssen and she had leisure enough to think about him, for Willem and Mies were deep in a conversation of their own for the moment. But presently they remembered that she was there, excused themselves laughingly on the plea that they had been reminiscing and began a lighthearted chatter which lasted them through the starters and the Sole Picasso.

It was while Lucy was deciding between crêpes Suzette and Dame Blanche that she happened to look up and see Mr der Linssen sitting at a table on the other side of the restaurant. He had a stunning redhead with him this time, but he wasn't looking at her, he was staring at Lucy who was so surprised that she dropped the menu and ordered a vanilla ice cream—something, she told herself silently, she could have had at home any time and wasn't really a treat at all. She took care not to look at him again, something she found extraordinarily difficult because she wanted to so badly, but it wasn't for a little while that she realised that Mies knew that he was there, which would account for her animated conversation and her gorgeous smile, as well as the casual way her gaze swept round the place every minute or so. He hadn't been staring at her at all, Lucy concluded, but at Mies; they had both known the other was to be there.

They must be terribly in love. She frowned. In that case why hadn't they dined together? The redhead couldn't be anyone very important in his life if he was so smitten with Mies, and poor Willem could have taken her out without Mies planning this dinner and no one would have been any the wiser, and much happier. For Willem had seen him now; Lucy could see him thinking all the things she herself had just mulled over, because he looked puzzled and worried and then put out. He made it worse by asking Mies if she knew that Fraam was sitting nearby and when she said Oh, yes, of course, wanted to know if she had known before they had arrived at the restaurant.

Mies gave him one of her angelic smiles. 'Willem, that's why I wanted to come.'

Lucy plunged into what she could see was fast becoming a ticklish situation.

'I thought it was a farewell dinner party for me,' she said lightly, and was instantly deflated by Mies' 'Oh, Lucy, that was a good reason for coming, do you not see?'

She swallowed her hurt pride. 'Then why not have just dined with Mr der Linssen? Willem and I would have been quite happy in a snack bar.'

Mies said huffily: 'He already had a date, I found that out, but now he can see me, can he not, and that is better than nothing.'

Willem had remained silent, but now he began to speak. It was unfortunate for Lucy that he did so in his own language, but whatever he was saying he was saying in anger—nicely controlled, but still anger. Something which so surprised Mies that she just sat and listened to him, her lovely mouth slightly open, her eyes round. What was more, she didn't answer back at all. Lucy, her coffee cooling before her, sat back and watched them both and was glad to see that Mies was actually paying attention to Willem, even looking at him with admiration. When he had at last finished she said something softly in quite a different voice from the one she usually used when she spoke to him, and then smiled. Lucy was pleased to see that he didn't smile back, only went on looking stern and angry and somehow a lot older than he was, then turned to her and said with great dignity: 'I am sorry, Lucy, that we have spoilt your last evening here. You were quite right, you and I would have had a pleasant evening together. Mies has behaved disgracefully. I have told her that she is spoilt and has had her way far too long; it is time that she grew up, and I for one do not wish to have anything to do with her until she has done so.'

It seemed a little severe. Lucy gave him a rather beseeching look which somehow she managed not to change to one of understanding when the eyelid nearest her winked. Willem, it seemed, was a man of parts.

Mies, of course, hadn't seen the wink. She said softly still: 'Oh, Willem, you're joking,' and then when he didn't reply: 'You are, aren't you?'

He gave her a long steady look across the table. 'You and I will have a talk, Mies, but not now. We are giving Lucy a farewell dinner party, are we not?'

And Mies, to Lucy's surprise, agreed meekly. They finished the meal in an atmosphere of enjoyment, even if they all had to work rather hard at it, and when they left presently, Mies did no more than nod across at Fraam as did Willem. Lucy didn't look at him until the very last moment and then only for a few seconds. He smiled so faintly that she wasn't sure if he had or not. They went home in a taxi, on the surface in good spirits. It wasn't until Lucy was in bed and on the edge of sleep that she began to wonder who was in love with whom; whichever way she looked at it, she hadn't helped much. True, Willem had pressed her hand and thanked her when she had wished him goodbye, but she wasn't quite sure why, and as for Mies, she was her usual gay self, only she didn't mention Fraam at all. Lucy wasn't sure if that was a good sign or not.

She was to return on the night ferry to Harwich and go from there straight to St Norbert's where she was due on duty the following morning, which meant that she still had the whole day in Amsterdam. Packing was something which could be done in half an hour—indeed, she had it almost finished by the time she went to breakfast. Doctor de Groot bade her goodbye at the table, for he had a day's work before him and was going on to a meeting in the evening, so that he wouldn't get home until she had left, but Mies was free and the two of them planned a last look at the shops with coffee at one of the cafés or in the Bijenkorf and after lunch at the flat, one last canal trip through the city. True, Lucy had taken the trip twice already, but she found it fascinating and as she pointed out to Mies, it would fill in the afternoon very nicely and the weather was too good to waste it in a cinema.

The canal boat was only half full and they sat as far away from the guide as they could, so that Mies could point out the now familiar highlights of the trip to Lucy. 'Oh, I'd like to live here,' breathed Lucy, craning her neck to see the last of the smallest house in the city.

Mies turned to look at her. 'Well, all you have to do is to marry someone who lives here,' she observed.

'I don't know anyone...'

'That is not so; you know Willem and you know Fraam.'

'But Willem never looks at anyone but you, Mies, and Mr der Linssen...' Lucy sighed, 'well, take a look at me, and then think of all those lovely girls I've seen him with.' She added firmly: 'Besides, he's not my type.'

Mies hadn't been listening. 'Willem doesn't look at other girls?' she wanted to know.

'You know he doesn't. He talked about you all the time when we were out.'

'But he is angry with me. Perhaps I shall never see him again.' Mies sounded worried.

'Oh, pooh, of course you will, but I think he'll read you a lecture when he does.'

'Read a lecture?'

Lucy explained. 'And you'd better listen,' she declared, 'unless you're really in love with Mr der Linssen or he's in love with you.'

Mies looked a little shy. 'It would be such a triumph,' she confided. 'He would be a prize which would make me the envy of all.'

'You make him sound like an outsize fish—you ought to make up your mind, Mies.'

Her friend turned thoughtful blue eyes on to her. 'You wish Fraam for yourself, perhaps, or Willem?'

'Good lord, no!' Lucy was genuinely shocked. Willem was a dear, but the only feelings she had for him were motherly, and as for Mr der Linssen...she stopped to think about that; certainly not motherly. She decided not to pursue the matter further.

It had been decided that it would be better for her to catch an earlier train to the Hoek. The boat train was invariably full and it was far better to get on board before it arrived. The two girls had tea out and then went back for Lucy to finish the last of her packing before having a light supper. Lucy felt a vague sadness when it was time to leave; she had had a lovely holiday, she declared to Mies, who had gone to the station to see her off. 'And you must come and see us.' She kissed Mies warmly, 'and I hope you...' She tried again: 'I hope that whatever you decide, you'll be very happy. Let me know.'

She hung out of the window, waving for as long as she could see Mies on the fast-receding platform. The station wasn't exactly beautiful, but it was clean and airy and had an atmosphere of bustle and faint excitement and in the gathering dusk of a fine September evening, it looked romantic too—anything could happen, she thought vaguely as she turned away and sat down—only not to her, of course. Anything romantic, that was.

She occupied her journey staring from the window, watching the lights in the villages and towns as the dusk deepened, conscious that she would have liked to have got out at each stopping place and got on a train for Amsterdam. She fell to wondering what would happen if she followed her inclination instead of obeying circumstances; Mies would be surprised but nice about it and so would her father, but she suspected that it would fall very flat the second time round. She would have to go off on her own—she became rather carried away here—get a job and somewhere to live. Her sensible head told her that there were things like money, work permits and an ability to speak the language standing in the way of her fantasy, and it would be more sensible to concentrate upon her future in England.

Less than a year now and she would take her Finals. She tried to imagine herself as a staff nurse, even as a ward Sister, but failed singularly in her efforts to get enthusiastic about it. She went back to peering through the dusk at the placid countryside. But now it wasn't placid any more; the train was running through the busy Europort, its chimneys and refineries mercifully hidden by the evening dark, and then it had slid to a quiet halt in the Hoek station. The train wasn't very full. Lucy waited until most of the passengers had got out and then got down on to the platform and turned round to haul out her case. Her hand was actually about to touch it when Mr der Linssen's calm voice said, 'Allow me,' from somewhere behind her, causing her to shoot round like a top out of control and go smack into his trendy waistcoat. 'Well,' said Lucy, 'I never did!' She retreated a few inches and looked up at him. 'I mean—you here and whispering at me like that—I nearly took off!'

She gave him a questioning look and he said at once: 'Doctor de Groot couldn't get away to see you off. I hope you don't mind me standing in for him?'

She was surprised but nicely so. 'That's awfully sweet of him to think of it, and nice of you. Did you happen to be coming this way?'

'Er—yes, in a manner of speaking.' He spoke with a soothing casualness which made it all seem very offhand and relieved her of any feelings of guilt that she might be wasting a perfectly good evening for him.

'Have you got your ticket?' He had conjured up a porter and handed over her case. 'There's time for a cup of coffee—it will give everyone else a chance to go on board. The boat train isn't due in for some time yet.'

A cup of coffee would be nice, thought Lucy, it must have been the thought of that which made her feel suddenly quite cheerful. They walked through to the restaurant, full of travellers, heavy with smoke and smelling of well-cooked food. There weren't any empty tables; they sat down at one in the window, opposite a stout middle-aged pair who smiled at them and wished them good evening and then resumed their conversation over bowls of soup.

'Hungry?' asked Mr der Linssen, and when she hesitated: 'I am. Let's have soup before the coffee.'

'I did have a kind of supper before I left,' explained Lucy, 'but the soup smells delicious.'

She smiled across at the woman opposite her, who beamed back at her and spoke in Dutch. Mr der Linssen answered for her, falling into an easy conversation in which only a word or two made sense to her, and when he shook his head and laughed a little she asked a little impatiently: 'Why do you laugh? What are you talking about?'

The soup had come, he handed her pepper and salt and offered her a roll before he answered. 'The lady thought that we were man and wife, but don't worry, I put her right at once.'

'I'm not worried,' Lucy said tartly, 'why should I worry about something so absurd? This soup is quite heavenly.'

Her companion's eyes gleamed momentarily. 'We make good soup in Holland,' he offered with the air of a man making conversation. 'My mother is a splendid cook and makes the most mouth-watering soups.'

'Your mother?' Lucy swallowed a spoonful and burnt her tongue. 'I didn't know you had a mother.'

He considered this, his head a little on one side. 'I don't remember you ever asking me,' he pointed out placidly. 'I have a large family, as large as yours. I hope that you will give my regards to your parents when you see them. Do you go home?'

She spooned the last of her soup. 'No, I'm due back on duty at two o'clock tomorrow. I'll go home as soon as I get days off, though.'

'And you take your Finals soon?' he asked idly.

'Next summer.' Their coffee had come and she handed him a cup.

'Ah—then I presume you will embark on a career?'

'Well, I haven't much choice,' said Lucy matter-of-factly. 'I expect I shall like it once I'm in a—a rut.'

'You have no wish to get out of a rut? To marry?' He added: 'To—er—play the field?'

What a silly question, she told herself silently. She turned her green eyes on him. 'Me? You're joking, of course.' She went on kindly: 'I expect you're so used to taking out beautiful girls...

they're the ones who play the field, though I'm not quite sure what that means...that you don't know much about girls like me. Parsons' daughters,' as if that explained completely.

Apparently it did. He sat back in his chair, very much at his ease. 'You know, you're quite right. What an interesting little chat we are having.' He glanced at the paper-thin gold watch on his wrist.

'Unfortunately I think you should go on board; the boat train is due in ten minutes or so.'

Lucy got up at once. Her companion might have found their chat interesting, but she had not, although she didn't quite know why. She thanked him politely for her soup and coffee, reiterated her hope that he hadn't wasted too much of his evening on her and went to the ticket barrier.

Mr der Linssen stayed right with her. As she got out her ticket he said: 'I could of course give you a meaningless social peck on your cheek. I prefer to shake hands.'

She was conscious of deep disappointment; a peck on the cheek from someone like Fraam would have done a great deal more for her self-esteem than a handshake. She stuck out a capable little hand and felt his firm cool fingers engulf it. 'I've had a very pleasant holiday,' she told him, for lack of anything more interesting to say.

He let her hand go. 'The finish of a chapter,' he observed blandly, 'but not, I fancy, the end of the book. Run along now, Lucy.'

The porter was ahead with her case, so she went through the barrier and didn't look back. A long time ago, when she had been a shy teenager, spending her first evening at a village dance with the doctor's son, he and a friend had taken her home at the end of the evening. They had said goodbye at the gate and she had turned round halfway down the short drive to the Rectory to wave, and surprised the pair of them laughing at her. She had never turned round since—not that she had had much chance; she didn't go out all that much. Perhaps Mr der

Linssen was looking at her in that same hateful mocking way; she longed to know, but she wasn't going to take any chances.

On board she was ushered into a stateroom with an adjoining shower, a narrow bed and all the comforts of a first-class hotel.

'There's a mistake,' she told the steward. 'I'm sure Doctor de Groot didn't book this cabin for me.'

He gave her an impassive look and fingered the large tip in his pocket. 'This is the cabin booked for you, miss.' He added in a comfortable tone: 'The ship's half empty, I daresay that's why.' He nodded to the dressing table. 'There's flowers for you, miss.'

A bouquet, not too large to carry, of mixed autumn blooms, beautifully arranged. The card with it was typed and bore the message: 'Happy memories, Lucy.' It wasn't signed; Mies must have sent it, bless her. Lucy sniffed at the roses and mignonette and Nerine Crispa tucked in between the chrysanthemums and dahlias and carnations; they would make a splendid show in her room at the hospital. She felt a return of the vague longing to rush back to Amsterdam, but ignored it; it was a natural disappointment because her holiday was over, she told herself as she unpacked what she would need for the night before going up on deck to watch the ship's departure.

St Norbert's looked depressingly familiar as the taxi drew up outside its grimy red brick walls and her room, even when the flowers had been arranged in a collection of borrowed vases, looked like a furnished box. She unpacked quickly, had a bath and in her dressing gown went along to the pantry to see if any of her friends were off duty. Beryl, from Men's Medical, was there, so was Chris, on day duty on Children's. They hailed her with pleasure, invited her to share the pot of tea they had made and adjourned to her room for a nice gossip until it was time to don uniform and go to lunch.

The meal, after the good living in Doctor de Groot's flat, seemed unimaginative; Lucy pushed a lettuce leaf, half a tomato and a slice of underdone beef round her plate, consumed the milk pudding which followed it and took herself through a maze of passages to the Principal Nursing Officer's office.

Women's Surgical was to be her lot; day duty for three months and would she report herself to Sister Ellis at once, please. The Principal Nursing Officer, a majestic personality with a severe exterior and a heart of gold, pointed out that as several of the nurses on that ward had fallen sick with a throat bug, Lucy's return was providential and she must expect to do extra work from time to time. Time which would, it was pointed out to her, be made up as soon as possible.

Lucy said 'Yes, Miss Trent,' and 'No, Miss Trent,' and hoped that life wasn't going to be too hard; Sister Ellis was an elderly despot, old-fashioned, thorough and given to reminiscing about her own training days when, it seemed, she worked for a pittance, had a day off a month, worked a fifty-six-hour week and enjoyed every minute of it. She never tired of telling the student nurses about it, always adding the rider that she had no idea what girls of today were coming to. No one had ever dared tell her.

Women's Surgical was on the top floor, a large, old-fashioned ward with out-of-date sluice rooms, side wards tucked away in awkward corners and bathrooms large enough to take half a dozen baths in place of the old-fashioned pedestal affairs set in the very centre of their bleak white tiles. Lucy climbed the stairs slowly because she still had a few minutes to spare, and pushed open the swing doors which led to a kind of ante-room from which led short passages to Sister's office, the kitchen, the linen cupboard and a small dressings room. Straight in front of her were more swing doors leading to the ward; she could hear voices, curtains being pulled and the clatter of bedpans coming from behind them. Just nicely in time for the B.P. round, she thought sourly as she tapped on Sister's door. Amsterdam seemed a long way away.

CHAPTER FIVE

LUCY, A HARD WORKER, found her capacity being stretched to its limits; even with Sister Ellis's splendid and uncomplaining example, her days were gruelling. One of the staff nurses went off sick on the day following her arrival on the ward and she found herself doing the work of two. Something, as Sister Ellis assured her, she was perfectly capable of doing, and indeed that was true, only it left Lucy too tired to think two thoughts together by the end of the day. But she had her reward; after a week the nurses began to trickle back from sick leave and two days later, she was given her days off with an extra one added on to make up for the extra hours she had worked. Sister Ellis had given her an evening off too so that she packed her overnight bag during her dinner hour, raced off the ward at five o'clock, tore into her clothes, and leaving Chris to clear up the mess, made for Waterloo Station, determined not to miss a moment of her freedom.

Her mother met her at Crewkerne because her father had a Parish Council Meeting and Lucy prudently offered to drive home. Mrs Prendergast had learned to drive a car of necessity, not because she particularly wanted to and she treated the Ford as an arch-enemy, only waiting to do something mean when she was driving it; consequently she gripped the wheel as though she had been glued to it, braked every few yards, ill-treated the clutch and never went faster than forty miles per hour. Fortunately her family had nerves of steel and patient dispositions; all the same, they ganged up to prevent her driving whenever possible. Lucy took the wheel now, and since her mother wanted to talk, didn't hurry overmuch, answering her parent's questions with all the detail that lady liked to have. 'And that nice man who brought you home,' enquired Mrs Prendergast, 'did you see him?'

'Oh, yes,' admitted Lucy cheerfully, 'several times. He lives in Amsterdam and knows Doctor de Groot quite well—he and Mies are very thick.'

She didn't see her mother's face fall. 'She must be a good deal younger than he is...'

'Mies is a year younger than I am, Mother. There's someone else after her, though, such a nice young man, Willem de Vries. They grew up together.'

'He'll find it difficult,' observed Mrs Prendergast.

Lucy said 'Um,' in a non-committal manner. She had changed her mind about Willem, he was a dark horse. True, someone like Fraam der Linssen could make rings round him if he had a mind to, but surely if he had wanted Mies he would have made sure of her ages ago.

'What are you thinking about?' asked her mother suddenly.

'Mies,' said Lucy promptly. 'She's so lovely, Mother, you have no idea. She has gorgeous clothes too...'

'You didn't have the right dress for that dance,' observed Mrs Prendergast far too quickly.

Lucy took the car gently through Beaminster and out into the narrow country road leading to home. 'It was perfectly all right,' she declared. 'You wouldn't have liked the dresses most of the girls wore—nothing on under the bodice—I mean, they were cut so low there just wasn't room.'

Her mother made a shocked sound. 'Don't tell your father, darling.'

Lucy giggled. 'Of course not, but it's quite the thing, you know—I didn't see any of the men minding.'

Her mother shot her a sideways look. 'I don't suppose they minded at all.' She frowned. 'All the same, you must get a new dress before the winter, darling.'

Lucy nodded. 'O.K., but I'll wait until I'm invited, Mother dear, otherwise it's just a waste of money. And there's a lot of life in that green dress yet.'

'There's a lot of life in the old tweed coat I wear when I feed the chickens,' declared her mother briskly, 'but that's no reason to wear it to church.'

'I'll buy a new dress,' promised Lucy, and pulled up tidily at the front door of the Rectory.

The stone-flagged hall smelled of wax polish and lavender mixed with something mouth-watering from the kitchen. Lucy sighed with deep content as she went in. It smelled of home, and hard on the thought was another one; that Fraam der Linssen's house smelled of home too, despite its grandeur. A wave of something like homesickness caught at her throat and she told herself that she was being ridiculous; one wasn't homesick for a house one had seen only once, and that fleetingly. It was because she was tired, she supposed as she followed her mother into the kitchen and then back into the dining room with her supper on a tray.

She spent a good deal of her days off talking, relating the day by day happenings of her holiday in Amsterdam. Her parents hadn't been there for many years and it was difficult for them to understand that it had changed. 'Though the *grachten* are just the same,' she consoled them. 'Some of the houses are used as offices, but they look just the same from the outside.'

'And where does that nice man live?' asked her mother guilelessly.

'Mr der Linssen? He's got a mansion in a dear little side street with a canal running down the centre. I went inside one day—just into a sitting room, with a cat I found—he's given it a home.'

It sounded rather bald put like that and she could see her mother framing a string of questions which she forestalled with: 'Doctor de Groot's clinic is pretty super—he works frightfully hard, a lot of the medical men give him a hand there.'

'Mr der Linssen?' asked Mrs Prendergast.

Lucy gave a soundless sigh. Her mother had the tenacity of a bulldog, she would end up by extracting every detail about him. 'He goes there, too. I didn't see much of him, though, although he's so friendly with Mies.' She drew a breath. 'He avoided me as much as he could; he was always polite, of course, but he told me that he—he tried not to see me.'

This forthright speech didn't have the desired effect. Her mother paused in her knitting to look at nothing. 'Now why should he say that?' she asked no one in particular. But she didn't mention him again for the whole of the three days in which Lucy was home, and nor, for that matter, did anyone else, a fact which she found decidedly frustrating. After all, she had seen quite a lot of him while she had been in Amsterdam, but she found bringing him into the conversation very difficult. She decided to forget about him and busied herself around the house with her mother, or drove her father through the quiet lanes when he went visiting. They were delightfully empty now; the summer visitors, and they weren't many, had gone and the local inhabitants had returned to their rural activities, and with autumn advancing the village social life was waking up. Handicrafts, knit-ins, whist drives were very much the order of the day. Lucy obediently put in an appearance at a knit-in, hating every moment of it, for she couldn't knit well and the conversation tended to centre round little Tom's adenoids, old Mrs Drew's rheumatism and the mysterious ailment which had attacked Farmer Will's pigs. After a little while she found her thoughts wandering. That they should wander to Mr der

Linssen was natural enough, she told herself; he had been part and parcel of her holiday, and that was still fresh in her head.

She went back to St Norbert's refreshed and ready for work. And that was a good thing, for there was plenty of it. There had been no empty beds when she had gone off duty three days earlier; now, although four patients had been discharged and their beds filled, there was a row of beds down the centre of the ward as well. Five in fact, occupied by ladies of various ages and all a little ill at ease, situated as they were in full view of everyone around them. Of course they wouldn't stay there long, as soon as their turn came for the operating theatre they would exchange beds with someone convalescent enough to spend the day out of bed and retire to the centre of the ward at bedtime. But in the meantime they sat up against their pillows trying to look as though they always slept in the middle of a room anyway, with a constant stream of people brushing past them on either side. Lucy, racing methodically to and fro, found time to feel truly sorry for them and at the risk of not getting done, paused to have a quick word with them in turn. They were all rather sweet, she decided; the old lady in the first bed was really only there because there was nowhere else to put her; she was a terminal case which stood a small chance of recovery if she were operated upon and none at all if she wasn't. There were those who might argue that she was taking up valuable space when it was needed so urgently for those who had a better chance and were younger, and that she was of the same opinion was obvious from her apologetic air and anxiety to please. Lucy, doing her best to dispel that look, gave the old dear a second helping of supper and a pile of magazines to look at. The girl in the bed behind her was young and pretty and terrified. She had a troublesome appendix, to be whipped out during a quiescent period, and no amount of reassuring both from the other patients and the nurses could convince her that she would survive the operation.

'You'll be sitting in a chair this time tomorrow,' Lucy promised her, 'or almost. Here's Mr Trevett to look at you, he's a poppet and he's got two daughters about the same age as you.'

She attended the consultant while he made a brief examination, exchanged the time of day with his houseman, saw them to the door and returned to go round the ward, checking the post-operative cases and then reporting to Sister in her office. Today had been busy, she reflected sleepily as she went off duty; tomorrow would be even worse, with six cases for theatre and she didn't know how many more for X-ray. She yawned widely, accepted the mug of tea someone had ready and plunged, inevitably, into hospital talk.

The day began badly. There had been a bad accident in during the early hours of the morning and the main theatre in consequence would start the list late; the six apprehensive ladies would have to wait. It was a pity that Maureen, the girl with the appendix, coaxed to calm by the day staff when they arrived on duty, and the first to go to theatre, should be delayed for more than an hour, for by the end of that time, even though sedated, she was in a fine state of nerves. Lucy, walking beside the trolley at last, holding a hand which gripped hers far too tightly, couldn't help wishing the day done.

The old lady went last and by then the morning had slipped into early afternoon, with everyone going full pelt and getting a little short-tempered what with curtailed dinner, two accident admissions and the routine of the ward to be fitted in. The part-time nurses came and went and Lucy, off at five o'clock, saw little chance of getting away until long after that hour; the old lady had proved a tricky case and didn't return from theatre until well past four o'clock, and then only because Intensive Care were so full they were unable to keep her. Sister Ellis, bustling about with her sleeves rolled up, exhorting her staff to even harder work, took an experienced look at the tired old face, still barely conscious, and appointed Lucy to special her in the corner bed which had been vacated for her.

It was after seven before she was relieved, although she

hadn't noticed the time; her patient was a challenge and she had taken it up with all the skill she possessed. The operation had been successful and would ensure at least a few more years of life, but a successful operation wasn't much good unless the after-care was of the best. Indeed, Lucy would have stayed even longer if it had been necessary, for she was sure that the old lady would recover, but she handed over, said goodnight to Sister Ellis and went wearily off duty. She was almost at the Nurses' Home when she remembered the letter in her pocket she meant to post to her mother. Sighing a little, she retraced her steps and went out of the hospital entrance; there was a letter box on the corner of the street which would be cleared that evening. She had slipped the letter in and was turning to go back when she saw the Panther de Ville, going slowly with Fraam der Linssen at the wheel and for a wonder, no one beside him. He didn't see her, nor did he go into the hospital entrance. She watched the elegant car out of sight, conscious that she had wished that he had seen her. Probably he wouldn't have stopped, she told herself robustly, and marched back to her supper and a reviving pot of tea in the company of such of her friends who were off duty. That she dreamt about Fraam der Linssen all night was pure coincidence, she told herself in the morning.

The old lady was better. Lucy, bustling round with charts and checking drips, was delighted to see that, and Maureen, helped from her bed and made comfortable in a chair, admitted with a grin that there hadn't been anything to get into a panic about, after all. And the other ladies were coming along nicely too; yesterday's hard work had been worth it.

Lucy had a lecture in the afternoon, one of Sister Tutor's stern discourses about ward management delivered in such a way that they were all left with the impression that their futures were totally bound to hospital life for ever and ever. Lucy, going back on duty, felt quite depressed.

It was a couple of days later when a notice on the board bade all third-year nurses, all staff nurses and as many ward Sisters as could be spared to attend a lecture to be given by Mr der Linssen. It was to be at two o'clock on the following day and Lucy, who was off duty for that afternoon, decided immediately that she wouldn't go, only to be told by Sister Ellis that her off duty had been changed so that she might attend the lecture. 'Because you've worked very hard, Nurse Prendergast,' said Sister Ellis kindly, 'and deserve some reward. Mr der Linssen is an exceedingly interesting man.'

Lucy agreed, although privately she considered him interesting for other things than lecturing. She would sit well back, she decided; there would be a large number of third-year student nurses and they would take up a good many rows—the back one would be at least halfway up the hall.

Her friends had kept a seat for her in an already full hall and she settled herself into it. Just in time; punctually to the minute Sister Tutor's procession advanced across the platform, followed briskly by Fraam who advanced to his desk, acknowledged the upward surge of young ladies rising to their feet and then quite deliberately looked along the rows. He found Lucy easily enough, he stared at her for a long moment and without looking any further, began his lecture—this time about Parkinson's disease and its relief through the operation of thalamotomy, to be undertaken with mathematical precision, he observed severely, and went on to describe the technique of making a lesion in the ventro-lateral nucleus of the thalamus. Lucy, making busy notes like everyone else, listened to his deep, calm voice and missed a good deal so that she had to copy feverishly from her neighbours.

At the end, she filed out with the rest of the nurses, not looking at the platform where several of the Sisters had intercepted Mr der Linssen as he was about to leave, in order to ask questions. He must have answered them with despatch because he and Sister Tutor were coming towards her down the narrow passage used as a short cut back to the main hospital and there was no way of avoiding them unless she turned tail and walked away from them. She wished now that she had gone the long way round with the others, but the lecture had run late and she was already overdue; Sister Ellis would be wanting to go to her tea and so would Staff. Not sure whether to look straight ahead or look at them as they passed, she compromised by darting a sideways glance. Sister Tutor gave a brisk nod and went on saying whatever it was she was engaged in; Mr der Linssen gave her a cool unsmiling look which left her wondering if she were invisible. By the time she had reached the ward she was quite cross about it; after all, they had seen quite a lot of each other not so long ago, enough to warrant a nod, surely. Her small, almost plain face wore such an expression for the rest of the day that several patients asked her if she felt ill and Sister Ellis, more forthright, wanted to know if she were in a fit of the sulks, because if so, her ward wasn't the place in which to have them. Lucy said she was sorry meekly enough and pinned a smile on to her nicely curved but wide mouth until she went off duty, when she allowed it to be replaced by a scowl.

The scowl was still there when she reached her room and because she wasn't in the mood to drink tea with her numerous friends, she declared that she would have a bath and go to bed early. She was indeed in her dressing gown when the warden, a thin, ill-tempered woman, came grumbling up the stairs. 'It's for you, Nurse Prendergast. Eight o'clock and I should be off duty, heaven knows I've had a busy day.' A gross exaggeration if ever there was one; she had come on duty at one o'clock, but Lucy let that pass. 'There's someone to see you—at the front entrance of the home. You'd better dress yourself and go down.'

'Who is it?'

The warden shrugged. 'How should I know? Didn't give a name, said he knew your parents.'

The vague idea that it might have been Fraam died almost before it was born; it sounded like someone from the village, probably with a parcel—her mother had on occasion sent cakes and such like bulky articles by parishioners going to London for one reason or another.

'I'll go down,' said Lucy. 'Thanks.'

She dressed again, this time in slacks and a sweater because her uniform had already been cast into the laundry bin. She didn't bother overmuch with her hair but tied it back with a bit of ribbon, barely looking in the looking glass as she did so, thrust her feet into her duty shoes and went downstairs.

The Home was quiet but for the steady hum of voices from behind its many closed doors. There was a very comfortable sitting room on the ground floor, but everyone much preferred sitting cosily, packed tight in someone's bedroom, gossiping and drinking pots of tea until bedtime. Lucy crossed the rather dark, tiled hall and opened the heavy front door and found Fraam der Linssen on the other side of it.

She was aware that her heart was beating a good deal too fast and she had to wait a second or two before she could say in a steady voice: 'Good evening, Mr der Linssen. You wanted to see me?'

'Naturally I wished to see you, Lucy. I have messages from Mies and a scarf which you left behind and have been asked to deliver to you.' And when she just stood there: 'Am I allowed to come inside? It is now October, you know, and chilly.'

She opened the door a little wider. 'Oh, yes—of course. There's a room where we may receive visitors.'

He looked around at the rather bleak little room into which she ushered him. 'Designed to damp down the strongest feelings,' he observed blandly. 'I wonder how many young men survive a visit here?'

She answered him seriously. 'Well, if they're really keen, it doesn't seem to matter,' she told him, and wondered why he smiled. She glanced round herself at the upright steel chairs and the table with the pot plant. 'It is rather unfriendly, I suppose. I've only been here once before.'

'Was he—er—put off?' asked Mr der Linssen in an interested voice.

'It was my godmother on a visit from Scotland,' she explained. 'Is Mies well?'

She had sat herself on one of the awful chairs but he, after a thoughtful look, decided to stand, towering over her. She thought how alien he looked in the anonymity of the visitors' room. She would, she supposed, always associate him with the lovely old house in Amsterdam.

He took his time answering her. At length: 'She is very well and sends her love. I took her out a few days ago, she looked very beautiful and turned all heads.'

Lucy nodded. 'She's one of the loveliest girls I've ever seen.' She stared across at him. 'Don't you think so?'

'Indeed I do. She made me promise to take you out for a meal while I was over here. Will you come now?'

She looked at him with horror. 'Now? Like this? You're joking!'

'You look all right to me, but change into something else if you wish to.' He glanced at his watch. 'Is ten minutes enough? We'll go somewhere quiet.'

Where he won't feel ashamed of me, thought Lucy, and was on the point of refusing when he repeated: 'I promised. I like to keep my promises.'

She got to her feet. 'Ten minutes,' she told him, and went back to her room. They were going somewhere quiet, he had said. She decided what to wear while she took a lightning shower. The tweed coat, an expensive garment she had bought years ago and which refused to wear out, and the Marks & Spencer velvet skirt with a shirt blouse. She pinned her hair with more regard to neatness than style, spent a few minutes on her face and sped downstairs. At any rate, she wouldn't disgrace a steak bar or a Golden Egg.

Mr der Linssen had other plans. He helped her neatly into the Panther and drove gently through the evening traffic, chatting about this and that. It wasn't until she saw that they were going down the Brompton Road that she stirred uneasily in her comfortable seat. 'Knightsbridge?' she queried doubtfully. 'I'm not dressed...'

'The Brompton Grill.' His voice reassured her, and she was still further reassured when they reached the restaurant and she saw that many of the tables were occupied by people dressed like themselves. Not, she decided, casting a sideways glance at her companion, that she was wearing anything to equal Mr der Linssen's beautifully cut suit. She forgot all that presently; the sherry he ordered for her sharpened her appetite, for she had skipped supper, and she agreed happily to caviar and toast for starters, Poussin en Cocotte to follow and a lemon syllabub to round off these delicacies, while her companion enjoyed a carpet-bag steak followed by the cheese board. And all the while her host carried on a gentle conversation about nothing at all.

But over coffee he suddenly asked briskly: 'And how are you getting on, Lucy? Your Finals are not so far off, are they? Have you any plans?'

She eyed him over the table and shook her head.

'Perhaps you plan to get married?' He sounded casual.

'Me? No.'

'I rather thought that Willem fancied you.'

She poured them each more coffee. 'Did Mies tell you that?'

He gave her a little mocking smile. 'My dear Lucy, I have eyes in my head and I might remind you that I've been around for quite a while.'

It was difficult to know what to say, so she decided not to say anything but asked instead: 'Are you and Mies going to get married?'

He dropped the lids over his eyes so that she couldn't see their expression. His face was so bland that she said quickly: 'No, don't answer, I can see that you aren't going to anyway...'

'You haven't answered me, either, Lucy.'

She frowned and he went on: 'It's difficult to lie when you're an honest person, isn't it?'

She threw him a startled look. 'Yes. You were very rude after the lecture. I don't understand you at all, Mr der Linssen. Here you are taking me out to dinner and yet you looked right through me only an hour ago.' She went pink as she spoke, remembering that he had once said that he tried not to see her.

He studied her face before he spoke. 'I wonder what Sister Tutor would have said if I had—er—greeted you with any degree of familiarity? I thought it best to keep to our roles of nurse and lecturer, and as for taking you out to dinner, did I not tell you that Mies made me promise to do so?'

Indignation almost choked her, but she managed an: 'Of course, stupid of me to have forgotten.' She put down her coffee cup. 'Would you please take me back now? It was a delicious dinner, thank you. You'll be able to tell Mies that you did exactly as she asked.'

He looked surprised. 'Now what on earth?...ah, I see, I put that very badly, did I not?'

Her eyes glowed green. 'No—you're like me, you find it difficult to tell lies. I should have hated it if you'd said how much you'd enjoyed meeting me again.'

He didn't answer her, only lifted a finger for the bill, paid it, helped her into her coat and accompanied her out to the car. Driving back he asked quite humbly: 'You won't believe me if I told you that I have enjoyed every moment of this evening?'

'No, I won't.' That sounded a little bald, so she added kindly: 'There's no need, you know. I think it was nice of you to take me out just because Mies wanted you to.' They were turning into the hospital forecourt. 'Will you give her my love, please? It was a lovely holiday—and Willem—will you give him...' she hesitated, 'my regards?'

He got out to open her door and she held out a hand. 'I hope you have a good journey back,' she observed politely, and then a little rush because she had only just remembered: 'How is the cat?'

'In splendid shape—you wouldn't recognise him, he has become so portly.'

'You were very kind to him.' She tugged at her hand which he was still absent-mindedly holding, but he didn't let it go.

'Kinder than I have been to you, Lucilla.'

She tugged again and this time he let her hand go. 'You've been very kind,' she repeated, longing for poise and an ability to turn a clever sentence. 'I must go.'

He caught her so close that the squeak of surprise she let out was buried in his waistcoat. 'I almost forgot,' his hand came up and lifted her chin gently: 'I had to give you this from Mies.'

She had never been kissed like that before. When he released her she stood staring at him blankly until he turned her round, opened the door and popped her through it. Even when he had shut it gently behind her she went on standing there until the warden, muttering to herself, came out of her little flat by the office to ask what Lucy thought she was doing. 'Gone midnight,' stated the lady. 'I don't know what you girls are coming to, coming in at all hours—no wonder you never pass your exams!'

Lucy turned to look at her, not having heard a word. 'It was a lovely evening,' she said, and added: 'But of course, he didn't mean the last bit.' She smiled at the warden, tutting and muttering by her door. 'Have you ever been kissed, Miss Peek?'

She didn't wait for that lady's outraged answer, but wandered off up the stairs and into her room where she undressed, got her clean uniform ready for the morning and went along to lie in far too hot a bath while she tried to sort out her thoughts. But she was tired and they refused to be sorted; she gave up in the end and went to bed to fall at once into a dreamless sleep, so deep that she missed the night nurse's rap on her door and only had time to swallow a cup of tea and half of Chris's toast on her way to the ward.

As the day advanced her common sense reasserted itself.

Fraam der Linssen had gone again and probably she wouldn't see him any more, and he had done just what Mies had asked him to do, hadn't he? Perhaps he had pretended that he was kissing Mies. Lucy let out a great sigh and Maureen, having her neat little wound re-sprayed, giggled. 'What's up?' she wanted to know. 'You look as though you'd had your purse stolen.'

Lucy laughed. 'That would be no great loss; it's two weeks to pay day.'

If secretly she had hoped to see Fraam again, she was to be disappointed; he had disappeared as suddenly as he had arrived and although she wrote to Mies later in that week, she took care not to ask about him, only made a lighthearted reference to his visit and that very brief. She didn't mention his visit when she went home, though; her mother, like all mothers, would read romance into a dinner *à deux*; there was plenty to talk about anyway, for on that particular trip home her brothers and sisters were all there too. They all teased her a great deal, of course, but being the youngest girl she came in for a little spoiling too. The weather had turned uncommonly cold too; they went for long walks, breathing the frosty air and the smell of bonfires and windfall apples rotting in the orchards, and in the evening they sat round a fire, roasting chestnuts and cracking the cobnuts they had picked on their walks. The days had never gone by so quickly. Lucy went back to St Norbert's with the greatest reluctance, only cheered by the thought that she would be returning in three weeks' time; she had five days' holiday still to come and Sister Ellis, always fair to her nurses, had promised that she should add them to her days off so that she would have a whole week at home. She would have to do some studying, of course, but most of the day would be hers in which to potter round the Rectory, drive into Beaminster for the shopping and help her father with the more distant of his parish visits.

These simple pleasures were something to look forward to; she reminded herself of them each day as she did the dressings, urged unwilling patients to get out of their beds when they didn't want to and urged those who wanted to and weren't in a fit state to do so to remain in bed for yet another day. The old lady was back too; she had been discharged to a convalescent home, but her condition had worsened and she was in her old bed in the corner by Sister's office, and this time there would be no going to the convalescent home or anywhere else. The nurses quietly spoilt her—extra cups of tea, the best books when the library lady came round, a bottle of Lucozade on the locker because she had faith in its strengthening properties and a constant stream of cheerful talk from whoever was passing her bed. She appreciated it all, making little jokes and never complaining, and during the last few days, when she was drowsy from the drugs to ease her, she would manage to stay awake long enough to whisper some small word of thanks. She died very quietly the day before Lucy was due to go on holiday, holding her hand while Lucy talked calmly about this and that until there was no need to talk any more. Sometimes, thought Lucy, going off duty, nursing was more than she could bear, and yet perhaps that had been the best way. The old lady had had no family and no friends, she might have gone on living in a lonely bedsitter with no one to mind what happened to her. Lucy, a tender-hearted girl, had a good weep in the bath and then, a little red-eyed, packed ready for her holiday.

CHAPTER SIX

THE OLDER MEMBERS of her father's parish had told Lucy that it would be a severe winter, and she had no reason to doubt their words as she left St Norbert's very early the next morning. The bus was crowded and cold and the sky hung, an ugly grey, over the first rush of earlier commuters. Lucy, going the other way, found Waterloo surprisingly empty once the streams of passengers coming to work had ended their race out of the station. She had ten minutes before the train left; breakfastless, she bought herself a plastic beaker of tea, which, while tasting of nothing, warmed her up. She had just enough time to buy some chocolate before the train left; she munched it up, tucked her small person into the corner seat in the almost empty carriage and went to sleep.

The guard woke her as the train drew in to Crewkerne and she skipped on to the platform, refreshed and ravenous, to find her father deep in conversation with the doctor from Beaminster, on his way to London. She was greeted fondly by her parent and with a friendly pat on the back from the doctor who had known her from her childhood. Both gentlemen then finished their conversation at some length while Lucy stood between them, her head full of pots of tea, home-made cakes and the cheese straws her mother always kept on the top shelf of the cupboard. She promised herself that she would eat the lot—if only she could get to them.

In the car at last her father observed apologetically: 'Doctor Banks and I were discussing Shirley Stevens—young Ted's wife, you know. She's expecting her first child very shortly and he's trying to get her into hospital a few days earlier. They're very isolated and even in good weather the lane is no place for an ambulance.'

'There's the district nurse,' offered Lucy helpfully.

'Yes, dear, but she has her days off, you know, and when she's on duty she has an enormous area to cover—she might not be available.'

'Where does Doctor Banks hope to get a bed?'

'Wherever there's one in his area. He's gone to London to some meeting or other. He'll try Yeovil on the way back; Crewkerne say they can't take her before the booked date.'

'Poor Shirley,' said Lucy, 'let's hope he's lucky at Yeovil—there's Bridport, of course.'

'Fully booked.' He turned the car into the Rectory drive. 'Here we are. I daresay you're hungry, Lucilla.'

She said 'Yes, Father,' with admirable restraint and rushed into the kitchen. Her mother was there, preparing vegetables, so were the cheese straws. Lucy, with her mouth full, sat on the kitchen table, stuffing her delicate frame while she answered her mother's questions about the journey, her need for a good meal and whether she had been busy at the hospital. But her usual catechism was lacking, and Lucy, who had been looking forward to tell all about her dinner with Fraam der Linssen, felt quite let down.

But not for long; over a late breakfast the three of them discussed her week's holiday and there was more than enough to fill it; a whist drive at the Village Hall, the W.R.V.S. meeting and how providential that Lucy should be home because the speaker was ill and she could act as substitute. 'First Aid,' murmured her mother helpfully, 'or something, dear, it's only for half an hour, I'm sure you'll be splendid.'

'Me? Mother, I've forgotten it all.' A statement which called forth amused smiles from her parents as they passed on to the delights of country dancing on Thursday evenings.

It was lovely to be home again, free to do exactly as she pleased and yet following the simple routine of the Rectory because she had been born and brought up to it. There was no hardship in getting up early in the morning when she could go straight out into the country for a walk if she was so inclined, something she combined with errands for her father in the other parishes, the distribution of the parish magazine and visits to the ladies who took it in turns to do the flowers in the little Norman church. The week slid away, each day faster than the last; the First Aid lecture was pronounced a rattling success, she won the booby prize at the whist drive and spent an energetic evening dancing the Lancers and Sir Roger de Coverley and the Barn Dance, partnered by a local farm hand, who proved himself a dab hand at all of them. She woke the next morning to the realisation that it was her last but one day. On Sunday she would have to go back and, worse, in six weeks' time she was due for a move. Women's Surgical had been busy, but she had been happy working there. Ten to one, she told herself, tearing into slacks and a sweater, I'll be sent to that awful Men's Medical. But she forgot all that; it was a cold day with lowering skies again and everyone in the village forecast snow; just the weather for a walk, she decided, and armed with sandwiches, set off for an outlying farm where there was an old lady, bedridden now, but still someone to be reckoned with. She liked her weekly visit from the Rector, but today Lucy was to fill his place; there was urgent business at the other end of the wide-flung parish and he couldn't be in two places at once.

She enjoyed the walk. The ground was hard with frost and there was no wind at all, although as she gained higher ground she heard it sighing and howling somewhere behind the hills. And the sky had darkened although it was barely noon. She hurried a little, her anorak pulled cosily close round her glowing face, her slacks stuffed into wellingtons. She would eat her sandwiches with the old lady and make tea for them both, since the men would all be out until two o'clock or later; they would be getting the cattle in, she guessed, against the threatening weather.

The farmhouse was large and in a bad state of repair. But it was still warm inside and the furniture was solid and comfortable. Old Mrs Leach was in her usual spot, by the fire in the roomy kitchen, sitting in a Windsor chair, her rheumaticky knees covered by a patchwork rug. She greeted Lucy brusquely and after complaining that it was the Rector she liked to see, not some chit of a girl, allowed Lucy to make tea and ate some of her sandwiches. The small meal mellowed her a little; she treated Lucy to a lengthy complaint about non-laying chickens, straying sheep and the difficulties of making ends meet. Lucy listened politely. She had heard it before, several times, and beyond a murmur now and again, said nothing. Mrs Leach was very old and got confused; she had never accepted the fact that her grandson who now ran the farm was making it pay very well, but persisted in her fancy that they were all on the edge of disaster. She dropped off presently and Lucy cleared away their meal and washed up, then put a tray of tea ready. The grandson's wife would be back from Beaminster shortly and the old lady liked a cup of tea. She sat down again then and waited for Mrs Leach to wake up before bidding her goodbye and starting off home again.

She wasn't surprised to see that it was snowing, and worse, that the wind had risen. The countryside, already thinly blanketed in white, looked quite different and although it was warmer now, the wind, blowing in gusts and gathering strength with each one, was icy. Lucy was glad to see the village presently and gave a sigh of content as she gained the warmth of the kitchen where she took off her wet things and went to find her parents, the thought of tea uppermost in her mind.

It was already dusk when Lucy went into the kitchen to get tea; an unnaturally early dusk by reason of the snow, whirling in all directions before a fierce wind. They hadn't had a blizzard for years, she remembered, and hoped there wasn't going to be one now. The howl of the wind answered her thought and when she went to peer through the window she had the uneasy feeling that the weather was going to worsen. She carried in the tea tray and put it on the lamp table by her mother's chair, then went to find her father. His study was at the end of a long draughty passage and the wind sounded even louder.

He looked up as she went in, observing mildly: 'Bad weather, I'm afraid, Lucy. If this snow persists there will be a good many people cut off, I'm afraid.'

They had their tea by the fire, in the cosy, shabby sitting room, while Lucy made a list of parishioners who might need help if the weather got really bad. She finished the list over her last cup of tea, handed it to her father and went off to the kitchen again with the tray, saying cheerfully as she went: 'I don't suppose it will be needed…there aren't any emergencies around, are there?'

She was wrong, of course; she was drying the last of the delicate fluted china which had belonged to her grandmother when there was an urgent banging on the kitchen door, and when she opened it Ted Stevens, one of the farm hands at Lockett's Farm, rushed in, bringing with him a good deal of snow and wind.

'Trouble?' asked Lucy. 'Sit down and get your breath.' She poured a cup of tea from the pot she hadn't yet emptied and handed it to him, and when he had gulped a mouthful:

'I'd say, Miss Lucy—the wife's expecting and the baby's started. I thought as 'ow I'd telephone from 'ere, but nothin' will get through—the snow's already drifting down the lane and the road's not much better.'

'And Nurse Atkins is in Yeovil—it's her day off.' Lucy

started for the door. 'I'll see what Father says, Ted—finish your tea; I won't be a minute.'

She was back in a very short time, her parents with her. 'Lucy will get to your wife,' declared the Rector. 'She knows her way—you stay here, Ted, and I'll telephone and see what's to be done—you'll have to act as guide when the ambulance or whatever can be sent arrives.' He turned to Lucy, already struggling into her wellingtons. 'And you'll stay with Shirley until someone gets through to you, my dear…and wrap yourself up well.'

Mrs Prendergast hadn't said a word. She was stuffing a haversack with the things she thought might be useful to Lucy and then went to fetch an old anorak into which she zipped her daughter with strict instructions to take care. 'And I'll get the spare-room bed made up just in case it's needed.' She added worriedly: 'I wish one of your brothers were home.'

They exchanged glances. Lucy, very well aware that her mother disliked the idea of her going out into the blizzard on her own, grinned cheerfully. 'Don't worry, Mother, it's not far and I know the way like the back of my hand.'

An over-optimistic view, as it turned out, for once outside in the tearing wind and the soft, feathery snow, she knew that she could get lost very easily in no time at all. And once she had started valiantly on her way, she knew too that it was going to be a lot further than she had supposed. True, in fine weather it was barely twenty minutes' walk, now it was going to take a good deal longer. But thoughts of poor Shirley, left on her own and probably in quite a state by now, spurred her on. She followed the country road, fortunately hedged, and came at last to the turning which led to the Stevenses' cottage. It wasn't so easy here; several times she found herself going off its barely discernible track, but at length she saw the glimmer of a light ahead. It was plain sailing after that, if she discounted sprawling flat on her face a couple of times and almost losing a boot in a hidden ditch. She stopped to fetch her breath at the cottage door and then opened it, calling to Shirley as she went in.

The wind and snow swept in with her so that once in the tiny lobby she had to exert all her strength to get the door closed again. 'Just in time,' she told herself as she shook the snow off herself, and repeated that, only silently, when she opened the living room door and saw Shirley.

Her patient was a large, buxom girl, rendered even more so by the bulky woollen garments she was wearing. Her hair, quite a nice blonde, was hanging round her puffy, red-eyed face and the moment she set eyes on Lucy she burst into noisy sobs.

'I'm dying,' she shrieked, 'and there's no one here!'

'Me—I'm here,' Lucy assured her, and wished with all her heart that she wasn't. 'I'll make a cup of tea and while we're drinking it you can tell me how things are.'

She walked through the cluttered little room to the kitchen and put on the kettle, then went back again to ask one or two pertinent questions.

The answers weren't entirely satisfactory, but she didn't say so; only suggested in a placid voice that Shirley might like to get undressed. 'I'll help you,' went on Lucy, 'and then if you would lie on the bed—how sensible to have had it brought downstairs—we'll work out just how long you've been in labour and that might just give us the idea as to how much longer the baby will be.'

Having delivered this heartening speech she made the tea, assisted the girl to get out of her clothes and into a nightgown and dressing gown and turned back the bedcovers. And it had to be admitted that in bed, with her hair combed and her poor tear-stained face mopped, Shirley looked more able to cope with whatever lay before her. They drank their tea with a good many interruptions while she clutched at Lucy's hand and declared that she would die.

'No, you won't, love,' said Lucy soothingly, busy calculating silently. It didn't make sense; from what she could remember of her three months on the maternity ward, Shirley should be a lot further on than she was. She cleared away the tea things and assuming her most professional manner, examined her patient; there wasn't a great deal to go by, but unless she was very much at fault, the baby was going to be a breech. She had seen only one such birth and she wasn't sure if she would know what to do. She suppressed a perfectly natural urge to rush out of the cottage into the appalling weather outside, assured Shirley that everything was fine and set about laying out the few quite inadequate bits and pieces she had brought with her, telling herself as she did so that things could have been worse; that at any moment now help could arrive. She gave a sigh at the thought and then gulped it down when someone outside gave the door knocker a resounding thump.

'We're in the sitting room,' she shouted. 'How quick you've been...' she looked over her shoulder as she spoke and let out a great breath, then: 'I didn't expect you!'

'I can see that,' agreed Fraam affably. He towered in the narrow doorway, covered in snow, which he began to shake off in a careless fashion before he divested himself of the rucksack on his back. 'And leave the questions until later, dear girl. Sufficient to say that I happened to be hereabouts and it seemed a good idea for me to—er—act as advance guard.'

He looked very much the consultant now, in a beautifully cut tweed suit and a silk shirt. It was a pity, Lucy thought wildly, that he had had to stuff his exquisitely cut trousers into wellingtons; she was on the point of mentioning it when he asked blandly: 'This is the lady...?'

She made haste to introduce him and then listened to him putting Shirley at her ease; he did it beautifully, extracting information effortlessly while he gently examined her. When he had finished he said: 'Well, I'm not your regular doctor, Mrs Stevens, but I don't think he would object if I gave you something to help the pains; you may even get a little sleep. It will be an hour or two yet and unless an ambulance can get through very shortly you will have to have the baby here. You will be quite safe. Nurse Prendergast is excellent and I won't leave you at all.'

'You're foreign.' There was a spark of interest in Shirley's eyes.

'Er—yes, but I do work over here quite a bit.' His smile was so kind and reassuring that she smiled back quite cheerfully. 'And now will you take this? It will help you considerably.'

Shirley tossed off the contents of the small glass he was holding out and Lucy tucked her in cosily while Fraam made up the fire and then went to shrug on his coat once more. 'I'll fetch in more wood,' he said.

'He's a bit of all right, Miss Lucy,' whispered Shirley, 'even if he is foreign.' She managed a grin. 'Between the two of you it'll be O.K., won't it?'

'Of course,' said Lucy stoutly. 'You're going to have a little doze, just as the doctor said, and everything's going to be fine.' And as Shirley grimaced and groaned, 'Here, let me rub your back.'

She had Shirley nicely settled by the time Fraam got back. He stacked the wood carefully, had another look at his patient and said casually: 'We're going to leave you for a few minutes, Mrs Stevens—just to discuss the routine, you know. Will you mind if we go into the kitchen and almost close the door? No awful secrets, you understand.' He sounded so relaxed that Shirley agreed without a murmur and Lucy, obedient to his nod, slid past him into the tiny kitchen, shivering a little at its chill, made even chillier by the wind tearing at its door and window.

She said in an urgent whisper: 'It's a breech, isn't it? I don't know a great deal about it, but it looked…'

'You are perfectly right, Lucy—it is a breech, at least the first one is.'

Her eyes grew round and so did her mouth. 'Oh, no!' she exclaimed in a whispered squeak. 'You must be mistaken,' and then at his bland look: 'Well, no—I'm sorry, of course you aren't.'

He inclined his head gravely. 'Good of you to say so, Lucilla.'

'And don't call me that,' she whispered fiercely.

His formidable eyebrows arched. 'Why not? Is it not your name?'

'You know it is—only—only you make it sound different...'

'I mean to—it's a pretty name.' He leaned forward and kissed her, brief and hard, on her astonished mouth and went on, just as though he hadn't done it: 'Of course the ambulance hasn't a chance of getting through—I suggested to your father that he tried to contact the army and get hold of something with caterpillar tracks; they might get her doctor through—if they can't then you will have to be my right hand, dear girl.'

She gazed at him in horror. 'Oh, I don't fancy that—I don't think...'

'You won't need to,' he pointed out blandly, 'I'll tell you what to do as we go along. Mrs Stevens should doze for another hour or so, on and off. Make a cup of tea like a good girl, will you, for once we start I don't expect we'll have time for anything. I'll get the things out of my case—there's some brandy there too. I thought Mrs Stevens might be glad of it when everything's over.'

He went back into the sitting room and bent over the bag he had brought with him while Lucy made tea again. He joined her presently, accepted the mug she offered him and whispered on a chuckle: 'I like the odds and ends you brought with you—practical even though not quite adequate.'

She gave him a cross look. 'Well, I wasn't to know it was going to be twins and a breech.'

He spooned sugar lavishly. 'True, Lucy. You didn't add any food to your collection, I suppose?'

'A tin of milk—for the baby, you know,' she pointed out kindly, 'and there's some chocolate in my anorak—it's quite old, I think...'

'We'll save it until we're starving, then.'

She poured tea for them both. 'How did you get here?'

He chose to misunderstand her. 'Through the snow—your father gave me the direction.'

'Yes, of course,' she said impatiently, 'but how did you get here—to the village, I mean?'

'Ah, yes—well; there was something I wanted to ask you to do for me, but this is hardly the time. We can have a nice little chat later on.'

She let that pass. 'Yes, but did you come by car?'

He looked surprised. 'How else? Doctor de Groot sent his love, by the way.'

She re-filled the teapot; it wouldn't do to waste the tea and he had said that there might not be time... 'You've seen him recently?'

'Yes—he's ill again.' He added infuriatingly: 'But no more about that; let us go over the task lying ahead of us.' He handed her his mug. 'Now as I see it...' He began to instruct her as to what she might expect and she listened meekly, inwardly furious because he was being deliberately tiresome.

He made her repeat all he had told her, which she did in a waspish little voice which caused a very pronounced gleam in his eyes. All the same, she had cause to be thankful towards him later on; Shirley continued to doze on and off for the next hour or so, but presently she wakened and the serious business of the evening, as Fraam matter-of-factly put it, began. Lucy, well primed as to what she must do, nonetheless had the time to see how well Fraam managed. Shirley wasn't an easy patient, expending a great deal of useful energy on crying and railing at her two companions, but he showed no sign of annoyance, treating her with a kindly patience which finally had its reward as Shirley calmed down after he had repeatedly assured her that she wasn't going to die, that the baby would be born very shortly and that she would feel herself in excellent spirits in no time at all.

The first baby was a breech, a small, vigorously screaming boy whom Lucy received into a warmed blanket. 'A boy,' Fraam told his patient, 'a perfect baby, Mrs Stevens. You shall hold him in just a minute or two, we'll have the other baby first.'

He had chosen the exact moment in which to tell her. Shirley, delighted with herself and no longer frightened, took the news well and except for exclaiming that they couldn't afford two babies, she made no fuss, and Fraam, bending over her, reassured her with a comfortable assurance that she would undoubtedly get help. 'You'll get the child allowance, won't you, and I'm sure your husband's employer will be generous.'

Lucy wasn't too sure about that; Farmer Lockett wasn't a generous man; it looked as though her father would need to come to the rescue, as he so often did. She heard Fraam say comfortably: 'Well, we must see what can be done, mustn't we?' and felt annoyance because it was easy for him to talk like that; he would be miles away as soon as he decently could and would forget the whole thing. But in the meantime at least, he behaved with exemplary calm, making tea while Lucy made the excited mother comfortable and when they had all had a cup, suggesting in a voice which expected no opposition that Shirley should have a nice sleep for an hour while they kept an eye on the babies.

There was only one cot; Lucy found herself sharing the heat of the fire with Fraam, each of them cradling a very small sleeping creature, cocooned in blanket. Fraam, wedged into an armchair much too small for him, had the infant tucked under one arm and his eyes closed. How like him, thought Lucy crossly and rather unfairly, to go to sleep and leave her with two little babies and a mother who at any moment might spring a load of complications...

'I'm not asleep,' Mr der Linssen assured her, still with his eyes closed. 'Both infants are in good shape and I expect no complications from their mother. I will warn you if I feel sleepy, I have shut my eyes merely as a precaution.'

He didn't say against what, but Lucy remembering his remark—a long while ago now—that he tried not to see her, went a bright pink and went even pinker when he opened one eye to study her. 'You look very warm,' he observed, 'but I think that you will have to bear it.' His glance fell on the small bundle she was holding so carefully. 'I'll have another look at them later on. If all goes well, you can have them both while I get in more wood and forage round a bit. Once Mum's awake it will ease the situation.'

The eye closed and Lucy was left to her own thoughts. Why was he here? He had said that he had something to ask her and that Doctor de Groot was ill again, but surely a letter would have done as well? Or perhaps he was on holiday? Was it something to do with Mies? Her thoughts chased themselves round and round inside her tired head and were snapped as if on a thread when the old-fashioned wall clock let out a tremendous one.

She turned her head to make sure she had heard aright and whispered: 'Isn't anyone coming?'

'Well, hardly.' He had opened both eyes again and smiled at her kindly. 'They'll have to wait for morning, you know.' They sat listening to the howl of the wind encircling the little house and he added comfortably: 'We're fine here for the moment. Close your eyes, Lucy, I'll catch the baby if you drop it.'

She gave him an indignant glance and he smiled again. 'You'll have chores later on,' he insisted gently, 'and you'll be in no fit state to do them.'

It made sense; she shut her eyes meekly, secretly determined to stay awake. The clock was striking four when she opened them and Mr der Linssen was sitting exactly as he had been, only now he had a little baby tucked under each arm. Miraculously they were still asleep.

'Oh, I'm sorry,' began Lucy, to be stopped by his: 'Feel wide-awake enough to take these two and keep an eye on Mum? She hasn't stirred, but she will very soon. I'll have a look round.'

He handed her the tiny pair and stretched hugely and went soft-footed into the hall for his jacket. Lucy felt the rush of air as he let himself out and then heard no more above the sound of the wind. He would, she judged, have some difficulty in reaching the woodshed. She looked across at Shirley, who was showing signs of waking; she would want some attention and a cup of tea, but how to do that with her arms full of babies? She was still pondering her problem when Mr der Linssen came back. She could hear him in the hall, getting out of his jacket and taking off his boots, and presently he came on his enormous socked feet into the room.

He grinned across at her. 'There's a goat,' he informed her softly, 'and chickens. I've dug a path through the drift behind the cottage and brought down enough coal and wood to keep us going for the rest of the day.'

'Where are they?' asked Lucy urgently.

'In the shed almost at the end of the garden. Can you milk a goat, Lucy?'

She said matter-of-factly: 'Well, of course I can. I'll go and see to the poor thing as soon as possible, but Shirley's beginning to rouse.'

He came and took the infants from her. 'Good, I'll sit here—there's nowhere else I can go with these two—while you cope with her. Let me know if there's anything worrying you, but if everything's as it should be she can have them while you see to the livestock and I get the tea.'

Shirley, now that she was the proud mother of twins, had assumed an assurance which was rather touching. Between them, she and Lucy managed very well, ignoring Mr der Linssen's impersonal broad back which had, of necessity, to be there too. Washed, combed and comfortable, Shirley sat up against her pillows and delightedly took possession of her family.

Mr der Linssen, taking her pulse and temperature, congratulated her on their beauty and size while he listened to Lucy's gentle slam of the door.

'The goat,' he explained to his patient, 'and the chickens. Lucy's gone to see to them.'

Shirley nodded. 'Oh, I'd forgotten them—there's Shep and Tibby, too...'

'Dog and cat? I didn't see any sign of them. I expect they're sheltering somewhere, if they don't turn up I'll go and look for them. Now I'm going to make some tea and then we can decide on our breakfast.' He added comfortably: 'I daresay someone will be along soon, now.'

He sounded so sure and certain that Shirley only nodded; she had her twins and she was content.

Outside Lucy found things rather worse than she had imagined. The wind was as fierce as ever and the snow, still falling, had piled against the side and back of the little house. The path Mr der Linssen had dug was already covered over and she seized the shovel he had prudently left by the door; she might need it.

The goat was housed alongside the woodshed and the chickens next door. She found fodder for the goat and feed for the chickens, then found a bucket and milked the beast before going in search of the eggs. There were quite a few, so at least they wouldn't starve. She piled them into an old basket, set fresh water and prepared to go back to the house. She was shutting the hen house door when a faint sound made her look down; a small cat had emerged from under the hen house floor and was eyeing her.

'Come on indoors, then,' invited Lucy, and started down the path, rather weighed down with eggs and milk and shovel. The little beast darted ahead, looking back to see if she were following, and then sat down outside the door beside a sheepdog, waiting patiently to be let in. He looked cold and hungry, but he obviously belonged; Lucy opened the door and the three of them went in together.

Mr der Linssen welcomed them with a cheerful: 'Ah, there you are. Shirley was wondering what had happened to Shep and Tibby. I'll feed them, shall I? There's tea in the pot, Lucy.'

'Shep went after Ted,' explained Shirley, 'he's that fond of him.' A faint anxiety creased her placid face. 'I wonder where my Ted is?'

Mr der Linssen answered from the kitchen where he was feeding the animals.

'I imagine he's in the village waiting to guide an ambulance here,' he observed placidly. 'There's a good deal of snow about and they might not be able to find their way.'

Lucy drank her tea feeling peeved; no one had mentioned the goat or the chickens. She took her cup out to the kitchen and filled the kettle; the twins would need attention in a little while and she wanted some cool boiled water. She was joined almost at once by Mr der Linssen, who closed the door gently behind him before he spoke. 'Not too good outside, is it?' His eyes lighted on the eggs and milk. 'I see that you've been your usual practical self—you must show me sometime.' He poured the milk into a saucepan and put it on to boil.

'What are we going to do?' asked Lucy. She felt cross and grubby and longed above all things for five minutes at her own dressing table.

'Breakfast, my dear. Porridge, I think, don't you?' He was at his most urbane, his head in a cupboard. 'Eggs, bread and butter,' his voice came from inside, 'tea, we have them all here.'

She gave his back an exasperated look. 'I didn't mean breakfast...'

He straightened up and closed the cupboard door. 'Wait, dear girl, wait. So far Shirley is quite satisfactory and the babies are warm and content. We'll take a look at them and get them to feed—if they do, that will take us over the next few hours.'

'But supposing they don't? We might be here for the rest of the day.'

He nodded his head with a calm which made her grind her small even teeth. 'I should think it quite likely, although there is a good chance that a helicopter will get here sometime before dark.'

She felt better. 'You think so? I'm on duty tomorrow.'

He spooned tea into the pot while she stirred the porridge.

'The trains will be delayed and I doubt if anything much could get through the roads.'

'You mean I'll not be able to get back?' She wasn't quite sure if she felt pleased about it or not.

'Do you mind?' He sounded amused.

Lucy didn't answer that. 'The porridge is ready,' she remarked rather more sharply than she had meant to. 'Are you hungry?'

He was busy with plates and spoons. 'Famished. Lunch yesterday was my last meal.'

'Oh, Fraam!' she had spoken without thinking, her voice warm with concern. 'I'll cook you three eggs...' She remembered then that she had called him Fraam and added hastily, 'Mr der Linssen.'

'I don't know about him, but Fraam could eat three quite easily, thank you. Have we more than this bread?'

'There's half a loaf in the bread bin...much more than we shall need.'

He looked as though he were going to speak, but instead he spooned the porridge into three bowls, put them on a tray and carried it into the living room.

Breakfast was a cheerful meal, the infants tucked up and still sleeping while the three of them fell upon the food, and when they had finished and Mr der Linssen had gone into the kitchen to do the washing up, Lucy dealt with her three patients.

It was light now, as light as it would be while the snow continued. She tidied the little room, made up the fire, fed Shep and Tibby again, found a place for them to settle before the hearth and then, leaving Mr der Linssen to keep an eye on everyone, went upstairs to the tiny bedroom and did what she could to tidy her person. Even when she had washed her hands and face in the old-fashioned basin and combed her hair, she didn't think she looked much better, but at least she felt rather more so. Her face was clean and her hair reasonably tidy; not that that mattered; when she went downstairs Mr der Linssen glanced at her with a casual, unseeing look which made her wish most heartily that she hadn't bothered.

But he pulled up a chair to the fire, put the cat on her lap and told her to go to sleep in a kind enough voice. 'I'll rouse you the moment anything happens,' he promised.

She hadn't meant to close her eyes, but she was weary by now. She didn't hear the helicopter, nor did she stir until the cat was taken gently from her lap and she was shaken just as gently awake.

'They're here,' he told her quietly. 'I'll go out to them. Get Shirley wrapped up, will you?'

She already had everything necessary packed in a case, and was nicely ready when Mr der Linssen came back with the pilot, carrying a light stretcher between them, as well as a portable incubator. The twins were small, they would fit into it very nicely. Lucy left the men to get Shirley on to the stretcher and turned her attention to the infants; and that done to her satisfaction, put on her anorak.

'Don't bother with that,' Mr der Linssen's voice held quiet authority. 'I'll come back for the infants.'

She stared at him. 'But aren't we going too?'

'No. Ted's waiting at the Rectory, they'll pick him up and take him on to Yeovil with Shirley and he'll hope for a lift back or get on to a snowplough if there's one coming this way. He wants to get back as quickly as he can—we'll go as soon as he arrives.'

She had no answer to this but bade Shirley a warm goodbye and went back to the incubator. Mr der Linssen was back again inside five minutes and took that away too with a brief: 'They're rather pushed for room, but they'll manage.' He had gone again before she could answer.

She stood in the room, untidy again, listening to the helicopter's engines slowly swallowed up in the noise of the wind, feeling let down and lonely. How awful it would be if Fraam had gone too and left her alone. She shivered at the very idea, knowing it to be absurd but still vaguely unhappy. Shep's whine disturbed her thoughts and she got up to let him out.

There was nothing to see outside and only the wind blowing, although the snow had stopped now. She shut the door and went back to the mess in the room behind her, telling herself to stop getting into a fuss about nothing; there was plenty of work to get on with and if one worked hard enough one didn't think so much. She picked up a broom and started on the great cakes of snow in the little hall. 'The wretch!' she cried pettishly. 'He needs a good thump—if he were here…'

CHAPTER SEVEN

'BUT I AM HERE,' Fraam's cheerful voice assured her as he opened the door and then stood aside as she swept the snow outside. 'Although from your cross face, I don't think I'll ask why you were wanting me.' He took the broom from her. 'The snow has stopped and the wind is lessening, but I'm afraid the lane is completely blocked—it will need a snowplough.' He gave her a long, deliberate look. 'Now hop into bed, Lucy. I'll make up the fire and then I'm going outside to clear a path round the house.'

She was glad to obey him without arguing, for she was peevish for want of sleep. She got on to the bed without a word and was already half asleep as he tucked the quilt round her.

She awoke to the domestic sound of something sizzling on the stove and saw that the table had been laid and pulled close to the bright fire. She tidied the bed, poked at her hair before the looking glass and went to peer into the kitchen.

Mr der Linssen was frying eggs, and beans were bubbling in a saucepan. He looked completely at home and somehow very domestic. His casual: 'Slept well?' was reassuringly matter-of-fact and calm, as though he made a habit of cooking scratch meals in snowbound cottages.

Lucy, good-humoured again, thanked him politely and asked if there was any news.

'None.' He turned the eggs expertly. 'The telly doesn't work and there's no battery for the radio.' He turned to smile at her. 'Just you and me, Lucilla. Two eggs?'

They ate their meal cosily before the fire and halfway through it Lucy remembered to ask if he had cleared the path.

He nodded. 'Oh yes, and I've widened the one to the shed.'

'Then I can milk the goat and see to the chickens.' She poured more tea for them both. 'Do you suppose we'll get away before dark?'

He leaned back and the chair creaked alarmingly under him. 'Perhaps.' He sounded casual about it. 'I would suggest attempting it on foot, but we can't leave the animals, and I don't like to leave you here alone.'

Lucy went a little pink. 'You don't have to worry about me. I would be perfectly all right.'

'Certainly—all the same I have no intention of leaving you.' He finished his tea and went on: 'I should imagine they will get a snowplough through to us and bring Stevens with it; he'll stay and we'll go back.'

'That sounds too good to be true,' observed Lucy, and started to clear the table.

But it wasn't. She was cooking a hot mash for the chickens and explaining just what she was doing to Fraam at the same time when they heard the drone of a snowplough, although it was half an hour before it reached the cottage with Ted Stevens on it just as Mr der Linssen had prophesied, and over cups of tea Ted told them that Shirley and the twins were safely in hospital and that he would stay at the cottage, going down to the Rectory each day to get news of them. He was profuse in his thanks although a little in awe of Mr der Linssen's elegance and great size, even in his stockinged feet and rolled-up sleeves. He wrung their hands, thanked them once again, pressed a dozen eggs on Lucy and walked with them to the snowplough, with old Tom Parsons, who had driven it there, striding ahead. It was a bit of a squeeze; three of them in the cab and Lucy, perched between the two men, was glad of Fraam's arm holding her steady. It was a bumpy, sometimes slow ride and cold, but she felt content and happy. She wasn't sure why.

They were expected at the Rectory; the kitchen door was opened the moment they began to make their way up the kitchen garden path and Mrs Prendergast welcomed them with a spate of questions as she urged them to take off their jackets and go straight into the kitchen where they found a table laden with home-made bread, soup, great pats of butter, pots of pickles, cold meat and a large fruit cake.

'I didn't know when you'd be back,' she explained, 'so I thought a little of everything would do. Never mind about washing and tidying yourselves; you'll need a good meal first.' She beamed at them. 'I've a pan of bubble and squeak all ready and bacon and fried bread, and tea or coffee...' but here she was interrupted by her husband, who had come hurrying in with a bottle of whisky under one arm and glasses in his hand. 'To keep out the cold,' he explained, putting them down carefully before embracing his daughter and greeting Mr der Linssen warmly. 'We are very anxious to hear your news,' he observed, 'we were a little worried at first,' he glanced across at his guest. 'Indeed, before you came, we were very worried about our little Lucilla. We were relieved to hear from the helicopter pilot that you were both in good spirits and safe and sound.'

He poured whisky and then went down the cellar steps to fetch up a bottle of port for the ladies.

'You don't mind if I sit down to table like this?' asked Mr der Linssen.

'Heavens, no—food first and baths afterwards. You'll stay the night, of course—we've put your Range Rover in the barn, by the way.'

Mr der Linssen swallowed his whisky with pleasure. 'You're very kind, Mrs Prendergast.' His glance slid to Lucy, sitting on the table swinging her legs, sipping port. 'I should like that very much.' And when Lucy glanced up at his words, he smiled at her. She wasn't sure if it was the port or his smile which was warming her.

They made a splendid meal, for after the soup Mrs Prendergast set on the table there was the bubble and squeak and everything which went with it as well as the cake and a large pot of tea. She sat at the foot of the table smiling at them both and when she judged they had eaten their fill, she urged: 'Now do tell us all about it—your father has his sermon to finish and supper will be late.'

So Lucy began, but when she got to the bit where Mr der Linssen had arrived, he took over from her, very smoothly, making much of what she had done to help him, until she exclaimed: 'Oh, you're exaggerating!'

'No—how would I have managed without you? You forget the goat and the chickens—why, before today I had never heard of hot mash.'

They all laughed, and he added: 'And of course the babies—I'm not very experienced with infants.'

Mrs Prendergast made an unbelieving sound. 'And you a doctor—I simply don't believe you!'

'A surgeon, Mrs Prendergast,' he corrected her gently, 'and I haven't delivered a baby since my student days.'

Lucy, nicely full of delicious food, was losing interest in the conversation. Mr der Linssen's deep voice came and went out of a mist of sleepiness. It was very soothing; she closed her eyes.

She was dimly aware of being picked up and carried upstairs, two powerful arms holding her snugly. She wanted to tell Fraam to put her down, but it was too much bother. She tucked her untidy head into his shoulder and slipped back into sleep.

'Worn out,' observed her mother, briskly turning back the bedclothes. 'We'll leave her to sleep for a while.'

Mr der Linssen laid Lucy gently on her bed, bent down and deliberately kissed her sleeping face, then waited while Mrs Prendergast tucked her in. 'The darling's absolutely out cold.'

'The darling's absolutely darling,' remarked Mr der Linssen at his most suave.

Mrs Prendergast bent over her daughter with the deepest satisfaction. Her dear plain little Lucy was loved after all, and by such a satisfactory man. She beamed at him as they left the room.

It was quite dark when Lucy woke up and when she looked at the clock she discovered that it was almost ten o'clock. She got up and opened her door; lights were on downstairs and she could hear voices. Fraam would be gone, she supposed, the Range Rover would be able to follow the tracks of the snow-plough and there was no reason why he should stay, even though her mother had invited him to do so. She had a shower, got into a nightie and dressing gown and wandered downstairs, wondering about him. He would have been on his way somewhere or other; she hadn't asked and now she worried about it; he hadn't had much sleep...

For a man who hadn't slept, he looked remarkably fresh, sitting opposite her father in the sitting room, with her mother between them, knitting. She stopped in the doorway, muttering her surprise as the two men got to their feet and her mother turned to look at her. It was Mr der Linssen who came to meet her and take her arm. His 'Hullo, Lucy,' was cheerfully casual as he pushed her gently on to the sofa beside her parent.

'You ought to be in bed,' said Lucy, 'you've had almost no sleep.'

He smiled but said nothing and went and sat down again, and Mrs Prendergast asked sharply: 'No sleep?'

'I had a good nap while Lucy cleared up my mess,' he assured her.

'All the same, you must be tired—I should have thought... Finish the row for me, Lucy, I'll get supper. Toasted cheese?' she suggested, 'and there are jacket potatoes in the Aga,' and when everyone nodded happily, she swept out of the room with: 'You men will want beer, I suppose. Lucy, you'd better have cocoa.'

Lucy said 'Yes, Mother,' meekly and went on knitting, suddenly conscious of Fraam's eyes on her. It disconcerted her so much that she dropped a stitch and decided to go and help her mother.

The kitchen was warm and comfortable in a rather shabby fashion; Lucy could remember the two chairs each side of the Aga and the huge scrubbed table since she was a very little girl. She set the table now and called the men to their supper and watching Mr der Linssen tucking into the simple food with obvious pleasure, wondered if he found it all very strange after his own lovely house. It seemed not; he washed up with her father to the manner born and then went back to sit by the fire while she and her mother went upstairs to bed, sitting back in his chair as though he had done it every day of his life. She kissed her father goodnight, smiled a little shyly at their guest and got into her bed, vaguely content that he should be there in her home, looking so at ease. She would have liked to have pondered this more deeply, but she went to sleep.

There would be no leaving on the following day, that was plain enough to Lucy when she got up in the morning. True, the snow had stopped, but there had been a frost during the night and there was still enough wind to make the clearing of the drifts a difficult matter. The telephone wasn't working and the snowplough had gone off to the main road again and the country road it had cleared was covered once more. Save for the impersonal voice on the radio telling them what bad weather they were having, Dedminster, Lodcombe and Twistover were cut off from the rest of the world. Lucy didn't mind; in fact, when she stopped to think about it, she was rather pleased. And Mr der Linssen seemed to have no objections either. He ate a huge breakfast and then volunteered to shovel snow. Lucy, helping her mother round the house, found herself impatient to join him, but it wasn't until they had had their morning coffee that she felt free to do so. He was clearing the short drive to the gate and beyond a casual 'Hullo' he hardly paused in his work as she settled down to work beside him. It was hard work, too hard for talking, and besides, she only nibbled at the easy bits while he kept straight on however deep the snow, but it was pleasant to work in company.

But presently she remembered something and paused to lean on her spade and ask: 'Why did you want to ask me something?'

Fraam heaved a shovelful of snow to one side before he too paused.

'Ah, yes—Doctor de Groot asked me to find you while I was over here. He is ill, I told you that—perhaps you don't know that he has Raynaud's disease? In its early stages—he wants me to operate, he also wants you to nurse him. Mies is no good at nursing and after the first day or so he refuses to stay in hospital—his idea is for you to look after him at the flat.'

Lucy stood looking at him. 'But I'm not a qualified nurse and I don't know much about Raynaud's disease or its treatment.' She went red under his amused look, reminding her plainly that if she had stayed awake during that lecture of his, she might not be so ignorant, but he didn't say that, only: 'I'll prime you well; there's not much to it. But can you get leave?' He added casually: 'I daresay that if I made a point of asking for you, your Nursing Officer might consent.'

She looked doubtful. 'Miss Trent? She might. I've got two weeks still, though I'm not supposed to have them until after the New Year...'

'You wouldn't mind giving up your holiday?'

'I wasn't going anywhere, only here, at home.'

He nodded. 'So if it could be arranged, you would agree? I intend operating soon—a week, ten days, that gives him a chance to enjoy Christmas. He'll need a few weeks' convalescence, he plans to spend it with Willem's people in Limburg.'

'Willem? Oh, does that mean that he and Mies... I mean, are

they going to get married? I thought—that is, she told me she was going to marry you.'

He gave a great bellow of laughter. 'My dear girl, I've known Mies since she was in her cradle. Whenever she falls out with Willem and there's no other admirer handy, she pretends she's in love with me—it fills the gap until she's got Willem on his knees again. Only this time he stayed on his feet and she was so surprised that she's agreed to marry him.'

Lucy breathed a great sigh of relief. 'Oh, I am glad!'

He stared hard at her. 'Are you? He appeared to be taken with you while you were in Amsterdam.'

'That wasn't real; you see, he thought—at least, I thought that if he took me out once or twice Mies might mind, but then I wasn't sure because you might have been in love with her...'

'My God, a splendid tangle your mind must be in! It takes a woman to get in such a muddle.'

Lucy picked up her shovel and attacked the snow with terrific vigour. 'Nothing of the sort,' she observed haughtily. 'Men don't understand.'

'And never will. Now, are you going to nurse Doctor de Groot?'

'If he really wants me to and if Miss Trent will let me have another holiday, yes, I will.'

He was shovelling again, but he paused long enough to say: 'Not much of a holiday, I'm afraid.'

'I've had my holiday,' said Lucy soberly.

He stopped shovelling to look at her, studying her slowly, his head a little on one side. 'Are you rationed to one a year?' he wanted to know.

'Of course not!' she had fired up immediately and then went on with incurable honesty: 'Well, actually, I do only have one a year—I mean, to go away.'

'To dance in a green dress—such a pretty dress, too.'

Her pink cheeks went a shade pinker. 'You don't need to be

polite,' she assured him rather severely. 'I've had that dress for three years and it's quite out of fashion.'

'But it suits you, Lucy.'

Because I'm the parson's daughter, she thought wryly, and wished suddenly and violently that she was a rich man's daughter instead, with all the clothes she could possibly wish for and a lovely face to go with them so that Fraam would fall in love with her... She attacked the snow with increased vigour to cover the rush of emotion which flooded her. Of course that was what she had wanted—that he should fall in love with her, because she was in love with him, hopelessly and irrevocably, only it wasn't until this very minute that she had known it.

'You look peculiar,' observed Fraam. 'Is anything the matter?'

Lucy shook her head and didn't speak, for heaven knows what she might have said if she had allowed her tongue to voice her thoughts. She would die of shame if he were ever to discover her feelings; he would be so nice about it, she felt that instinctively—kind and gentle and underneath it all faintly amused. She would be nonchalant and frightfully casual, as though he were someone she had just met and didn't really mind if she never saw again. And indeed for the rest of that day and the day after that too, she was so casual and so nonchalant that Mr der Linssen looked at her even more than usual, his eyes gleaming with something which might have been laughter, although she never noticed that. Mrs Prendergast did, of course, and allowed herself the luxury of wishful thinking...

Fraam drove Lucy back on the following day, the Range Rover making light work of the still snowbound roads, and because he had seemed so sure that Miss Trent would grant her a further two weeks' holiday, she had packed a bag ready to go to Holland, explaining to her mother while she had done it.

Her mother had expressed the opinion that it was a splendid thing that she could repay her father's old friend by nursing him. 'Just as long as you're home for Christmas, darling,' she observed comfortably, and Lucy had agreed happily; Christmas was weeks away.

She had been decidedly put out when they arrived at St Norbert's that afternoon, for Fraam had carried her bag inside for her, said rather vaguely that he would be seeing her and driven off. And what about Doctor de Groot? she asked herself crossly as she went up the stairs to her room. Had he thought better of having her as a nurse? Had Fraam changed his mind or his plans and forgotten to tell her? Was she to go meekly back to the ward and wait until wanted? She wouldn't do it, she told herself roundly as she unpacked her case, pushing the extra things she had brought with her in anticipation of another stay in Holland into an empty drawer.

And nobody said anything to her when she reported for duty, relieved to find that she was still on Women's Surgical. The ward was busy, not quite as hectic as it had been, but still a never-ending round of jobs to be done and she plunged into them thankfully, resolutely refusing to think about Fraam, which wasn't too difficult while she was busy; it was when she was off duty, doggedly studying for her Finals, that she found it hard not to pause in her reading and think about him instead, and worst of all, of course, was bedtime when, once the light was out, there was nothing at all to distract her thoughts.

It was during the evening of the fifth day that a junior nurse came down the ward to where Lucy was readjusting Mrs Furze's dressing and told her that Sister wanted her in the office.

Lucy paused, forceps poised over the gauze pad. 'Two ticks,' she objected, 'I can't leave Mrs Furze half done. Is it desperate?'

'I don't know—Sister poked her head round her door and told me to find you.'

Lucy began to heave her patient up the bed. 'Well, will you tell her I'm on my way?'

Her junior scurried off and she finished making Mrs Furze comfortable, collected her bits and pieces on to a tray and bore them off to the dressings room. She was quick about it, only a few minutes elapsed before, her tray tidily disposed of and her hands scrubbed spotless, she tapped on Sister's door and went in.

Sister Ellis was sitting at her desk, looking impatient. Fraam was standing by the narrow window, looking as though he had all day in which to do nothing.

'And what,' Sister Ellis wanted to know awfully, 'kept you so long, Nurse Prendergast? Not only have you kept me waiting, but Mr der Linssen, with no time to spare, has been kept waiting also.'

Lucy's mild features assumed a stubborn look; she was overjoyed to see Fraam, but the joy was a little swamped at the moment by the knowledge that she wasn't looking her best. She was tired, her hair was ruffled and her nose shone. Not that these would make a mite of difference to his attitude towards her, so that it was ridiculous of her to mind, anyway. She said meekly: 'I'm sorry, Sister, but I couldn't leave Mrs Furze at once...'

Sister Ellis snorted. 'In my young days...' she began, and then thought better of it. 'Mr der Linssen wishes to speak to you,' she finished. She settled back in her chair as she spoke, intent on missing nothing.

Fraam took his cue smoothly, with a pleasant smile for Sister Ellis and a gentle 'Hullo, Lucy,' in a voice which sounded as though he were really glad to see her again and quite melted her peevishness. He went on to explain that he had spoken both to Miss Trent and Sister Ellis and both ladies had been so kind as to make it possible for Lucy to take the remainder of her annual holiday. 'Seventeen days,' he commented, 'which should give Doctor de Groot ample time to get over the worst. You are still agreeable, I take it?' he wanted to know.

Lucy tucked away a strand of mousy hair. 'Yes, of course. When am I to go?'

'Tomorrow evening, if you are willing. I shall be operating early on the morning of the following day and would be obliged if you would take up your duties then.' He looked at

Sister Ellis. 'If I may, I will have the tickets sent here tomorrow morning. I shall be returning to Amsterdam this evening, but I will arrange for someone to meet you at Schiphol and bring you to the hospital.'

Sister Ellis nodded graciously; Mr der Linssen was behaving exactly as she considered a distinguished surgeon should, no familiarity towards her nurse—true, he had called her Lucy, but the strict professional discipline had altered considerably over the years—and a gracious acknowledgement of her own help in the matter. Lucy Prendergast was a good little nurse, one day she would make an excellent ward Sister. She said now, ready to improve the occasion: 'You will learn a good deal, I hope, Nurse; other methods are always worth studying, and any knowledge you acquire will doubtless come in useful when you sit your Finals.'

Lucy said: 'Yes, Sister,' and stole a look at Fraam. She wondered why he looked as though he was laughing to himself. Really he seemed quite a stranger standing there so elegant and cool, it was hard to imagine him shovelling snow and making tea. She found his eyes upon her and knew that he was thinking the same thing, and looked away quickly.

'If Mr der Linssen has given you all the instructions he wishes, you may go, Nurse. Send Night Nurse in to me in five minutes and then go off duty. Goodnight.'

'Goodnight, Sister. Goodnight, Mr der Linssen.' She didn't quite look at him this time.

She had expected to see him again, she had to admit to herself later; she had gone off duty, eaten her supper and repaired to her room, accompanied by a number of her friends, to undertake the business of packing, and all the while she had her ears cocked for the telephone, only it had remained silent and she had gone to bed feeling curiously unhappy. There had been no reason why Fraam should have tried to see her again; the whole arrangement was a businesslike undertaking, planned to please Doctor de Groot—and what, she asked herself miserably, could be more proof, if proof she needed, that Fraam wasn't even faintly interested in her? She tossed and turned for a good bit of the night and went on duty in the morning looking so wan that Sister Ellis wanted to know if she felt well enough to travel that evening.

She went off duty at one o'clock and obedient to the instructions she had received with her ticket, took herself to the airport and boarded a flight to Schiphol. It was a miserably cold evening and it suited her mood exactly.

It was cold at Schiphol too and she shivered as she followed the routine of getting herself and her luggage into the outside world again. There hadn't been many people on the flight and the queue before her thinned as they reached the main hall. She wondered who would meet her; someone from the hospital presumably, but how would she recognise him or her? She put her case down and it was picked up again at once by Fraam.

'A good flight, I hope?' he wanted to know. 'I thought it better if I fetched you myself, in that way we can save a lot of time; I can give you the facts of the case as we go.'

'Good evening,' said Lucy on a caught breath, 'and yes, thank you, the flight was very comfortable.' And after that brief exchange they didn't speak again as he led her to the car park. He had the Mini this time and what with her case and him she found it rather cramped. She sat squashed beside him while he drove into Amsterdam, listening carefully to his impersonal voice taking her through the case, and because she had expected that he would take her straight to the hospital, she was taken aback when he stopped the car and when she peered out, discovered that they were outside his house. 'Oh,' said Lucy blankly, 'I thought...'

'Supper first.' Fraam was already out of the car and at the same time the door of his house opened and Jaap's portly figure stood waiting for them, framed in the soft shaded lights of the hall.

Lucy got out then, because Fraam was holding the car door

open for her and besides, it was cold. He took her arm across the narrow brick pavement and ushered her up the steps and into the warmth beyond to where Jaap was waiting, holding the door wide, smiling discreetly at them both. And there was someone else in the hall; an elderly very stout woman, with pepper-and-salt hair dressed severely, and wearing an equally severe black dress, neatly collared and cuffed with white.

'This is Bantje,' explained Fraam, 'Jaap's wife, she will take you upstairs. I'll be in the drawing room when you're ready.'

Lucy went up the lovely carved staircase behind Bantje, trying to see everything at once; the portraits on the wall beside it, the great chandelier hanging above her head, the great bowls of flowers...and once in the gallery above, her green eyes darted all over the place, anxious not to miss any of the beauty around her. She hadn't much time, though, for the housekeeper crossed the gallery and opened an elaborately carved door and smiled at her to enter. The room was large by Lucy's standards, and lofty, with a handsome plaster ceiling and panelled walls. The furniture was a pleasant mixture of William and Mary and early Georgian, embellished with marquetry, against a background of dim chintzes and soft pinks. Left alone, she did her hair, washed her face in the pink-tiled bathroom adjoining and then spent five minutes looking around her. Even if she never saw it again, she wanted to remember every detail. Satisfied at last, she did her face in a rather perfunctory fashion and went downstairs. Fraam was in the hall, sitting in one of the huge armchairs, but he got up when he saw her and took her arm as she hesitated on the bottom step.

'It's a little late,' she observed. 'Oughtn't I to go to the hospital? Don't they expect me?'

'Of course they expect you. I told them that I would take you there not later than midnight.'

High-handed. She had her mouth open to say so and then closed it again as they went into a very large, very magnificent room; dark oak and crimson was her first impression and she had no chance to get a second one because she saw that there were people already in it: a handsome elderly couple standing before the enormous hooded fireplace, a young man so like Fraam that she knew at once that he was his brother and a pretty girl who could only be his wife. Her first feeling was one of annoyance that he hadn't warned her; she was, to begin with, quite unsuitably dressed; a nicely cut tweed skirt and a shirt blouse with a knitted sweater on top of it were suitable enough for travelling but hardly what she would have chosen for an evening out. She eyed the other ladies' long skirts as she was introduced; Fraam's mother and of course his father, his brother and as she had guessed his wife, all of whom welcomed her charmingly.

'My family, or at least part of it, happened to be in Amsterdam,' observed Fraam coolly, 'and now how about a drink?'

Lucy could scarcely refuse, so she asked for a sherry and prayed that it wouldn't have too strong an effect on her empty insides, but when it came she found to her relief that it was a small glass and only half full; perhaps that was the way they drank it in Holland. She sipped cautiously, answering her companions' pleasant questions, and was relieved when Jaap opened the door and announced that supper was ready.

A rather different supper from the one her mother had produced for them in the Rectory's kitchen not so long ago; pâté and toast, a delicious dish of sole cooked with unlikely things like bananas and ginger and pineapple followed by small wafer-thin pancakes, filled with ice cream and covered with a brandy sauce. A potent dish, Lucy decided, and was glad that she had had only one glass of the white wine she had been offered.

They had their coffee in the drawing room, which, after the restrained simplicity of the Regency dining room, seemed more magnificent than ever. Lucy, feeling a little unreal, sat on an enormous buttonbacked sofa and talked to Fraam's father; a nice old man, she decided, who must have been as good-looking as his son and still was handsome enough. She felt at ease with him, just as, surprisingly, she had felt at ease with his mother, a rather formidable lady with a high-bridged nose and silver hair who nonetheless had a charming smile and a way of making her feel as though she had known everyone in the room all her life. She had talked to Leo, Fraam's brother, too, and his wife Jacoba, and as she got up to leave presently she was aware of deep envy for the girl Fraam would eventually marry; not only would the lucky creature have him for a husband, she would have his family too, to welcome her with warmth into their circle and make her one of them.

She sighed without knowing it and Mevrouw der Linssen said at once: 'You are tired, my dear, and no wonder. Fraam shall take you to the hospital at once—we have been most selfish keeping you from your bed.' And she had kissed Lucy goodnight. So, for that matter, had everyone else, except Fraam of course. He had driven her back quickly, handed her over to one of the night Sisters, wished her goodnight, expressed the hope that she would remember all that he had told her and gone away again. She had felt a little lost, standing there at the entrance of the Nurses' Home, but she was sleepy too; she accompanied the night Sister up the stairs to a pleasant little room on the first floor, listened with half an ear to instructions about uniform, to whom she must report, and where to go for breakfast, and went thankfully to bed. She had plenty to think about, but it would have to wait until the morning.

And when the morning came, she had no time. A pretty girl who introduced herself as Zuster Thijn and begged to be called Ans fetched her at breakfast time, sat her down at a table with a dozen others, supplied her with coffee and bread and butter and cheese, introduced her widely and then hurried her along to the Directrice's office.

That lady reminded Lucy forcibly of Miss Trent; kind, severe and confident that everyone would do exactly as she wished them to. She outlined Lucy's duties in a crisp, very correct English, struck a bell on her desk with a decisive hand and when a younger and only slightly less severe assistant appeared, consigned Lucy into her care.

She would never find her way, thought Lucy, skipping along to keep up with her companion's confident strides. The hospital was old, added to, modernised and generally made over and she considered that unless one had been fortunate enough to grow up with the alterations, one needed a map. They gained the Private Wing at last, and she was handed over to the *Hoofdzuster*, a placid-looking woman somewhere in her forties, with kind eyes and a ready smile and a command of the English language which while not amounting to much, was fluent enough.

'Doctor de Groot is in a side room,' she explained, 'he will go to the *operatiezaal* in an hour, so you will please renew your acquaintance with him, give him his injection and accompany him, there to remain until Mr der Linssen has completed the operation. It has been explained to you what is to be done?' She nodded her head. 'So you will know what is expected of you, you will remain with him for the rest of this day and you will be relieved by a night nurse. You will receive free time on another day. You understand me?'

'Yes, thank you, Sister. I understand that Doctor de Groot is to go home within a few days.'

'That is so. Now I take you to your patient.'

Lucy had expected to see Mies there, which was silly, for visiting would hardly be allowed before the operation. Doctor de Groot was propped up in bed looking ill but quite cheerful and talking with some vigour to Fraam, who was leaning over the end of his bed, listening. They both looked at Lucy as she went in, said something to the *Hoofdzuster*, who smiled and went away, and then stared at Lucy once more. She bore their scrutiny for a few moments and then wished them a rather tart good morning.

Her patient grinned at her. 'Hello, Lucy, I'm very glad to see you, my dear. I can't think of anyone I would rather have to look after me. My little Mies is no good as a nurse, not this sort of nursing at any rate. We're going home in three days' time—I've Fraam's promise on that. And now,' he added testily, 'what about giving me my pre-med?'

Fraam nodded at Lucy, not in greeting, she was quick to see, but as a sign that she could draw up the necessary drug in the syringe lying ready in its little dish. She did so without speaking, gave it to him to check, administered it neatly and gave Doctor de Groot a motherly little pat.

'We'll have a nice chat when you're feeling like it,' she promised.

He stared up at her. 'I'm the worst patient in the world!'

'And I'm the severest nurse,' she assured him. 'Now close your eyes, my dear, and let yourself doze—I'll be here.'

She went to get rid of the syringe and then to look at the charts and papers laid out ready for her once the operation was over. Fraam was still there, indeed he hadn't moved an inch, but he wasn't Fraam now, he was the surgeon who was going to perform the operation and she was the nurse in charge of his case. 'Was there anything more that I should know about?' she asked him calmly.

'Not a thing,' he assured her, 'at present. I daresay I'll have a few more instructions when you're back here.' He moved then, going soft-footed to the door. 'I'll see you later.'

An hour later Lucy, swathed in a cotton gown and with her hair tidied away beneath a mob cap which did nothing for her at all, stood by Doctor de Groot's unconscious form, ready to hand the anaesthetist anything he might require. Mr der Linssen was there, naturally, with his assistant, a houseman or two, theatre Sister and a team of nurses, and it all looked exactly the same as the operating theatre at St Norbert's, only of course they were all speaking Dutch. Not that much was said; Mr der Linssen liked to work in peace and quiet; bar the odd remark concerning some interesting phase during the operation, and a quiet-voiced request for this or that instrument, he worked silently, completely absorbed in his task; the division of the sympathetic chain of cervical nerves so that his colleague's right arm might become normal again, free from pain and the threat of gangrene quashed once and for all.

He worked fast, but not too fast, and despite his silence the people around him were relaxed. Bless him, thought Lucy lovingly, he deserves all the pretty girls he dates and his lovely house and his nice family; thoughts which really made no sense at all.

He straightened his long back at last, nodded to his assistant and left the theatre and in due time Doctor de Groot was borne back to his bed. He had already opened his eyes and muttered something and gone directly back to sleep again. Lucy, arranging all the paraphernalia necessary to his recovery, was too intent on her task to notice Mr der Linssen in the doorway watching her. When she did see him she concluded that he had only just arrived and informed him at once about his patient's pulse and general condition. 'His hand is warm and there's a good wrist pulse,' she went on. 'Do you want half-hour observations?' After the shortest of pauses, she added 'sir.'

His manner was remote and courteous, they could have been strangers. 'Please. I want to know if you are uneasy about anything—anything at all. Zuster Slinga will be in from time to time.'

He went to bend over his patient and then without saying anything else or even looking at her, went away.

He returned, of course, several times, to study her careful charts, check Doctor de Groot's pulse and scribble fresh instructions. Lucy, who had been cherishing all the dreams of a girl in love, however hopelessly, did what she had to do with meticulous care and calm and when, later in the day, she had a few minutes to herself, she tucked the dreams firmly away; they didn't go well with the job she was doing. You're a fool, she told herself as she sipped a welcome cup of coffee, and fools get nowhere—stick to your job, Lucy my girl, and leave day-dreaming to someone with the time for it.

An excellent maxim which she obeyed for at least the rest of that day.

CHAPTER EIGHT

IT BECAME APPARENT to Lucy within the next day or so that they could have managed very well without her. Certainly Doctor de Groot was a very bad patient, ignoring everything that was said to him, ordering his own diet in a high-handed fashion and using shocking language when his will was crossed. Lucy took it all in good part, coaxed him in and out of bed, obediently held mirrors at the correct angle so that he could inspect the ten neat stitches Mr der Linssen had inserted alongside his spine and rationed his visitors with an eagle eye to the length of their visits. Mies came each day, of course, prettier than ever and usually with Willem in tow. She had a ring now, a diamond solitaire which sparkled and shone on her graceful hand. Lucy admired it sincerely and tried not to feel envy at Willem's air of complacent satisfaction. It would have been better if she had had more to do, for once Doctor de Groot had recovered from the operation there was little actual nursing to be done. The wing was well staffed, a nurse could have been spared to look after him easily enough. She puzzled over it and on the third day, when Fraam came to pay his evening visit, she broached the subject, following him outside into the corridor as he left the room. But to her queries he made only the vaguest of answers, saying finally: 'Well, Doctor de Groot likes you, Lucy, you are contributing to his recovery—besides, I'm allowing him home the day after tomorrow.' He gave her a questioning look. 'You're happy? They're kind to you? You get your off duty?'

'Oh yes, thank you, everyone's super. I'm glad Doctor de Groot is doing so well. I didn't know that he was ill, he never mentioned it.'

Fraam smiled. 'No. But he began to lose the use of his fingers and it was noticed…'

'By you?' Lucy smiled with a warmth to light up her ordinary face. 'Can he do a bit more when he's home? He's sometimes a bit difficult—I mean, wanting to go back to work…'

'Out of the question for a little while, but we must think up something—someone from the clinic could call round each day and give him particulars of the cases… I'll see about that.' His eyes searched hers. 'You're to have a day off once he's settled in—I'll get a nurse to relieve you.'

'I'm all right, thank you. I wouldn't know what to do with a whole day to myself.'

'No? We'll see.' He turned abruptly and strode away from her and she went back to her patient, sitting up in bed and grumbling because someone had forgotten to send some books he had particularly asked for.

The move back to Doctor de Groot's flat was made with the greatest of ease; the patient was getting his own way so he was his normal pleasant self, a gentle elderly man with a joke for everyone. Lucy prayed that his mood would last as she installed him in his own room and equipped the dressing room leading from it with the necessities she might require. And it did, but only until that evening, when Doctor de Groot exploded into rage because no one had been to see him. 'Probably the clinic is in a complete state of chaos,' he barked at Lucy. 'Why has no one kept me informed? Why hasn't Fraam been to see me?'

As though in answer to his question the telephone rang and

Lucy hurried to answer it. Fraam's voice was quiet and calm. 'Lucy? Can you get Doctor de Groot to the telephone? I'm tied up at the hospital, but at least I can give him some details about the clinic. Is he anxious about it?'

'Yes,' said Lucy baldly. 'I'll get him.'

She gave her patient an arm across the room, pushed a chair under him and went out of the room and returned ten minutes later to find him quite cheerful again. 'Willem is coming round in the morning,' he told her. 'He's down at the clinic now, so he will have the very latest reports. Fraam won't be over for a time.' He cast Lucy a quick look and she schooled her features into polite interest. 'Plenty of work at the hospital,' he explained, 'and his social life is rather full at the moment.'

'Indeed?' Lucy wondered which girl it was this time—perhaps it was the right one; she was bound to turn up sooner or later. She sighed soundlessly and said brightly: 'Mies will be back tomorrow, won't she?' Mies was staying with Willem's family for a couple of days.

Three days went by. On each of them Fraam telephoned for a report on his patient and Willem, when he called, examined him before he sat down to recount the happenings at the clinic. It was quite late on the third evening, while Mies and Willem were at the *bioscoop*, that the front door bell sounded and Lucy went to answer it. 'Hullo,' said Fraam, 'rather late for a visit, I'm afraid, but I've managed to fit it in.'

Between what? Lucy asked herself silently. He was in a dinner jacket, so presumably he was either on the way to or from some social function.

She wished him good evening in a rather colourless voice and led the way to her patient's room. Doctor de Groot was sitting by the fire, a table loaded with books and papers at his elbow. He thrust these aside as his visitor went in and welcomed him with real pleasure, to plunge at once into a series of questions, brushing aside Fraam's enquiries as to his own health. He did pause once to ask Lucy to make them some coffee and when she had done so and poured it out for them both, suggested that she might go to bed. 'We'll be talking for some time and I'm quite able to get myself into bed later on.'

It was Fraam who answered him. 'I'm going to take those stitches out—they're due out in the morning, and an hour or two sooner won't matter. Then Lucy can get you settled in bed and if you still want to talk, we can carry on from there. I can't come tomorrow—I'm operating in the morning and I've a date after that.'

'If you say so,' grumbled Doctor de Groot. 'I shall go down to the clinic tomorrow.'

'No, you won't. I'm free, more or less, on the day after, though; we'll all three go, but don't imagine you're going to do any work. Willem can take over for a week or two. And Lucy must have a free day—after you've convinced yourself that the clinic is still standing, I shall hand you over to Mies for the rest of the day—Lucy needs a change.'

Lucy stood listening to him, not all that pleased that he was arranging everything without a word to her. Supposing she didn't want a day off? No one had consulted her about it—besides, in another week she would be going home again. She would have liked to have told him so, but he forestalled her by asking her where her own coffee cup was and when she said she didn't want any, suggested that she should make ready for the removal of the stitches.

Everything she needed was in the dressing room. She laid scissors and forceps and a sterile towel and swabs ready and waited there quietly while the two men drank their coffee. When they joined her presently Fraam asked, half laughing, 'Don't you like us any more, Lucy?'

She didn't answer but took his jacket when he took it off and then offered him a clean towel with which to dry his hands. The stitches took no time at all; Fraam whisked them out, laid them neatly on a bit of gauze so that Doctor de Groot might check them for himself, sprayed the neat incision and washed his hands again. 'Shall we finish our talk?' he wanted to know.

'Certainly. Lucy, go to bed.'

She eyed him calmly. 'I can't—not until Mies comes in, she's mislaid her key so I'll have to open the door.'

'I'll do that.' Fraam sounded a little impatient. 'I'll see that Doctor de Groot gets into his bed, too. Goodnight, Lucy.'

She wished them both goodnight in a quiet voice which betrayed none of the annoyance she felt.

And the next morning Doctor de Groot told her happily that Fraam would be calling for them the following morning and could she be ready by ten o'clock. 'A brief visit to the clinic,' he explained airily, 'and then you are to have the rest of the day to yourself. Mies will come for me in a taxi.'

'When?'

'Oh, don't worry, you will be able to see me safely into it before you go off.'

'But Doctor de Groot, I'm not sure that I want to have a day off—I've no plans.'

He waved a vague hand. 'Plans? What does a young thing like you want with plans? All Amsterdam before you and you want plans! Go out and enjoy yourself—have you any money, my dear?'

'Yes, thank you, enough for a meal and that sort of thing.'

'Ah, good. If it's not too cold outside, we'll walk to the corner and back, shall we?'

She had both of them ready by ten o'clock, Doctor de Groot well muffled against the chilly wind and herself buttoned into her winter coat. She was wearing a sensible pair of shoes too; if she was to spend the day walking around the city, she had better have comfortable feet. 'What time shall I come back?' she asked.

'Any time you like, Lucy—take a key and let yourself in.'

She had a clear mental picture of herself filling in the evening hours with a cinema and then eating a *broodje* as slowly as possible. She hadn't enough money to go to a restaurant and she wasn't sure that she wanted to even if she had.

Fraam was punctual, driving the Rolls so that the doctor should have a comfortable ride. Mies had gone on ahead, for she had continued to work while her father was ill, but she would leave early that day in order to go back home with him. She had been a little mysterious when she had told Lucy the evening before, but Lucy hadn't asked questions; it would be something to do with Willem, she supposed.

The clinic was crowded with patients. Fraam, leading the way down the passage to Doctor de Groot's room, sat him in his chair and said: 'You may have half an hour.'

'My dear Fraam, what can I do in that short time?'

'Nothing much, that's why I said half an hour. Longer tomorrow, perhaps. Now, what do you want to do first? See Willem—Jo's here, too, and so is Doctor Fiske.'

'Willem and Fiske, then. What about you?'

'I'll see a couple of patients while I'm here.' Fraam's eyes slid to Lucy, standing between them. 'Will you wait for half an hour, Lucy? Perhaps with Mies.'

She couldn't really see why she had to wait. There were plenty of people to see the doctor back to his house; on the other hand, there would be less day to get through... She nodded and went to find Mies and give her a hand with the patients' files.

It seemed less than half an hour when Fraam put his head round the door: 'Mies, your father's ready to leave.' He had his own coat on again, too, so presumably he was driving them back after all. Lucy got up too and went to the door with Mies, to find a taxi there and Doctor de Groot already in it. He called cheerfully to her as Mies got in and she smiled and waved and then turned away to start walking into the city. Mies had said it wasn't a very nice part for a girl to walk alone, but she wasn't worried about that.

Fraam's hand on her arm stopped her before she had gone ten yards.

'Wrong way,' he observed blandly, 'the car's over here.'

'I should like to walk,' she told him, 'thank you all the same.'

'So you shall, but I can't leave the car here, I'll take it home and we can start walking from there.'

'We?' she asked weakly.

'I told you that I had a day off.'

'Yes—but...'

'Well, we're going to spend it together.'

It didn't make sense. 'It's very kind of you,' she began, 'but there's no need. I mean, I don't suppose you get many days off and it's a pity to waste one.'

'Why should I be wasting it?' He sounded amused, standing there on the pavement, looking down at her.

'Well,' she began once more, 'with me, you know.'

There was no one about, the bleak street was empty of everything but the wind, the shabby buildings around them presented blind fronts. Fraam bent down and kissed her very gently. 'For a parson's daughter,' he said in a gentle voice to melt her very bones, 'you talk a great deal of nonsense.' He took her arm and stuffed her just as gently into the Rolls and got in beside her. 'I'm going to marry you,' he told her. 'You can think about it on the way to the house.'

Of course she thought about it, but not coherently. Thoughts tumbled and jostled themselves round her head and none of them made sense. They were halfway there before she ventured without looking at him: 'Why?'

'We'll come to that later.'

'Yes, but—but I thought—there's a girl called Eloise...' She paused to think. 'And that lovely girl who was in the car when the little boy ran across the road...'

'For the life of me I can't remember her name. She was just a girl, Lucy, like quite a few others. Eloise too.' He allowed the Rolls to sigh to a dignified halt before his house and turned to look at her. 'Do you mind?'

'No, not in the least.' A whopping great lie; she minded very much, she was, she discovered, fiercely jealous of each and every one of them.

'No? I'm disappointed, I hoped that you would mind very much.' He didn't sound in the least disappointed.

Jaap had the door open and his dignified smile held a welcome. 'Coffee is in the small sitting room,' he informed them, and led the way across the hall to throw open a door. Lucy, following him, thought that Fraam must be one of the few people left in the world whose servants treated him as though he were something to be cherished.

The room was small and extremely comfortably furnished with deep velvet-covered chairs and sofas in a rich plum colour. The walls were white and hung with paintings—lovely flower paintings, delicately done. There was a fire burning in the small marble fireplace and as they went in a stout, fresh-faced girl brought in the coffee tray.

'Take off that coat,' suggested Fraam, 'and sit over here by the fire.' He had flung his own coat down as they had entered the hall and she put hers tidily over the back of a chair and sat down, wishing she was wearing something smarter than the tweed skirt and woolly sweater she had considered good enough for her day out.

She was feeling awkward too, although it was obvious that Fraam was perfectly at ease. He gave her her coffee and began to discuss what they should do with their day, but only to put her at her ease, for presently he said: 'Supposing we don't do any sightseeing and go to my mother's for lunch?'

She choked a little on her coffee. 'Your mother? But does she...where does she live?' She tried to sound cool while all the while all she wanted to do was to fling down her delicate coffee cup and beg him to explain—there must be some reason why he wanted to marry her, he couldn't love her, and surely she wasn't the kind of girl with whom a man got infatuated? Perhaps she was a change from all the lovely creatures she had seen him with?

She heard him laugh softly. 'You're not listening and I can read every thought in your face, Lucy. Mother lives in Wassenaar. If you like, we'll have lunch with her and my father and then go for a walk—there's miles of beach—it's empty at this time of year.' He got up to fill her coffee cup. 'You don't believe me, do you? Perhaps when we've had our walk, you will.'

They set out half an hour later, Fraam chatting easily about nothing that mattered and Lucy almost silent, a dozen questions on her tongue and not daring to utter one of them.

Fraam's parents had a house by the sea, with the golf course behind the house and the wide sands only a few hundred yards away. The house was large and Edwardian in style, with a great many small windows and balconies and a roof which arched itself over them like eyebrows. It was encircled by a large garden, very neat and bare now that winter was upon them, but behind the flower beds there were a great many trees, sheltering it from the stares of anyone on the road. Lucy, who still hadn't found her tongue, crossed the well-raked gravel beside Fraam and when he opened the door beneath a heavy arch, went past him into a square lobby. They were met here by a bustling elderly woman who opened the inner door for them, made some laughing rejoinder to Fraam's greeting and then smiled at Lucy. 'This is Ton—she housekeeps for my mother. If you like to go with her you can leave your coat.'

He spoke in a friendly way, but there was nothing warmer in his manner than that; Lucy, following Ton across the hall to a small cloakroom, began to wonder if she had dreamt their conversation. She still looked bewildered when she returned to where he was waiting for her in the hall, but it hadn't been a dream; he bent and kissed her hard before taking her arm and ushering her down a short passage and into a room at the side of the house. It was high-ceilinged, as most Dutch houses are, with a heavily embossed hanging on the walls, a richly coloured carpet covering most of the parquet floor and some quite beautiful William and Mary furniture.

Fraam's parents were there, standing at one of the big windows looking out over the garden, but they turned as they went in and came forward to greet them, looking not in the least surprised. And although nothing was said either then or during the lunch they presently ate, she couldn't fail to see that she was regarded as part of the family, so that presently, walking briskly along the hard sand with Fraam, she was emboldened to ask: 'Do your parents know—about—well, about you asking me to marry you?'

He had tucked a hand under her arm, steadying her against the wind. 'Oh, yes—I mentioned it some time ago.'

She turned her head to look at him. 'Some time ago? But you never said...' She trailed off into silence, and watched him smile.

'No. I had to wait for the right moment, didn't I?' He stopped and turned her round to face him. 'And perhaps this is the right moment for you to give me your answer.'

He hadn't said that he loved her, had he? But he wanted to marry her. She would make him a good wife; she was sure of that because she loved him. She put up a hand to tuck in a strand of hair the wind had whipped loose.

'Yes, I'll marry you, Fraam. I'm—I'm still surprised about it, but I'm quite sure.'

'Why are you sure, dear girl?'

She met his steady gaze without affectation. 'I love you, Fraam; I didn't know until that day we were shovelling snow...'

'I know, Lucy.' His voice was very gentle.

She looked at him, startled. 'Oh, did you? How?'

He had pulled her close. 'I'm a mind-reader, especially when it comes to you.' He kissed her slowly. 'We'll marry soon, Lucy—there's no reason why we shouldn't, is there?'

She rubbed her cheek against the thick wool of his coat. 'Yes, there is. I have to give a month's notice.'

'I'll settle that,' he told her carelessly. 'You won't need to go back to St Norbert's.'

'Oh, but I must—I mean, it will all have to be explained.' She frowned a little. 'I can't just walk out.'

'We'll sort that out later on.' Fraam started to walk again, his arm round her shoulders. 'We'll telephone your mother and father when we go back.'

'They'll be surprised.'

He said on a laugh: 'Your mother won't.' And then: 'You'll be able to leave Doctor de Groot in a couple of days and come to my house until we can go back to England—I've several cases coming up, I'm afraid...'

'Oh, but I can't do that!'

She felt his hand tighten on her shoulder. 'You haven't met my young sister yet, have you? She's coming to pay me a visit—you'll enjoy getting to know her.'

'Oh,' said Lucy again, 'well, yes, I shall.' The wind was in their faces now and the seashore looked bleak and grey under the wintry sky—the bad weather had come early, there had been no mild days for quite a while. She was cold even in her winter coat but so happy that she hardly felt it. None of it seemed real, of course; just a lovely dream which could shatter and become her mundane life once more with no Fraam in it. 'I can't think why...' she began, and caught her breath.

'You're still scared, aren't you? When you're quite used to the idea, I'll tell you why.' He smiled so kindly that she felt a lump in her throat. 'Mama wanted us to stay for dinner, but I thought we would go somewhere and dine together. Would you like that?'

Lucy nodded and then frowned. 'I'm not dressed for going out.'

'You look perfectly all right to me—we'll go to Dikker and Thijs, it'll be quiet at this time of year, we can stay as long as we like.'

It was a lovely evening. Lucy, lying wide-awake in bed that night, went over every second of it, fingering the magnificent ruby and diamond ring on her finger. Fraam had taken it from his pocket during the evening and put it there and by some good chance it had fitted perfectly. It was old, he had explained, left to him by his grandmother when he had been a very young man; he had promised himself then that he would keep it until he could put it on the hand of the girl he was going to marry. Lucy sat up in bed and turned the light on just to have another look at it. It was so beautiful that she left the light on and sat up against her pillows and went on thinking about the evening.

Fraam's parents had been kind. They had welcomed her into the family with just the right kind of remarks, told her that she was to come and see them again as soon as possible and expressed their delight at the idea of having her for a daughter-in-law. And Fraam had been a dear. She repeated that to herself because right at the back of her mind was the vague thought that he still hadn't said that he loved her and his manner, although flatteringly attentive, had been almost like that of an old friend, not a man who had just proposed. She wanted too much, she told herself; more than likely she wasn't a girl to inspire that kind of feeling in a man. It was surely enough that he wanted her for his wife. She went to sleep on the thought and by morning her doubts had dwindled to mere wisps in her mind.

Mies was flatteringly impressed but disconcertingly surprised too. She exclaimed with unthinking frankness: 'I am amazed, Lucy—Fraam has had eyes only for Adilia, who is beautiful—when you returned to England he took her out many times. What will your parents say?'

'They're delighted.' Lucy tried to speak lightly, but she frowned as she spoke. Here was a new name and a new girl. 'Adilia—I don't think I've heard about her. Did I ever meet her?'

Mies thought. 'Fraam danced with her at the hospital ball, she was wearing a flame-coloured dress, very chic. They've known each other for ages. I quite thought...' She looked at Lucy's face and added brightly: 'But that means nothing; he has had so many girl-friends, but Adilia he sees more than the others. But not of course now that he is engaged to you.' She added hastily: 'You must not be worried.'

'I'm not in the least worried,' declared Lucy, consumed with enough worry to sink her. She would ask Fraam; he would probably see her during the day. She cheered up at the thought and went along to see how Doctor de Groot was and to break the news to him. He wasn't in the least surprised, indeed he suggested that she might like to leave then and there. 'I'm quite able to look after myself,' he told her, 'and Fraam did mention something about his sister paying him a visit—I daresay he plans for you to go and stay with him while she's there.'

'Well, yes, he does. But don't you want me here? I never did have much to do, I know, but you're not going back to work yet...'

He looked benignly at her. 'Just an hour each day,' he murmured. 'I've already discussed it with Fraam—I'll go away for Christmas as I said I would, but I just want to keep my hand in. Now run along, my dear, I daresay Fraam will be along to see you.'

But Fraam didn't come—he telephoned at lunchtime to say that he wouldn't be able to get away but could she be ready if he called for her after breakfast the next day? He sounded remote and cool, and Lucy, anxious for her world to be quite perfect, put that down to pressure of work and perhaps other people listening to him telephoning. All the same, she thought wistfully, he could have called her dear just once. She shook her head to rid it of the doubts which kept filling it; just because Mies had told her about Adilia; probably it was all hot air...

She was ready and waiting when he arrived the next morning and his hard, urgent kiss was more than she had expected—a great deal more, she decided happily as they made their farewells and she got into the Mini beside him. Mies must have got it all wrong about Adilia. She responded to Fraam's easy conversation with a lightheartedness which gave her a happy glow.

His sister came into the hall the moment they entered the

house and before Fraam could speak volunteered the information that her name was Lisabertha, that she was delighted to meet Lucy, that they were almost the same age and that she was quite positive that they would be the firmest of friends. She paused just long enough to give Lucy a hug and then throw her arms round her brother's neck. 'Dear Fraam,' she declared, 'isn't this fun? And may I ask Rob to dinner this evening?' She turned to Lucy. 'I'm going to marry him next year,' she told her. 'He works in Utrecht, but he said he could get here by seven o'clock.'

Fraam chuckled. 'So he's already been asked to dinner?' He smiled at Lucy. 'If you two like to go into the sitting room I'll get Jaap to take the cases up.'

He stayed and had coffee with them and then left them to their own devices with the remark that he had work to do and would see them that evening. Lucy, who would have liked to have been kissed again, got a friendly smile, that was all.

The day passed very pleasantly. Lisabertha was obviously the darling of her family and had a great fondness for her eldest brother; she talked about him for a good deal of the time and Lucy listened to every word, filling in the gaps about him with interesting titbits of information. He had been in love several times, his young sister informed her, but never seriously. They had all begun to think that he would never marry, and now here was dear Lucy, and how glad they were. Where had they met and when was the wedding to be and what was Lucy going to wear? To all of which Lucy gave vague replies. Their meeting had been most unglamorous and the less said about it the better, she decided, and she had no idea when they were to marry. Fraam had suggested that she left the hospital at once, but at the back of her mind she wasn't too sure about that. Supposing he were to change his mind? If she worked for another month, that would give him time to be quite sure. But even as she thought it, the other half of her mind was denying it. Fraam wasn't a man to change his mind.

Certainly there was nothing in his manner to give her any

cause for doubt that evening. The three of them dined together and then sat round the fire in the drawing room, talking idly, until Lisabertha declared that she was going to bed, and when Lucy said that she would go too, Fraam begged her to stay a little longer. 'For I have hardly seen you,' he protested, 'and we have so much to discuss.'

But the discussion, it turned out, wasn't quite what she had expected: whether they should visit his parents on the following day or the one after, and had she any preference as to when she returned to England.

'Well, I hadn't thought about it,' said Lucy. 'If I give a month's notice I suppose the quicker I go back to St Norbert's the better.'

He frowned. 'You seem determined to do that,' he observed rather coldly. 'I told you that it could be arranged that you left at any time...' He got up and strolled over to the window and looked out into the dark night, holding back the heavy curtains. 'You are not anxious to marry me as soon as possible, then, Lucy?'

'Yes—well, no. It's...' she paused, at a loss for words. 'I mean, supposing you changed your mind and it would be too late.'

'You think that I might change my mind?' His voice was silky.

It seemed a good opportunity to take the bull by the horns. 'I'm not at all the kind of girl everyone expected you to marry; Mies said, and so did Lisabertha, that you liked pretty girls—not like me at all.' She drew a little breath and asked in a rush: 'Who is Adilia?'

He didn't answer her for a long moment but stood by the window still, staring at her. Finally he said: 'I have rushed things too fast, I believe. You are uncertain of me, Lucy—indeed, possibly you don't quite trust me. I will tell you who Adilia is and then we will forget this whole conversation and return to our former pleasant task of getting to know each other. She is a girl I have known for some years; I have never had any wish to marry her, just as I have never had any wish to marry any of the girls I have taken out from time to time.'

He walked over to her and pulled her gently to her feet. 'I have never asked anyone to marry me before, Lucy.' He bent and kissed her lightly. 'Go to bed, my dear. I wish I had all day to spend with you tomorrow, but I'm not free until the late afternoon. We'll put off going to Mama's and we'll go out to dine, just the two of us.' He put up a hand and touched her cheek. 'You're a dear, old-fashioned girl, aren't you? You need to be wooed slowly; I should have known that.'

He was as good as his word. He came to take her out the following evening and by the end of it Lucy had almost made up her mind to leave the hospital at once and marry him just as soon as he wanted her to. They had dined at a quiet, luxurious hotel and danced for a while afterwards, and she couldn't help but be flattered by the attention they received. Fraam was obviously a well-known client and although he took it all for granted, she was made a little shy by it. They had walked back through the quiet, cold streets afterwards, and when they had got back into the house she had actually been on the point of telling him that she would do as he wished, but the telephone had rung and when he had gone to answer it, he had bidden her a hurried goodnight and left the house.

She saw him at breakfast, but as he was on the point of going as she reached the table, there was no time for more than a quick kiss and an assurance that he would be home for lunch.

As indeed he was, but with a guest. 'Adilia,' he introduced her coolly, and Lucy, instantly disliking her, greeted her with a sweetness only matched by her new acquaintance.

'We met outside and since Adilia tells me that she is at a loose end I invited her for lunch.' He added carelessly: 'I told Jaap as we came in. And what have you two been doing with your morning?'

He sat down between Lisabertha and Adilia, opposite Lucy, and it was to her he looked. Lucy began some sort of a reply, to be interrupted gently by Adilia, who demanded, in the prettiest way imaginable, that she might be given a drink. And after that she kept the conversation in her own hands, and during lunch as well, even though Lisabertha did her best to start up a more general conversation so that Lucy might join in; for how could she do that when the talk was of people she didn't know and times when she hadn't even known Fraam. She looked composed enough, made polite rejoinders when she was addressed and seethed inside her. Adilia might only be a girl Fraam had known for years, but she was a beautiful one and she had a lovely voice, a low laugh and the kind of clothes Lucy had hankered after for years. She decided that the wisest course was to attempt no competition at all and was pleased to see presently that Adilia found it disconcerting. All the same they parted on the friendliest of terms, and Lucy, talking animatedly, managed to avoid Fraam, calling a casual goodbye as he went through the door with Adilia, who had begged a lift, beside him.

'You do not like her,' declared Lisabertha instantly, leading the way back to the sitting room.

'I can't say I do,' agreed Lucy, 'though I daresay I'm jealous of her; she's quite beautiful and she wears gorgeous clothes.'

'And you also will wear such clothes when you are Fraam's wife, and you may not be a beauty, but he has chosen you, has he not?'

Lucy said 'Yes' doubtfully and because she didn't want to talk about it, said that she had letters to write and had better get them done and posted.

And that evening, when Fraam came home and they were having drinks before dinner, he asked her what she had thought of Adilia. It would have been nice to have told him what she did think, but instead she said rather colourlessly that Adilia was beautiful. He laughed then and added: 'So now you know what she's like, my dear.'

CHAPTER NINE

LUCY HAD SPENT an almost sleepless night wondering exactly what Fraam had meant. He hadn't said any more; dinner had been a pleasant affair, just the three of them, and the talk had been of the family dinner party at their mother's house the next evening. 'Have you got that green dress with you?' Fraam wanted to know, and when Lucy answered a surprised yes: 'Then wear it, my dear, it suits you very well.' He had smiled to send her heart dancing: 'There will be more family for you to meet; there are a great many of us...'

'Aunts and uncles,' chimed in Lisabertha, 'and cousins. I suppose that horrid Tante Sophie will be there.'

'Naturally, and you will be nice to her, Lisa, although I think that we must all take care that Lucy doesn't fall into her clutches.'

'Why not?' asked Lucy.

'She is malicious. Perhaps she does not mean to be, but she can be unkind.'

'Well, if I don't understand her...'

'She speaks excellent English. But don't worry, we'll not give her a chance to get you alone.'

All the same, Lucy found herself alone with the lady the next evening. Dinner was over, a splendid, leisurely meal, shared by some twenty people and all of them, it seemed, der Linssens. They had had their coffee in the drawing room and had broken up into small groups the better to talk, and someone or other had delayed Fraam as they had been crossing the room, and Lucy found herself alone. But only for a moment. Tante Sophie had appeared beside her and no one had noticed her taking Lucy by the arm and leading her on to the covered balcony adjoining the drawing room.

'I'm really waiting for Fraam,' began Lucy. 'He's just stopped to speak to someone...'

'He will find us here,' beamed Tante Sophie. 'I have been so anxious to have you to myself for just a few minutes, Lucy. Such a sweet girl you are, you will make an excellent wife for Fraam; so quiet and malleable and never questioning.'

'Why should I question him?' asked Lucy curiously.

Tante Sophie looked arch. 'My dear, surely you know that Fraam is what you call a lady's man? That is an old-fashioned term, is it not, but I am sure that you understand it. So many pretty girls...' she sighed, 'the fortunate man, he could have taken his pick of any one of them, but he chose you. You haven't known him long?' Her voice had grown a little sharp.

Lucy didn't answer. She wondered if it would be very rude if she just walked away, but Tante Sophie still had a beringed hand on her arm.

'Of course, my dear Lucy, we older ones find it difficult to understand you young people—not that Fraam is a young man...' Lucy opened her mouth to make an indignant protest, but she had no chance. 'You are permissive, is that not the right word? Why, I could tell you tales—but wives turn a blind eye these days, it seems, just as you will learn to do.'

Tante Sophie had small, beady black eyes. Like a snake, thought Lucy, staring at her and trying to think of something to say. The lady was so obviously wanting her to ask all the questions she was just as obviously wanting to answer. When she didn't speak Tante Sophie said tartly: 'Well, it is to be hoped that he won't break your heart; he's never loved a girl for more than a few days.'

Lucy felt Fraam's large hand on her shoulder. Its pressure was reassuring and very comforting. 'He's never loved a girl,' he corrected the old lady blandly, 'until now. Have you been trying to frighten Lucy, Tante Sophie?' His voice was light, but Lucy could feel his anger.

'Of course not!' The elderly voice was shrill with spite. 'Well, I must go and talk to your mother, Fraam.' Her peevish gaze swept the room behind them. 'Such a pity it is just family. A few of those lovely girls of yours would have made the evening a good deal livelier.'

They watched her go, and Fraam's hand slipped from Lucy's shoulder to her waist. 'Sorry about that,' he observed easily. 'Do you want to call our engagement off?'

He was laughing as he spoke and she laughed back at him. Now he was there beside her, all the silly little doubts Tante Sophie's barbed remarks had raised were quieted. 'Of course not! She must be very unhappy to talk like that.'

'Clever girl to see that. Yes, she is, that's why we all bear with her.' He smiled down at her and for a moment Lucy thought that he was going to kiss her. But he didn't—perhaps, she told herself sensibly, because someone might turn round and see them, but it didn't matter; he loved her and everything was all right.

All right until lunchtime the next day. She and Lisabertha had been out shopping and while they were waiting to cross the busy street at the Munt, she saw the unmistakable Panther de Ville coming towards them. And Adilia was sitting beside Fraam. Lucy watched it pass them in silence and it was Lisabertha who exclaimed: 'Well, what on earth is she doing with Fraam? He told me he was working until at least three o'clock.'

'Perhaps he finished early,' Lucy heard her voice, carefully colourless, utter the trite words, and her companion hastened to agree with her. But Lucy didn't really listen; she was thinking about Adilia. In the few seconds during which the car had passed, Lucy had had the general impression of loveliness and chic and beautiful clothes, and an even stronger impression that Adilia had seen her...

By the time they got home she was in a splendid turmoil of temper, hurt and doubt. She could hardly wait until Fraam returned so that she might unburden herself; men who were just engaged didn't go riding round the city with other girls, nor did they tell lies about working until three o'clock when they weren't. When he did get home she was sitting in the drawing room alone, for Lisabertha, sensing her mood, had retired discreetly to her room. Fraam barely had time to close the door behind him when she told him icily: 'I saw you this afternoon—at lunchtime—with Adilia. You said you would be working until three o'clock.' She added waspishly: 'I suppose you took her out to lunch.'

His expression didn't change at all and she couldn't see the gleam in his eyes. 'Er—no, my dear.' She waited for him to say something more than that and when he didn't she got up and started for the door. She knew that she was behaving childishly and that she would probably burst into tears in no time at all; she had been spoiling for a nice down-to-earth quarrel and Fraam had no intention of quarrelling. Was this what Tante Sophie had meant? Was this learning to turn a blind eye? A sob bubbled up in her throat and escaped just as she had a hand on the door, but she never opened it. Fraam had got there too and turned her round and caught her close.

'Now, now, my love,' he said soothingly, 'what's all this?' He kissed the top of her head. 'I believe Tante Sophie's hints and spite did their work, after all.' He turned her face up to his and carefully wiped away a tear. 'I told you I would be working until three o'clock, but what I didn't explain was that I had a list at another hospital. I was driving there when Adilia stopped me and asked for a lift. And I didn't have lunch with her—indeed, I haven't had lunch at all.'

'Oh, aren't I awful?' Lucy said woefully, 'jumping to conclusions, and you going without your lunch. I feel mean and a bit silly.'

'You're not mean and you're not silly, but supposing we get married as soon as we can, then you'll be quite sure of me, won't you?'

'You mean I'm not quite sure of you now?' she asked him quickly. 'Well, no, perhaps I'm not. But don't you see, while I'm not then how can I marry you?' She went on earnestly: 'I think I should go back to St Norbert's and—and not see you for a bit and then you'll be sure…'

'Sure of what?' His voice was very quiet.

'Well, wanting to marry me.'

'And you? Would you be sure then, Lucy?'

She looked at him in surprise. 'Me? Oh, but I'm sure—I mean, sure that I love you.'

'So it is for me that you wish to go back to hospital? Not for yourself?'

She nodded. 'Yes. You do have to be quite certain.'

'And you think that I am not. Shall I tell you something, Lucy? The world is full of Adilias, but there is only one Lucy.' He pulled her to him and kissed her slowly. 'I can't teach you to trust me; that's something you must do for yourself, and I think that you do trust me, only you have this ridiculous idea that every girl in the world is beautiful except you, and because of that you have this chip on your shoulder which prevents you from accepting the fact that anyone could possibly want to marry you.'

'I have not got a chip on my shoulder,' said Lucy pettishly. 'I'm trying to be sensible.' She wanted to cry again, but she didn't know why.

'All right, no chip.' He kissed her again. 'We won't talk about it any more now; I have to go back to my rooms after tea, but after dinner this evening we'll talk again, and this time I shall persuade you to change your mind and marry me as soon as possible.'

She leaned her head against his shoulder and thought that probably she would be persuaded because that was what she wanted to do really. She said quite happily: 'Yes, all right—I like being with you and talking, Fraam.'

They had tea together presently, and Lucy had felt utterly content. This was going to be marriage with Fraam; quiet half hours in which to talk and knowing that he would be home again in the evening. Just the sight of him sitting opposite her, drinking his tea and eating cake and telling her about his day at the hospital, made her feel slightly giddy with happiness. Her matter-of-fact acceptance of her plain face was being edged away by a new-found assurance stemming from that same happiness and after all not many girls had green eyes. When Fraam had gone she went upstairs and washed her hair and wound it painstakingly into rollers while she did her face. The results were not startling but at least they were an improvement. She would buy a new dress or two, she thought happily, and when later that evening they would have their talk, she would agree to anything he said. He had been right, of course; the reason why she wasn't quite sure of him was because she hadn't quite believed that he could prefer her to other girls. She skipped downstairs to wait for him.

He didn't come. There was a telephone message a little later to say that there had been an accident—one of the surgeons on duty—and Fraam would stay in his place until he could be relieved. The two girls dined alone and the evening passed pleasantly enough discussing the clothes Lucy would like to buy. 'Get all you want,' advised Lisabertha. 'Fraam has a great deal of money and he will pay the bills.'

'I'd rather not—at least, not until he suggests it, if he ever does. I've some money, enough to buy a dress.'

They went to bed presently and Lucy, thinking of Fraam, slept dreamlessly.

He was at breakfast the next morning, immersed in his letters, making notes in his pocketbook and scanning the newspaper headlines. He got up when she joined him, settled her in a chair beside him, declared in a rather absent-minded way that she looked as pretty as a picture, kissed her briefly and went on: 'I have to go to Brussels this morning—there's a patient there I've looked after for some time and his own doctor wants me there for a consultation. I'm flying down, Jaap will take me to Schiphol, and I should be back this evening—wait up for me, Lucy, there is something I want to tell you.'

'Can't you tell me now?' She tried not to sound anxious. His 'no' was very decisive.

Lucy was alone in the sitting room after lunch when Jaap came into the room.

'There is a visitor for you, Miss Prendergast,' he announced uneasily.

Adilia looked lovely, but then she always did. She brushed past Jaap as though he weren't there and addressed Lucy. 'I've come to fetch some things I forgot to take with me.'

Lucy felt puzzled. 'Things?' she asked, and added politely: 'Well, I'm sure Fraam won't mind if you collect them—where did you leave them?'

Adilia gave her a wicked look. 'Upstairs, of course—where else do you suppose? In the Brocade Room.' She gave a little laugh. 'Fraam called you the parson's daughter, and you really are, aren't you?'

She sank down into one of the large winged chairs, apparently in no hurry, arranging herself comfortably before she observed: 'Why do you suppose Fraam is marrying you, Lucy? He needs a wife...' she glanced round the beautiful room, 'someone to run his household and rear his children. That's not for me,' she shrugged briefly. 'I'm all for freedom, so he can't have me—not on a permanent basis—and now he doesn't care who he marries. You will do as well as any, I daresay—probably better.'

Lucy felt cold inside and there was a peculiar sensation in her head. All the same she said sturdily: 'I don't believe you.'

Adilia got up, stretched herself and yawned prettily. 'It's all the same to me. You will be an excellent wife, for you will never allow yourself to wonder if Fraam is really in Munich or Brussels at some seminar or other, or ask where he has been when he comes home late.' She nodded her beautiful head. 'It is a great advantage to be a parson's daughter—he sees that too.'

Lucy was on her feet now, her small capable hands clenched on either side of her. 'I still don't believe you,' she said, and somehow managed to keep her doubts out of her voice.

'You don't want to. Fraam is in Brussels, is he not, or so he told you.' Adilia tugged the bell rope and when Jaap came: 'Jaap, you drove Mr der Linssen to Schiphol, did you not? We are both so silly, we cannot remember where he was going.'

Jaap marshalled his English. 'To London, Juffrouw—the ten o'clock flight.'

Adilia nodded dismissal and he went away, looking puzzled and a little worried; Miss Prendergast had looked quite ill when he had said that...

'You see?' asked Adilia when the door had been closed. She crossed the room and tapped Lucy on the shoulder. 'Jaap does not lie—you have to believe him. And now you will have to believe me; I am going to London too.'

She went to the door. 'There is one thing of which you may be very sure: I am very discreet. But what should you care? You will have what you want—this house, Fraam's money and a clutch of children—they will be plain, just like you.'

She had gone, closing the door very quietly behind her, and Lucy stood speechless, the strength of her feelings tearing through her like a force-ten gale. Rage and misery and humiliation all jostled for a place in her bewildered head and for the moment at any rate, rage won. She tore at the ring on her finger and then raced from the room, up the stairs and into her bedroom, there to fling on her coat, tie a scarf over her hair and snatch up her gloves. She was in the hall and almost at the door when Jaap came through the little arched door which led to the kitchens.

'You go out, miss?' he asked. He didn't allow his well-schooled features to lose their blandness, but his voice was anxious.

'Yes. Yes, Jaap.' She looked at him quite wildly, still re-living those terrible minutes with Adilia. 'I'm going away.' She darted past him, got the heavy door open and was away before he could stop her.

She had no idea where she was going, but she wasn't thinking about that. She had no idea in which direction she was walking either; she was running away, intent on putting as much distance between her and her hurt as possible. She hurried along, thinking how strange it was that she had been so happy and that just a few words from someone could sweep that happiness away like sand before the wind.

She walked on, right through the heart of the city, without being aware of it, and when the street she was in merged into the Mauritskade, she turned along it and then into Stadhouderskade and so into Leidsestraat. She trudged down that too, and if it hadn't begun to rain she might have gone on and on and ended up at Schiphol; as it was she turned round and started back again towards the centre of Amsterdam. She was tired now and she wasn't really thinking any more, aware only of a dull headache and an empty feeling deep inside her. It had grown from afternoon dusk to wintry evening and she realised that she was cold and hungry and needed to rest, and over and above that, it was impossible for her to go back to Fraam's house ever again. She would go home, of course, but just at the moment she was quite incapable of making any plans, first she must have a meal.

She had reached the inner ring of the *grachten* again and there were hotels on every side. She recognised one of them;

Fraam had taken her there to dine only a short time ago. She went inside and booked a room at the reception desk, for she had to sleep somewhere and she remembered that he had told her that it was a respectable hotel. She didn't ask the price of the room; her head was still full of her own unhappy thoughts and she brushed aside the receptionist's polite enquiry as to luggage, following the bell boy into the lift like an automaton and when she was alone in the room, sitting down without even taking her coat off. But presently she bestirred herself and looked around her. The apartment was luxurious, more so than she had expected, and the adjoining bathroom was quite magnificent. She washed her white face and telephoned for a meal. It was while she was waiting for it that she realised that she had no money. And no passport either.

She ate her dinner when it came because whatever trouble lay ahead of her, and there would be trouble, it would be easier to face if she were nicely full; all the same, she had no idea what she ate.

When the room waiter had cleared away she undressed, had a bath and got into bed. She already owed for her dinner, she might as well owe for a night's rest as well. She really didn't care what they would do to her, although she wondered what the Dutch prisons were like. But her thoughts soon returned to Fraam. She would have to send him a message or write to him—probably from prison. She chuckled at the thought and the chuckle turned into tears until, quite worn out with her weeping, she slept.

She woke in the night, her mind clear and sensible; all she had to do was to telephone Jaap in the morning and ask him to send round her handbag. All the money she possessed was in it, and so was her passport. It was a pity she would have to leave her clothes behind, but they weren't important; she would be able to pay the bill and go to Schiphol and catch the first flight possible. She wondered if she had enough money; as far as she could remember there had been all of fifty pounds in her purse, surely more than sufficient. She closed her eyes and slept again.

It was after breakfast, taken in her room, and an unsatisfactory toilet that she went down to the reception desk. There was another clerk on duty now, a sharp-faced woman who bade her a grudging good morning and asked her if she wanted her bill.

It seemed the right moment to explain. Lucy embarked on her story; she had left the house without her purse and could she telephone to have it sent to her at the hotel. It wasn't until she had come to the end of it that she saw that the clerk didn't believe a word of it. All the same she gave her the number. 'It's Mijnheer der Linssen's house,' she explained. 'He is known here, isn't he?' And when the woman nodded grudgingly: 'Well, I'm his fiancée.' Too late she saw the woman's eyes fly to her ringless hands. She had plucked off her lovely ring and left it... where had she left it? She had no idea.

'I'll call the manager,' said the clerk, still polite but hostile. And when he came, elegant and courteous, the whole story was repeated, but this time in Dutch and by the clerk, so that Lucy couldn't understand a word. At the end of it the manager spoke pleasantly enough. 'By all means make your call, Miss...' he refreshed his memory from the register before him, 'Miss Prendergast. Perhaps you wouldn't mind waiting in your room afterwards?' He smiled. 'Your handbag shall be brought to you there.'

Lucy sighed with relief and went to one of the telephone booths. Jaap sounded upset, but she didn't give him a chance to speak. 'My handbag,' she urged him, 'it's on the dressing table in my room, please will you send it round as soon as you can? You do understand?' She heard him draw breath and his hurried 'Yes, miss,' but didn't give him a chance to say anything else. 'And Jaap, don't tell anyone I'm here—not anyone. Here's the address, and do please hurry. And thank you, Jaap.'

She went upstairs at once since the manager had been so insistent; perhaps they thought it would be easier and save time if they knew where she was. It was a little irksome to stay there, though, for the urge to get away was getting stronger every minute. An hour passed and she became more and more uneasy; she didn't think that it would take all that time to come from Fraam's house, she decided to go down to the desk and see if it had been delivered and forgotten.

She had been locked in. She stared at the door in disbelief and tried the handle again, fruitlessly, and when she lifted the receiver no one answered. Not a girl to panic, she went and sat down and tried to think calmly. In a way it was a relief to have something to worry about; it stopped her thinking about Fraam. She thought of him now of course and tears she really couldn't stop spilled from her tired eyes and ran down her unmade-up face. If he had been there, this would never have happened, she told herself with muddled logic. But he wasn't there, he was in London, possibly even now waiting eagerly at the airport for Adilia. The thought made the tears flow even faster and she uttered a small wail. The sound of the key turning in the lock sent her round facing the wall so that they shouldn't see her face. When the door was opened and shut again she cried in a soggy whisper: 'Oh, do please go away!' only to swing round at once, because of course if they went away she wouldn't get her bag...

Fraam was standing there with a white and furious face, her handbag in his hand. He said in a bitter voice she hardly recognised: 'You wanted this? Presumably you left home so fast that you forgot it.'

He looked enquiringly at her, his brows raised, but she didn't answer him.

'You should be more careful,' he told her. 'You need both money and passport when you run away.' His eyes swept over her tatty person. 'Make-up too, and a comb.'

Surprise had checked her tears, but at this remark they all came rushing back again. How dared he poke fun at her! She meant to tell him so, but all she said in a wispy voice was: 'They locked me in.'

His mouth twitched. 'And quite right too. They weren't to know whether you were lying or not, were they? And you were lying, Lucy. I found your ring in your teacup—an extraordinary place—so I must take it that you are no longer my fiancée.' He added sternly: 'There is a law against false pretences.'

It seemed to Lucy that she was getting nowhere at all. She had the right to upbraid him, but she had had no chance. To point out his duplicity, confront him with his two-faced behaviour. Suddenly indignant, she took a deep breath and opened her mouth. She was dreadfully unhappy, but an angry outburst might help her to forget that.

'And before you launch your attack,' said Fraam in a surprisingly mild voice now, 'I want an explanation.'

She choked on the words she had been preparing to utter. 'You want an explanation? It's me that wants one!' Her voice rose to a watery squeak. 'Adilia said...'

'Ah, now we are getting to the heart of the matter.'

Her rage had gone, there was nothing but a cold unhappy lump in her chest.

'Don't joke, Fraam—please don't joke,' and when she saw how good-humoured he was looking now, she added pettishly: 'Why do you look so pleased with yourself? Just now when you came in you were furiously angry.'

He was leaning against the wall, his hands in his pockets, looking, she was shocked to see, as though he was enjoying himself. 'My dear girl, no man worth his salt likes to find his fiancée—ex-fiancée—locked in an hotel bedroom because she can't pay the bill. Over and above that, I was roused from a night's sleep by Jaap's agitated request that I should catch the next plane and return home because you had left the house rather more hastily than he liked. I've had no breakfast and I'm tired, and until a few minutes ago, the most terrified man on earth. And now tell me what Adilia said to cause you to tear away in such a fashion.'

'You went to London,' Lucy pointed out in a wobbly voice,

'and you told me you were going to Brussels, and Adilia said—she said that she was going to London too and that I was a parson's daughter and you only wanted to marry me because she wouldn't have you.' She sucked in a breath like a tearful child. 'And she said I'd have p-plain children, just like me.'

A spasm passed over Fraam's handsome features. He dealt with what was obvious to him to be the most hurtful of these remarks. 'Little girls with green eyes and soft mouths are the most beautiful of God's creatures,' he said in a gentle voice, 'and as for the boys, they will be our sons, Lucy, with, I hope, their mother's sweet nature and my muscle.'

He left the wall so suddenly that the next thing she knew she was wrapped in his arms. 'You silly, silly little girl,' he observed, 'did you not know that I would come after you wherever you went?'

Lucy sniffed. It was very satisfying to feel his tight hold, but they still hadn't dealt with the crux of the matter. 'Adilia said...' she began, and was interrupted by Fraam's forceful: 'Damn Adilia, but since you have to get her off your chest, my darling, let us hear what the woman said and be done with it.'

It was a little difficult to begin. Lucy muttered and mumbled a good deal, but once she got started the words poured out in a jumble which hardly made sense. But Fraam listened patiently and when she paused at last, not at all sure that she had made herself clear, he had the salient points at his fingertips. 'Dear heart, will you believe me when I say that Adilia has never, at any time, stayed at my house? There was nothing of hers in the Brocade Room or anywhere else in my home. Why should there be? You have been the only girl, Lucy. She was making mischief—people do, you know; they're bored with their own lives and it amuses them to upset those of other people.'

'Of course I believe you,' declared Lucy, and added after a moment's thought: 'You went to London—she asked Jaap, you know, and he told us. Because I didn't believe her.'

'I went to London, my dearest darling, to see the Senior

Nursing Officer of St Norbert's, for it had become increasingly clear to me that getting married to you was more important than anything else and all this hanging around for a month until you could leave was quite unnecessary. I saw your father briefly too and asked him about a licence. If you would agree, we could be married within the week.'

'But you didn't say a word...'

'I was afraid you would have all kinds of arguments against it, my love.' He kissed the top of her head. 'No time to buy clothes, you would have said, certainly no time to arrange for bridesmaids, no time to send out invitations...'

Lucy considered. 'I don't mind about any of those things,' she told him, 'though of course I must buy a dress...'

'My dear sensible girl, and so beautiful too.' And when she looked at him she saw that he meant it. 'At your home? And your father, of course. My family can fly over,' his eyes narrowed in thought, 'I'll charter a plane.'

'But that's extravagant!'

'Surely one may be forgiven a little extravagance at such a time, my darling.' He loosed her for a moment, found her ring in a pocket and slipped it on her finger. 'Why a teacup?' he wanted to know.

'I don't know—I don't remember, I was so unhappy.'

'You shall never be unhappy again, dear heart.' He kissed her slowly. 'And now we're going home.'

Lucy received the manager's apology with a smile. She was so happy herself that she wanted everyone else to be the same, only she longed to wave her hand with the ring once more upon it under the clerk's nose.

They hardly spoke as Fraam drove through the city. It wasn't until they were in the hall with a beaming Jaap shutting the door on the outside world that Lucy spoke.

'Fraam, were you ever in love with Adilia, or—or any of those girls you danced with at the hospital ball?'

He turned her round to face him, holding her gently by the shoulders.

'No, my love, just amusing myself while I was waiting for you to come along, and when you did I was so afraid that you would have none of me... I think I am still a little afraid of that.'

Lucy flung her arms round his neck. 'The first time you saw me—at that lecture, you looked as though you wanted to shake me.'

'Did I? I wanted to get off that platform and carry you off and marry you out of hand... I fell in love with you then, my darling.'

She leaned back the better to see his face. 'Did you really? And I looked such a mess!'

His hands were gentle on her. 'You looked beautiful, my darling, just as you look beautiful now.'

She leaned up and kissed him. 'That's such a satisfactory thing to have said of one,' she commented. 'I'm not sure that it's quite true, but oh, Fraam, I'm so glad I'm me!'

Jaap, coming from the dining room, looked carefully into the middle distance and coughed. 'There is breakfast,' he mentioned with dignity.

They both turned to look at him. 'Jaap, old friend, you think of everything,' remarked Fraam as Lucy left him to take Jaap's hand.

'Thank you,' she said. 'I hope you'll be my old friend too.'

Jaap beamed once more. 'It will be my pleasure, Miss Prendergast.'

He watched the pair of them go into the dining room and then closed the door. On his way to the kitchen he ruminated happily on the days ahead. Such a lot to do; a wedding was always a nice thing to have in a family. He nodded his elderly head with deep satisfaction.

* * * * *

New release – out next month!

The Rough Rider

by

NEW YORK TIMES BESTSELLING AUTHOR
MAISEY YATES

Return to Four Corners Ranch for a marriage of convenience between two unlikely souls — a hopeless romantic and a man who has long given up hope.

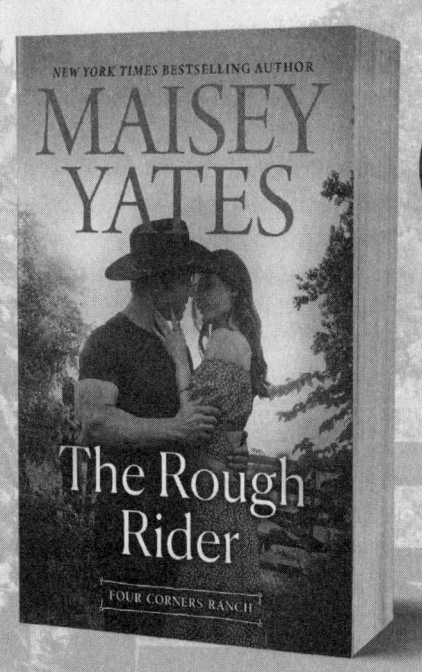

NEW RELEASE

In stores and online August 2023.

MILLS & BOON

millsandboon.com.au

MILLS & BOON

Want to know more about your favourite series or discover a new one?

Experience the variety of romance that Mills & Boon has to offer at our website:

millsandboon.com.au

Shop all of our categories and discover the one that's right for you.

MODERN

DESIRE

MEDICAL

INTRIGUE

ROMANTIC SUSPENSE

WESTERN

HISTORICAL

FOREVER
EBOOK ONLY

HEART
EBOOK ONLY

f @millsandboonaustralia @millsandboonaus

Subscribe and fall in love with a Mills & Boon series today!

You'll be among the first to read stories delivered to your door monthly and enjoy great savings.

MILLS & BOON SUBSCRIPTIONS

HOW TO JOIN

1

Visit our website
millsandboon.com.au/pages/print-subscriptions

2

Select your favourite series
Choose how many books. We offer monthly as well as pre-paid payment options.

3

Sit back and relax
Your books will be delivered directly to your door.

MILLS & BOON

JOIN US

Sign up to our newsletter to stay up to date with...

- Exclusive member discount codes
- Competitions
- New release book information
- All the latest news on your favourite authors

Plus...
get $10 off your first order.
What's not to love?

Sign up at **millsandboon.com.au/newsletter**

f @millsandboonaustralia @millsandboonaus